MR ROY BL
1 GREENBA
COLEBROOF
PLYMPT
PLYMOUTH
TEL: 01752

GUESTS OF TH̶̶̶̶̶̶̶̶̶̶̶̶

by

Roy Blackler

Included within the text of this memoir are pictures drawn and painted by the author during his captivity in Singapore, Thailand, and Japan. Pens and paper were difficult to come by in a prison camp, so he used materials obtained by whatever means necessary to record the events that took place

quasar

First published in Great Britain
By
Quasar Publishing Agency
59 High Street, Bathford, Bath BA1 7SZ

Copyright © Roy Blackler 1999

This book is sold subject to the condition that it shall not, by way of trade or otherwise, be lent, re-sold, hired out, or reproduced by any means without prior permission of the publisher or the author

ISBN 0 9533 2365X

Antony Rowe Limited
Chippenham, Wiltshire

CONTENTS

Foreword	1
Acknowledgements	2
My Early Days	4
Collect of the Royal Engineers	10
Nearing our Pass Off	17
The Body	25
A Near Shave!	26
Back to Chatham and Duty Party	28
To be Field Engineers	30
Blackdown – The First AA Battalion	33
The Girl from Bristol	34
Adolph becomes a nuisance	36
Draft Leave	45
Embarkation HMT Lancashire	51
The Troop Ship	52
So this is Singapore	63
Let us get home	78
Building up	79
The Haunted Engine Room	79
"Tekon" Ghost Train	82
Engine Rooms on the Coast	84
All the Sixes	85
Write Home Jack	87
War Clouds over Asia	90
A Letter from Bristol	91
Prelude to the Disaster	92
Still Talking	95
We Visit the Queen	96
The Final Word	97
HMS Prince of Wales	98
We Still visit the City	99

"Tommy" Poem by Rudyard Kipling	99
December 1941	100
The Balloon Goes Up	100
The Attack Comes!	101
Our Questions Answered	104
The Other Disaster	106
Roads to Singapore	113
Japanese Intelligence	115
A Trip to Paula Ubin	118
Spies – Espionage – Third Column	138
We Build a Still	143
1943	145
Off to Siam and Burma	146
So this was Siam	148
We were known as "Y" Battalion	152
Kanu I	154
The Kanu Kid	167
Down the River	170
The Death Tent	178
In the Death Tent	184
Dolly Grey	188
Tarsao	200
Working Parties at Tarsao	201
I am a thief	209
The Burial Party	210
A New Game for Little Men	211
Our Wonderful Doctors	212
Corporal Yamamoto's Chitterlings	215
Japanese Civilians Take Over	219
The Japanese Planter in Malay	236
Another Raid on the Train	238

The Operations	239
The Geisha Ladies	240
Jap Troop Train	242
Japan on the Cards	243
Non Pladuk	246
Nakhon Pathom	247
We Leave Siam	250
A Journey into Hell	254
The Swim	260
So this was Japan	262
Hell Below	266
The Soya Bean Fields	269
The Reaper Called at Night	270
Time goes on into January 1945	271
Fire Watchers	272
Fish for Fags	275
More Air Activity	276
Air Raid Shelters	277
Extract from the book Banzai You Bastards	278
We are Now into May 1945	280
June 1945	281
July 1945	282
We have a Meat Issue	283
Truly a Great Day	303
We Board HMS Implacable	314
Through Canada	317
Il de France	324
Home Again	326
Drink was our Valium	330
An Unusual Pet	332
List of Men Left Behind	337
Japanese Hell Ship – Hakasoka Maru	342

FOREWORD
by the Chief Royal Engineer, General Sir John Stibbon KCB OBE

It is a great privilege to be invited to write the foreword to this remarkable story, reconstructed from diary notes written by a private soldier when a prisoner of the Japanese during the Second World War.

It covers the period from school days, enlistment and early training as a regular soldier in the Corps of Royal Engineers, posting to Singapore in 1939, the Japanese invasion and the horrific experiences as a prisoner of war for 3½ years in Changi Gaol, on the infamous Burma-Siam railway and his later internment in Japan.

The original diary notes were scribbled on paper salvaged from used cement bags. That they survived repeated searches by camp guards is remarkable in itself; but it is their translation into this book in the author's own simple style which makes the telling all the more forceful and poignant.

It is a personal account of terrible atrocities, hopelessness and, at times, bitterness - but it is also a story of the courage of ordinary people, both military and civilian, of fortitude and resourcefulness and of remarkable acts of kindness in adversity.

Reading this book is a humbling experience of the author's inner strengths, drawn from the steadfastness of his Christian beliefs, the memory of this time spent with his beloved Grandfather and his sense of humour. It is one soldier's story of man's inhumanity to man and is published as a tribute to those of his comrades who did not return. It should be a lesson to us all - and yet today we see the horrifying examples of ethnic cleansing.

Will we ever learn?

ACKNOWLEDGEMENTS

I am truly indebted to so many people in helping and encouraging me in the production of this book. I find it impossible to thank them all. It too has been such a long gestation period.

* * * * * * * * *

Firstly to the loving memory of my late wife MARCIA, I met her on the first night home after captivity in November 1945, we married in 1950. She stood by me in all the setbacks that I know we all endured in those years after release, fits of depression - the black holes. She passed away in 1989, it was a tragic loss. The writings were shelved for many years. May she Rest in Peace.

* * * * * * * * *

Next I would like to thank my so very good friends of forty years or more, we met at Ripon during Army Service, YVONNE & JOHN ADAMS, they have encouraged me, read the script, corrected items and advised on many points.

* * * * * * * * *

Now their daughter JULIE EASTER, she has put the story on computer disks, altered, re-written - a mammoth task. She has been so kind, nothing too much trouble - thankyou Julie.

* * * * * * * * *

My partner KATE, she has helped, encouraged and advised, thankyou Kate for your friendship and companionship in what could have been such lonely years.

* * * * * * * * *

A special thankyou to GENERAL SIR JOHN STIBBON KCB OBE, Chief Royal Engineer, for his outstanding foreword written for this book. I shall be forever grateful to him.

* * * * * * * * *

Lastly, to my old and dear friends in captivity, the British Servicemen, always at hand to help each other, always that sense of humour when it is most needed. Men of many Regiments, as well as my own, Gordon Highlander, the Argyll and Sutherland Highlanders - too many to mention and those little Gurkhas not to be forgotten.

With these writings, let's hope the haunting will cease.

R.C BLACKLER

Plymouth 1999.

MY EARLY DAYS

I was born in Devonshire, the South West of England.

My Mother died when I was aged seven years. From that date to leaving school at the age of fourteen, my Grandfather brought me up with the aid of an old maiden aunt. She was a bad tempered, vicious person and she made my life a living hell as she did my Grandfather. If we had jam on our bread we did not get margarine. If we had margarine, we had no jam. She used to beat me with anything she could lay her hands on. My Grandfather to me was a Saint, he was so kind. I only wish at a later date that I could have paid him back for what he had done for me in my early years. Just before I reached the age of thirteen, my Grandfather had just about had enough of the "old devil" as he used to call her and we moved to live with an Aunt and Uncle. Grandfather got very crippled with arthritis, he could hardly walk. Then came the awful day, I saw him taken off to the hospital and after a few weeks he died. It seemed as if my world had ended, I saw no tomorrow.

I LEAVE SCHOOL

After Grandfather had passed away, it was only a matter of months and I reached the school leaving age of fourteen.

My first employment was in a pottery at Bovey Tracey. We started work at 8.00am and finished at 5.00pm, having had one hour for lunch. On Saturday we worked from 8.00am to 12 noon, a total of 44 hours per week. I walked three miles to work and three miles back. My wage packet was 12s 6d per week (62½p by todays reckoning). I could not say that I was happy at Bovey in spite of having to work with very nice people.

Heathfield:-

Most of my school friends were working at Tile and Brickworks at Heathfield. This was one of the main employers in the area. I felt I would like to get work there as the wages were a little higher and I could get with more of my friends.

My chance came after nine months, one of my friends said that they were taking on a few hands. I took a day off work at Bovey and went to Heathfield and got an appointment to see one of the firm's directors. I explained that I had pottery experience at Bovey but would be much happier in employment at Heathfield. I also told him that, being an orphan and living in lodgings, the extra wages that I could earn would be of great benefit to me. He was very sympathetic and said that he would consider my case.

It was almost a month after that I received a letter from the director telling me to start work the following Monday at 7.00am, I was delighted.

So I started work at Heathfield. At first I was employed in the Press Room at a higher wage of 14/9 per week, or todays reckoning 74½p. I was better off each week by 11½p. Candy, Heathfield was a much bigger firm than at Bovey and made the Devon Fireplaces, as well as bricks and pipes, a small department also made vases of all sizes.

At this time, my landlady charged me 14/- per week for my lodgings. This left me with the worldly amount of 9d per week. I had to buy my own clothes out of this, so I joined a clothing club, into which I paid 6d per week. This is how I clothed myself. After about one year, I asked the foreman if he could find me a position where I could earn more money. I was given a job on a big press on peace work. My pay rose to between 18/- and £1 per week. After two years, I was transferred to the dipping shed, glazing the tiles before they were fired. Once again my pay rose to 25/- to 30/-

(£1.25 or £1.50). At no time did I tell my landlady that I had had these rises in my pay packet, so I was much better off and had a bit of cash to myself. In the dipping shed, I worked with the ladies and the young girls. I quite enjoyed it.

During this time, I still attended the Church of St Michael at Ilsington, where I sang in the choir and attended at least twice on a Sunday.

When I started work at Heathfield, I had been given an old cycle by a friend, it would save me the long walk to and from my work. Now that I was getting better wages and putting a bit by, I bought myself a new bicycle, a Raleigh at £5/19/6. At this time, we young lads in the village started a "Wheelers Club". At weekends we would ride to the seaside resorts at Exmouth, Teignmouth, Torquay and Paignton, even to Dartmouth and Slapton Sands. We would swim in the sea. We were young and enjoyed every moment of our young lives. We played cricket and football, if we didn't play, we watched the senior sides, so much for leisure.

Vase Shed:-

One day, the foreman asked me if I would like to work in the vase shed, I agreed to this. I found it very interesting. At this time, the firm started to make lovely plaques and other products for King George V and Queen Mary's Silver Jubilee, we also made the Jubilee mugs.

After the death of King George V, we started on a big scale to make mementoes for the Coronation of Edward VIII. Thousands of articles were made in this line - then came the abdication. Potteries throughout the country must have lost thousands of pounds. I, with one or two others, spent weeks taking these items to the tip and putting them through the crushing machine. I often wish I had kept a few, they would have been worth a fortune today but we were always supervised on this work. Next phase was the Coronation of King George VI and Queen Elizabeth, so we started all over again, we were kept very busy. My wages by this time were up to £2 per week. At times I could get as much as £2-10s.

After the Coronation, work in the vase department dropped, so I had to return to the press room. I was by no means happy about this, as we had a nice set up - all the workers got on well together.

I had been back in the press room only a short time when I got involved in a fight, a lad had thrown a piece of clay and he hit me in the eye. I told him he was stupid to do such a thing and he took a punch at me, so I struck him back, we were in the middle of our set to when in walked the foreman. He told us both to go to the office and collect "our cards" in a weeks time. This shook me to the roots, me out of a job, whatever should I do. I dare not go home and tell them that I was out of work. Every day I went to the foreman and pleaded with him to give me back my job or I would be turned out into the street, to which he replied "you should have thought about that before - you are paid to work in this pottery - not to fool about - and start fighting".

He kept me on a string for almost the week, I didn't sleep, nor did I eat much as work was so scarce and getting the sack above all things, I never once mentioned it at home. At the end of the week, the foreman told me to go to the office. I thought "well this is it, I'm getting my cards". Well I got one of the biggest lectures I had ever had, a right dressing down. Then to my relief he said "Well Sonny! I will overlook it this time but watch yourself in future". Thank God, what a relief, I had got my job back.

I was then sent to the dipping shed, back with the girls. I was then employed glazing small sample tiles, I was very proud of my work as these samples were sent all over the world to get orders for fireplaces and tiles running into thousands of pounds. I felt very uplifted on this job. This went on for a few months.

Then came the bombshell, a lot of us were made redundant due to lack of orders in pipes, bricks and other products. We worked our weeks notice and then "ON THE DOLE". We used to meet at the Dole Office. We were given little cards and told to go to places where men were wanted. But when we got there, the jobs were already taken.

At that time, we were getting about 30/- (£1.50) per week dole money.

We had been out of work for two months and a friend of mine from Newton Abbot said that he was going to Plymouth to join the Royal Navy. I thought this was a good idea - we got on our cycles and went to the Recruiting Office at Plymouth. We filled out the forms and went for our medical examinations. We both wished to join the Navy as "Stokers". My friend passed, I failed to get in as a Stoker as I had false teeth but I could have joined as a "Seaman" and re-mustered at a later date. I wished to go with my friend, so I turned the offer down. I went back to the dole for a fortnight. Then I thought of joining the Army. What Regiment or Corps, I had no idea. When we were at first unemployed, a few of us joined the 5th Battalion the Devonshire Regiment T.A. We went on our first camp to Bulford Camp on Salisbury Plain. Being the latest recruits, we were not called upon to take part in any manoeuvres. We were given general fatigues and instruction in small arms i.e rifle and the famous Lewis gun.

The weather at Bulford was very hot and dry, a beautiful Summer. We were billeted in the big round Army tents. The food was top rate, I enjoyed every morsel.

We spent a lot of time playing all kinds of sport. The highlight of the fortnight was a visit to the Tidworth Searchlight Tattoo. We were taken there in the big Army transports, lorries like I had never seen before. The Tattoo was a fantastic show, Military Bands in mass, marching and counter marching. The Scots in their kilts and spats - a beautiful spectacle. This was followed by other displays. Gun drill by the Royal Artillery. P.T displays by other

Regiments. Last of all a bridging display by the Corps of Royal Engineers. All this had a great impression on me. Perhaps I would join the Army!! Yes! I would join the regular Army, I had made up my mind.

When we got back home, I went to see our PSI (Permanent Staff Instructor) T.A to see if he would advise how to go about it, he said "you are a big tall lad - why not join the Coldstream Guards". I was 6'2" tall. Then I had visions of the smart uniform, the big occasions like "Trooping the Colour" or even "Taking part in displays such as the Tidworth Tattoo". Wonderful I thought and so off to Exeter Higher Barracks to join the Coldstream Guards. It was about the 12 September 1937.

At first we had an educational exam, it was quite easy. I say "we" as another lad went with me, he wanted to join the Tank Corps. I then had to go before the Medical Officer, he asked me a lot of questions, I had to think very hard before answering some. Then he sounded my chest, he gave it a good going over, my heart gave quite a flutter. Then he declared me "fit for service". I was delighted, I had now got a good job which I think I was going to enjoy.

When I got home I met my Uncle who had served through the Great War 1914-18. When I told him that I had joined, or was hoping to join the Coldstream Guards, he went spare, as he had been in the Royal Engineers and told me, in no uncertain terms, that I had made a mistake, the Guards was a very hard life. Then I went to see the PSI again and said that I wanted to join the Royal Engineers and he said that if I had not been attested and had not taken the Kings Shilling, they had no hold on me I could refuse to join all together. The other lad that went with me also wanted to join the R.E, so we had to wait until we were called to Exeter again.

We, my friend and I, then got letters telling us to report to Exeter on 23 September 1937 for "swearing in". We were confronted by the Recruiting Sergeant, a massive man from the Guards, he had a voice like a bull. I thought he was going to have a heart attack when we said "Please Sir! We wish to change our minds". "Change your minds" he bellowed, "What the bloody hell next". Getting very red in the face "You can't bloody well do that". We very timidly said "But Sir - we haven't been sworn in, we both want to go home again". "Go home" he roared. "Yes Sir" - he was blowing a gasket. Then he calmed down a little and asked "What do you want to do?". "We both want to go into the Royal Engineers". He then said "I will see what I can do". He took down a big ledger from a shelf and started to thumb through the pages, then said "There are just two vacancies - you are very lucky". We were attested, we took the Kings Shilling and our travel warrants, a days pay - ration allowance. We were on our way to Chatham, Kent. We had to cross London on the underground, we had never been so far from home before - the great adventure had started. We were booked into the Nursery late at about 7.00pm 23 September 1937.

All our civilian clothes were taken away from us, we were issued with underclothes, canvas jacket c/w 5 g.s buttons, canvas trousers, long puttees, a forage cap (without badge). We were a motley crowd, from all parts of the Great British Isles. We could not understand each others brogues. We two were proper "swede bashers"!

First thing next day Reveille sounded at 6.00am. The nursery Corporal shouting "Get up, feet out on the floor" this was the first taste of the regular Army.

Collect of the Royal Engineers

O God, whose righteousness is exceeding glorious, may it please thee to send out thy light and thy truth so to lead us the servants of the Corps of Royal Engineers that everywhere we may be enabled to do our duty and so glorify thee our Father in Heaven. For the sake of Jesus Christ our Lord.

Amen.

At 6.30am after washing and shaving, we were marched off to the cookhouse and dining hall for our first breakfast - porridge, bacon, egg, sausage, bread, margarine and marmalade. This was good. After our breakfast we were marched off to the Medical Centre. We were all in the bare buff (nude) awaiting to be called into the Medical Officer by the Orderly. A lot of us had never had this experience before, so were a bit embarrassed. There were all sizes, some with hair some without, some dark, some ginger, some blonde, some were fat, some were thin. My name was called, I went before the M.O. Height was taken, weight checked, chest measurements, then a very strict medical examination. Hearing was checked, it was a medical more strict than we had had at Exeter. After this, we were taken back to the Nursery by the Corporal "Dodger" Green, whom I might add, was an old soldier. I think he had served in the 1914-18 War. He wore quite a few medals. After our lunch, we were taken on to the verandah overlooking the Holy Land (the barrack square), where squads of men were being drilled. How smart they looked, some had only been in a few weeks, would we ever attain these standards. The Corporal explained all the movements - the turning, the timing etc. We were very taken up by the SDI (Senior Drill Instructor). He had a voice like a lion roaring, would we get to the standards shown?
We were then taken to a small square behind the main cookhouse. Out of sight, where another L/Corporal took us on the elementary drill - left turn, right turn, about turn, saluting by numbers and told that we must always salute an Officer, no matter how far away he was.

I remember well one day I was walking towards the main gate when I saw an Officer coming towards me, I thought "Now is my chance, my first salute, I will do what I have been told" my hand shot up to the saluting position "Up 1-2-3-4-5 down". I was very pleased with my first effort. Until the Officer bade me go to him and stand to attention. He upbraided me and told me that I was a silly little man. "What are you"? "A silly little man Sir". He then told me that he was the RSM - the Regimental Sergeant Major. The Holy man himself.

When I returned to our billet, I told the others of my first salute, we all had a good laugh -the Corporal said that I was not the first one to make that mistake. I had to put up with quite a lot of leg pulling.

Then, as regards saluting, I don't know how far it was true but we had a "scouse" from Liverpool, he was quite a wag. He told us that he was walking by the square and he met an Officer who enquired "Why didn't you salute me when you passed"? To which our wag replied "Well Sir! I have been told never to salute an Officer, when I got a fag in me mouth". The Officer told him what he should do in such circumstances - if it happened again he would find himself an extra fatigues.

On about the third day, we were marched to the Regimental Dental Centre by a young L/Corporal. The Centre was used by all the Forces in the Chatham area i.e Army, Royal Navy, Royal Marines and RAF. After my inspection, I was told to return the next day when I would have five teeth filled. I don't think any of us got away scot free. The Dental Centre was a big building with big white curtains as partitions. One could hear all that was going on behind these curtains.

When I returned the next day, we were waiting in the room provided, when we heard a Military Band passing. Being new to service life, we all got up to look at the parade going by. The Band belonged to the Royal Marines. All their instruments were draped in black. We discussed between ourselves and wondered why this should be. A very old and wisened soldier who had been sitting in the corner of the waiting room then stood up and came to the window and looked out. He then came out with a statement or explanation "They have just been to a Military Funeral up at the Garrison Church. A Marine bloke - was in here five days ago - 'e 'ad a tooth out - then gangrene set in - they put 'im away today".

His face was expressionless. My God!! We have to go in there for treatment. Our faces drained of all circulation. My name was called Sapper Blackler, I had to go to the furthest cubicle. As I passed the curtained off sections, I could hear the "Ahhs and Ohhs" and the drills working. There were not many electric drills then, the dentist worked a treadle with his foot to keep a good speed up - he had to be very active. I thought about that Military Funeral. My legs were like jelly. Once I got into the chair, there was no turning back, the dentist was a very pleasant fellow - he hit the nerve once or twice - my fillings were done all in the one sitting. Was I glad that was all over.

After two or three days, two of the lads that arrived on the same day as my friend and I were told to report to the Regimental HQ. When they returned, they looked very dejected, they had to hand their kits in and collect their civilian clothes - they had been discharged due to medical grounds. One had perforated ear drums, the other had hammer toes.

We were given a large piece of brown paper and string, together with our civilian clothes. We had to tie up the parcels, put our home address on, the Army would pay the postage and dispatch same. We knew then for sure that we had been accepted. The Corporal then told us that we had to wait for our Regimental numbers. Seeing that I had been in the Devonshire Regiment T.A, I had to wait for confirmation from Higher Barracks Exeter. At last, after a day or two, my number became 5619438. Sapper Blackler R.E.

We had only been at Chatham two days when two young lads came into the nursery, they looked very pitiful, their trousers were at half mast, just pullovers and shirts, much too small, on their feet, shoes, which we used to call sandals, the rest of their kit was in small carrier bags. I have said they looked pitiful and half starved. I got into conversation with one of them, he said that they had come down from the North East of England the Durham area. They had been coal miners and they had been on strike for some time, they had asked for ½d per hour, they worked an eight hour shift i.e 4d per day. In those days, they worked a six day week, they were therefore asking for 2/- (10p) extra per week. The mine boss said that in no way could he see his way clear to pay this amount, so he closed the mine down. They could not go on the dole, how could they live? They joined the Army hoping to use their experience as miners. We all felt very sorry for them. After a day or two, one of these lads was very upset, he had had a letter from his mother, she was distressed. His father was getting on in years and he had been on strike as well from the same pit as they called it. Dad was too old to join the Army, he took the easy way out - he had committed suicide, he had hung himself. Why are these people allowed to treat people in this way, the boss was allowed to do this deed, he could afford to close the mine. The young lad had to go for an interview with the Welfare Officer. I don't know if he was discharged or not. I never saw him again.

Another week we were formed up into our party 231. We left the nursery to C Block the main Barracks at Brompton. We then drew our full kit. S.D suits, shirts, boots, the full kit complete full marching order. We were shown to our rooms, had lessons on how to clean our equipment. The main item being our D.P (Drill Purpose) Rifles. We were told all the elementary points on cleaning, how to blanco our equipment.

We were now recruits in 231 Party C Company. The T.B.R.E (Training Battalion Royal Engineers) Brompton Barracks, Chatham, Kent.

We were getting pay as recruits 14/- (70p) per week. We drew 10/- (50p) per week 4/- (20p) per week went into credit out of which, if required, we would pay barrack room damages, perhaps 6d per week would be stopped. The rest went into our credit to be paid out on our first leave home. That will be next Christmas.

We were not allowed out of Barracks for the first month before gracing the streets of Chatham.

We now started our drill instruction on the main square, we had new instructors and we had a good Corporal - Johnny Leek. He was very patient with our efforts. Although we had practised behind the cookhouse we were now in full view of the Holy Land under the eyes of the Drill Sergeant, the SDI and the RSM and of course our Officers all with eagle eye. Every spare moment we were practising our movements, we wanted to be the best.

We marched, drilled and became quite good at squad drill. We now came on to our rifle drill and after a week we became very efficient and our instructor was quite pleased as was our Party Sergeant (Sergeant Kimber) who I am sure took a bit of pleasing, the least mistake or mis-timing he was on to us like a ton of bricks.

Things started to hot up now, we had breakfast then go to the gym. We would take our rifles and bayonets with us, we had an hour in the gym, practised rope climbing, walking the beam, jumping the horse and all such exercises. We were feeling fit and hungry all the time.

After the gym, we donned our canvas trousers, boots and puttees. We took our rifles and bayonets on to the assault course where we practised the art of bayonet fighting stripped to the waist. We would go out there in the snow and frost. We felt fit for anything.

We had practised our squad drill, we began to drill as a party, everyone was watching us and the SDI took us over - we found this more difficult. Keeping our dressing etc, the SDI told us that if we were going to pass off by Christmas, we had to buck up.

We were allowed into town on our first time out of Barracks for a month, we all made for the Jerome photo studios to have our photographs taken to send home, just to let them see that we were doing OK.

We were always hungry, we could never get enough to eat but I must say the Army food was great, I enjoyed every morsel. When we went for supper at night, we always had cocoa and cakes but we used to find a loaf of bread, another lad would get margarine, another would get a tin of marmalade, smuggle the goods out of the dining hall to the Barrack Room, give the fire a good stoke up, then it would be toast all around the billet. We would take it in turn to pinch the ingredients.

On Saturday evenings we used to have a good tuck in, it was always the "Cooks Special" an "all in pie", it had all the leftovers for days, it was put into a big pie dish - a pastry on the top then baked in the oven, it had hosts of ingredients, cabbage, potatoes, scraps of bacon, pork, beef, we could have as much as we could eat.

I remember I went into the dining hall one Saturday evening, I was starving. I had one helping, then I went back for the second and got it. We were all sitting around the table and I got a piece of something in my mouth, I couldn't chew it and I couldn't swallow it, so I took it out of my mouth and put it on the side of my plate saying "excuse me lads", then I finished off the remainder of my pie. We sat at the table for a while and had a smoke with our cup of cocoa. Curiosity got the better of me and I had to have a look at the stubborn piece of food that I couldn't get the better of. I poked it about a bit and unravelled it, my God - it was the cook's finger bandage!. All the lads said "Bloody hell - ooooh"!. But you know it never put us off the "all in pie", we were always there on a Saturday night - that is if we were in Barracks. Later on in our course, we were able to go out on Saturday evenings. We used to go to the cinema, we could also go to the live theatre, where we saw Lew Prager and his Accordian Band, we also saw other big bands which were on top in those days.

NEARING OUR PASS OFF

Our drill is progressing, we are now practising the Ceremonial Drill. Every Sunday we had to attend Church Parade, that is the Church of England. I had always been brought up to go to church and to be a believer. I think these Church parades put a lot of men off religion. I remember several of them were put on charges or extra fatigues for some silly little fault the Party Sergeant or Officer had found. I quite remember well one lad in our section was put on a charge for having a bit of dirt in the 'O' of Royal on one of his great coat buttons. He had four days C.B. This was very drastic or extreme but I suppose that was discipline. It was an awful bind to have to do the extra duties that "jankers" entailed. These men were expected to report to the Guard Room to be inspected by the Sergeant Guard Commander and the Orderly Officer, they would come back to the Barrack Room and change into fatigue dress and report to the cookhouse to wash dishes and pans in the tin room. this was a dirty and greasy job. As I have said before, this did not help a man to turn to religion, it turned him away if anything but after the inspection was over, we marched to the Garrison Church. All Companies were on parade and the Training Battalion Band would lead the way. On the way we would then join up with the Depot Battalion with their Band from Kitchener Barracks. En route we would be joined by the Royal Navy, Royal Marines and, of course, other Regiments of the line and the Royal Artillery, all with their own Bands.

We all felt very proud and the regimental marches were very stirring, it made one feel on top of the world. The streets were crowded with spectators. We all tried to show our skills. After the parade we returned to our Barracks where the Band would form up and play music on the square. Visitors were allowed in for the occasion. We used to flirt with the young girls.

As time went on, we were getting efficient in all things, Squad Drill, Rifle Drill, Ceremonial Drill. We were hard at work now practising for the Pass Off. Christmas was getting nearer, we must pass off or we go back a party or two, so pass off is the objective now, then our first home leave.

We were marching and counter marching early in December, it was very cold and the square was covered in a sheet of ice, we were marching in quick time and the instructor shouted "HALT", the front four men fell and pulled the lot of us down. As we fell, one of the lads broke wind - a rasper. Of course we thought that very funny and started to laugh - that was a sin - to laugh on the square - the Holy Land. The instructor doubled us around the square with our rifles above our heads. He halted us and said that we could now see the funny side of life. I couldn't help it, I burst into laughter. He told me to stand by the bell. The bell was a bell that General Gordon brought back from China. It was a favourite place to be sent when in disgrace. After the parade, the instructor took me to the Guard Room. I was given one evening's extra fatigues. I had to report to the Guard Room with the Janker lads at 6.00pm. My fatigue was to scrub down the stairs from the SDI Office to the ground floor - three flights. The SDI was in his office but I didn't know that at the time. When I had scrubbed down half way, I thought I had better get clean water in my bucket, so I left the scrubbing brush and soap on the stairs. While I was away the SDI decided that he had worked long enough, he switched off the lights and came down the stairs. He came down very fast after treading on my bar of soap - he wasn't at all pleased. The Guard Commander came out to see what all the commotion was all about, just as I was coming up with my bucket of clean water. They both set upon me, the language I had never heard the like before. I was given an extra nights fatigues. So the next evening I took the bucket, soap and brush with me. Good job he didn't break his leg, I would have been in the guard room for the rest of my service. When I got back to the billet and told the lads what had happened, they thought it very funny and said that I would be a marked man. I was never in trouble again in the Training Battalion.

All this time we had been going to school to learn the Regimental history, together with the 3Rs in readiness to take our 3rd Class Army Certificate of Education. We also learn about geography, of Generals and other high ranking officers. We get questions on the square when we pass off like "what is the Colonel's name? Who is the O.C of A Company?" and such like. We were now practising the Pass Off, perhaps three times a day. We went through the same ceremonial procedure as with "Trooping the Colour". We knew that we were getting near the final as the Senior Drill Instructor takes charge of the parade and the full R.E Band is in attendance. Everything was going well, we had all passed our Squad Drill and Arms Drill. Then we were asked our oral questions. I was very lucky, my questions and answers were:-

Who is the CIGS?= General Ironside
Name two R.E V.Cs= Sapper Thomas Hackett R.E
L/C Jarvis R.E
Who is your C.O=Lt Col Wolner R.E
Who is your O.C=Capt H.C.T. Faithful
Who is your R.S.M=R.S.M "Buck" Speary

Yes, five questions - five correct. I felt good.

I am afraid to say that the friend who joined the Corps with me has been put back a party, he has had to go to the Medical Centre a few times - he has an injury to his foot. So we have to part company.
We left the gymnasium for a five mile run, then went on to the assault course to pass off on our bayonet fighting, stripped to the waist, it was snowing.

We had all of our gym tests i.e the high beam, rope climbing, wall bars, ground exercises and the vaulting of the high horse. I got an average mark in the gym. I didn't mind at all as long as I have passed.

A few weeks before, we were walking the high beam when we saw an awful accident. A young recruit from another section slipped and fell with one leg on either side of the beam, he turned over and landed on his head. They say that he had a broken neck.

This accident upset us quite a lot for a day or two, we had lost our confidence, the instructors were good and we soon got it back again.

The great day had come, we were up early in the morning putting the last touches to our kit, which had to be immaculate. Boots, chinstraps, rifle and brasses to be highly polished, our Blanco had to be put on with an even coat.

We marched, counter marched, advanced in review order as the R.E Band played "Wings", it was a very proud day.

Our Colonel told us that we were one of the best parties he had ever seen. We stuck our chests out, we were very proud. I had often wondered - how many parties had been told the very same thing, still it made our day.

We now went on leave, our very first home leave - it was Christmas 1937.

Three whole weeks leave. We packed our cases in readiness the night before, we were all full of excitement going home in uniform for the first time.

We drew our pay, this included all we had in credit since the first day we joined. We were issued with our train warrants and off we went. The lad I joined with, although he had been put back due to sickness, was going on leave, so we travelled together. We were a bit apprehensive about getting across London but found it very easy. Staff on the underground were always very helpful. We got to Paddington in good time - a ten minute wait and we're going home.

The train clacked away, every station we stopped at we had to look out and see where we were - Bristol - Exeter - next stop Newton Abbot.

On my first leave, I stayed with my cousin, it was better to be in town than living in the country and my Auntie was getting older.

I went around to see all my old friends and neighbours. They were all pleased to see me. The friend of mine that joined the Navy - he was on leave, also some of the lads I had worked with had joined the RAF, we went around together.

As I went out to the place where I used to be employed, I saw a lot of my old pals, good friends that I had worked with, they were glad to see that I was happy in the Forces. I went to the dipping shed and saw again all the girls that I had worked with, we joked about the old days. They were glad to see that I was in good health and wished me well for the future. Going around the old place and seeing the conditions I had worked in, I was very glad that all that was behind me. Whilst there I met the Foreman that I had had the encounter with over the fighting incident, he shook me by the hand and said that he was glad to see me again, I said "no hard feelings - little did you know at the time when you gave me my cards, you had done me a great favour". I left the old place feeling very elated after seeing my old friends working in those awful conditions.

Together with my old friends, I visited all the old public houses. The Star Inn, The New Inn, The Anchor and The Claycutters where we used to play darts in the old local leagues. We all came away feeling merry.

I visited my old Aunt and Uncle with whom I had lodged. They were glad to see me and they said that I had done the best thing by joining the Army. My Uncle was very glad to see that I had taken his advice and joined his old Corps. He told me of his adventures in France during the 1914-18 War and hoped that I would never have to endure the same as they had. He had been in a road construction company, they had to keep the roads open, filling the shell holes thus enabling supplies to go through to the front line. He was a definite survivor of some very hard times.

The time came to go around and say "cheerio" to all the friends and neighbours. I think I was glad in a way as my wallet had taken a bashing and I was getting very short of cash.

So back to Brompton Barracks, our three months on the Square completed, it was now January 1938. We had to pack our kits and prepare for the march to Shornmead Fort on the banks of the River Thames. We set off from Brompton in good spirits across Rochester Bridge. We saw the experimental pick a back planes Mercury and Mao anchored on the Medway River. This they said would revolutionise the air mails throughout the World, we were very impressed.

We kept marching, we had a Corporal in charge of our party, as we continued he taught us quite a few of the old soldier songs like "Two German Officers cross the Lines Taboo! Taboo!" and "Mademoiselle from Armentieres" – very rude but a good laugh. We also sang "Pack up your troubles in your old kit bag" and "It's a long way to Tipperary". Songs that our Uncles and Fathers had sung twenty years before. We were the next generation. We completed the march by late afternoon, on the way we had been attacked by low flying aircraft. One Gypsy Moth the other an old Bristol Bulldog, so famous in the dog fights over France. this had given us an insight into what air attack was like and how to take cover.

By the time we got into the Fort, we were all starving. The cooks had got a lovely stew, this went down in quick time and the second helping. We were allocated to our Barrack Rooms. The Fort was not the best of accommodation, it had been built in the early 1800s to fend off attacks against any French invasion coming up the River Thames to Gravesend and finally London. Such places were not built for comfort. We got a coal issue to last us a week but I didn't think it would last that long. Most of it was slack and slate. On the first night, we made our beds down and were soon asleep.

I have not mentioned before but we had come here to do our Small Arms Training. The Rifle Ranges were quite near here. So far we had only done elementary training with the small calibre .22 Arms.

Our first day was spent laying arms with rifle rests which the instructors checked to see your accuracy in sighting. The instructors were top rate and gave us all the encouragement they could.

Next day we went on to the open range at 100 yards. The day was spent in zeroing our rifles, getting the sights accurate. After a slight adjustment, my rifle was dead on. When the time came, I hoped that I would be able to put it to good use.

We completed the first few days by firing in the laying position at 100x, 200x, 300x, 400x, 500x that last 600x. We did butt duty i.e marking the targets and pasting over the holes. As I have said before, we had very good instructors. One is the R.E Corps top shot and had fired in competitions at Bisley. One day one of the lads, a very timid type, just couldn't hit the target at 500x, so this instructor said "Give me your rifle lad", he got down on to one knee, held the weapon into his shoulder with one hand and put three shots in quick succession right in the centre of the bull. He then said "There is nothing wrong with your rifle laddie". We were all dumbfounded, such was our instructors.

Our next exercises were Fire and Movement. During this period, we had quite a few snow storms and we found it hard going on the open ranges at this time, with the cold east winds blowing up the Thames Estuary. Our fingers were frozen but we had to carry on.

We started at 600x. As the targets rose we would drop to the ground and fire five rounds. We would then advance at the double to 500x. During the advance I saw a large pool of water which I ran round. I received a blast from the Sergeant Instructor - "Get down you idiot, in action you would have been killed, as the enemy would be firing at you". I went down, felt the water pour into my skin and fired my five rounds. This action was continued at 400x, 300x and 200x. When we reached 100x we had to remain in the standing position to fire the five rounds.

The muzzle of my rifle was going around in circles as I was out of breath and panting. I finished with a score just above average.

The instructor gave me an ear bending about not getting down when the targets appeared. "The next time" he said "you will be on fatigues for a day or two". He could see that I was wet through and I said that I was. "Better to be wet than dead lad". I suppose I agreed.

Lads who lived near enough were allowed to go on leave but very few did as it was such an awkward place to get to. The nearest place to go was Gravesend. We used to walk there on a Saturday evening, have a pint or two and chat up the girls. Our best route was to walk along the canal bank. On Sundays, we would take a walk along there, girls used to walk to meet us, we walked and talked with them. Some of them worked in a gas mask factory. One I remember well was "Gas Mask Rosie". She was quite a comedienne and a good sport.

THE BODY

We found that with the very cold weather, our coal issues did not last very long, so to subsidize our supply, we used to walk along the banks of the Thames picking up driftwood that had come up with the tide. We would collect piles and put it outside the billet door, then start the fire off with coal, then pile the wood on the top in the great open fireplace. If one went outside you could see the flames coming out of the large chimney. The baron barrack room became like an oven.

We were out one Sunday morning collecting our pile of driftwood when, in the distance, we saw an object had been washed up on to the high water line of the beach. We wondered what it could be, there were four of us in the party. One was a cockney lad, Harry Adrian, quite a wide boy. As we approached, we found that the object was a body of a young man. The cockney lad said "Right giz a hand, get 'im back in the water". It was not a pretty sight but we managed to do as he asked, then he said "'ang on to 'im" and he went off to get the Police. He phoned from our guard room to the Police in Gravesend. After some time, a Police Officer arrived on a bicycle. We let the cockney do all the talking. "Did you recover the body from the River"? asked the Constable. "Yes" replied our friend, "we had to wade out to get 'im in". "Very good" said the Policeman. The body was taken in to the Fort Mortuary. An ambulance came the next day to take the body away. He was a poor lad that had fallen off a barge near London, he had been in the water about four or five days. The cockney lad had to attend the inquest some days later, as he seemed to be the one in charge of things. When he returned, he had ten shillings (50p) which he shared with those who had been with him on that day. I then asked him if he remembered suggesting putting the body back into the river and why, it seemed odd to me at the time. The cockney lad stuck his chest out and said "Well it's like this mate, if we had said that the body was on the beach, we would 'ave only 'ad 'alf a crown, saying we got it out of the water, we got 'alf a nicker". So that was that. "The Crafty Cockney"!

I remember one day we were all in our barrack room, not much to do, so we all thought we would write our letters home or to the girlfriends. This same cockney had said to me "Hey Blackie" How do you spell fout"? to which I replied "F-O-R-T". "Not that fout, I mean the fout what you fink with, not the fout that you fights in". So I spelled out "T-H-O-U-G-H-T". He was a good lad, full of fun.

As time passed, we all qualified with the rifle, I was a first class shot but failed to get marksman. I can tell you, there were only a few of our party to achieve that and I envied them that honour. They were allowed to wear the crossed rifles on their lower sleeve.

The next part of the course was the "Lewis Light Machine Gun". This was very interesting. The gun with all the stoppages to remember and one had to remember them all to get through.
To change all those parts and springs when our hands were freezing was no picnic. To operate the Lewis we had to work in pairs, number one fired the gun and number two helped to fill and change the magazines. We trained on the open range, we advanced up the range the same procedure as with the rifle. We fired at moving targets being towed by light aircraft.

Then came the night exercises, going up the range in the dark and firing 303 tracer bullets. We just couldn't see where we got down to fire, great ponds of water (too big to call pools). When we came in off these exercises, we were all wet through and cold. Always ready to eat and drink. We were now getting to the end of our course at Shornmead Fort.

A NEAR SHAVE!

One evening we had a trip down to Gravesend. We were coming back along the canal bank when we started having a snow fight. It had been snowing hard that morning and we were having a fight with another section. The cockney lad suggested that we get back to the Fort and get a big snowball and drop it on these lads as they came through the main gain from the old guard post above. We rolled the big snowball up and took it up onto the old look-out post. I don't know how we got it up there as it was massive - we got it in position to push off onto the unsuspecting lads. We kept very quiet, then we heard footsteps and voices. "That's 'em" said the cockney. "Wait a tick - 'ere they come". We saw the shadowy figures below. "Together - shove". Our missile was on it's way - wham a direct hit, then the language - enough to make your hair curl. We had bombed the Orderly Officer, the Orderly Sergeant and the Corporal of the Guard. The Officer and Sergeant were knocked flat. We'd better move, we flew down the stairs back to our billets and into bed - fully dressed boots and all. After ten minutes the lights went on, the Officer and Sergeant went to each bed - but saw no movement and left. The other section who we were snow fighting with were on their way to their billets and were accosted by the two. They were told to go to the guardroom where they were accused of the offence in that they did drop a large snowball onto the Orderly Officer and Orderly Sergeant - thus knocking them to the ground. They tried to deny the offence. The Orderly Officer said that it was funny that they were the only people out of bed. They were given two days fatigues - spud bashing. The next few days they accused our section of the offence and they said that they would get us in due course. We told them not to be so silly and make a good job of peeling the spuds and dig all the "eyes" out. This made them even worse - we had to be on our guard.

We came to the end of the course. We had all got reasonable results, so once again we packed our kits for the return to Chatham. Goodbye Shornmead, we were glad to be shot of you, you were not too comfortable in that hard cold weather and so we marched back to start another part of our training at St Mary's Barracks. Before our course could start, we had to do six weeks "Duty Party". This entailed many duties throughout the Garrison.

BACK TO CHATHAM AND DUTY PARTY

We arrived at St Mary's Barracks and were told to watch daily orders where we would find all details of the work we had to do and the guards and duties we had to perform.

It appeared on orders that I had to go to the R.E Yacht Club and report to a civilian who was the Skipper of the R.E Yacht Ubique. There were two of us for this duty. It was now February 1938. We reported to the gentleman concerned at 8.00am. He seemed to be a grump old Scot. "Get your boots and socks off - and roll up your trousers". He gave us buckets and ropes and brooms then said "Swab the decks". We were in bare feet all the morning. Then we put on our soft shoes, we then had to blanco all the ropes and clean the brass. We were glad to change duties after a week - he was a miserable old sod.

I then found myself on coal fatigues, delivering coal to the married families in the area. There were four of us on that with a horse drawn G.S Wagon. We collected the coal from the central store then made our rounds. We tried to give all the O.R Wives the best coal. I remember the SDI quarter, someone said "Give 'im a load of slack" so we did - next day we were told to go and collect it and give him a better ration, we didn't gain much. I'm glad he didn't see me, thinking of the soap on the stairs episode. We also supplied the barrack rooms issues, our room always had a full bunker.

Whilst we were on duty party, we also supplied the main guard at Brompton. This duty lasted 24 hours. Five Sappers, Full Corporal and L/Corporal and Sergeant of the guard mounted at 8.00am with a bugler from the boys depot at Kitchener Barracks.

On my first guard, I spent about three evenings cleaning my kit. We had to be immaculate, even looked at the bottoms of our boots and the backs of our cap badges to see that there were no specks of dirt. I always remember one lad saying "They look up your arse to see if you have cleaned the backs of your teeth". When the guard was inspected, this was carried out by the RSM. He was very strict. He would pick out the first stick, the second stick, the remaining Sappers did the beat two hours on and four hours off. This was carried out for the 24 hours. During this time, the Orderly Officer could come at any time and turn out the guard for inspection. At times they have been known to turn out the guard during the night. The Sentry had a beat of 20x, he would be expected to salute all Officers within view "butt salute" below the rank of Field Officer, present Officers above this rank. Many mistakes were made. At that time, there were many foreign officers attending courses at the SME (School of Military Engineering). I remember quite well there were two Japanese Officers attending courses at that time. Their uniform insignia differed from ours, they had red background to their stars. At a distance, they could be mistaken for one of our high ranking officers.

On one occasion, I remember it was a very cold and dry night and one of my friends was on Sentry. He was on just as daylight was breaking and a big stray dog wandered on to the square, it made it his business to cock it's leg against the Sentry Box. Just after the incident, the Orderly Officer turned out the guard for an inspection, he also inspected the box. My friend was accused, the Orderly Officer put him on a 252 (charge sheet) in that he did, at Brompton Barracks, urinate against the Sentry Box during his two hour beat. My poor friend was awarded seven days confined to barracks. Being confined to barracks meant extra fatigues, maybe in the pan room of the O.R or Sergeants Mess, washing up the greasy tins. this was Eric Moreton. If on C.B, one could be up very late at night cleaning kit for the next day. Even sitting in the toilets where there would always be light - after lights out at 10.00pm. So much for discipline.

Before being relieved on the guard change, we would again be inspected. After being on guard all through the night, the Medway fog would descend around us. Our buttons, badges and highly burnished bayonets would become tarnished, all was expected to be as clean as when one mounted guard the day before, many a man on the last beat was charged for not being up to standard. So much for discipline.

While on duty party, I was detailed for three guard duties. The first one I was on the beat (the chicken run) the second I got the second stick. This was the guard room orderly, running messages etc. The third guard I got the first stick or Commandants Orderly. On this duty one stood guard outside the Commandants Office. He was at that time Major General L.V Bond. To get the first stick was quite a proud moment. You wore the white belt and bandolier with a big pouch on the back with the Royal Coat of Arms. You also carried a special cane. This duty only lasted half a day, the rest of the day was spent cleaning the equipment you had worn, it was then taken to the guard room and inspected and made ready for the morrows guard. So much for guard duties.

Other duties carried out while duty party was the fire piquet - mess orderlies, both in the Sergeants and Officers Mess. I was never called upon to do the latter two. I did fire piquet -this entailed fire drill and potato peeling which was a bit of a bind.

Throughout this time, we were going to school studying for 3rd and 2nd Class Certificates of Education. I got my 3rd Class Certificate very early on, so was studying for my 2nd.

TO BE FIELD ENGINEERS

Duty Party over, our next phase was Field Engineering. For the first part, we stayed at St Mary's Barracks. Firstly we start on elementary field engineering. We learn knots and lashing, this being the basics for all bridging and lifting equipment. Old soldiers always called it sticks and strings. We were taught how to tie all size ropes from the simple thumb knot to the square and diagonal lashing. We were taught formula to define the strength of rope, blocks and tackles for lifting. Then on to what was known as the ravlin, where we built improvised bridges with giant spars all lashed with ropes. We erected Derricks, shear legs and gyns, all instruments for lifting heavy weights. This was very hard work but we were as fit as could be at this time. The bulk timbers that were used were very heavy, some 30ft in length and 2ft in diameter. It took 15 to 20 men to lift them. I remember well on one occasion a lad was on the bulk end and, for some reason, he was left holding all the weight, we saw his predicament and rushed to take the weight, he came from under the timber almost too doubled with pain in his back. He was very distressed. The next day he went sick but the Medical Officer accused him of swinging the lead. He was given M & D - "medicine and duty". He was up all that night in intense pain. The next day he reported on sick parade again. The MO then gave him M & D in red ink, which automatically stated that the poor lad was a malingerer. He tried to get to work and the instructor saw that he was very ill (why the MO at that time couldn't see, God only knew). So he sent him back to the barrack room. When we got back to the room we found him to be delirious. We got a message to the Orderly Officer who came and took one look and sent for an ambulance. The lad was taken away. Two days later he died of Meningitis. There was never an inquiry about this affair, we always thought that if he had been given medical treatment in the first instance, he could have been saved. All the lad's kit was taken away and fumigated, as was our barrack room. The MO was dashing about full of his own importance, it was much too late then. The Sapper was buried with full military honours in his home town somewhere up in the North of England. Very tragic, this was the first death we had had, we were all very upset at the circumstances, he should never have died.

After having mastered our sticks and strings, our next instruction was on demolitions. At first it was all elementary lighting safety fuse with matches. Then safety fuse and detonator. The actual detonations were done under a giant igloo built with chainmail. Six men would enter with the instructor, taking it in turns to ignite ones charge. When ignition had been achieved, you would shout "Fire one, fire two, fire three" until all six charges were burning, as soon as number six was alight, we would stand up and walk out of the igloo. Many men would panic as they saw their fuses burning away. Never run away from a charge, you may fall and be injured. Demolitions never worried me, it was my favourite subject. As a lad of eight or nine years of age, I used to accompany my Grandfather to his quarry where he told me a lot about explosives, he used to let me place dynamite charges into the bore holes to blast out the limestone rock, I even lit the safety fuse. It was in my blood as it were. We graduated on to larger charges with guncotton, plastic explosives. We were taught how to blow up railway lines and bridges, to blow craters in roads by using lifting charge like Amatol and Amunol using special equipment. I found this all very interesting.

Our next phase of instruction was mining, we drove shafts into the chalk hills and were taught to shore up the roofs and sides. The miners amongst us were in their element. Whilst here, we learned how to dig trenches as used in the 1914-18 War. Dogleg, bastion trace with fire steps, dugouts and communication trenches, all so far behind the times.

Next part of the course was watermanship, when every morning we rowed cutters across the River Medway to Upnor Hard. We raced against the other sections across the river. Competition was very high, we rowed like mad with our instructors acting as coxes. Even on those cold frosty mornings with our very cumbersome cork life jackets on, we would reach the other side of the river bathed in sweat, we loved every minute. It so helped to build us up into strong lads. The wet bridging was good where we rowed pontoons into position to take the heavy box girder bridges. At this time, the Bailey had not been invented. At the end of our field engineering course, we went to the Depot Battalion R.E St Mary's Barracks, all we did was change barrack rooms. We were here to await postings to other units in the R.E network throughout the country. A lot of the tradesmen went to field companies. I, with many of my friends, were posted to the 1st Anti-Aircraft Battalion at Blackdown in Hampshire. Trucks picked us up at St Mary's, took us to Chatham Station where we caught the train early in the morning. We crossed London and it wasn't a very long journey to Blackdown so another adventure was about to begin.

BLACKDOWN
THE FIRST AA BATTALION

The first few weeks were spent on general duties. We were employed as mess waiters, dishwashers, some of us went to the truck parks to clean all the different types of vehicles from the 10 Ton Crossleys, Guys down to Austin 7s and motor cycles. We also did piquets at night around the camp, where all the searchlights and other equipment were stored. Discipline was very relaxed here after the Training Battalion. We had been here a few weeks and we were joined by more men from other recruit parties at Chatham.

We were then formed up into parties and moved to Haslar Barracks to join No 12 Defence Electric Light Course. We were trained in all the duties to be carried out in searchlight crews. This entailed driving, aircraft spotters, searchlight operators. Whilst we were on this course, there were very little regimental duties to perform. Just the odd twelve hour guard at night from 6.00pm to 6.00am. Regimental Police took over during the day. After we had done our lessons and completed our notebooks for inspection, we had plenty of time to relax. As it was now summer, we spent a lot of time on the sea wall overlooking The Solent which led up to Southampton Water. Here we did a lot of swimming, we became very strong in this sport.

We used to watch all the big liners passing up to Southampton, these lovely big ships, the Queen Mary, Queen Elizabeth I, The French Normandy, The German Brennan and many others, it was quite fascinating.

At weekends, we could go into Gosport, Portsmouth and Southsea, it was summer and a lot of the folks took their holidays in the area. I must not forget the Isle of Wight.

Some nights we would go out for a swim in the moonlight, we were often joined by the nurses from the Royal Naval Hospital, they would bring out food in the form of a picnic. They also brought a wind up gramophone, where we would listen to all the latest big bands, Bing Crosby - this was a lovely time.

At about this time I had been told that my old school friend, Harry Howard, had joined the Royal Marines and was at Eastney Barracks, Portsmouth. I went to visit him but was told that he was in Haslar Hospital, only 100x from our Barracks. I went into the hospital to visit him and was told that he had ben discharged, he had joined his unit so back to Eastney goes I, this time I was lucky, I met him in his billet. He was still very sick and was not allowed out, he had had septicaemia very bad. We had a good old talk about the old days. Might see him one day on leave. "May be home for Christmas" he said as I left.

THE GIRL FROM BRISTOL

One Saturday, while in Southsea with a friend, we met two very nice girls on holiday from Bristol. They were on the first day of a fortnights stay. We walked around the sea front and promised to see them the next evening. We were in - we had clicked, as we used to say.

On the way back on the ferry from Portsmouth, I sat in a patch of grease. Whatever could I do for tomorrow evening. I asked one of my mates "Can I borrow your suit tomorrow as you are on guard"? "Yes" he answered "but it will cost you half a crown". "OK" says I, "you're on". I couldn't afford to miss this date. So the next night I met the girl again in a borrowed suit. She said "You look quite smart this evening". We spent a lovely evening together, went on all the rides in the fun fair. She said that she had enjoyed my company. I made a date for later in the week as duty called. I was on guard one of the nights and pay was a bit short. We met again midweek and went to the cinema. I promised her that I would meet her again at the weekend, Saturday evening. So I asked my mate if I could again borrow his suit, to which he replied "No! I'm going out myself", to which I said in jest "I hope you get drunk and fall in the Sea". "No fear of that" he said. I put on my sports coat and trousers and went to meet my girl. Whilst I was in Southsea, I met my friend wearing his suit, the sod - he came up and spoke to me and the girl. She did not recognise the suit. We went for a walk along the sea front then to the fun fair, another good evening.

I caught the last ferry but one back to Gosport. I got in in plenty of time. The next morning early we heard a bit of a commotion. The friend I had borrowed the suit from had been brought back to barracks by the Water Police. He had been running to catch the last ferry, had missed his footing and gone down between the stern end of the boat and the pier. The Police had fished him out and brought him back to barracks. When I saw him the next day, he said "You wished that on to me you bugger". It never spoiled our friendship.

As regards to the girl, I saw her all the last nights of her holiday. She had to go back to Bristol on the Saturday. It was very hard to say goodbye as she had been such good company, very sporty. It was quite a wrench on the Friday evening. We promised to write to each other. I kissed her goodbye.

The course continued, we all became more expert in the handling of our equipment - the large trucks, trailers and searchlights. We did night runs all around the outlaying country, aircraft were flying and we had to pick them up, it was all very interesting.

At the end of the long course, I think most of us passed with good results. I passed as a searchlight operator and No 6 of the crew. This was always recognised as the 2i/c the detachment, I was very happy.

ADOLPH BECOMES A NUISANCE

In other parts of Europe things were not so good. Adolph Hitler was stirring up the war clouds. Since coming to power as Chancellor in 1933, he had invaded the Rhine area. The British and French Forces withdrew their forces, this being the Army of Occupation (BAOR) since the end of the 1914-18 War. His next move was to occupy Austria. Then Czechoslovakia. His next move was Poland. This was the last straw, the British Forces mobilized in 1938. We watched the destroyers, frigates and other warships coming and going in and out of Portsmouth Naval Base. We also watched the minelayers in action. We thought "This is it"!! We received orders to pack our kits for the return to Blackdown Camp. We travelled back full of expectations. Every station en route was packed with servicemen, a lot of them Reserves, called back to the Colours. We arrived back at Blackdown, all our searchlights, lorries, generators and other equipment was tested and made ready for issue to the Territorial Army from other parts of the country. This task over, we had to equip ourselves. We had to go to the Royal Ordnance Depots to collect brand new equipment. This was all preserved in grease and wax and took a long time to clean. If I remember, it took us two days. The Lewis Guns were stored in grease cocoons, they took up a lot of our time. All the actions were very stiff due to the newness. When we had prepared all our kit, we were told to be ready to move out to unknown destinations. Our convoy moved off early in the morning, we were loaded with blankets, tents, field kitchens and large primus stoves. We wound our way northwards past the outskirts of London. We all thought that we were going to defend our capital but it was not to be. Onward we went through Oxfordshire, Buckinghamshire, Bedfordshire, Cambridgeshire and we then thought we were bound for East Anglia. We were wrong again, we came into Lincolnshire. Our destination was to be the Castle Bytham area, this was to be our Headquarters. Here the convoy of lorries were to be split up. Our detachment of which I was the No: 6, was to go out to a little hamlet called Clayhill.

Our detachment commander was a L/Sergeant Jones. He was a welshman and not at all happy, he had finished with the colours twelve years and been discharged from the Army nine months before. He had gone into business as a builder with his elder brother and they were doing quite well. Then came the crisis and he was called back to service from the reserve. In no way could he be a happy man, he was a grumpy old sod.

Clayhill was to be our home, not too long we hoped. It was September and to be in tents, sleeping on groundsheets, didn't seem like luxury. We got the searchlight in position, the sound locator ready for action and all cables ran out to the lorry generator. "Come on Jerry, we are waiting" some wag said. The Lewis Gun was erected on its stand and all the magazines had been filled with .303 ammunition.

Next duty was to erect our bell tent, this had a pole in the middle, we slept around on the outside, feet to the pole. Attached to the pole was a rifle rack on which we hung our weapons. At this time, it began to rain and the field became a quagmire, very soft to put the tent pegs into.

After a while, we got the large primus stove to go (all was wet). We made a bully stew. This I might add went down honey sweet. All the time our happy go lucky Sergeant was moaning "I should never be here - bloody Hitler". I suppose it was understandable.

We were ready for action. A lookout man was always on duty looking for a rocket which would be fired from the HQ Company. This would be the signal to expose our light and search for aircraft. We had a code of signals.

It was now bedtime - "Let's get our heads down". We made our beds down after a fashion. The cockney lad was with us from my Shornmead days, we had quite a few laughs with him and his dry humour. We got into our beds, it was pouring with rain. I don't think any of us slept very much that first night. Our lookout had to keep knocking in the tent pegs during the night.

At last, dawn came. We had not dug a gulley around our tent, so the water had been draining right through under our groundsheets. Our blankets were saturated. The next day we were issued with a three sided lean-to shed, this was a great asset and was to be used as a cookhouse. It took us half a day to erect. We soon had the primus going to brew tea. Where would a Tommy be without his tea? We were also issued with a 65 gallon drum, this was to make an Aldershot Oven.

The hedges around our field had plenty of trees, so plenty of firewood, it was mostly ash which burns very easily when wet. We were lucky in this aspect. The ration truck came once a day, all rations had to be cooked on our primus or in the Aldershot Oven. The lean-to shed also acted as our dining hall, this was our community centre. After we had checked our equipment, we spent a lot of time in the lean-to preparing our food and making suggestions for improvement.

Our Sergeant said to me "Can you take charge here No 6"? "Yes Sir". "Well I'm taking the bike and I'm going to see if I can find a pub". "Good idea" we all agreed. The cockney had said "Hope the miserable old bugger comes back in a better temper". Again we all agreed.

The Sergeant returned at about 3.00pm, he was quite red faced and happy. He said that he had found a lovely little pub, it was about a twenty minute walk. It was only a little hamlet and the people he had met were quite friendly. They had bought him a pint or two I guess. He said that he would work out a roster so that we cold take it in turns to visit the Inn. We were lucky in as much that out of our nine detachment, we had four non drinkers. They said that they would stay behind.

We had three or four nights having to stand by on full alert. By now we were in touch by telephone with our Headquarters, so did not have to have the lookout on duty watching for the rocket.

On about the third night, we had an awful storm. It rained, hailed and blew. We were all in bed, the tent began to rock at about 2.00am, the whole lot went. All the rifles and tent pole fell on our beloved Sergeant - oh boy did he go, He was not at all chuffed, then he caught the cockney laughing, that was the end, he gave a bellow "He'd never seen such bloody idiots in his whole life - buggering Hitler". We spent the rest of the night in the lean-to. The rain eased the next morning and we altered the position of our tent and put a big trench around to run the water off, we had also put straw on the floor to keep our groundsheets off the ground, we got the straw from a barn just down the road. It seems to be very snug, let's hope we get a better kip than last night. We took it in turns to get up early in the morning to make the tea.

One night it was pouring with rain, it had been all day. At about 11.00pm we saw lights come into the field, we were all down and snug, some of the lads were asleep. The Orderly Officer came to the tent and told the Sergeant that he had brought a rum ration for all ranks, i.e nine rations. The Sergeant asked the Officer if he could leave the ration in our lean-to cookhouse, as he did not want to disturb those that were asleep. The Orderly Officer said that he would, he called back to say that he had left the spirit in a steel basin and he had put a saucer on the top to keep the dirt out. "Thank you Sir" said our Sergeant. "We'll have that in our tea in the morning". We were soon all asleep having had a poor night the night before. One of our spotters, a lad called Blackman, was listed to make the tea the next morning. One of the lads gave him a shout at about 7.00am. I might add that he, Blackman, had been asleep when the Orderly Officer had called the night before. He got up, made the tea and gave us all a shout at about 7.30am. Our Sergeant was first out, he went to the shed. Then we heard him bellow "You bloody little idiot" - "called back I am and what a lot of bloody fools I'm asked to soldier with". We all thought what the devil is wrong with him now. We went out to see what had happened. The Sergeant had gone out, he had had his eyes on the rum - he poured out his tea and asked Blackman where the rum was. "What rum Sir? I haven't seen any rum". "It was left here last night by the Orderly Officer - he put it in a basin on the table". "Oh that Sir" said Blackman "I thought that was cold tea, I threw that away". It took the Sergeant about four days to simmer down. So much for our rum ration.

Our rations were quite good but I always thought they could be improved upon. We had all gone down to the little pub at Clayhill, it was only a little place. On the way to the Inn, I saw turnips, swedes and potatoes growing in the fields. One day I asked an old fellow in the pub if he could get me a few rabbit snares, the wire type, he said that he would bring me in some the next day. I went the next day and he had brought me in six, at two pence each, quite a bargain at one shilling. I went around our field and set the snares for the next night, the rabbit runs were easily seen in the long grass. The other lads asked what I was about, to which I replied "Leave it to a country lad and you'll never starve". I told them they may be fly in their cities and on their barrows, just wait till the morrow.

Early the next morning, I went out and found that I had snared three good sized rabbits. I was quite pleased with my efforts. When I got back to our cookhut the lads asked what I was going to do. I told them that I had to paunch them. "Do what" they asked. "Paunch them" I said again "then I will skin them". At this point, I took my jack-knife and slit the belly of the first one and proceeded to take out its insides, some of them looked away, the cockney lad said "You dirty bugger". He turned away and immediately threw up. I cleaned the other two then skinned the three, we got an oval camp kettle and I then put them in salt water to soak. I asked the Sergeant if two or three of us could go to the field and pinch a few swedes, turnips and potatoes. He gave us permission and said "Don't get caught". We were not long away and we returned with quite a load. We then got a big square cooking pot, I cut the rabbits into pieces. We peeled the vegetables, cut them up small and put the pot to cook. I made a few dumplings which were put in the pot later. By about 1.00pm the stew was smelling lovely. "Time to lob out" said the Sergeant. Some of the lads were a bit doubtful at first, after the first taste they thought it was beautiful. They, or we all had about two mess tins full each. Whilst we were there, we always had the stock pot going. It helped out our Army ration. One day I caught two rabbits and we put them in a large baking dish and cooked them in the Aldershot Oven - a rabbit pie, the pastry was a bit hard but we ate the lot.

While all this was going on, Mr Neville Chamberlain was meeting Adolph Hitler in Germany, what would be the outcome?

We became very popular with the people in the little hamlet, there were a few girls full of giggles. At that time, we wore the long puttees from the knee down. One young girl asked one of the lads "How did we put on our twisted trousers"? This caused quite a laugh.

Another incident, we went into the pub one evening (we were on stand down awaiting results from Germany), at the end of the bar room was a large wooden chair by the fireside. I took it upon myself to sit there. An old man with a beard and smock said "Hey, you can't zit there, that be squire's chair - you musn't zit there". "But" I said "the squire is not here". "That's no matter" he said "he will be yer zoon and he'll be right upzet if 'ee zees 'ee zitten there". "I'll wait till he comes" I said "and I'll get up then". "Well take it on yerself". After a while a man came in and everyone looked at me and the old man said under his breath "That be the squire u'm ver it". "Who's in my chair"? asked the gent in plus two's and deerstalker hat. I got up and asked "Is this your chair"? I carried on "You must be pleased to meet me" and I shook his hand. All was taken in good part.

The weather was changing for the better now, the sun came out and the ground began to dry out. We were on stand down awaiting the outcome of the talks in Germany. Things here were not too bad at all, we were more organised and our cooking was good. Bacon and egg for breakfast, stew or pie for dinner, anything that was going for tea. Late at night we always had bread and cheese and cocoa. We were doing quite well.

We then got orders to break camps. Mr Neville Chamberlain returned from Germany waving his famous piece of paper "Peace in our Time" he had made a pact with Adolph Hitler. We didn't know at the time but it gave us just enough time to get a few arms together.

We packed up our camp and returned to Castle Bytham, formed the convey and returned to Blackdown Camp. The Sergeant was delighted, he would soon be going home again and back to his business as a builder. Before he went, he shook all the crew by the hand and thanked us for all we had done. He told Blackman to always smell the tea before he threw it away.

All our equipment had to be cleaned, checked, re-greased and returned to the RAOC stores. It was now the end of September 1938.

We were not long at Blackdown before things returned to the normal routine. Small courses were started and we learned how to become despatch riders. We took motor cycles out on to the moorland surrounding the camp. We learned truck driving, telephonists etc.

Rumours started to circulate that drafts were being sent overseas in the very near future. We watched orders every day to see if the rumours were to become fact.

At about the first week in November, two draft lists appeared, one for Gibraltar, the other for Malta. My name was on neither.

After a few days, two draft lists appeared for Hong Kong and Singapore. My name appeared on the latter.

We moved huts and formed up in our respective drafts. Next we had all the inoculations etc. Some of the men who moved into our hut are older soldiers. They have been to Singapore before, one was a L/Corporal, another was a Corporal. The others were about three Sappers. They were telling us all about the Far East. We listened quite eagerly to all their stories. They told us of the beautiful girls and the night clubs. The Malay Dollar 2/4 Eight to the Pound. Beer 18c per pint. Blimey, that's 44 pints to a £1. Cigarettes were 4c or 6c per packet of ten. It must be lovely out there. Showing off a bit as well, they were speaking Malay, we thought this was great. We were going on a new glorious adventure and were all looking forward to it.

Whilst we were awaiting our draft, we had a very relaxed time. To keep us in trim, we had a lot of cross country running, we had to run eight to ten miles. I had done the run about five times and was getting a bit fed up with it, so took my time and got in amongst the last five or six. One day two of us (Bill Hydon) decided that we would take a short cut. We jumped through a hole in the hedge of a small copse. The run came back towards the camp on the other side of this copse. We stopped and had a cigarette or two in the thicket. When we thought we had been in long enough, we looked to see that there was no-one in authority about (a Sergeant Major used to do the course on a cycle, just to gee us up). The coast was clear and we ran back to the camp guard room and checked in. The P.T Instructor was there and he said that we had done well, I was 10th back, my mate was 11th. A few days later we found out that the course had been lengthened by two miles. It appeared on orders that I had been picked in one of the teams of five to represent the A/A Battalion at Aldershot in the inter unit Cross Country Competition, so much for fiddling. I ran there and came in about 20th, not bad I suppose against all the other Regiments in the Command.

During our leisure hours in the evenings, we used to drink in a pub at Frimley Green. We were always made welcome there. Most of us used to drink the 4d beer.

Outside the camp was a mobile cafe. We used to love the meat pies that the gentleman sold, they went down lovely after a pint or two of the old 4d.

One evening we were in the pub at Frimley Green. I think there were about six of us. A Corporal we knew from another company was away on a twelve week course. His wife was at a loose end and came into the pub with another lady. The Corporal's wife told us that her husband was away six weeks and that she was fed up. She took a shine to one of our company. He was a very shy type but she made a bee-line for him and chatted with him all the evening. When we got our rounds in, we all bought her and her companion a drink. When closing time came we all left the Inn together. We had to pass the Married Quarters on our way. When we got there, the Corporal's wife invited our mate back for coffee, we chaffed him and said that she fancied him and we would put pillows in his bed to make it look as if he was in and asleep. He went with the lady to the quarters. We all said "Lucky sod - he will be OK there, he'll get his leg over tonight"! We had only been back about an hour and a half. We had all been saying "Wonder if he is abed yet - I bet she'll give him some zip"! The Barrack room door opened and in he came, we were amazed. "That was a quick jump" we all shouted "what happened"? "Well" he said "she made a cup of coffee and I drank that" then he added "she started kissing me and playing with my tool. She even locked the door so I jumped out of the window - bugger that - if her old man was to find out, I'll be on Jankers for the rest of me service". "Bloody fool" we all said "wish I'd had that chance". "We shall be in Singapore before he finished that course". "It's alright for you lot to say that" then he added "if it had been any of you, you would have jibbed when the cards were down". It took him quite a time to live that down.

44

We often saw the Corporal's wife but she had got another male companion.

Some evenings we would go to the Ubique Cinema where we saw all the latest films and cartoons. Our favourites here were Betty Grable, Dorothy Lamour (in jungle scenes), Rita Hayworth, Mae West (bubbling over), Jane Russell, Hedy Lamar, Carole Lombard and many others could be mentioned, notice we didn't think about the men.

Time drifted by, we had all our inoculations, we were all passed fit for overseas service. Our draft leave drew nearer, the last before we started our next big adventure to which we were all looking forward. We had been issued with our tropical kit, K.D for the Far Eastern Stations, we all tried on our brand new topees, some put on their full tropical uniform and had their photographs taken. An old gentleman had a licence to come into the camp to take photos and he used to do quite a good trade. Only cost half a crown for large size, good photographs.

DRAFT LEAVE

About mid December we went on our draft leave. At this time I had got my No 1 blue uniform, of which I was very proud, with of course the swagger cane, with which no soldier was without.

Before going on leave, I had received a letter from my cousin saying that they had moved house and I had to go back to the village to stay with my Aunt and Uncle. I should be seeing all my old school buddies and visit old friends that I went to school with, some of them had joined the forces, RAF, Royal Navy and Royal Marines. At this time one of my oldest friends, Harry Howard, had joined the Royal Marines and he was on leave at the same time. I saw him at Eastney Barracks, Portsmouth. He was on leave before joining the ship HMS Repulse. I spent quite a lot of time with him. His father was an old salt and had been in the Royal Navy about 35 years. He had been in the 1914-18 War and he told us of the great battles. If one ever said to him "You were in the Navy Mr Howard" he would retort with some venom "I was in the Royal Navy, please Sir". Still a very proud old man. I remember him showing us his medals. "This one from the Emperor of Japan - I was there doing rescue work in Japan during the earthquake in the 1920s. This one was from the King of Italy when Mount Etna erupted". What adventures he had had. Then he turned to me one night and said "You will be going over a lot of the ground that I have covered in my time". "Well" I said "I don't suppose I shall go to Japan as you did". "It is a beautiful country" he added "if you get the chance to go - you go". Little did I know what was in store.

I visited the pottery where I was once employed, saw a lot of my old workmates. I was pleased when they said that I looked smart and a lot better in health, this I knew as I had put on a lot of weight and the open air life was my salvation. I was so glad that I had joined up when I saw a lot of my dust infected old workmates.

One day whilst in the town, I met my old girlfriend. I asked her how she felt, she was adamant that she had not changed her mind. I took her to the picture house one evening. After I took her to the bus depot, it was at this point I told her that I had met a girl from Bristol and was writing to her. She looked very surprised but did say "You won't write to me then when you are in Singapore". "There is no point you said you wanted to forget the past". Well that was that, I didn't mind. "No hard feelings" I said "I'll still think of you for old time sake". "And I'll be thinking of you at times I expect" she said. "We must see how things go, remember you will be away for three years". The bus took off and that was that.

Our gang went around the pubs. We were drinking quite a lot. The 4d beer I might add. My Aunt and Uncle lived in a bungalow on the outskirts of the village. My cycle was still available, this was very handy as I could ride it to the village and leave it with one of my friends. In the meantime, my cousin had fallen on hard times and lost his job, so he, his wife and baby daughter came to live with his mother and father. It was a small bungalow with only two bedrooms. I didn't have much option but I was asked if I would sleep in the spare front room. As I have said, I had no option, so agreed to this arrangement. They put an old sofa against the wall. To make extra width, three chairs were put along the side, on to this set up was placed a big feather tick. This was my bed. Another draw back was the fact that the electric at that time had not been connected, so the only illumination available was oil lamps and candles, a bit Heath Robinson. Still never mind, I had three weeks of my leave to go. The bed was quite OK as long as I didn't turn over. The crunch came when one night I had been to the Star Inn and had had one too many. All was quiet when I got home. All were asleep, it was about 11.30pm. I took my uniform off and was getting into bed, I tried to stand on the bed and my feet went down into a void between the chairs and sofa. The whole lot collapsed and I fell in between and couldn't move. It woke everyone up including the baby - then all hell was let loose. The sitting room door shot open, in came my Uncle and cousin. "What the hell is going on"? "I'm sorry" I said, to which he replied "I thought it was a bloody earthquake". I was helplessly jammed on the floor. They had to get me out. My Aunt then appeared "What's up"? she asked. "It's alright" said my Uncle. "He's bloody drunk" said my cousin. After that episode the feather tick was laid out on the floor.

One day I went to Newton Abbot and I met the friend that had joined the Army on the same day as I at Exeter. His occupation before going to the pottery had been a pastry cook with a large bakery. As I said before, he left me at Chatham so it was nice to see him again. He had had a foot injury in the gym. He was now employed as a pastry cook with a field company at Aldershot. He was quite happy to be working in his trade. I told him that I was on draft to Singapore. He said that he wouldn't care much for that. We went out and had a drink or two together.

Then one day I thought I'd take a walk alone through the woods where I had played as a small boy, where I had walked with my dear old Grandfather. He had a great philosophy, he told me tales of bygone days when he was a child. He taught me the names of all the trees and the birds. "Listen my boy" he would say "that is a blackbird" or "that is a thrush". He taught me how to make a whistle from a piece of ash or hazel wood. How to find the hazelnuts and edible mushrooms. This is where a badger lives, a holt it is called. He also showed me how to lay a snare to catch a rabbit. "Look my boy a fox has been here". He would pick a leaf from a tree and ask "what sort of tree is this"? "That is the English Oak" I would reply "That's good" he would say. Yes, in that wood I was happy and that day I felt very near to my dear "Boppo" as I called him when I was a small child. My dear Grandfather had been dead for six years. I only wish he could be here to see me now, I wonder what he would have said?

Then I went to our Church at Ilsington, where I sang in the choir and was a server. I asked God to guide me in the adventure that was ahead. The Vicar had been changed since I joined the Army, so I did not see my very old friend. As I entered the Church, I heard the bells ringing as they welcomed everyone to prayer. Our England, would I miss all this whilst I was away. Then I thought "it's only for three years". After the Church service, I visited my Mother's grave, she had died of TB when I was only seven. I often think of her, it sticks in my memory as she lay dying of that dreaded disease, they took me to her, she was in a semi coma and they said "Here is Roy come to see you", she rallied, put her arms around me and said "Promise me you will always be a good boy". She kissed me and slipped again into the coma. Her long black hair came down to her waist, she had been a beautiful lady. She died that evening in June 1925.

At the foot of her grave my Grandfather and Grandmother lay buried. I did not know my Grandmother, she died in 1906, my Grandfather remained a widower for the rest of his life. I stood at the foot of the grave and thanked him for all he had done for me. He brought me up until he died in 1932. I left the churchyard and walked away home with my thoughts and memories.

The week before I was due to return to my unit, I went to my old school, I saw the Headmaster and other teachers, it was only a church school and not very big, so the teaching staff was not many, the Headmaster and three lady teachers. They were very pleased to see me and wished me well in the adventure ahead. I was leaving and walking across the school playground, I looked at the three giant oaks where we climbed and played as kids, in one was still the big bird nesting box that I had made and fixed there during our woodwork lesson. I wonder how many birds had built in it since I had put it there about six years ago. Let's hope they would have the pleasure of nesting there when I am far away. I wondered if it would still be there when I came back again. I think how patient our teachers were in educating us through the years. I think of the girls who have since left that I thought I was madly in love with, carrying their cases and buying them the odd 2d bar of chocolate. One of these girls had been misbehaving and the Headmaster was giving her the stick across the hand, I very bravely stood up and shouted "Don;t hit her, or you will have to hit me". "Come here boy" he says "bend over and he gave me six of the best with his best cane. She (the girl) thought that I had been very brave. So I leave my memories behind.

Two nights before I was due to return, I went to see my friend Harry, the Royal Marine and his family. Harry, his father and I went to the local inn The Anchor at Chudleigh Knighton. We had a good evening and partook in too much ale and rum, I had to ride my cycle back to my Uncle's bungalow. After our farewell, I set off, not at all steady I might add, I had about four miles to cover, with my meandering I think I must have covered twenty four miles or more. As I neared home I felt the beer and rum mixture begin to churn over in my stomach - then suddenly I was violently sick over the handlebars of the cycle. I staggered home and got to bed feeling the worse for wear, I soon was in a drunken sleep. The next morning I awoke and went to clean my teeth but what teeth I hadn't any, I looked high and low searched my pockets but no sign. Only one answer I must retrace my steps. Well I found them - there they were - just outside a farm gate. The farmer had earlier taken his cows in from a field opposite, milked them and taken them back to the field again - well you know what cows are like, there were my teeth embedded in the largest cowpat I had ever seen. I took them home cleaned them and let them soak in milton for two or three hours, I must tie them in with string on my future drinking bouts.

The day of my return had arrived, I had to say farewell to all my folks. My Uncle told me to look after myself, I think he was a little proud to see me wearing the uniform of a Sapper, as he had done all through the 1914-18 War with distinction in the fields of flanders. He shook my hand and said "Good luck my boy". I kiss my Aunt goodbye and she said "I shall never see you again", this was very upsetting, as I knew she was getting on in years.

I shook hands with my cousin and kissed his wife. I took their child, the baby girl Anne in my arms and kissed her, she was my Godchild. I knew the tears were in my eyes, she was only 18 months old. I handed her back to her Mother, I did not wish to make a fool of myself. I picked up my suitcase. It was snowing as I went out of the front gate, it was now January -I had had a good Christmas and New Year. The local bus arrived and took me away as I waved goodbye to them all.

I got on to Newton Abbot station and had an hour to wait for my train. It was snowing quite hard. I waited in the restaurant when a Sapper came in and told me that he was going back to Blackdown Camp. He was in another company and he told me that he was on draft for Malta. So I had company to go back with. We talked about service life and were both looking forward to our foreign service. It seemed that we had got over the 1938 crisis - Adolph seemed to behaving himself. Of course there were troubles in Spain with General Franco, Italy had attacked and bombed Addis Ababa, the Japs were at war with China. We did not think that any of this would affect us. We should be alright for a year or two at least. We got back to Deepcut, the duty truck was there to take us back to Blackdown Camp. It had been snowing quite heavy here and it was quite deep. There were a lot of the lads awaiting the truck, all in good spirits, they had come from all parts of the British Isles. It wouldn't be long now and we would leave all this snow behind.

EMBARKATION HMT LANCASHIRE

Orders were posted, we found that the Hong Kong and Singapore drafts would leave Southampton on board His Majesty's Troopship Lancashire. On 16 February 1939, We now knew the date was fixed. We had just a month to do general duties i.e mess waiters, piquet duties. We got to school and I sat my Second Class Education Certificate (Army). To my delight, I passed. This certificate allowed one to reach the rank of Sergeant. At this time, I was thinking of completing my six years with the colours and coming out and joining the Devon County Police Force. I should then be 25 years of age. I should be just inside the limited age.

We had quite a few snow storms here whilst we were awaiting the boat. One old soldier told me that we should be glad of a bit of snow in two months time. Our sporting activities were hampered, no football, rugby or cross country running. I didn't mind about the latter.

We went to the pub at Frimley Green at weekends or to the cinema, we just couldn't get away quick enough.

The last day came and we arranged to have a draft party at the pub in Frimley to spend the last of our english money. We got to the pub and it was packed with people who had come to see their sons and loved ones before they left the next day. A L/Corporal's girlfriend and his parents were there, he had got engaged at Christmas, they said they would be at Southampton the next day to see our draft depart. There were several people from the London area came to see their sons depart, sisters had come to see their brothers off. We had a lovely evening all singing together.

It was spoiled by some idiots on the way back to camp, they started to smash the street lights and pull up trees in peoples private gardens. I didn't see the reason for such behaviour, a few of us tried to stop it but a small majority were acting like idiots. The Police took over, together with the Military Police. Quite a few of the vandals who were responsible were put into the guard room cells to cool off, a lovely night out spoiled by such fools, it gave our Corps a bad name.

THE TROOP SHIP - 16 FEBRUARY 1939

Well our embarkation date had arrived. We handed in our bedding and our accommodation is checked for breakages. Our kits are packed, we drew our haversack rations and we awaited the transport that would take us to the railway station at Deepcut, then out on to the main line for Southampton.

The two standby men were ordered to get ready for embarkation, they were taking the places of the two who were in the cells at the guard room. At the last minute, the two were released and charges would be served against them when they arrived at the Singapore Garrison. Not a very good start for them out there. The two reserve men were a bit disappointed at not being able to go.

We got on to the trucks with all our kits. It was still very cold, we had a fall of snow again the night before. The truck took off and we waved to all our friends who were left behind. They wished us luck, my God we were to need it!!

We arrived at the docks and there she was awaiting us, His Majesty's Troopship Lancashire of the Bibby Line. Well I had seen her before, I remember I was on our choir outing, a trip up the River Dart, she was tied to the sister ship HMT Dorsetshire, little did I think then as a small lad that I would one day sail in her. When trooping was out of season, these ships laid up there for cleaning and repainting and of course repairing.

She looked a lovely ship from the dockside. We went aboard at about 1400 hours. We found things differed. We drew hammocks and were detailed twelve to a mess. Our hammocks hooks were allocated, it was very cramped. A month of this before we reached our destination.

Many of the people we saw in the pub at Frimley Green were on the dockside, sisters, brothers, Mums, Dads and sweethearts had come to see their loved ones set sail. I remember well the lad from London, the L/Corporal, his Mother, Father and the girl he had got engaged to the last night we were there. The gang plank came up, no jumping off now!! The ship's siren gave a mighty blast, then that first movement, a judder as the tugs took her in tow. You felt that sinking in the stomach, this was it, we were off. A few hundred yards off the shore the ship's engines started to pulse, in no time at all we were out into the Solent and deep water. Another stage of service had started. The coast of England glides by on the starboard, the Needles were to the port, we slipped into the English Channel, it was not long and the ship began to roll a bit. I went up on deck, I felt a bit homesick as I saw the coast of my beloved Devon to starboard. I wondered what they were thinking about, were they saying "He is on his way". I pictured their faces at our front door as I passed through the garden gate on my return from my last leave.

We now turned southward and we saw the coast of Brittany to port, we now headed out into the dreaded Bay of Biscay. I had heard so much from my old friend Harry's Father. The ship now took on a definite pitch and roll. I saw several lads dash to the rail to be seasick, so early I thought. We went below, slung our hammocks after a meal. Then it was bed time, or should I saw hammock time, to us it was a pantomime, jump in one side and fall out the other. We had a draft of Royal Navy men on board, they were going to Hong Kong to join a ship out there. They slung their hammocks and were in with no bother, well after all it was their life. We had to take some stick from them - "Land Lubbers - Bloody Pongos". After a while, they came and taught us the tricks of the trade, like putting a stretcher between the strings of the hammock, grab the bulkheads and swing up into the hammock and drop right in, it was easy really. They were a good lot of lads, we all got on well together.

A list of duties were posted, I found that I had to go to the Married Families Mess as a mess waiter. This turned out to be quite a good duty. There were about thirty ORs ladies who were going out to join their husbands. I had to wait on three tables. After the meal, we all mucked in to clear the pots, pans, knives, forks, spoons etc. We had time off then until the next meal. After the first day, very few of the ladies came to meals, sea sickness was taking its toll. I wasn't too bad at this stage. Then early one morning, I was on my way to the dining hall and I saw some of the lads bringing their hearts up, even that didn't upset me, I got into the dining hall and they had put up kippers for breakfast. I had to dash upstairs to the rail - well up it came, I was sick for two whole days. I wasn't required in the dining hall as there were only two ladies in for meals. It was a terrible feeling - not knowing where the next meal was coming from, I'm sure I brought up a toenail at one stage. The Bay of Biscay was rough some said, it was only the Blue Line around the side of the ship that was keeping her together. The sea then began to quieten down.

We now saw Gibraltar ahead, we watched as it grew bigger. We slowed to a stop and dropped anchor. A tender came from the shore to take off mail and stores.

It was here that we saw the first bumboats, the owners selling their wares, we lowered baskets with our money and we then pulled the baskets back in board with the goods that we had purchased, I only bought a few postcards to send home, it was easier than writing letters. But these small boats were like bees around a honey pot, all jostling for position. We only stayed at Gibraltar for about four hours. It was a mighty fortress, we saw guns poking in all directions, it was an impressive show of strength. It had a great water catchment area as the main water supply was only rainwater.

Some came from Spain but could not be relied on due to the political state of our countries. At this time, the Spanish Civil War was in progress.

After a while, we weighed anchor and proceeded through the Straits of Gibraltar into the Mediterranean Sea. So blue, so calm. The blue was so very deep it fascinated me. We watched the flying fish, they broke the surface to fly or glide seventy or eighty yards before disappearing into the blue. At night, we had a full moon and went to the bows of the ship to watch the dolphins playing in the bow phosphorus waves, all was so fascinating to us watching these beautiful creatures. Our sea sickness was now all forgotten, it was beautiful and calm. We carried out our duties and had plenty of leisure time on our hands. For exercise, we used to pace the decks in pairs, some of us got up very early and gave ourselves a task of running around the deck six or seven times. We found that as each day passed, the temperature rose. We had surely left the snows of England behind.

On the starboard side of our trooper, the coast of North Africa was pointed out to us. Where so many battles were to be fought in the coming years. On the portside the coast of Sicily was now in view many miles away.

Our next port of call was Malta, we arrived early in the morning and dropped anchor. We were allowed ashore here for a few hours, which gave us a good chance to stretch our legs. We went to the R.E canteen. We met a few of the lads who had left us a few months before. We took in a good fill of beer and, before we knew, we were due back to the ship. We said our farewells to our old mates, quite a few of whom were to pay the extreme and final sacrifice in later years. In no time at all, we once again set sail. The Lancashire ploughed her way through the calm blue sea.

There were many rackets on board ship, hot sweet tea or hot sweet coffee. At night one could buy from the vendors hot sweet cocoa. I didn't quite know how this was done, I noticed the vendors were all men with at least two good conduct badges "old sweats" who had travelled these routes many times before, all out to make a fast buck as we used to say. I often wondered if it was our own rightful rations we were buying, who knows? I do know it was better tea than we had on our mess rations or we could buy in the canteen. In the evening we could drink beer. Well beer, if you could call it that, we could buy Alsops mild, we called it Allslops, we could also buy MacQuans??? It may have started as a good brew but how many voyages it had made to Hong Kong and back to the UK, one would never know. A gang of about eight men would chip in together and buy an enamel bucket full, about three gallons. We would dip our china one pint pots in and sup up. Many a man was free from sea sickness until he had had a few jugs of this brew, you would see them run to the ship rail and throw up. During these drinking sessions, we would play an old forces game "Ships at Anchor" known to old sweats by another very familiar name. It was quite a good laugh, with many forfeits having to be paid. At other times, we played tombola. I think the old sweats always ran that as quite a lot of the old sweats always won - it was uncanny at times. We would walk away on the next house, as the numbers dwindled, low and behold a young soldier would win, then back we would all go to be fleeced again as the number of tickets sold would mount - for the old sweat to win again. I wonder, could it be sheer luck. A lot never drew their pay till just before they reached their destination or disembarkation.

So with engines throbbing and many vibrations, we ploughed our way through the Mediterranean toward Port Said, our next port of call. We found the temperature begin to soar. we had been issued with salt water soap, this we used when taking showers at numerous times, it was like rubbing oneself all over with a pumice stone, no lather whatsoever.

Port Said came into view, we were all on deck to see this mystic middle eastern city come into view, having heard and read stories of Laurence of Arabia and the romantic Middle East.

About four days before our arrival, it had appeared on orders that Arab Town was out of bounds to all ranks. We all wondered why, was there some unknown mystery?

Lancashire approached Port Said very slowly. We tied up to a pontoon pier at about 0900 hours.

We were told that we could go ashore at 1030 hours and had to be back by 1600 hours, so we had a nice trip ashore of 5½ hours. We could have a nice walk around to stretch our sea legs and get the muscles and circulation working. We were all excited as we crossed the pontoon pier in our little parties. Six sappers with a Corporal in charge. We met the vendors of filthy postcards, other pictures of the Sphinx and the Pyramids. We bought some to send home. In our letters, we cheated a little by sending these photos - we saw none of these things - but it would impress the folks at home. We had small boys approach us with proposition of "you good English soldier, you jig jig my big sister", pestering us "she big girl - you like very much" we laughed about this and thought of the awful VD pictures we had been shown both before leaving and on our voyage.

We were pestered by young children begging, some were very deformed, some were blind. We gave a few pence to these unfortunates, within no time at all the crowd swelled. One of the old soldiers told us that it was wrong to give to these beggars, they were professionals, the were maimed at birth or blinded and as very small children were sent on to the streets to beg to supplement the family income. We thought this was terrible and felt so sorry for them. How unfortunate that such things were allowed to happen in the world. We saw men with hands missing and were told that they were thieves who had been caught stealing, they had been tried and sentenced to have their hands amputated, how awful, but that was their justice, their way of doing things - how barbaric.

Then one of the lads had a very bright idea and suggested that we made a visit to Arab Town. You might have guessed, it was our cockney friend. So, in spite of being warned on daily ships orders that it was out of bounds to all troops, we set off with an Arab guide who said that he could show us around for a few bob. We had a whip around and off we went. The Corporal in charge of our party wasn't too keen but was out-voted and he couldn't go back to the ship without us, to say he wasn't too keen was an understatement - he was worried sick. We were taken through winding streets, everyone was trying to sell us goods of some kind, pornographic picture postcards and other such literature was to the fore. The cockney lad saw a man with a very black beard looking out of an upstairs window, he shouted to him "Hello! you black bearded old bastard" the guide tried to keep him quiet but he insisted on shouting. We moved on to the low dives. We were asked if we wanted to see naked ladies dancing, we couldn't resist this, it wasn't too bad about five young Arab girls were doing belly dancing, they were quite attractive in fact. Then the touts were after us, selling their wares, did we wish to see jig jig exhibition, big man with girl very good to see. It was at this point that the Corporal put his foot down and said "Back to the boat". I was quite in favour, we were getting a little bit out of our depth as it were. Things could have gotten a little nasty, so we beat a hasty retreat out of Arab Town. As we were making our way back, we had to pass the bearded gentleman's abode, we had forgotten all about him - but he had not forgotten our cockney pal, as he passed under the window, a bucket of muck cascaded down on him, to put in plain language, it was pure crap and it covered our friend from head to toe, it couldn't have been a better shot had it been fired from a large blunderbuss, the smell was awful - we couldn't get near him. We had a few hours of our shore leave to go but he had to go back aboard. When he reached the gang plank, they would not allow him aboard, everyone walked away from him. Eventually they got buckets, filled them with sea water and swilled him down. All his kit that he was wearing was destroyed and he had to got the Medical Officer and get some special injections against disease. I doubt if our old friend would ever forget Arab Town. and the black bearded old bastard!

As we had time to spare, we went into the town and found a Regimental canteen and partook in a little beering session - quite enjoyable. On our way back to the ship, a few of us had our photographs taken wearing fezzes and riding a camel with a backcloth of the Sphinx and Pyramids. After an hour the photos were developed, quite a good service - black and white of course. Very impressive to send home to the folks.

So our trip ashore at Port Said came to an end. I thought we had all enjoyed the experience but I don't think I would like to be stationed in the Middle East.
We went aboard Lancashire, tired out having done quite a lot of walking around. A blast of the ships horn, we set sail once again.

We enter the Suez Canal pass De Lesseps monument. We were all eyes to see one of the greatest engineering marvels of all time. The canal was just one hundred miles long with no locks. It connects the Mediterranean Sea with the Red Sea, the Arabian Desert on the starboard side and Arabia to port. Our ship passed through with ease but I think our big ships such as the Hood, Rodney and the aircraft carriers such as the Eagle must have found it hard to manoeuvre with not a lot to spare. So as we sailed, night was upon us. It was a great pity as the scenery was none such as we had seen before. On one side we had sand, on the other grass and palms. The sunset was the most beautiful I had ever seen. So to our hammocks for the night, we had had a lovely day, a bit of excitement and we had seen a bit of Port Said it had been quite an experience to our young eyes.

We chaffed our cockney pal but he took it all in good part and said that if the bearded gentleman was as good a shot with a rifle as he was with a bucket of crap, he would be a good soldier.

Early the next morning, we were up to carry out our various duties, I was still a waiter in the Married Families Mess. Quite a few of these ladies were going to Singapore to join their husbands. In the course of our duties, we got to know them well. As soon as our chores were completed, we went on deck to see all the canal activities. Before we left Port Said, we took on a Suez Canal Pilot.

He took control of the ship for its passage through this waterway. We also took aboard two small boats with two Arab seamen in each. One boat on the bow, the other on the stern. If we had to tie up to let another ship pass, these boats were lowered and the men rowed to the side of the canal with ropes. In turn they pulled long hawsers ashore and made fast the ship to bollards. We pulled in to a kind of lay-by. The canal was a very busy line of communication, we were always stopping to let ships pass, or they pulled into their lay-bys to let us pass. On one occasion, we pulled in to one lay-by and were tied up to let a French submarine pass, they waved to us, we waved back - quite a friendly affair. Not like the Italian ship full of troops we saw in Port Said.

Next day we were at Port Suez, we entered the Gulf of Suez after having passed through the Bitter Lake. We gathered speed as we were more or less in the open sea. Within a short time, the Lancashire was in the Red Sea. We were again fascinated by the dolphins playing in the bow wave of the ship. Flying fish were again in evidence.

Our next port of call was Aden. Only about four men disembarked here. "Good luck" I thought to myself. What a God forsaken place it was, it appeared to be only sand and bleak rocks, not a happy place to be I guess.

We passed through the Gulf of Aden and into the Indian Ocean. We were now ordered to don our K.D uniform and shorts. This was where our knobbly white knees came into view.

It was now becoming very hot indeed, we were issued daily with very strong lime juice. This they say was to combat or keep our sex urges under control, not that we could do much if we cannot.

Life continued in the same vein as before, hot sweet sugary tea, hot sweet coffee. The Crown and Anchor board was still in evidence as the tombola sessions with the old sweats calling the numbers. We were still drinking that horrible beer by the bucket full, so life continued as did our ship on it's voyage.

We then spotted a few sharks with their triangular fins cutting the surface of the water, a very sombre sight to be sure.

Our next port of call was Colombo Ceylon. As we approached, we saw the beautiful greenery of the tea plantation on the hillsides. What a contrast with those barren rocks in Aden, this looked a paradise. As we got closer, we saw the giant sign above all the other buildings "Liptons Tea". We were proud to think that was part of our great British Empire. Once again our ship was tied up and we were allowed eight hours ashore. We went ashore in our same little parties with the same NCO in charge. We at first got on a conducted tour of the tea plantation. This was very interesting as we watched the native girls picking the tea and putting it into the baskets attached to their heads. I remember as a small boy at school seeing pictures of these activities, never dreaming that one day I should be able to see these things at first hand. After the tour of the plantation, we returned to Colombo to have a look around the city and do a bit of shopping, postcards to send home. We were very interested in the shops selling beautiful silks and brassware. We finished up in a British NAAFI and met quite a few who were stationed here from our own Corps, some of whom were attached to the Indian Army. They told us that they had good postings. All too soon our stay in Colombo came to an end. We went back aboard Lancashire, without mishap, our cockney mate had behaved himself and was totally clean on his return and did not disgrace himself as he had at Port Said. As the evening approached, we took up anchor and set sail further south in the Indian Ocean toward our destination Singapore. We had been on the ship just three weeks, we were all looking forward to getting off and settling down to our normal service life. It was getting very hot now as we approached the Equator. We were warned against sunbathing but it was too late for some of our fair skinned friends, they looked like lobsters, others had giant blisters on their backs. Keep your shirts on we were warned, even when the sun is covered by cloud, the ultra violet rays can still burn your skin, this we were to find out to be very true as we continued our service in the tropics.

We had heard so much about service life in Singapore, we were all looking forward in anticipation to a good three year posting. We will be sailing home again in 1942 when, I hope to finish my service life and join the Devon County Police Force.

During the next few days, routine was still the same on board ship. We entered the Straits of Malacca and knew that it would not be long now and we could even smell the magic of the Orient as the green palms came into view, as we voyaged down the west coast of Malaya. The green vegetation looked beautiful, as we got closer to the coast, we saw the giant coconut palms and the sandy shores, it looked like a paradise.

We were told to get below, pack our kits and make ready for disembarkation. We were all full of excitement at the thoughts of our new adventures ahead. We made ready, cleaned our mess deck, hand in our hammocks and bedding. Once everything had been inspected by the ships staff, we were allowed on deck.

Singapore Island came into view, we inched our way into Kepple Harbour, the shipping lanes were very busy. This was a very busy port, the docks were full of merchant vessels, oil tankers and other such shipping. The tugs took us in tow, it was not long before we were tied up and the gang planks put into position. A regimental band was on the dockside to greet us. We noticed the Chinese junks that were busy around all the other shipping, they were carrying cement, sand, coal and all such cargoes. We were told that they ply goods to Sumatra, Java, Borneo and the other islands in the vicinity.

We were told to get below and prepare to leave Lancashire, it had been our home afloat for exactly one month. It had been 28 days since we left Southampton on 16 February 1939, today was 16 March 1939.

SO THIS IS SINGAPORE

We were met on the docks by the administration staff of the Fortress R.E Changi. We embarked on to trucks driven by Chinese drivers. These were civilian trucks with board seats laid across the sideboards of these trucks. We set off from the docks, through the streets of this cosmopolitan city. The smell of open drains and the different types of cooking took us by surprise. We had never been told about this, it was a bit obnoxious, the smell of ghi (goat fat) used by the Indians, the smell of coconut oil by the Chinese, this was truly a new experience. Would we ever get used to it? We leave the city area with all its temples, the smell of joss sticks, we passed through the kampongs with their attap roofs. Changi Gaol was pointed out to us, it looked a very sinister place.

These Chinese drivers hadn't had much instruction before taking over their vehicles. They all seemed to start up, point into the direction they wished to go and foot down, it was certainly a very hairy ride with many near misses on the way. We were glad when we reached Changi Garrison in one piece. We unloaded at the R.E Garrison HQ office block, we were marched on to the square and were detailed off to our different companies. There were three companies at Changi, 30th, 34th. These were anti aircraft searchlight units. I was detailed to the 41st Fortress Coy, this was a coastal defence searchlight company. I was disappointed at this posting as I wanted to stay with the AA S/L units for which I had been trained. We bid farewell to our friends who had joined the other companies and marched off to H Block in Changi Barracks which housed 41st Coy. It did not take us long to settle in, we were made very welcome by the rest of the company. Of course we had to put up with a bit of the banter "Get your knees brown" and "Oh! you do look pale - are you ill". This of course was the usual mickey taking on all the new drafts.

We were told that we would be excused all parades for the first few days, as they wanted us to get acclimatized, we found it very hot. Singapore being only 2° off the equator. We were told that at all times we had to keep our shirts and topees on when going into the sun, as we were told on the ship to beware even on cloudy days. We were allowed to go to the pager to swim. When swimming, beware of jelly fish, never swim outside the pager (fence) because of the sharks. After swimming, dry the feet and ears and wash with medical spirits as a precaution against Singapore Ear and Chinese Feet which could be very painful.

We had a very stern lecture by the Medical Officer about VD with slides and photographs, it made one feel sick at what could happen after going with these girls of ill repute. We said we would never go with a woman again, it put the fear of God into one to hear of the horrors this MO had told us about.

We visited the canteen but found the beer very bitter and did not at once take to it. I think one had to get acclimatized to the beer as well as the heat. The most popular beer is of course Tiger, Chop Remau. At that time, it was 18c per pint, just under six pints to a $ which was valued at 2/4 (12p).

I had been in Changi just five days before my 21st Birthday. When it came, I hadn't a cent to my name, so I had a very quiet 21st Birthday. I would celebrate at a later date.

After a few days, we joined the morning parades and were soon shown the routine. Our barracks were the most modern in the world, all air conditioned, the canteens were well equipped with billiard and snooker tables (full size). Everything was done to make life as comfortable as possible, we were encouraged to partake in all the sporting activities such as rugby, football, boxing, water polo, swimming and diving. I found that I liked the latter and became a very good swimmer and not too bad a diver. I loved the warm waters of the tropics. Our day started early at 6.30am, we had breakfast, first parade was at 7.00am. We were inspected and taken to work on our own transport. We finished at midday, when our trucks brought us back to barracks.

We were re-trained in coastal defence and did every duty from the direction stations, engine driving, searchlight operators. I found it to be most interesting and was glad that I did not get posted to an anti aircraft company. We were always under good cover from the tropical storms, whereas the A/A crews were under tentage and were in the elements when operating their positions. They were also vulnerable to the hoards of mosquitos in their jungle sites and outposts. Coastal defence was better after all, I was quite happy with my lot.

We had been settled in for a few weeks when an enquiry was held into the vandalism caused by the few of our draft on our last night in the UK. Those who were thought to be responsible were made to pay through stoppage of pay for the damage caused, it was a great pity that they had acted so foolishly on our last night at home.

We were allowed to wear civilian clothes when off duty, it didn't take long before we kitted ourselves out in the white duck suits.

These were very smart and looked quite nice when laundered by our expert Chinese, we were the cats whiskers.

We had our own servants, one boy would look after four or six men, clean all our kits, boots, shoes, buttons and sweep our bed areas every day. We had to clean our own rifles and bayonets, the rifles were locked in a large rack at the end of each barrack room. This had always been tradition in the East since the Indian Mutiny.

One could employ an Indian Barber to shave one before reveille. I had this man shave me a few times but it always gave me a shock to awake to find this gentleman standing over me with a cut throat razor in his hand, so I chickened out and always shaved myself.

We had the Chinese Sew Sew ladies, they came around the barrack rooms calling "Sew sew -sew sew". They would do any repairs to our kits, sew buttons and such, they were very good and very skilful. Would do a very good job at a very reasonable price.

Yes! Life in Changi was good. Discipline was very laxed, our NCOs were very friendly. Not at all like in the UK. We found that our officers were very good, any problems, they would do their best to put right.

We were trained up in the duties of coastal defence. Our training was done at Changi Beach and Betin Kusa Beach. Our searchlights were on the sea edge. We did night exercises, exposing on moving targets with the Royal Artillery firing blanks from their six inch guns at Changi Battery and other outlaying positions. We were confident that Singapore was well protected from any sea invasion from the seaward side to the south.

After a few months, we were detailed for duty on the outstations. These were Penerang and Tekon, we went across daily to these positions by boat, which we boarded at Changi Pier. During the early days, there were only skeleton crews on these sites. We tried and tested the equipment i.e the engines, searchlights, telephones and other pieces of equipment such as small arms which were used for our own protection. This all done, our days work was completed, so back to Changi by noon.

The unwritten law of the barrack room was "In bed or out of barracks". The old soldiers I might add liked their afternoon kip. A lot of the young soldiers, myself included, went to the pager to swim and sunbathe, we had got ourselves used to the tropical sun by this time. If the tide was out, we would take a trip to Selerang Barracks and by courtesy of the Gordon Highlanders we would swim in their fresh water bath. This pool was up to the then olympic standard complete with high diving boards and spring boards. If of course we had had a late night out the night before, we would join the old soldiers in kip for the afternoon.

During this part of my service, I would like to mention that I met and made friends with some of the best men one could ever meet in ones life. I will mention their names at this point:-

Harold Grey (Dolly) Eric Morton
Reggie Mullins Bill Hydon
Neville Vaughan John Collins
David Englefield Taff Kennard
Arthur Fenn

These were some of the men that I spent a lot of my leisure time with, our trips to town, in trouble, out of trouble, we had excitement together, we had fun together, this was our little gang.

We spent quite a lot of our leisure at the swimming pools during off duty spells. At night we went to the Ubique cinema. This cinema was more or less central in the Changi garrison. We saw all the latest films imported from the UK and the USA. Our favourite stars to name but a few:-

Deanna Durbin Ginger Rogers
Mae West Vivian Leigh

Olivia de Havilland Lana Turner
Dorothy Lamour Clark Gable
James Stewart George Raft

If the films were not too good we would go to Roberts Barracks where the Royal Artillery would be holding tombola session ("bingo" today). For 50c we could buy a book of five tickets. The snowball at times would be as much as $100, on our pay this was quite a small fortune. Most times the snowball was the last house of the evening and had to be won in the lowest amount of numbers called, say 50 numbers or below, the next evening it would be called in 49 or below and $10 would be added to the amount to be won.

At other nights, we would go to the Married Families Club where small sessions of the game would be played, this club was just below our barrack block, 'H' Block.

Then of course we had the NAAFI canteen. By this time, we were getting used to the Tiger Beer. In fact, had acquired a good taste for it, our intake was getting bigger and better, we began to enjoy a good session.

We used to put ourselves on short pay for three weeks of the month, draw just enough to keep one in a few pints, a few cigarettes and our cleaning materials, then at the month end draw out the credits and enjoy a good weekend on the town.

Big pay days were always staggered with the other regiments. Our pay day was always on a Thursday, the Royal Artillery on a Friday, the Gordon Highlanders on a Wednesday, the Argyll and Southerland Highlanders on a Tuesday. This was organised to keep us all apart in the City, during the day there was very little trouble, it was after the drinking bouts in the evenings that the Military Police were kept very busy in the night clubs and dance halls.

I always remember the very first day out in the City, four of us went out to explore this wonderful place, gateway to the Orient with all its splendour and mystery. We set out with our kodac brownie box cameras to record our adventures.

To the smell of joss sticks burning, we visited the Chinese Temples. The Indian Temples with all their carvings, it was with sheer wonderment that we took in all these sights, our cameras clicking in quick time as we posed before these exciting buildings.

We visited Raffles Museum and the monument to this great man's memory in Raffles Square, we went on to Raffles Place. I remember we took photographs outside the famous Hotel named after this great man, please note I said on the outside of the Hotel. This building was out of bounds to all ORs at all times, not that we wished to mix with the people that used it, not that I suppose they would wish to mix with us. As we used to say that they were too "toffee nosed" to even speak to us. We used to see the planters down from Malaya, up country as they used to call it. Then of course there were the tin miners all earning a living on the backs of the native population. We found out later that they were indeed a load of snobs.

After a day in town, we would wend our way back to the Union Jack Club, this again was the serviceman's paradise, everything was laid on for us. We could get a shower here and a good spruce up, a good meal and a few pints of beer. We were then ready to explore this City at night. We usually made our way to the infamous Lavender Street with the cafes with names such as The Modern, The Moonlight, Mickey Mouse, The Green Circle, The Red Moon, most of these places were run by the Chinese. Had to get to these places early to get a table. On entry one bought a book of dance tickets about 25c, the beer was very dear and watered down, not a good buy at all, the spirits were even worse, we often said that they were diluted with a good portion of methylated spirit. The girls would sit on high stools at the bar and we would ask them to dance, we gave them one of our tickets, if we asked them to sit at our table they would ask for a drink before sitting down. The drink would be brought up by a waiter 50c for coloured water. Once in your company, they would proposition you to accompany them to their room at a price of $2 short time, $5 or $6 longer time. I might add that one could take your pick of all races, Chinese, Malay, Indian at times white Russian. There were beautiful Eurasian girls. Some of the lads used to go with these girls.

Some soldiers kept girls in the town and spent quite a lot of their leisure time with them at weekends they had living out passes.
Other pastimes were of course the cinemas, there were quite a selection in the City - Cathay, Capitol, Roxie and The Palace. These showed all the up to date pictures from America and the UK. At times in the Roxie and The Palace we could see foreign films from the continent such as French and German.

Other places of entertainment were The Happy World, The New World and The Great World. These were big amusement parks with every type of entertainment available from Circus to Cabaret. Chinese Opera, Malay Opera, every type of culture could be seen. Then of course the dance halls, where you again bought a book of tickets.

Towards the end of the evening, we always found our way back to Lavender Street. How it got its name I will never know as the smell was far from that of lavender. The smells were all part of this mystic Eastern City. At this late hour the dance halls were always packed to capacity. It always paid to look in the door before entering to see how things were progressing, one could always get involved in trouble without asking.

When it came to about 11.00pm it was time to look for a taxi back to Changi, they were big open taxis carrying five or six passengers, we used to club together and the driver would take us back to our guard room by 2359 hours. Most times the taxi drivers were Sikh.

Back in barracks tired, happy and perhaps a little the worse for drink.

Such were the happy days.

WAR CLOUDS

We had been in Singapore three or four months, we were always kept closely in touch with the UK and the latest news.

Herr Hitler was of course on the warpath again. He was declaring his intention to expand his German Empire. This he had done in 1938 would he go further than he did then?? Would Mr Chamberlain be able to pacify this Dictator? Then the maniac invaded Poland. As the whole world now knows, we declared a state of War between our two countries on Sunday 3 September 1939.

We had been in our paradise just six months, it came as a great shock to us all "The Peace in our time" meeting in 1938 between Mr Chamberlain and Hitler lasted just a year. We were now at War.

At once our out stations were to be manned 24 hours a day. Our Company was divided into shifts, details were published for outstations and the local positions on the island. We went to the outstations for two weeks and back at the local positions for four weeks. This wasn't too bad at all, we were quite happy, some men volunteered to stay on the outstations. We had bedboards and blankets in the engine rooms, direction stations and in the searchlight positions. One man was always alert in the D.S (Direction Station). We had alarm bells at Action Stations. It was a bit difficult to get to sleep in the engine rooms with the auxiliary engines chumping away but after a time we became used to it. Most of the day we could use as leisure time as the searchlights were never needed, only at night. The Royal Artillery Gunners

were always on the alert, in case of any attack up the waterways to the Naval Base.
It was published in orders that at all times when outside our barracks areas we must wear uniform, this we thought was a bit of a bind.

When not on duty, we were still able to go on our visits to the City, having to wear uniform, we were easily recognised by the Military Police who, since the start of hostilities, were always in evidence around the places we always liked to frequent.

It was about this time (November 1939) that the Royal Artillery began taking over the searchlights, both Ack-Ack and coastal. We still had to maintain the engines and run same. I was now a Regular Engine Driver and was driving the six cylinder 200 HP Rustons at Changi Spit. These were brand new engines and engine rooms built as an extra defence. At Anti Motor Torpedo Boat positions there were six searchlights on fixed positions. As there were now more Sappers available due to the R.A take over, a Field Section had been formed in the 41st Company. I volunteered to join it and was accepted.

The Field Section of the 41st Fortress Company:-

This section was formed to improve the defences of the whole island of Singapore. Defences such as Anti Aircraft Gun Pits, Field Gun Pits, Machine Gun Emplacements and Rifle Pits three man, Machine Gun Emplacements on the Airfields. Auxiliary Roads to be built through the rubber plantations in the event of the main roads being bombed. Obstacles in the field of fire on machine gun emplacements had to be moved. New beach defences were to be built. The task ahead was a very big one.

Our first task was to remove obstructions in the field of fire for the fixed machine gun posts. This was where our experience with explosives came to the fore.

At first quite a lot of houses had to be demolished. One I remember quite well, it was a beautiful house. Lady Doctor Clarke had it built a few months before at the cost of $15,000. We arrived on site and marked out the holes to be drilled to take the plastic explosive. I was driving a Morris Compressor truck at the time. As I started to drill, this poor lady arrived and asked "What the Devil are you doing"? I told her that we had orders to demolish the house as it was an obstruction to the field of fire. She demanded that we stop until she had been in touch with higher military authority. We said that we had orders, she then began to fight us and push us around. At this point our Sergeant, Sergeant Stracchino, arrived and he told her that she should not have built the house in that position in the first place, she had been warned not to build and that was that. The poor lady cried, it was a pity. We took all her furniture out onto the lawn. They got a large van to take it away and into store. We started to put our charges in position, it didn't take us long to reduce this lovely house to a pile of rubble. Before we left the site, the Doctor returned, she was broken-hearted and I think all our sub section felt for her. We left a small outhouse as this did not concern us. She opened it and inside was a very large refrigerator. She opened it, it was full of bottles of beer, she said "This is all you have left me so you may as well take it, you have all worked very hard today". There were about ten bottles to each member of the sub section. We all, I think, felt very sad for this good lady, including our Sergeant.

Before going out on these demolition details, a conference was always held in our Section Officers Office. Details of the target were given together with the map reference. The final question from our O.C was "Any questions? Then OK off you go".
We set off early one morning as quite a few houses had to be demolished. We were full of enthusiasm and eager to get on with the days work. On this day, we had a very efficient L/Corporal who, without doubt, knew his job. He got to his site, he had been detailed to demolish 38A in this certain road. He turned the Malay people out, they carried what they could, the remainder he had put

out on to the lawn. He turned to one of his Sappers and said "Queer, these people haven't been told before - still let's get on with it". He completed his task - raised the place to the ground. He reported back to HQ that he had carried out his task. He was then told that he had blown down the wrong building, he should have demolished 38A and not 38B. "Oh dear" he said.

THE NEBONG PALM TIMBER DEFENCE

We blew up many houses around the coast together with piers and pagers, as this could offer cover or even landing places to any invading forces coming from the sea. Once all these obstacles had been removed, we started to repair the gun pits, many of which had been invaded by termites, such as white ants attacking the woodwork, thus weakening the whole structure. This again was a very big task. Our next big task was to build up the beach defences. The anti-landing devices. These were in the form of large palm tree trunks called nebong being bolted together to form a framework. This type of palm trunk is such that the longer it remains in sea water the harder it gets. It had to be imported from Java. It was floated in and landed in the timber yards at Beach Road Singapore, where it was cut to size. Sappers were employed on this work. Many months were spent on the building of these defences, all along the South Coast. Once the framework had been built, we laced it with coils of barbed wire. Mines and booby traps were laid in position around and on these obstacles at a later date. These were such that it would have been impossible for landing to be made on this coast, all of course covered by heavy machine gunfire.

THE MACHINE GUN POST SCANDAL

At this point in time, I was detailed to report to the C.R.E (Chief Royal Engineer) Office with the Morris Compressor Truck complete with drills and spare drill bits. I had with me another Sapper, Evans by name, he I might add was a very good friend of mine, so whatever this task, I knew I was in good company.

On reporting to the CRE we were told to go to the Works Services Department where we would be working with a Captain R.E who would give us daily orders. The job in hand was a very important one which we were to carry out to the best of our ability. We of course wondered what this job was to be?

On meeting the Captain, he gave us the run down. All around the coast of Singapore were numerous fixed machine gun posts in which the infantry had four and five heavy machine guns such as the .303 Vickers, some also had .303 Bren guns. These were the very positions that a few weeks before we had made good their field of fire by demolishing the houses and other buildings.

All the walls of these machine gun posts were at least one foot thick. We were given a stopwatch to time our drilling, a box to catch the residue drilled out and a pro forma to fill in stating if we had struck any reinforcement in the concrete. We started off in the Changi area and worked our way along the south coast from East to West.

One of the first posts we drilled under the supervision of the Officer i/c the project. We drilled in the middle directly under the gun slot, it took us approximately fifteen minutes to drill through the one foot thick concrete, we struck reinforcement rods, we caught all the residue that was drilled out of the 2" hole we timed with the stopwatch. When he saw that we were experienced enough, he left us to get on with the task. Before leaving he gave us the map references of five or six positions he wanted us to deal with that day. The first ones we did we found that the drilling time varied, anything from twelve minutes to twenty minutes. At times we struck reinforcement, in others we did not.

On the second day we advanced down by Betin Kusa Beach. These posts we found were easier to drill, the holes took about eight to ten minutes, we struck very little reinforcement and the residue was very fine.

Then we came to a post near Bedoh, we found this very easy and went through one foot of concrete in eleven seconds, struck no reinforcement and the residue was only very fine sand. We took another drilling - it took eight seconds, we were amazed at what we discovered. We contacted the Officer i/c and he said that surely you have made a mistake, no way could this be. We invited the Officer to see for himself. The Captain came with a Major R.E. We drilled again with the same results. They were full of disgust and openly showed their feelings. The Major then remarked "This is what we have been looking for, it has brought out into the open what we have suspected for a very long time". then he added "The bastard will have to pay for this - carry on the good work lads - you are doing a good job".

We carried on, the rest of the posts varied anything from ten seconds to fifteen minutes. We found very little reinforcement at all.
Why we were doing this task, we did not know we were completely in the dark. Our task completed, we returned to our unit. We often thought of the machine gunners of the Manchester Regiment the Loyal Regiment or anyone for that matter whose lives depended on good solid positions to man their guns against invasion from the sea. At no time at all during the War were these posts used. Thousands of pounds spent were wasted in these contracts.

A while after all these tests were carried out, a Royal Engineer Officer Captain on the Works Services was Court Martialled at Fort Canning and sentenced to three years imprisonment at Changi Gaol. A lot of our infantry friends thought he should have had ten years or even hung for his treachery and deceit.

In the evidence against this man, it was said that good portland cement had been imported from the UK to be used in this work. He had sold this cement to the Chinese who had put the lower grade cement in the portland bags, even stitched the bags as they were before. Freshwater sand had also been imported, this treacherous man had sold this and used sea sand in these buildings instead.

Other projects that he had been responsible for were found to be faulty. Like an engine room that was built on marshy ground, it had not been piled as it should have been. After a few months the engines with their intense weight began to sink, the engine room fell into two halves, this was a disgrace. Mens lives depended upon these structures.

Rumour had it that when this criminal was being led up the steps of Changi Gaol to his cell, he noticed a pool of water on the floor that had come in through a crack in the roof, he stopped, looked at the ceiling and said "Some bastard made a pile when they built this place".

When the Japanese invaded and took Singapore, they visited Changi Gaol, they questioned the said Officer (well he wasn't an Officer as he had been discharged in disgrace). They were said to be very interested in his previous activities, as he had been a military "Foreman of Works" he knew quite a lot about things they wanted information on, it is said that he was often seen riding around pointing out different installations to his captors, such as drains, water supply which he knew all about.

I don't know if he survived the Jap occupation or not. I know one thing, if he had been with us he would not have.

It was said later that his wife had been evacuated to Australia.

It was also said that the money he made out of his foul transactions was in his wife's name and could not be recovered. Such is Justice.

LET US GET HOME

The War in Europe had progressed quite a while, about a year and we had been hearing about the fighting in Europe, the bombing of our home cities like Plymouth, Coventry and London. Volunteers were asked for to form special forces like the airborne, glider pilots, parachutist, commandoes and such units. Quite a number volunteered. Our O.C said that he was quite pleased with the response but we must bide our time - our chance would come at a later date.

LETTERS HOME

With all the activity, I always found time to write letters home, at least once a week I would write to my Aunt and Uncle or my cousin and his wife.

I wrote to the girl in Bristol quite regular and she always answered.

With all the shipping being sunk of course a lot were lost and letters were not quite as regular as they could have been.

We had quite a good air mail service, due to air attacks the mail did not go all the way by air, so there were delays.

At about this time I received a letter from home stating that my old school friend Harry Howard had been captured and taken Prisoner of War by the Germans in the Battle for Crete. Harry had been on HMS Repulse when I last heard from him. He had been dropped off to reinforce the Armed Forces in that area.

When I answered the letter, I asked if my folks could find out where he was, as I could then send him cigarettes etc. I hoped he would soon be liberated.

Sad news I also received was that the lad who joined the Royal Engineers with me and transferred to become a cook was killed at Dunkirk during the evacuation of the beaches. Dear old Sid, we had had some happy times together.

BUILDING UP

During these months after the concrete machine gun posts had been found to be so useless, we spent quite a long time building emplacements with sandbags and revetted gun pits in the Katong area and the approaches to Kallang Airfield. It was whilst we were working at Katong that we adopted the four ducklings that came out of the undergrowth. That is a story that I think should be told later, the ducks deserve a chapter of their own.

We built defences all around the airfields at Kallang, Seletar and Sembawang this took us many months.

At this time, our M.T Section was reinforced by five extra trucks. As I was a driver, I was transferred to the M.T Section. We had quite a good section - Corporal Roberts (Taff) M.T Corporal, Sapper Evans (Kipper) Fitter M.T, Sapper Reg Mullins, Sapper Shepherd, Sapper Hydon, Sapper Grey, Sapper Wilson and myself Sapper R.C Blackler and Tommy Atkins also a driver. The M.T Officer was Lieut Calthorpe, we were quite a happy little unit. We drove ration trucks, stores to and from the ordnance depots. We drove the trucks to the working parties then worked on the defences all day then brought the men back.

We still got quite a lot of recreation football, swimming and whatever sport one was interested in and we still had time for a few beers at night in the canteen. We still took our trips to town.

THE HAUNTED ENGINE ROOM

After a few months in Changi I passed my driving test to drive heavy goods vehicles anywhere in the Federate Malay States. Within a few months of this, I was given the chance to take a course in "Driving and Maintenance" of stationary engines, these engines were used to generate power for the searchlights on coastal defences, they also supplied power to the coastal gun batteries, including the 15 inch and 9.2 inch around the island of Singapore. At this time, I found this to be very interesting work to be always learning something new.

After having completed the course and got a good mark, I was posted to my first outstation at Penerang. My duty here would last a month, then back to Changi for two months. Penerang was across the water in the state of Johore.

I was shown around my new living quarters and then the engine room which supplied power for the three searchlights and the 6 inch gun battery and the command posts. I also had with me a Malay Sapper who, I might add, was keen and efficient. I was shown my duties by a L/Cpl who was later to become a great friend of mine.

The first week or two I found the work very interesting and I had no problems whatsoever. We did a few exercises, the guns fired out to sea, the searchlights exposed, all was well with the world as far as I was concerned.

To enter the engine room, one had to pass through a blastproof door, this was of solid steel. This had to be left opened when the engines were in action, due to the engines drawing in a supply of air. So in its place swung a big iron grill. The passage to the engine room was approximately sixty yards long and zig-zag to make it blastproof. To enter, one had to ring a loud bell, one also had to answer to a password.

Then one night, it was about midnight, I heard a shrill whistle come up through the corridor, I looked at the Malay Sapper and he was asleep on his trestle bed, as was allowed when on standby duty.

I waited a while to see if the whistle was repeated, then I walked down the corridor to investigate. I looked through the iron gate but there was no-one there. I waited a while, then the Gordon Highlander sentry came into view. It was his duty to patrol the pier and the surrounding buildings. When he came near enough, I asked him if he had seen anyone in the area, to which he replied that he had not. In fact it had been a very quiet and lonely night. I went on to tell him about the whistle I had heard and he again assured me that he had seen no-one.

At this point, I would like to point out that the main electric cables were laid in channels about nine inches deep. These were covered with steel plates ¼ inch thick. They were four feet long and one foot wide.
I was just on my third week in the engine room and we were on standby. The Malay Sapper was asleep on his bed boards and I was laid on mine, all was quiet. I was reading a book, the incandescent Lister engine was chugging away quite merrily ...... then, all of a sudden all hell broke loose. It was as if three or four of the steel plates were dropped from a great height. The Malay Sapper (Abu Hassen) jumped off his bed boards and I felt the hair on the back of my neck bristle. A shiver went down my spine and the place seemed to turn very cold "What was it"? We looked at all the steel plates and found them to be all in place. When I came off the shift the next morning, I told the L/Cpl of the happenings of the night before, to which he replied "You will get used to that in time, I didn't tell you about it before as I did not want to put the wind up you". He then went on to tell me about the steel bar that was used to bar the flywheel around on the big Ruston engine. It was always kept in place on a big tool display board. He went on to tell me that, before starting the compressor, to make sure that this bar was on the board, as at times it had been found to have moved down and across about three feet and lodged between the spokes of the compressor fly wheels. I finished my first tour of duty there and returned to Changi. I was telling some of my friends about the Penerang experience, to which one of them

replied that it gave him the willies over there as the bloody place was haunted".

I did several duties on Penerang after this but got used to these extraordinary ghostly happenings. Yes, on two or three occasions I did find the bar between the compressor flywheels.

The Malay Sapper asked to be relieved of his post, this request was granted. The Malays, some were of a very superstitious nature, some did not seem to bother at all.

After these happenings, a little research was made. It was found that this engine room was built on a Chinese Graveyard, much to the disgust of the local population, who again were very superstitious people.

Myself and others that served in this station never came to any harm, it was the fright that it gave one when it happened.

The ghost I have always thought of as a great practical joker.

"TEKON" GHOST TRAIN

There were four main outstations manned by the 41st Fortress Company, R.E from Changi. One of these was at Tekon, across the water from Changi. We had the usual searchlight position i.e lights, directing station and engine room. Power was also supplied to the 5'9" guns. On the station was also a light gauge railway. This was used to transport the ammunition from the pier landing place to the bottom of a very steep hill on which these guns were positioned. The ammunition was then winched to the top of the hill where it was stored in a large magazine. The train was also used to ferry men to the different positions on the island. All the trucks had attap (dried palm fronds) roofs.

I was returning from Penerang and I had just finished one of my tours of duty. The ferry called at Tekon to pick up men from there who had been relieved of their duties and were returning the Changi, as I was and were, no doubt, all looking forward to a few beers and a night or two in the city Singapore.

A Sapper Kibby came and sat with me for the journey back to Changi Pier. We talked about the duties we had just finished and things in general.

He then went on to tell me of a very funny happening that he had had about a week before. He said that he had been detailed to take a message down to the engine room from the directing station on top of the hill. He was told that he need not return until the next day and that he could stay in the billet by the pier. He said that it was very dark and he only had a small flashlight to light his way. He said that he was about half way through his journey when he heard the train coming and he thought for a while then came to the conclusion that he would wait and hitch a lift. This was the usual thing to do as the drivers were from our Company. So he waited by the side of the track and, as the train approached, he waved his torch for it to stop and give him a lift to the pier. To his utter amazement, it carried on straight past. It had all lights ablaze and it was full of soldiers, no-one seemed to speak or shout as was normal. He also noticed that all the occupants were wearing shorts and short sleeved shirts and pith helmets, this being dress for daylight hours. This was most unusual, the train carried on its way and out of sight.

When he got to the end of his journey, he met one of the railway engine drivers from our Company, a L/Corporal Hartshorn. He asked why the train was travelling so late and why it did not stop to pick him up. To which the Corporal replied that there had not been a train and the last train had come down from that direction in the late afternoon. My friend was baffled and said "Well it must have been a bloody ghost train"!!

No-one could ever account for this, no more than the ghost of the engine room at Penerang. I spoke to Sapper Kibby on many occasions on this matter, in fact at one time he said that he would swear on the Holy Bible. I have always believed his story.

A few months after this incident, there was a terrible accident at Tekon. There was a big exercise in progress and targets were out, searchlights were all exposed. All the guns were firing and from all around area i.e Changi, Johore Battery 15 inch, Penerang and Tekon.

The gunners were in fine fettle. Suddenly one of the 9.2 inch guns at Tekon backfired just as they were closing the breech. Three men were killed instantly and two others died in the Military Hospital Singapore. I can say the whole garrison were very upset about this incident.

I have often thought about this "ghost train" and if it was an omen to this terrible accident. I do know that it took us all a long time to recover from the shock, some of them we had got to know very well.

On the other hand, it could have been an omen of the terrible things that were in store for us when the Japanese invaded Malaya and Singapore?

ENGINE ROOMS ON THE COAST

One of the best sites I did duty in was on the south coast of the Island at Betin Kusa. It was not far from Changi, in fact Changi Beach and Betin Kusa were linked together. One could, when on standby, walk down the beautiful sandy beach and go for a swim in the sky blue surf. It was just a paradise to us all.

Whenever I think of Betin Kusa today, I think of all the good times we had there swimming in the surf. All this good life was spoilt when the Japanese invaded this tropical paradise. They came to desecrate, murder, rape and pillage. It was on this beautiful site that a number of the wars worse atrocities were carried out.

Hundreds of poor Chinese people were rounded up in the City of Singapore and brought here to be bayoneted or machine-gunned to death. These poor souls were left here for the tides to take their bodies away. We who were imprisoned at Changi could hear these executions taking place.

On another occasion, during the Selerang Incident, it was on this beach that the men reputed to have tried to escape were put to death by firing squad, after having been made to dig their own graves. One of which was only 17 years of age and he had been a drummer boy in one of the infantry regiments. I have, since the War, been back to this site but, knowing what happened there, the magic of the place had all gone and all I had were sad thoughts of those terrible days.

Many atrocities were also carried out on the beautiful beach at Changi. When going back there, it was so hard to think what kind of people do these terrible things to innocent men, women and even children. They turned this heaven into hell for so many. We all know that many were never brought to justice. For instance, the Indian Sikh Officer who took his officers and other ranks to join the Imperial Japanese Army. Many of which carried out many atrocities. Many of our men who were Prisoners of War were beaten and kicked by these people. They had sworn to serve the British Crown, the officer concerned of course held the Kings Commission. After India had got its independence, he became an MP in the Indian Government. So much for justice???

ALL THE SIXES

One evening we were on our way to the Garrison cinema, almost broke as usual, when one of the lads said "Let's pool our money and buy a few tickets in the R.A tombola", so this we did. Not a bean did we win till the last house, we were sweating on one number, then the caller shouted "All the sixes - clickety click", we all called as one "HOUSE". When they counted the numbers, we had also won the snowball - we had $120 between the four of us.

So back to barracks, change into best uniform and ordered a taxi - away to town - to the Green Circle what a night we had. The bloomer that we made was the Argylls were in town. Dolly Grey was dancing with a Chinese Eurasian girl, she was beautiful, I had just been dancing with her. The Scotsman said to Dolly "That's my girl - hand over", to which Dolly said "P off you", without warning the Scot butted Dolly in the mouth, I took a swipe at him, punched him in the face, then all his mates tore into the four of us. I remember a big mirror being hit with a full bottle of beer, it shattered into a hundred pieces. We were fighting with broken chairs, glasses, tables were over-turned, girls were screaming, it was bedlam. Then we heard the police whistles - as the Military Police came in the front bat wing doors, I saw an Argyll smash a chair over his head. We didn't wait any longer, we ran out into a back street by the back door. We quickly got a taxi and got back to Changi Guard Room by 23.59 hours. I had a black eye and a lump or two on the head. Grey was bleeding from the mouth, apart from that the four of us were OK. I saw one of the Argylls afterward, he said to me "Did ye enjoy the scrap"? So much for 66 and the snowball.

There were some very bad happenings in the Lavender Street area. One evening three or four Argylls were chased into the Green Circle, they entered and stood by the bat wing doors, a Military Police Sergeant stuck his head through the door looking for the quarry, the two men hiding by the doors kicked them shut upon the M.P's neck - he couldn't move, they drew a razor and took a slash, the unfortunate policeman fell to the floor, his ear was hanging on his shoulder - we got out fast. The injured man was rushed to the hospital, his ear was stitched back in place. Six weeks later he was back on the streets of Singapore looking for the two who had done the damage. I expect they kept out of town after that episode. It was very rare that our little party was involved in such activities, we never looked for trouble only if it was forced upon us.

WRITE HOME JACK

My family in our little village had been very friendly through the years with a family named Roberts. The old man of this family had worked for many years with my dear old Grandfather in the quarries in the area, as did his son who was the father of Jack who joined the Army, the Royal Army Service Corps as a boy soldier.

Jack was never one for writing home to his parents. I might add that I used to write home regularly.

Jack's Mother saw my Uncle one day and, in conversation, he told the lady that I was in Singapore. She asked if I wrote home, my Uncle said that I did - she said that she had not had a letter from her boy Jack for many months, would my Uncle ask me to visit him to see if he was OK and not sick and tell him to write home. He said that he would ask me.

Well I got the letter, knowing that he was in the Royal Army Service Corps, I paid a visit to their offices in Changi, I made enquiries as regards to Jack Roberts. At this time, I did not know what rank he was but I was soon to find out when the Sergeant Major of the unit said "Jack Roberts – you mean Mr Roberts he is a WOII". "Oh God" I thought, me going to him and telling him to write home to his Mother, I guess he'd soon tell me where to go. The Sergeant Major told me that Mr Roberts was on outstation at Paula Blakan Mati, I could phone him if I wished, or could write him a letter which would be despatched with the Military mail. So I wrote a letter telling who I was and my mission. Two days after I was called to our Company office, where a message had been received asking if I could visit the gentleman at the island outstation. I sent a message back saying that I would pay him a visit on the following Sunday.

During the course of conversation in our barrack room, I mentioned to Sapper Fenn that I was going to Paula Blakan Mati to visit an old neighbour of mine. He said that if I wished he would accompany me. I was pleased to have a bit of company, so agreed that we would go together on my mission.

We set off on the Sunday morning after our Church Parade. We caught the piggy bus from Changi to Singapore, we hired a taxi to Keppel Harbour where we caught a ferry boat to Paula Blakan Mati. We arrived at our destination at about midday. I enquired from one of the R.A.S.C men on the pier as to where I could find Sergeant major Roberts, he told me that no doubt he would be in the WOs and Sergeants Mess and directed me. We found the mess and enquired where Mr Roberts was, a mess boy said that he would get him for me. Mr Roberts came to the door and told us to follow him into the mess. this of course to two young Sappers was the Holy Land. Mr Roberts introduced us to all present as lads from his old village Liverton in Devon. He told how our families had been great friends for many years and how our Grandfathers had worked together 50 or 60 years ago. It was at this point that the drinking started, it wasn't very long before it was "Call me Jack".

We had had a few beers when in came a Captain R.E who enquired "What the hell are you two doing here, this is a mess you shouldn't be here". As this was an outstation, the WOs and Officer's shared the mess. The R.E Captain had once been our Sergeant Major and we had both fell foul of the gentleman in the past. Anyway, Mr Roberts explained the position and said that his Mother had sent us to him asking us to tell him to write home. This went down quite well. The Captain then asked us to have a drink with him, we said that we would have a beer, to which he replied "You will have a bloody John Collins - as Sappers we should know better". This started the session that lasted till about 5.00pm in the early evening. We all got stinking drunk. Fenn or I could not stand up. We were taken to a hut to sleep it off. We came to at about 7.00pm, the last ferry for Singapore had gone - what could we do to get back? It was about 8.00pm when Jack Roberts came around. It was a sin in the tropics to be dressed as we were - in short sleeve shirts and shorts, after 6.00pm one should have been wearing long trousers and long sleeve shirts as an anti malarial precaution. Roberts said that he could get us back to Singapore, we should have to then dodge the Military Police and make our own way to Changi. We said that was OK by us - get us back to Singapore. He called his servant boy who was Chinese and spoke to him in his own language, he then told us to go with him. The boy took us to the waterfront, he gave another Chinaman money, we then had to follow the second Chinaman. He took out a small rowing boat and he told us to lay in the bottom, this we did, he then pushed off, he stood up and rowed us back, with our weight the water was lapping over the sides. After about an hours rowing and being sick as the water was very choppy, we reached Keppel Harbour. We got a taxi to the Union Jack Club. We entered still in our shorts, everyone looked around at us as if we had just returned from a space mission. This was unheard of still in shorts at 9.30pm. We had two or three pints then thought we had better make tracks for Changi. As we left the Union Jack Club, we ran into two Military Police - a Sergeant and a Corporal. The Red Caps were on to us.

We called a taxi and told the driver to take us to Changi and we would pay him 50c extra to the fare. It was an open taxi, he was a good driver, we laid on the floor while he went at breakneck speed through the overcrowded city. the M.Ps followed us for quite a distance but gave up the chase at Katong a suburb of the city. We got back to our barrack room in good time to change into trousers and long sleeve shirts.

We reported to the Guard Room at 11.00pm still under the influence of John Collins and Tiger beer.

The next day the Red Caps visited our barracks to report that two Sappers had been seen in the City of Singapore improperly dressed.

I don't know if, after me telling Sergeant Major Jack Roberts to write home to his dear old Mother he did so or not. I do know that he was killed in a motor cycle accident at Kuala Lumpur. One of many to be left behind in Malaya, with a headstone - a piece of a foreign field that will be for ever England.

WAR CLOUDS OVER ASIA

The Japanese were in the early part of 1940 being squeezed financially by the great powers of the West. Their assets were frozen, this was mainly because of her attitude in China with whom she had been at war since the early thirties. Prime Minster Tojo came to power, he was always talking of war and threatening war on the Western powers. Of course he wasn't taken seriously as it was thought that the warring in China was keeping their economy poor. We were always being educated on the facts of the Japanese forces, their equipment was all out of date, they had very poor eyesight - couldn't see at night. The most up to date was their navy, even the Navy was only third class to ours and the Americans. All I can say is that our intelligence, together with that of the USA was in a very bad state, we were misled all along the line. Statements were always being made that the jungle in North Malaya would form an unpenetrable barrier against any invasion from the North, this was the great myth. So the North of Singapore Island was left naked of any defence whatsoever. Who was there to attack us from the North in any case?

Well the warning came in 1939 when the European War started, then in 1940 the threat came even greater when the Japanese occupied French-Indo-China. This is when the decision should have been made to reinforce the defences of the northern part of the island, or even a sound line in North Malaya. But I suppose commitments on the home front and in the Mediterranean zone were given precedence over the Far East. Time had run out for Singapore even at this early date.

Even now we were strengthening the defences on the South coast, we were still putting up the Nebong type timber defences that I have mentioned before. Anti motor torpedo boat defences were added to at Changi and a small island of Pulau Sajahat, these sites consisted of six searchlights on fixed bearings, so that the whole waterfront was floodlit, the area was covered by the six coastal defence batteries. Also on the beach were two pounder pom pom guns. It was a great shame that some of these defences couldn't have been built to defend the causeway, or the north coast.

A LETTER FROM BRISTOL

We have now got to mid 1941, I had been writing quite a few letters home and to the girl in Bristol but had had very few in return. I supposed that it was caused by the loss of shipping en route. We had had news that the shipping losses had been terrible. It must have been terrible for the poor seamen, especially those from the torpedoed oil tankers when the sea on the surface was all alight. These were truly very brave men. I had often wondered if all my letters had got through and was beginning to think if the girl in Bristol had got fed up with writing to me.
The post Corporal one day was handing out the mail and he said "One here for you Blackie from Bristol". I thought as he gave me the letters "Well she hasn't forgotten me" but the address was in a strange hand. I opened the letter with trembling hand, it was from the girl's sister, she told me that "Joan" had been killed in an air raid. She had been in a shelter at the Imperial Tobacco Company where she worked. The shelter had received a direct hit. I was quite shocked, to think that one so beautiful and so full of life when I last saw her in Southsea, should have had her life taken so violently. For the rest of the day I was quite numb, I was in fact devastated. No more letters from her so full of life, telling me all about home and how she enjoyed her life at work and in general. What a tragedy for her life to end at the hands of those German airmen. I shouldn't think there was ever a sign of malice in her young life. Now she was gone forever. I had only known her for that short time, yet I felt that I had known her all my life. I shall miss her very much. After a few weeks, the ache in my heart began to subside but I know that I shall never ever forget her. I think I was very privileged to have had that brief encounter and

will always be thankful for that meeting in Southsea. I often see her smiling face - her golden hair but never to see her again in reality -only dreams - only dreams. May she rest in peace forever and ever in God's good hands. Amen.

PRELUDE TO THE DISASTER

History tells us of plans laid down by the Prime Minster of Japan in 1927-28 for international plunder. He was Barnon Tanaka. The plan which became known as the "Tanaka Plan" was to better the Japanese race who were desperate, even so long ago and this was due to their population explosion of 800,000 growth per year. This plan was designed to conquer the whole of the World in this order:-
1. China
2. S.E Asia
3. India-Burma
4. Australia
5. Middle East
6. Europe
Finally the whole World.

The irony of all this is that this plan was photographed and sold to Russia by a Japanese employee in the Naval office in Tokyo for the very low sum of $3,000 to $4,000. In time it reached the great powers of the western world but no action was ever taken. With hindsight, it is easy to see what Japanese intentions were, even at this early stage. In 1931 the Japanese seized Manchuria, taking no heed of the League of Nations.

During 1937, they extended their movement into North China - saying that the "red" lawless factions were attacking their trading lines. They proceeded to invade the eastern province and put a puppet government in Nanking. Why was it that the interested great powers in the Far East didn't take heed at this time - countries like the USA, France, the Dutch and Great Britain. The meetings of these great powers and the taking of countries like

Siam, China, Burma and Indo China surely showed that the catastrophic Japanese War could have been avoided.

Japan's economic worries were piling up. Her industry had doubled, she had to find markets. She was short of oil, 80% of which came from the USA.
All this time she was building up her Military and Naval Forces, so her expenditure was very high.

In 1939 a non aggression pact was signed with Germany.

With the outbreak of War in Europe - France was overrun by Nazi Germany. The retreat from Dunkirk - the bombing of Great Britain, the great powers had their troubles at home, these were the powers with influence in the Far East.

The Japanese started their sabre rattling "Greater East Asia under Jap Rule". The Vichy French Government took over the administration of Indo China. At this time, Siam claimed back the provinces which were taken by the French. This of course caused friction between the Vichy and Siam. Japan then seized on this to set herself up as a neutral referee. She stationed troops to keep the peace between the two. This of course got her a footing. In came troops - planes and warships (to keep the peace). There was a token opposition by the French Vichy Government but to no avail, they gave in to Japanese demands. Within days they took over the Naval Base. A jump off point had been achieved to attack South East Asia.

This objective had been achieved in July 1941. In a few days the Naval Base at Camrank Bay was taken over by the Jap Navy and a convoy arrived at Saigon. This was just about 400 miles to the South West in line was Kota Bharu, Malaya. The Base was also within 700 miles of Singapore. Airfields built on the S.W point were only about 550 miles, so Malaya and Singapore became wide open to attack. Jap warships were soon cruising in the Gulf of Siam.

At this time, the US Government in the name of President Roosevelt asked the Japanese to withdraw from the area. If they failed to do as asked, he would freeze all Japanese assets of trade in the USA. The British and Dutch East Indies backed the USA, so within a few days Japan had lost her complete oil supply. What were they to do? Go to war or get out and lose face in Asia.

In America the Jap Ambassador was putting forward proposals and promises that his nation would withdraw from Indo china and go no further into South East Asia if the US would resume normal trade relations. This dilly-dally went on for three or four months. All this time, the Japanese were being very two-faced and lulled us into a false sense of security. They were massing for conflict, thousands of men were being disembarked, loaded on to motor transport and driven westward to the Siamese border. War equipment was to follow them.

Their Navy was mobilised. At this point, we must bear in mind that their Navy was third in size in the World. First being the US Fleet, then second was Britain. Due to our commitments in the Atlantic and the Mediterranean seas, we were totally outnumbered. In the Pacific we were relying on the USA Fleet. Intentions were in hand to build up our Sea force in these waters by early 1942.

Germany, after having made a pact with Japan, was flooding the country with aircraft technicians. Military missions were exchanged. One such mission was led by Lieut General Yamashita who was of course later to lead the attack on Singapore. Germany of course had the knowledge and experience from the Spanish War, as she sent a force on the side of General Franco. The German pilots had gained vast knowledge re fighters - dive bombers and high level attack from that war. Without doubt, this knowledge was passed to the Japanese Air Force by these technicians.

This was why the Japanese Navy was so successful both armament wise and with the drop tank technique developed to give the extra mileage. I think it was in May 1941 that one such plane was shot down over China. Details of this machine were forwarded to our Air Ministry in the UK and HQ - Air Force in the Far East. It appears that little notice was taken of this information. Such was our organisation and intelligence at that time. This was to be one of the main factors in the loss of Singapore - their air superiority was due a lot to this aeroplane. Their bomber force out stripped ours, no doubt the Germans gave the Japanese a superior force, one which gave the Jap pilots every confidence in their machines and manoeuvrability.

STILL TALKING

All this time, talks were going on between the USA, Great Britain and Japan. It was a case of who was stalling for time. We, that is the USA, Great Britain and Dutch when possible built up sea, land and air forces for the future. All this time while these "talks" were being held the Japanese had gathered 200,000 of their best shock troops in Indo China, including the elite Imperial Guard. A lot of these had gained experience in the War with China, a campaign that had been going on for a number of years. They were seasoned fighters.

They built airfields in the South West of Indo China. There were reported high level reconnaissance flights all over Malaya, Siam and even over Singapore. Their fleet was patrolling in the Gulf of Siam and well into the China Sea. They were preparing for a big major offensive.

The British Military Forces in Malaya and Singapore totalled about three weak divisions. Our Air Force, about 600 planes all out of date in comparison with the Japanese. We had the Brewster Buffalo Fighters, slow with a very poor rate of climb. Our torpedo bombers were of the old stringbag type. "Vickers Vildebeest" had been obsolete for almost two years. Our bombers were Blenheims, so we found our Air Force lacking well behind the superior Japanese.

WE VISIT THE QUEEN

During August 1941, I was at Changi when I saw the Queen Mary sail up the straits of Johore to the Seletar Naval Base. She had just delivered the first of the Australian troops to arrive in Singapore. Our company gave a few of us permission to visit this ship in the Naval Base dry dock. She was in for painting and repairs. A party of us was shown over this great ship. It was an experience that I never thought that I should ever have. She was painted in battleship grey and not as we had seen her when we saw her sailing up the Solent to Southampton water, during our training at Gosport. It was a steward that showed us around the ship, he had been with her since she was launched by Queen Mary. When he got to the dining area and bars, he told us how he had seen all the film stars of the day - he had seen Tommy Farr sitting on that very stool. "Tommy always sat there" he said. We were even shown the engine rooms, this of course was of great interest to us, the power of those engines produced the power and speed to out strip any Germany submarine wolf pack. This was a great ship.

This was a wonderful day out.

****

As the months passed we were, that is the Field Section of the 41st Fortress Company, still employed in building fortification around the North and the North East coast of the island. We put in extra machine gun posts, these were no doubt to defend Seletar and Sembawang Airfields.

We travelled daily to Sembawang from Changi. At this time, this airfield was manned by the Australian airmen, their aircraft were Hudson Bombers, at this field there were also Brewster Buffalo fighters. These were little hump backed machines and looked to be very short. The Australians said that they were very manoeuverable and they seemed to have every confidence in these machines.

Seletar was defended by fixed defences but we added a few A/A gun emplacements. At this airfield were the Vickers Vildebeest, these machines looked very out of date, like leftovers from the 1914-18 War, all with fixed undercarriages, top speed about 100 mph. The "erks" called them Flying Coffins, the bodies were shaped like coffins. Also here were a few of the British Blenheims, which looked more up to date but we were told that the Hudson Bombers were the best of the two, both in speed, bomb load and distance. When talking to these airmen, they were all confident of being able to take care of the Japanese, if ever the time for action came.

The RAAF at Sembawang, the RAF at Seletar always seemed to have a little rivalry between the two. Apparently when the Aussies first arrived at Sembawang they did a beat up over the Seletar air base, a bit of "show off" low flying. The very next day the RAF crews made a leaflet raid over Sembawang - they dropped a load of army form blank, i.e toilet paper - I wonder, did the Aussies get the message?

THE FINAL WORD

On November 26th, the Japanese delivered to Washington a "last and final word". They proposed to evacuate Indo China and making a settlement over China, make peace in the Pacific, eventually pull out of China - this in return for the much needed oil.

On November 26th, the USA Government replied giving ten main points to be followed. The Japanese must pull out all military, naval, air force and police forces from China and Indo China. General Chaing Kai Shek and the National Government only to rule over China at Chungking. We in Singapore watched developments very closely. One night three of us caught the piggy bus (being short of cash) to Katong, we were sitting in the Roxy cinema when a news flash came on to the screen:-

"All British and Australian Forces return IMMEDIATELY to their Units".

This was on the evening of 29 November 1941. Our reaction - "God are we being attacked"?

Things were certainly looking very bad, the International situation had worsened in the last week.

The next day we drew all our extra equipment, we were on a war footing. We drew from store the extra Lewis guns to be erected in case of air raids and for our own defence.

HMS PRINCE OF WALES AND HMS REPULSE ARRIVE

On 2 December, we were working at Changi when we saw those two beautiful ships steam up through the Straits of Johore to the Naval Base, we couldn't believe our eyes, it was the Prince of Wales and the Repulse accompanied by four destroyers. We were full of pride to see these great ships with their white ensigns fluttering in the tropical breeze. This would give our little yellow friends something to think about. They would protect us. I am sure that the native population were also glad to see this protection arrive. The Prince of Wales being one of the proudest and powerful ships in the Royal Navy.

At this time, I had cause to pass the airfield at Kallang and saw there were some of the sleekest fighter planes I had ever seen, this was the first Hurricanes I had ever seen. I think there were about six at this time. They were beautiful to watch as they took off. With the Brewster Buffalos, they would add to our air cover. We had read in the papers from home about these aircraft and their outstanding performance against the German airforce and their 109's during the Battle of Britain.

WE STILL VISIT THE CITY

During this period when off duty we still made our trips to Singapore City, to the Union Jack Club for a few beers. Then to the picture houses. Some would go to the houses of ill repute or the Japanese massage joints. It was very plain to see that the European population were living it up, they didn't seem to care about the crisis at hand, all still very aloof, never speaking to the low down "Tommy". We were very envious of their clubs. The ladies in their evening dress, the smell of the havana cigars when with their high living escorts, their chauffeurs drove up to the Raffles Hotel, the Cathay picture houses, it was all a false facade. I'm afraid the relations between these people and the military lower ranks was not at all healthy. To put it plainly, they did not like us and we did not like them with their sham carry on. We often said that a good 50% of these gentry would not hold a job in the UK. To look at these people, it made one think "is there a crisis"? "Is there any danger at hand"? Or were they all living in a proud cuckoo land with their evening dress, cigars, Daimlers, Rolls Royces etc. It made one wonder, one would think that with their careers at stake, they would have other things to think about except the social high life of dancing and dining that was going on at this time.

I often thought of the famous poem by Rudyard Kipling "Tommy".

How fitting to explain the attitude between these "Tuans" and the "British Tommy".

"TOMMY" POEM BY RUDYARD KIPLING

I went into a public 'ouse to get a pint o' beer,
The publican 'e up an' sez, "We serve no red-coats here".
The girls be'ind the bar they laughed an' giggled fit to die,
I outs into the street again an' to myself sez I:

O it's Tommy this, an' Tommy that, an' "Tommy, go away",
But it's "Thank you, Mister Atkins," when the band begins to play -
The band begins to play, my boys, the band begins to play,
O it's "Thank you, Mister Atkins", when th band begins to play.
I went into a theatre as sober as could be,
They gave a drunk civilian room, but 'adn't none for me;
They sent me to the gallery or round the music 'alls,
But when it comes to fightin', Lord! they'll shove me in the stalls!
For it's Tommy this, an' Tommy that, an' "Tommy, wait outside",
But it's "Special train for Atkins" when the trooper's on the tide -
The troopship's on the tide, my boys, the troopship's on the tide
O it's "Special train for Atkins" when the trooper's on the tide.
Yes, makin' mock o' uniforms that guard you while you sleep
Is cheaper than them uniforms, an' they're starvation cheap;
An' hustlin' drunken soldiers when they're goin' large a bit
Is five times better business than paradin' in full kit.
Then it's Tommy this, an' Tommy that, an' "Tommy, 'ow's yer soul"?
But it's "Thin red line of 'eroes" when the drums begin to roll -
The drums being to roll, my boys, the drums begin to roll,
O it's "Thin red line of 'eroes" when the drums begin to roll.
We aren't no thin red 'eroes", nor we aren't no blackguards too,
But single men in barricks, most remarkable like you;
An' if sometimes our conduck isn't all your fancy paints,
Why, single men in barricks don't grow into plaster saints;
While it's Tommy this, an' Tommy that, an' "Tommy fall be'ind",
But it's "Please to walk in front, sir", when there's trouble in the wind -
There's trouble in the wind, my boys, there's trouble in the wind,
O it's "Please to walk in front, sir" when there's trouble in the wind.
You talk o' better food for us, an' schools, an' fires, an' all:
We'll wait for extry rations if you treat us rational.
Don't mess about the cook-room slops, but prove it to our face
The Widow's Uniform is not the soldier-man's disgrace.

For it's Tommy this, an' Tommy that, an' "Chuck him out, the brute"!
But it's "Saviour of 'is country" when the guns begin to shoot;
An' it's Tommy this, an' Tommy that, an' anything you please;
An' Tommy ain't a bloomin' fool - you bet that Tommy sees!

DECEMBER 1941

Early in December, reconnaissance planes were seen high over South Malaya and Singapore island itself. "It must be ours - or they would be shot down". This is what we said amongst ourselves, but did our planes have the performance to reach them in time - it appears not!!

THE BALLOON GOES UP

We now know that the Japanese fleet left Japan as early as 25 November 1941 to attack Pearl Harbour and other ports in the Pacific seas. It would depend upon the talks between the United States of America and Japan in Washington, if an agreement could be reached in which Japan would not lose face, this massive fleet would be called back. As Japan was given a strong ultimatum to withdrew her forces from China, Indo China etc. She would not be allowed any trade with the Western world i.e trade restrictions would not be lifted, therefore no oil supplies, her assets would remain frozen. Japan was boxed in. On 1 December this fleet was ordered to proceed with the plan laid down. So the Fleet Commander Admiral Nagumo took Pearl Harbour by surprise, America was stabbed in the back, as no declaration of War had been made. Attack on the US Fleet was already planned many months before to take place on 8 December 1941.

On December 6th at about 12 noon, a Hudson Bomber of No 1 Squadron Royal Australian Air Force piloted by Lieut Ramshaw spotted a mine laying vessel 200 miles off Kota Bharu. Thirty minutes later he saw a battleship, five cruisers, seven destroyers and 25 merchant men.

An hour later at 1.00pm, another Hudson reported sighting another convoy consisting of two cruisers, ten destroyers and twenty merchant men. This second Hudson was set upon by a Japanese plane and chased away. The merchant ships involved in both these sightings were carrying manpower for an attack.

At this point, it was believed that these forces were being directed against Siam - "It was therefore none of our business".

Our forces were put on first degree standby.

On December 7th a reconnaissance Catalina flying boat was directed to sight and shadow these convoys - it was shot down.

On this very same day, the Japanese Ambassador in Siam delivered an ultimatum to that country - demanding free passage through. The British legation or intelligence were kept in the dark - it appears they knew nothing of this demand. I think the Siamese Government could have told our legation. It seems that the Japanese made a pact - they would not harm the people or their property if allowed this free passage.

During the night signals poured into Fort Canning and other military headquarters giving details of the Japanese shelling the coastal defences from the sea at Kota Bharu. They were also bombing the airfields in the North - troops were also landing from the assault barges.

THE ATTACK COMES!

In Changi H Block, it was a very heavy sultry night, one of those nights when the mosquitoes were active, sleep just would not come, the bugs were restless. I got out of bed, should I have a shower to cool down? I went for a shower, I then lit a cigarette and went out onto the verandah to look out over the padang and the

Straits of Johore. All bathed in the lovely tropical moonlight, it looked almost like day. On the verandah were other men who could not sleep - one of them was Bill Hydon. We talked about the military situation, the international position in fact. I might add that at no time then had we heard about the landings in North Malaya, only that the conveys were nearing Siam. What would be the outcome of it all. We chain smoked two or three cigarettes, giving no thought to our beds, other sleepless friends joined us. Were we unconsciously worried by the crisis that was at hand? It must have been, I had never had trouble getting to sleep at other times.

It was about 4.00am on that sweaty morning of 8 December when we couldn't sleep that we heard the approach of aircraft as they droned up Changi spit, they were flying over the waters of the Johore Strait. We started to talk excitedly amongst ourselves, our air forces were being reinforced!! They must be ours as all their navigation lights were on, there were two waves the first at 12,000 feet, the second at 5,000 feet. We watched from the end of the second floor of the barrack block looking west toward Seletar Airfield and the Naval Base. Were these planes going to land at Seletar or Sembawang Airfields?? Then my God!! the bombs started to fall on the Naval Base - these must be the Japanese attacking us - "attacking us - we haven't even declared War yet".
Then we saw the searchlights expose and the guns of the battleships HMS Prince of Wales and HMS Repulse. Then the A/A searchlights exposed and the A/A guns started to blast off. We didn't see any of these aircraft shot down. The barrage put up by the warships was very impressive. The multiple pom pom guns (the Chicago Pianos) put up fire like we had never seen the like before. We were confident that these great ships would protect us in any future emergency. By this time, everyone was out of bed, buzzing with excitement, all chattering at once. Have the high level talks fallen through? Have the Japanese attacked us without warning, have they stabbed us in the back? Would we soon be in action?

OUR QUESTIONS ANSWERED

The next morning, December 8th 1941, we were paraded early on the square at Changi and told the news that the Japanese had landed in Siam at two points without any resistance at all, this was in Siam at Singora and Patani. We are told that they came ashore clean and in parade order, so it seems we had been double crossed in as much as the Siamese Government had not in any way told our representatives of the Japanese intentions.

The situation painted a totally different picture for our Military leaders. A Military operation "Matador" had been planned as far back as the early part of August 1940. If invasion was threatened, we would take up positions on the beaches of Siam at Singora and Patani, thus catching the invaders by surprise and destroying them before they could get a foothold.

The British Government held back this authority for fear of provoking the Japanese and giving them a chance to "Go to the aid of Siam" or the Siamese people against an imperialist aggressor Great Britain.

Singora and Patani was of course the very landing places that the Japanese landed their forces.

Singora is a big port in the South, there were two strategically placed airfields both at Singora and Patani.

If operation "Matador" had been brought into action, we should have denied the Japanese the use of the port and the two airfields. There were also two main roads which ran south direct into North Malaya and of course the railway.

There was another defensive plan to stop the invasion of Malaya. It was to put a force on the ledge, the main road at this point was cut into solid rock on the cliffs, a good defensive position could have halted any invader.

If appears that "Matador" could not be activated without authority from the War Office or War Cabinet in London.

The authority was given on 15 December 1941 - the Japanese had landed on the 8th. We were seven days too late. Why? Why? Why?

Weeks before we had had reconnaissance reports that the Japanese had been massing their forces in Indo China. The Hudson Bombers of the Royal Australian Air Force had shadowed the convoys before the landing. It was at this time that "Matador" should have been brought into action.

Another landing was of course made on the North East coast of Malaya at Kota Bharu. Here the Japanese troops waded ashore from their assault craft, they met very strong resistance from the British Forces dug in at the beach heads.

The troops who formed "Matador" were briefed re the operation in hand. They were ready and waiting to go into action. They waited during a monsoon rain storm such as can only happen in the North of Malaya. Then rumours started to spread that the Japanese had already landed, had got a good foothold on the territory that they were going to defend. This and the weather conditions was very bad for their morale. These troops of course had a very bad start in the first battles in North Malaya.

I am of the opinion that the loss of initiative and the two airfields in these early days caused the loss of Malaya and Singapore. The fortress that the peoples in the Pacific had relied upon to defend their freedom was a sugar fortress.

THE OTHER DISASTER

Our section had worked all day from a very early hour building more defences around the coast. We returned to our barracks in Changi at 5.00pm. I had just taken a shower before going to the Mess Hall for our cooked meal. I dressed and went out on to the lawn at H Block. It was about 5.30pm on December 8th. I looked across to the Straits of Johore and saw a great force of ships steaming passed Paula Ubin. I called my friends from the barracks to watch this sight. It was Force "Z" consisting of the Prince of Wales, Repulse and four of our destroyers namely Electra, Express, Vampire and the Tenedos.

We watched with great pride to see the white ensigns waving from the sterns of these great ships.

Remarks were passed to the effect that this force would put the fear of god in to those convoys that were still piling forces and equipment into Siam.

Rear Admiral Sir Tom Phillips, Commander in Chief of the Far East Fleet which had just been formed thought that it was the ripe time to play a positive part during these early stages of the War.

We watched these great ships go out of sight and thought how lucky we were to have them on our side.

We all slept well that night, confident that things could look a lot better once these ships had dealt with the menace in the South China Sea.

Early the next day, 10 December, we were on parade, took our work details and set off to the coast to build more defences. Some of these projects were very hard work, digging in heavy clay soil. We put in large calverts under the roads that were built. The concrete was all hand mixed, this was very tiring work in the tropical sun but we loved every moment of it - it kept us fit.

We returned to Changi barracks at about 4.00pm, a little earlier than usual. We had two or three radios in our barrack room. One of the lads said "Let's get Radio Tokyo - and listen to Tokyo Rose and hear what bullshit she is coming out with today".

We had been told not to listen to these propaganda broadcasts as it could be bad for morale. So, when we listened to Tokyo Rose, we always had a lookout.

At about 4.30pm on came the propaganda broadcast from Tokyo. "This is Tokyo Rose calling, all forces in the Pacific areas - the news I have today will be, I am sure, of great interest to the British Forces in Singapore and Malaya - we have pleasure in telling you that we have today sunk your battleships. Prince of Wales and Repulse".

We all shouted and laughed "What a lot of bullshit - you lying old bag".

We just did not believe it could happen - another load of Japanese propaganda. It was only 48 hours ago that we saw those ships set out full of pride, keeping our flag flying. We expected these great ships to put paid to the Japanese landings, these ships that we had read about in the papers from home and how they had played so great a part in the chase and sinking of the German dreadnought Bismark. "Yes, Tokyo Rose, you're telling a load of bullshit".

Later that evening, it was confirmed on the BBC Radio that the two ships had both been sunk off the east coast of Malaya. What a blow to the British flag and our prestige in the whole of the Far East.

We that had listened to the announcement looked at each other dumbfounded, I had a lump in my throat the size of an egg and the tears ran down my face, there wasn't a dry eye in the block. "God - what a great disaster".

Not many of us slept that night, we spent most of the hours of darkness on the verandah, chain smoking and looking over the Straits of Johore, where we had seen our pride sail out to meet the unknown.

If only the clock could be put back 48 hours to perhaps start again.

No doubt at all, Singapore was full of spies, as was Malaya, we always thought after this disaster that an agent secreted in the Johore area had passed information to the Japanese HQ that this force was putting to sea, it was thereafter shadowed by aircraft or submarine.

From these two great ships, out of their total crews of 2,921 men, there were 2,081 survivors, so 840 souls went to their death on this very sad day including Admiral Sir Tom Phillips, Commander in Chief Eastern Fleet and Captain J.C Leach "Prince of Wales". Captain W.G Tennant "Repulse" went down with his ship but was later rescued.

On this very day, a meeting had been held in the War Cabinet at No 10 Downing Street to review the Naval situation in the Far Eastern waters. Mr Churchill had suggested that these ships should get lost in the many Pacific Islands, to keep the enemy guessing and to worry as to their whereabouts. They were then to move across the Pacific ocean to join what remained of the American Fleet who had taken such a battering at Pearl Harbour. With these combined forces, a decisive battle could perhaps be fought in this area. It would also strengthen the defences of Australia the New Zealand area. They, the War Cabinet, would give the idea considerable thought and come to a definite decision the next morning.

By that time, these two important vessels were at the bottom of the South China Sea.

Before leaving Admiral Phillips had asked Air Vice Marshall Pulford for air cover in the areas he intended to sail in.

1. Reconnaissance 100 miles ahead of his fleet from first light 9 December.

2. Recce to Singora and beyond, 10 miles off the coast 10 December.

3. Fighter escort and protection off Singora from dawn 10 December.

Air Marshall Pulford replied:-

1. He could provide.

2. He was very doubtful as he would have to use Blenheim planes, based at Kuantan, half way up the Malayan coast, it was not certain if the airfield would still be in operation.

3. Impossible as the airfields in the North had been bombed and were out of action.

The short range Buffalo fighters would be limited as travelling from distant airfields would limit their combat time as they would have to return to refuel. Anyway, if they went into combat in the China Sea, Singapore would be left without air cover. "Z" Force was already at sea. Signals were made and confirmed "There could be no fighter cover off the coast of Siam".

At midday, an aircraft spotter reported aircraft to port. It was an RAF flying boat, a catalina which signalled to Prince of Wales. "Japanese making major landing at Singora". Admiral Phillips was pleased to hear this news.
He at once made plans to attack the Singora landings.

Later a Japanese aircraft Nakajima Naka 93' appeared - then disappeared - how much it had seen of the "Z" Force one never knew.

Admiral Phillips intended to attack under the low cloud and retire, hoping that the Jap planes would not attack in the very frequent squalls. Also that the planes would not be equipped with anti-ship bombs or torpedoes.

As evening drew nigh, the skies began to clear and more enemy planes flew overhead, it was clear that they were being shadowed. At this point, the Admiral abandoned the plan to attack Singora and turned to the southward course.

At this time, the Japanese 22nd Air Flotilla intended to attack and bomb Singapore from their base in Indo China. They took off but had to return due to low cloud and bad flying conditions. They then loaded with torpedoes to attack "Z" Force but low cloud compelled them to return again to their base.

At midnight Admiral Phillips received a message from Shore HQ. "Enemy reported landings at Kuantan". Kuantan is on the east coast of Malaya 60 miles south of Kota Bharu, this was a very strategic position to the military with a very valuable airfield.

How he would like to surprise the Japanese at this point, it was also on his way back to Singapore.

A message was sent to Singapore saying that the fleet had turned back and was going to make for Kuantan. No further message was received at HQ.

No 453 Fighter Sqn was standing by for further orders from Prince of Wales, they could have got into the air and been in a position to protect the fleet at Kuantan. No further message was received from Admiral Phillips.

Later that night, another Japanese submarine radioed that the "Z" Force had turned back to the South, this brought an air search into action. This was followed by that formidable 22nd Air Flotilla of 34 high level bombers and 51 torpedo bombers.

Early on the morning of 10 December "action stations" were sounded, enemy aircraft had been seen but disappeared almost at once Prince of Wales and Repulse catapulted their aircraft to scout the coast and patrol for submarines. HMS Express also left the force to make reconnaissance in the area.

Earlier on the night before, an enemy force had approached Kuantan but land forces had opened fire on them and they withdrew. At dawn, our recce planes had signalled that the area was quiet. The destroyer Express found that all was peaceful there.

At this time, the fleet observed a tug towing a number of barges, these could be landing craft. The Admiral decided to check. The strike force of aircraft that had been reported earlier and had missed them had searched as far as Singapore - was now returning to their base. A Japanese recce plane that had been shadowing the fleet for quite a time, warned them that their target was right here. It was at 11.15 hours. The first high level bombers attacked at 10,000 feet in tight line abreast.

Before the initial attack came in, the bombers swooped down on Repulse drawing her fire power of ack ack guns - then swung again - a very clever diversion.

The multiple pom pom were busy, they shot down one Jap plane but fire had started in the hanger - joy was short lived.

The second wave then came in on to the Prince of Wales, they drew her fire power, at the same time she was struck by two torpedoes carried by planes at a very low level. Both port propellers were put out of action, as was her steering gear. She listed heavily, she was little more than a floating wreck.

HMS Repulse was then attacked by nine torpedo bombers, she turned away and was missed, high level bombers then came in, all their missiles missed their target.

Prince of Wales then came under attack again, she received three more direct hits on the starboard side. Another Jap plane was shot down. Repulse then took her second attack, her decks ripped open, her rudder jammed. In this attack she shot down two Japanese plans, her crew cheered this final hit back. She was hit again, it was her death knell, she keeled over and sank - her multiple pom pom guns still firing.

The Japanese allowed the British destroyers HMS Express and Electra to close with the Prince of Wales to take off the wounded sailors. The big ship was mortally wounded, she slipped beneath the waves at 1.30pm.
The initial attack had been in progress half an hour before the force sent its first signal, this was from Repulse, it was another half an hour before it was received at Air Headquarters. When our fighter planes arrived, all the Japanese planes had left the area, their task had been completed.

This was looked upon as a major disaster wherever the British Union flag was flying.

It was indeed a major disaster to the War in Malaya and played a great part toward the fall of Singapore.

The air supremacy of the Japanese had been very much underestimated. Our intelligence in the area of the Pacific and South East Asia must have been very sadly lacking.

What a shock this disaster must have been to the House of Commons when Mr Churchill told his hushed audience the next day. Mr Churchill had been awakened that morning by the First Sea Lord with a telephone message in which he could not camouflage his distress, with a slight cough he began:-

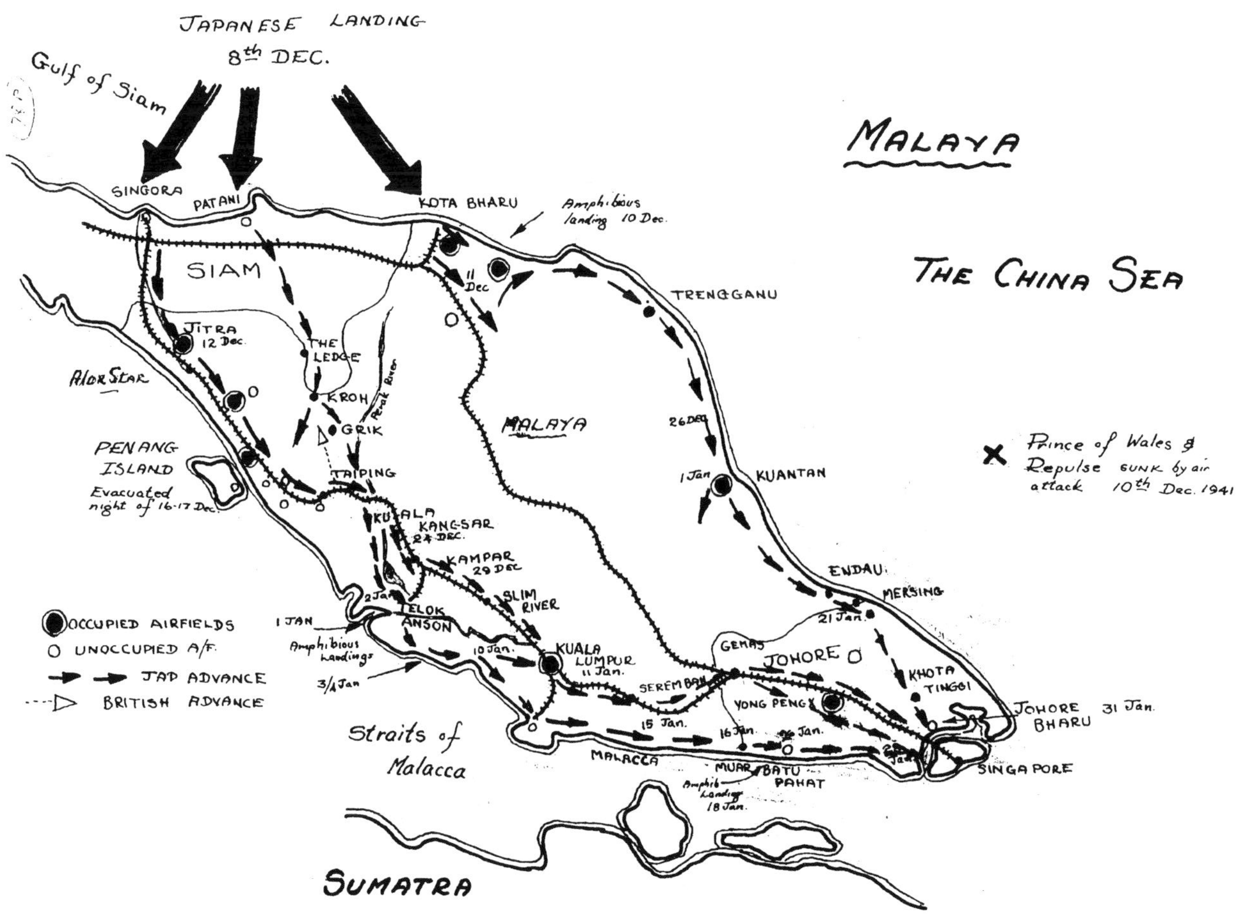
MALAYA
JAPANESE LANDING
8th DEC.
Gulf of Siam
SINGORA
PATANI
KOTA BHARU
Amphibious landing 10 Dec.
SIAM
11 Dec
TRENGGANU
THE CHINA SEA
JITRA
12 Dec.
THE LEDGE
KROH
GRIK
Perak River
Alor Star
PENANG ISLAND
Evacuated night of 16-17 Dec.
TAIPING
MALAYA
26 Dec
1 Jan
KUANTAN
Prince of Wales & Repulse sunk by air attack 10th Dec. 1941
KUALA KANGSAR
24 Dec.
KAMPAR
29 Dec
SLIM RIVER
2 Jan
TELOK ANSON
1 JAN
Amphibious landings
3/4 Jan
10 Jan.
KUALA LUMPUR
11 Jan.
ENDAU
MERSING
21 Jan.
GEMAS
JOHORE
KHOTA TINGGI
SEREMBAN
YONG PENG
JOHORE BHARU
31 Jan.
15 Jan.
16 Jan.
MALACCA
MUAR
BATU PAHAT
Amphib. Landing 18 Jan.
SINGAPORE
Straits of Malacca
SUMATRA
OCCUPIED AIRFIELDS
UNOCCUPIED A/F.
JAP ADVANCE
BRITISH ADVANCE

Island of Singapore
15th Feb. 1942

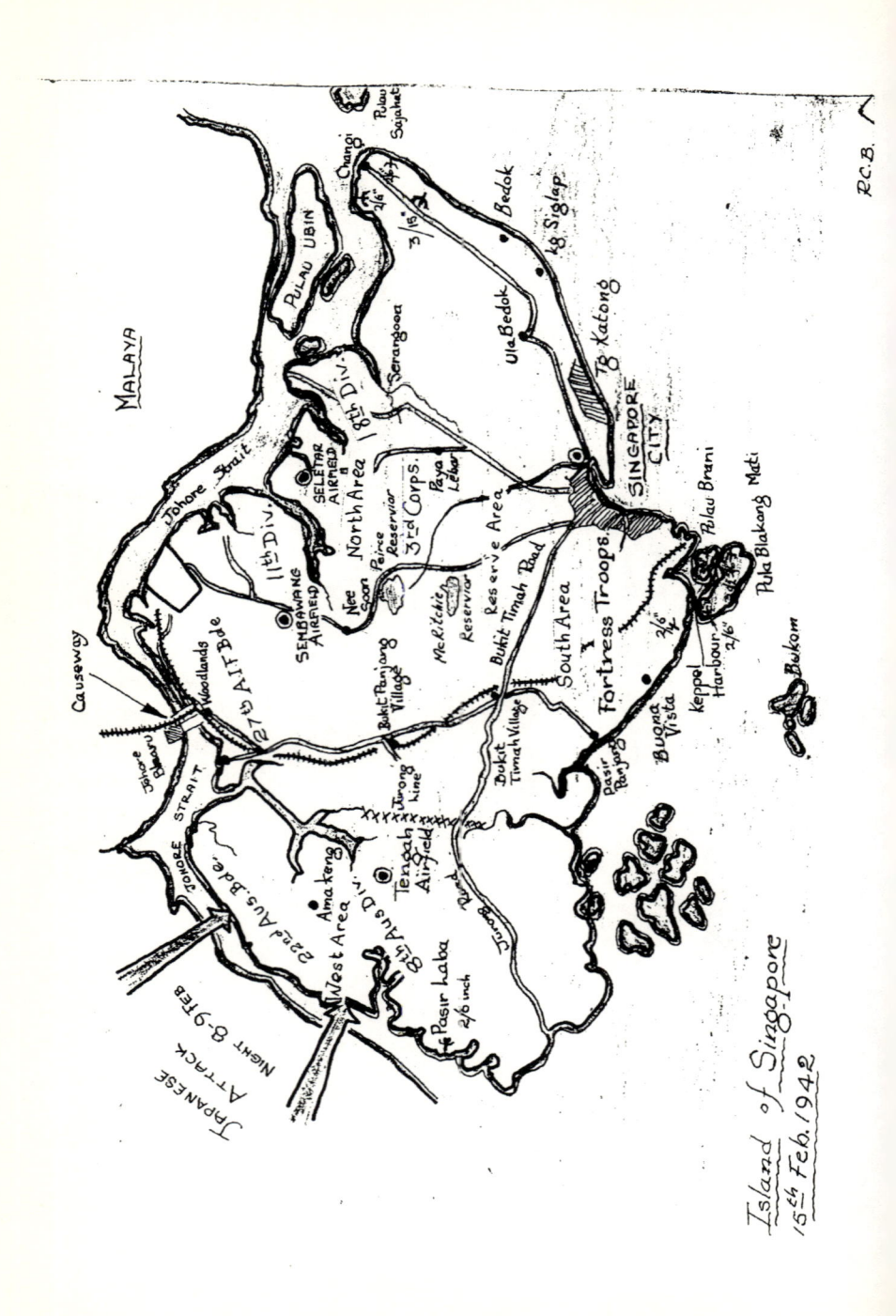

"Prime Minister, I have to report to you that the Prince of Wales and the Repulse have both been sunk by the Japanese - we think by aircraft - Tom Phillips has been drowned".

"Are you sure that this is true"?

"No doubt at all Sir".

Mr Churchill was shattered, he put the phone down - he was glad of the solitude.

If only the plan discussed the day before by the War Cabinet had been put into action. "Z" Force would have been on their way to America. Instead, these two great ships were laying many fathoms beneath the South China Sea.

ROADS TO SINGAPORE

Many books have been written about the battles fought down the Malay peninsula. The enemy were at the gates of Singapore by 28 January 1941. There are many stories told of this advance by the enemy, of their bravery. There are many stories told of the bravery of our forces but we must always bear in mind that we were up against a force of very disciplined men, well trained in the wars with China, whose sole aim was to die for their Emperor and beloved Japan.

We must also consider that their air supremacy out stripped ours, from the very start at Singora and Patani they had aircraft on the peninsula much superior to ours. With a bomber force coming from Indo China. Later they had the airfield of Malaya (see map).

We also read of the chaos in the battles fought by untrained soldiers. The confusion between the leaders, orders and counter orders, this was rife from the very start. There always seemed to be confusion between the different areas and sectors. Many of the Indian Regiments just fresh from India had very little training in this type of jungle warfare. The Indian Officers, many could not speak or understand the English language. When our forces evacuated Penang and many other ports and villages along both the east and west coasts of Malaya, large numbers of boats and small craft were left behind, we failed to destroy these as we should have done. The Japanese put these craft to good use by sailing down the coasts, both to the east and west and landing behind our lines.

Many of these landings enabled the Japanese to take up positions as snipers in trees and undergrowth, shooting at random on our retreating forces. From their tree positions, they dropped hand grenades into the retreating Bren gun carriers, causing havoc among the crews. One never knew where they (the enemy) were. Right throughout the Malay campaign, they seemed to bring off tactics of surprise to cause confusion from the north to the south. It boils down to the fact that our forces were not up to this type of warfare, in fact it was never expected in this jungle barrier.

During the retreat, there were many refugees on the roads and tracks, hundreds of these were Chinese, among these people on the run from the enemy were of course Japanese soldiers dressed in civilian clothes, many dressed as coolies and riding bicycles, all had concealed weapons with which to shoot our retreating army. Who amongst our green and untrained recruits could tell the difference between Chinese and Japanese when they were dressed the same in coolie garb?

It may be noted at this point that the roads, many were mere tracks in the early 1930s, were improved on by these Japanese managers, there were three main roads leading to Johore Bahru through the Johore state. One on the west coast from the River Muar to Johore via Batu Pahat, Senggarang and Benut. Another through the centre from Labis, Yong Pen and Kulai to Johore. The other road on the east coast from Endau, Mersing, Jemaluang on to Kota Tinggi thence to Johore. So we find the planning to be excellent that went into the Japanese campaign long before the hostilities started. All these roads were capable of carrying heavy tanks which the Japanese used to the full extent. The only track vehicles we had were the bren carriers. So another trump card in the Jap hand.

JAPANESE INTELLIGENCE

Many of the rubber plantations, iron and tin mines were owned and developed by the Japanese. These people built up understandings and friendships amongst the local communities. One of these gentlemen, it is believed, returned to Johore as a Colonel in charge of one of the enemy infantry regiments.

One such case I remember well at the Penerang coastal searchlight and 6" gun position. A coolie used to come daily to clean up our bucket type toilets, these buckets were taken out and their contents dumped in the sea. The coolie, we all knew him by the nickname of "Shit Charlie". He spoke very good broken english. We at times conversed with him and gave him the odd cigarette or two. After the fall of Singapore, we were on working parties in the city and on the docks. One of our men, Sapper Bill Long, was approached by a Japanese Officer, who gave him a cigarette and said "You very good man, you give me cigarettes a long time ago at Penerang - me "Shit Charlie". So we find that the Japanese intelligence service, together with the fifth column was very well planned.

No doubt other intelligence agents were employed in the camera and developing shops where, at times, I expect films for processing were of interest to these people.

There were the Japanese massage parlours, where soldiers used to frequent to pass an hour. I expect many a pay book was scrutinized when uniforms or clothing was left in the dressing rooms, particulars of regiments, company and other data were copied in detail.

Then we have the oldest profession to contend with, many of the brothels were Japanese run. No doubt the Japs had a field day in such places gaining information as some of the leaflets dropped on the city were to show at a later date, naming persons complete with regimental numbers and even next of kin. All these things were used to outwit and build up the surprise element to great effect. One such leaflet dropped was addressed to an Australian soldier telling him it was about time he packed in the fighting and returned home to his wife (giving her name) as no doubt she was now abed with an American serviceman whom the US President, FDR, had sent to defend his country while he was wasting his time here in Malaya. We always had a good laugh at these leaflets but it wasn't very nice for the persons mentioned on them. They seemed to know everything.

The Japanese forces were attacking down through the state of Johore at a very fast rate. It was discovered at this point that the odd gun or two of the coastal batteries could be fired in the direction of Johore instead of out to sea, as they were all designed to do. One of the 15" guns of the Johore battery could be fired north. Also one of the 6" at Changi. Our task was to fell all the very high trees, to clear a path for these projectiles. Many of these trees were at a height of 70 to 80 feet, it was quite a task. We were working from dawn to dusk as it was very essential to get the big guns planting their projectiles amongst the Japanese military who were massing for the final attack on the fortress of Singapore.

Many natives were recruited to help with the task, they were able to climb these massive trees with rope slings around the trunks, then walking up the side of the tree to the top, they proceeded to lop off the branches. I remember one day, it was quite early in the morning, one of these men (a tamil) was sawing off a giant branch. We told him to saw on the other side of his body, he just laughed and carried on sawing, we all made frantic shouts but to no avail. Then it happened, he had sawn off the branch on which he was sitting, the poor man crashed to the ground from a height of about

70 feet. He was badly injured and was taken to the local hospital. I never heard if he recovered.

We had another very bad accident to one of our own Sappers "Doc" Broadbent. A tree had been felled but the trunk had split taking the weight of the whole bulk.

I was driving the Karrier winch truck on the particular day. A long hawser had been attached to the top of the tree, I was instructed to take in on the winch hawser, the tree was felled to the position that was required but the trunk had split. The split section was taking the whole weight of the trunk which was about four feet in diameter with a weight of two or three tons. The Sergeant in charge of the detachment detailed Sapper Broadbent to get in and saw off the piece of wood holding the trunk in position. At the time it was suggested to the Sergeant that the hawser be attached to the trunk and winched to break the greenstick. He would not alter his mind, so poor Broadbent had to try and saw through the piece of tree. As he was sawing with a petrol driven saw, it hampered his movement and the whole two or three tons of trunk fell on to him. An ambulance was sent for and he was taken to hospital, where it was found that he had a broken spine, arms, legs and pelvis. He was in a very bad state. The sheer guts of this man I will later tell you about.

After a hard time, the offending trees were moved from the field of fire but only two guns could fire into Johore State, one of the 15" and only one of the 6".

As the Japanese Army were massing for the final assault, these two guns were fired but it was not of much success as they were armour piercing shells. They made quite a noise when in flight to terrorise the enemy I should think. When they reached the target, they buried themselves into the ground and failed to explode. They were meant to be used against armour plated ships out to sea at a distance of 12 to 15 miles away, we never heard that these guns did much damage to the enemy. I read a Jap Colonel's book and he said that the noise was terrifying.

Johore state was about to fall, our forces had been driven back on to Singapore Island. At this time, we were being told to hold out, we were to fight to the last man.

Tomorrow the skies over Singapore would be black with American Air Force aeroplanes, we kept looking and waiting for this to happen. The only planes we were to see were those with the fried eggs on their wings.

One day I was on detail to drive out towards Changi on the East Coast Road. As I passed the civil airport at Kalang, it broke my heart to see about ten or a dozen Hurricane fighter aircraft total wrecks, some were burnt out, others damaged by machine gun fire or bomb damaged by the high level bombers, these fighters and bombers had the freedom of the skies, they just flew at will wherever they wanted.

When we saw the Hurricane a few days before, it lifted our morale and we were looking forward to seeing the dogfights we had heard so much about in the Battle of Britain. We wanted to see the Jap Air Force shot out of the Singapore skies, we dreamed in vain. The air raid sirens would sound, the Hurricanes would take off at great speed and fly in the opposite direction to the approaching Japanese "zeros". We were all appalled to see this and did in fact say that the pilots were yellow. I am afraid at that time we did not know the true facts, apparently the planes came on one ship. Their armaments came on another which was sunk just off Singapore by enemy action, so these poor pilots had no option but to take off and get away as far as possible, with a view to getting armaments at a later date but it wasn't to be.

A TRIP TO PAULA UBIN

The company were paraded one morning earlier than usual. Our OC was present. He asked for volunteers to carry out an operation that had a few risks. I wasn't too keen having been caught a few times to carry the piano from the Sergeants Mess to the Officers Mess etc. It was always a pet of our Sergeant Major, I was never one to jump at any bait to volunteer. On this particular morning, I happened to form up with my best mate "Dolly" Grey, he stepped forward and said that he was going for a bit of excitement and let's get at the enemy. He looked at me and asked "Ain't you coming"? To which I replied "Not bloody likely". He then said "I didn't think you were yellow". Well this did hurt my pride, there was nothing else to do but step forward. Out of the whole company on parade, I think a good 75% had stepped forward. The OC said that he was very pleased with the response but he only wanted eight sappers. He then went down the ranks and picked the eight sappers, I was one of those, "Dolly" Grey was overlooked. The OC told us to stand by that evening and we would be told of the operation to be carried out. The task, if completed, would last all night. Dolly Grey came up to me and shook my hand and said "Well goodbye me old mate, give me the address of the folks at home and I will write and tell them how you got bumped off". I thought "You bugger - you are giving me good heart, if it hadn't been for you and your taunt, I shouldn't have volunteered". He then said "Give me your watch and other valuables and I will see that they get to your folks". To this I replied "Bugger off". In my heart I wished that he would have been with us, he was a good type to have around in crisis.

Our duty truck came for us just before dusk. Our party consisted of our OC, one Sergeant, a Corporal and eight sappers. We took with us two Lewis guns and four rifles, these weapons were for our own protection. The OC was wearing his .38 revolver.

We went to the magazine at Changi and drew explosives. About five boxes of guncotton slabs, the same amount of gelignite, together with all the primary charges. With all this equipment, we moved off to Changi beach where a Toncan was moved in and manned by Royal Navy personnel. The vessel came to the beach and we loaded the equipment. The craft was armed with a three pounder gun. We pushed off from the beach and at a steady speed we approached the east of Paula Ubin, all in darkness. The OC told us that the operation would be a piece of cake. At this point, the engines of the vessel were stopped, we were to drift in on the incoming tide. The tide was quite swift and we were drifting in on to the north beach of Paula Ubin, the state of Johore was on our starboard side. As I have already mentioned, Johore was occupied by the Japanese Army. Before we landed, the OC told us that we were to demolish three piers. A reconnaissance had been made recently and it was reported that one was of concrete structure, the other two were wooden, the job wouldn't take long. The piers had to be demolished to stop the Jap landing, at least it wouldn't be so easy for them. It was thought that they would use Paula Ubin as a springboard to land at or around the Changi area.

At last we hit the beach, we jumped ashore with our arms and explosives, as I dashed up the sandy beach I was challenged "God" I thought "we have been ambushed". I broke into a cold sweat, I heard our OC give the password, it was OK, I then heard a Scot say "It's OK, this is the RE". It was our old friends the Gordon Highlanders, they were there waiting to protect us. We could never have had better, we always got on well with them, a good steady battalion of men.

We made our way to the first pier to be demolished, the concrete one. We dug down between the pier legs and set the charges in position, we put guncotton on all the braces, this was ready to blow.

We then moved on down the beach to attack the remaining two wooden structures. To our horror we found that one of these was also concrete, so much for the reconnaissance that was made, the job was going to take longer than was at first estimated. We set about the task and got our charges in position, the explosive remaining was very little for the last wooden pier. We put cutting charges on all the wooden legs and cross beams. We linked all the charges together with the three means of firing, electric, F.I.D and safety fuse. We took cover, tested all circuits, we were ready for the big bang!!! We began to sweat, the mosquitoes were buzzing and biting. "God - don't let us have a misfire - or the Japs will be landing before we can get away". The wires were connected to the electric exploder - the OC turned the handle to generate the power, he then said "Stand by" and pushed the handle down, there was one almighty explosion. The piers went up skyhigh. "Well done lads - now let us get out, they will be on to us".

At this point, our own coastal defence searchlights exposed on us, they had not been warned that we were carrying out this operation. We dived for cover expecting our own coastal guns to fire upon our party. It was like day with the powerful lights upon us. The Japanese started to fire at Paula Ubin but were off target, with their small arms they did not cause us any trouble, the lights doused. We then proceeded to march back across the island. This was a very hazardous task in the dark, the tracks were hard to find, quite a lot of the ground was swampland and completely jungle. At this point, I might add, that I carried a fully loaded Lewis gun during this journey. We were all very glad to reach the south coast where the Navy were waiting to take us back to Changi in the old Toncan. We stayed the rest of the night at Changi in our old barracks before going back to Singapore. We had a brew up and bully beef sandwiches. I went to my old bed space to find that all my treasured possession had been looted, all my civilian clothes and photograph albums had gone, still there was a war on, I hope those that stole them were in more need than I. It was the natives I believe.

We left Changi as day was breaking and we looked across the Johore Straits to Ubin and there the "fried egg" (Jap flag) was flying. The big guns at Tekon Battery opened up and the flag soon disappeared from view. Without doubt, the Japanese had been landing on the island farther down the beach while we were preparing the demolition. The Toncan returned to the island to bring back our covering party of Gordon Highlanders, they said that they had not seen any signs of the Japanese. I think we were very fortunate not to have been attacked by the enemy.

When we got back to our camp area, Dolly Grey was the first one to greet the party. He told me that he had worried about the outcome of the operation and was glad to see me back safe and sound. He felt he had been responsible for getting me into the party in the first place. I said "You won't have to send and tell my folks how I got bumped off". As an afterthought I said "I don't suppose you would have written anyway as you are always up before the Colonel for not writing to your old mother you rotten sod".

After this episode, I went back to driving HG vehicles.

At this time, we were being attacked from all quarters. We were bombed from high level -dive bombed, fighter aircraft attacked us from low level with machine cannon and small calibre ammo. Artillery fire was with mortar from Johore and from the sea, Singapore was a hellhole. I saw many people killed by bomb-blast, many Chinese and Indians were dead in the streets, we could do nothing for them. One day I was taking rations to the front line - electricity cables were down, I had to avoid them. I saw a house in front of me - a red brick building, it shook and just exploded before my very eyes, I guess it must have had a direct hit, my truck was showered in debris. I got through with the rations.

About the start of February I was sent to Johore Battery to assist in blowing up the 15" guns and the engines - that I had tended to with such care. Our mission was complete and a success. After the fall of Singapore, the Breech Block of one of these guns was found quarter of a mile from the site, the guns were rendered useless to the enemy. At this time, we also blew up the magazine at Changi - it stored all types of ammunition from 15" to small arms, it made quite a bang. L delay fuses were used.

The Japanese forces had landed on the north coast, they came in their thousands running over the dead and picking up their arms. They were breaking through our lines. Snipers were all over the town, we kept plodding away at our task.

They say that the attacking forces are some of the best and very seasoned troops from the Japanese Imperial Guard. Some said to be over six feet in height and fearless to the point of being fanatical.

We had a big battle on the Bukit Tima Road, it was very difficult to tell who was who. The Japanese were known to be taking up many disguises, we could not tell the difference between them and the Chinese.

Whilst on one patrol, we were going from bombed building to bombed building. The smell of cordite and other explosives was terrible. Also the terrible stench of death as many bodies were left unburied.

We went into one building and there were people there that had been looting, they had been killed by the blast. One was sat at a desk with his head blown off, in his hands was the loot, two bars of chocolate. My friend said "That's no good to him now, he's too far gone". So we took the chocolate - had a bar each, we sat there and ate it. It's a callous War!!

At night we had bodies flitting from building to building, it was a case of when to shoot and when not to shoot.
On the night of the 14 February 1942, I was on patrol in Orchard Road with a very good friend of mine, going from building to building trying to flush out snipers. Many we were sure were from the 5th column. It was very nerve racking. I felt very afraid but, at the same time, quite calm. I felt as if someone was with me - I know I prayed to our God - or- maybe the spirit of my Grandfather was with me - who knows?

I know it was a terrible night, we shot at shadows - some were hit - but how many and who we know not.

A terrible night.

The next day was 15 February 1942. Guns ceased firing, IT WAS ALL OVER.

Some men could not take defeat - it was very hard, our pride had been severely hurt. We all thought that Singapore was impregnable!!

An Australian shot himself outside of the Cathy Building - a sorry end to perhaps a good soldier.

The Emperor of Japan has a lot to answer for.

It was not long before the Jap occupation forces marched into the city with their tanks flying the Jap flags (the fried eggs). Surely a terrible day.

We also saw Japanese flags appearing at windows of private houses. I wonder were they occupied by 5th column members.

A lot of the Indian population we know supported the Japanese in their greater East Asia campaign.

General Percival had surrendered to General Yamashita at the Ford Factory - 15 February 1942.

>"March into Bondage"
>"Banzai you Bastards"
>"Naked Island"
>"Bamboo and Bushido"

Just to name a few of the books published since the end of World War II but none can tell of the devastation we all felt on this day, utterly shattered, bewildered, dejected. We were all, that is my unit (41st Company Fortress Royal Engineers) assembled at Amber Mansions, Orchard Road, Singapore. We had to pile our arms to be collected by the IJA (Imperial Japanese Army) later that day. I had a .38 revolver that I had acquired very early in the heat of combat. I buried it in the flower garden wrapped in rags saturated in engine oil. I thought I would collect it at a later date. My rifle (.303) Lee Enfield (No V8700) I bashed it to pieces with a 7lb sledgehammer. I had become a marksman with that rifle, it was like killing a very dear friend, it hurt me very much to do this deed.

Later that day, our OC Major James Boyle OBE RE came to see us, he had been to a meeting at Fort Canning. He gave us instructions that we would be going back to the Changi Contonement. Most of us would march back but the drivers could take our trucks with as many stores as possible. I had to take a truck. The Major went on to tell us to be very careful of the Japanese troops, as a lot of them had been drinking and would think nothing of shooting us out of hand. If we were stopped en route, we should give them all they asked for and not put our lives at risk. He then broke down and cried and said that he was so sorry he could not have lead us to better things which he knew us to be capable of but not to think we were in disgrace. He was pleased with all we had done in our duties, we had done all that was expected of us. He then wished us good luck whatever was in store or what we had to face, as he cleared his voice and rubbed the tears from his eyes he said - "God bless our beloved homeland".

We drivers loaded our trucks and went in convoy to Changi. We took all the food stuff we could. We also took the very old soldiers and wounded on the top of our loads. I took off my wrist watch, I also took out my cap badge and put them together in the headlamp of my truck, just in case some "nip" tried to take them off me. (I still have the cap badge to this day - it was issued to me as a recruit and it is one of my most prized possessions).

We got back to Changi without incident. I, or we, were lucky, some of the trucks were stopped, the drivers were beaten and made to leave their vehicles complete with stores and march the rest of the way with the columns of troops.

After about three hours, we were allocated to our billet!! We were sent to our garages, this was where we usually kept our motor transport, there were no beds nor bedding, we had to sleep on the concrete floors. I, like many others, used by backpack as a pillow. The first night I did sleep well. It was good not to hear the pounding of guns, shells and bombs exploding around ones person. Before going to sleep, I said my prayers, I asked God to see me through the ordeal that we all would have to face. I asked that all at home would be taken care of, most of all that we would soon be liberated again.

At dawn I awoke, stiff and very cold as well as being very hungry. We had not eaten since breakfast the day before. When we did eat we were given hard biscuits and bully beef, I always liked "bully" so it was not a hardship to me.

I forgot to mention in the last story how I went to the Navy base at Selator where we loaded a truck full of condensed milk and other tinned food. I also took about ten 1lb tins of ticklers, a Navy tobacco. I gave some away but kept about five tins to myself, as I could not see the Japanese giving us cigarettes, so I could curb the hunger pangs for a while. The milk and tin foods were rationed out every day. It did not last long.

After approximately ten days, our rations were very low. It was at this point that the Japanese gave us our first rations. It was mostly rice with a little vegetables. As a child I used to love rice puddings. This was another matter, just boiled rice, it came as a solid lump, with vegetable water poured over the top - it was d-i-s-g-u-s-t-i-n-g!!!

After two days, news came through that one of our old soldiers who was made to get off one of the trucks and walk after being beaten had died. He was buried on the roadside - he was later exhumed and given a proper burial at the Changi Cemetery, later to be taken up again to be laid at Krangi Cemetery, as were all the others who were killed in action or died as Prisoners of War.

We could not get bread at any price, or flour to make it, our cookhouse was an improvised affair. We cut down oil drums to cook the rice, we laid oil drums on their sides and covered them with mud to make "Aldershot" ovens. We tried to make a bread by grinding the rice to a flour, it did make a change - but it was still rice. We tried all kinds of experiments, we boiled grass and mixed it with the rice, we boiled hibiscus* leaves and the flowers to make a change in flavour but all to no avail, we even put tooth powder in the rice.

*Hibiscus is a tropical plant or shrub with red bell like flowers. Dorothy Lamour used to wear them in her hair.

One day we had a big issue of rice. When we cut the sacks open, we found that the rice was infested with maggots and other grubs. It was disgusting. Our Officers complained, the Japs retorted "What do you expect - you have lost the War - not won it"!! The Officers were beaten up for their trouble. The League of Nations charter of the Geneva summit was mentioned, the Japs just laughed about this and said that they were not members. This was a pointer to things to come, where death and disease were to befriend us all along the way for the next 3½ years.

Our billets were not far from the sea by Changi Pier, we were allowed to go there to swim. We even caught a few fish with improvised fish hooks (from my poaching days as a lad) it helped to give a better taste - we also brought back seawater to cook the rice in - it was different!!

One day I was on the pier when some Chinese men rowed in a small boat and gave us bread, there were three of them, we were so grateful, we wanted to pay them with what little we had to offer, they refused to take anything and just rowed away again back around the coast.

The bread - it was manna from heaven - it melted in the mouth - such kind men these must have been to row up, throw us the bread and row back from whence they came.

Two days later these gentlemen rowed in again with bread, they threw some to us. Just then a Japanese truck came roaring along the road to the pier. With a screeching of brakes a group dismounted - they were screaming and shrieking at the Chinese like demented demons. They mounted a light machine gun - then before my very eyes they shot one of the men - the other two jumped into the water and swam underneath until their lungs must have been at bursting point. When they came up for air, the soldiers opened fire on their bobbing heads, they did this until both were shot dead - their bodies were washed ashore on a small island, they were there for many weeks - "as a warning to others" - so the Japs said. Like many other experiences, I shall never forget those so brave and benevolent men. Just around the corner on Changi Beach, many more were to meet their deaths by firing squad, we often heard the LMGs firing.

We stayed in this position for about two months, then the Japs moved us away as far as possible from the coast. We moved into Temple Hill, Changi. I had a billet beneath the servants quarters of an Officers House - so we had moved up market, it was dry but still on concrete, rations were still very bad.

As regards to work, we were employed around the area, we put the power lines in position, we got the water supply working, we cut the grass to keep the mosquito population at bay, trying to keep down the malarial fevers.

Beri beri began to come into being, we had never heard of such a thing, always having had the best of food. Beri beri is caused by malnutrition, otherwise a very poor diet. There are several stages of this disease. (i) Swelling of the lower limbs, ankles swell with water, when a person lays down to sleep the face and upper part of the body swells. (ii) At this stage, the swelling goes - but one gets what we called "happy feet", the feet and legs have a peculiar feeling crossed between an ache and an itch, just can't rest, have to keep moving about. It was awful to see men walking up and down outside the huts through the night and at daytime as well could not sleep for the awful feeling. (iii) The third stage could be a very bad attack of glossitis, all the skin peeled off the inside of the mouth and the tongue, this was a very painful stage of the disease, could not drink hot tea etc. Salt became very painful inside of the mouth. Without treatment, the disease progressed to stage. (iv) The whole body began to swell and cardiac trouble started. Many men died at this stage of heart attacks. The treatment to cure the disease was all the vitamins but mostly Vit B. This is why we tried to eat grass etc and rice polishings, i.e the rusks from the rice husks. We found that marmite was a good help - when we could get it.

Malaria began to get very bad, as we could not carry out anti-malarial precautions. Malaria is carried by the female mosquito. When she sucks blood from a person, she also lays her eggs in the bloodstream - this is the cause of the disease. There are mostly two main types MT and BT. MT being the most dangerous. Without treatment, it is a killer. A very frightening disease, without treatment it can be very serious. The only treatment we had (if lucky) was quinine. Today there are many medicines to combat this illness. The symptoms - very bad headaches, very cold shivers and sweating all at the same time hallucinations. It took ten days to clear and left one feeling very weak and listless. When I went into Siam (now Thailand) I had 15 attacks in 14 months. I hope to tell you about that adventure at a later date.

The next disease to hit us was dysentery. This I believe was the worst disease of all. It killed thousands of our number over the 3½ years in captivity under the Japanese Imperial Forces. This disease was carried by flies, mostly of the blue bottle type. This disease of course is a very acute type of diarrhoea. It is a disease - inflammation of the stomach, with frequent discharge from the bowels mixed with blood. It is a terrible infection.

If one got the two latter disease together, there was very little chance of recovery. As the quinine was inclined to make one run to the toilet, if one had dysentery this is the last thing one wanted. Now I have told you a little about these diseases so if I mention them later you will understand what I am telling you about.

We stayed in the Temple Hill district only a matter of weeks. We were moved to V Block which was the Married Families Quarters used by my Company - the 41st Fortress RE. It took us a few days to get settled in. We still worked in the garrison area. We built aldershot ovens and fireplaces to cook the meagre supplies which, by this time, had not improved by any means. Each man received a bowl of rice per day, with perhaps a few pumpkins thrown in. These were boiled to make a vegetable stew. Every Sunday, whenever and wherever, we tried our best to have a little Church Service. I saw men there praying and singing hymns who were the "hard cases" the "tough guys" who never at one time gave a thought to religion -the cards were now on the table. This was a different ball game. Things are not in any way easy.

We had a young Merchant Navy man join our Company, he had been in Singapore at the fall. Being M.N he would have been interned as a civilian. To overcome this situation, he was given the rank of a Sapper RE and a fictitious regimental number, he hoped to get a better deal as a POW than as a civilian internee. Now this lad had been a radio operator on a merchant ship that had been sunk in the China Sea. It was his ambition to build a radio set. This would enable us to get news from the outside world. It took about three weeks and he had a set working - we could pick up Radio

Delhi, India. It was very "Heath Robinson", the bits and pieces had been salvaged from Army radio sets, even some pieces from old barrack room sets. It was powered by 12v car or truck batteries. To charge the batteries we had a dynamo from an Army truck. The charger was something, a converted bicycle frame, upside down with a belt from the back wheel (without tyre) to the dynamo, we took turns to turn the pedals by hand getting up a good speed - it took about two or three hours to get enough juice to power the radio. It was worth all the hard work to hear the crackling voice from Delhi telling us that the Japanese forces were being halted in Burma, there were battles going on in the Solomon Islands etc etc. We also had the luck to pick up the UK radio with "bandwagon". The system of listening in was a pair of Army radio earphones split so that two persons could listen in as the news was read, we took down every other line - thus enabling us to compile a news sheet. If we had been caught it would have been curtains. The dreaded Kempi Tai (Jap Military Police) more dreaded than the German Gestapo. The radio was operated in the loft or attic of V Block. It was in use for about a month, we had worked hard to get power to the barracks. One day it arrived, the bicycle charger was discarded and the radio had to be adapted to 220-250 volt system. This was soon done. In about a week the radio was confiscated by our Officers, they said it was not safe to be operated under the present circumstances. Too many people were in the know. The radio went as did our radio operator. After this, news was very slow coming in. Well I suppose they were right at the time.

By this time, we had lost about five of our comrades, i.e 41st Company - they had died from malaria and dysentery. Many men were dying throughout the Changi area, a lot were dying from their wounds at Roberts Hospital.

We were all getting to the point of starvation at this time, we ate all we could get our hands on. Just outside the perimeter fence of barbed wire was quite a few coconut palms - with nuts ready to fall. I watched with interest. I was talking to two of my best friends one day about these nuts (Sapper Ackroyd and Sapper

Grey). If we could get a ladder, the nuts would be ours. So we went outside the fence to make a reconnaissance. Would you believe it, there was a long ladder on the ground in the long grass by the plantation. We were in luck. We took the ladder (it was about 30ft long) and placed it against the tree - remember we were outside the fence - now who was going to go up - we looked at each other, me being brave (I thought) said "I'll go up". I got to the top of the ladder and twisted the nuts off - they fell to the ground with a great thud. I'd got about four off - when I heard a crack and a whine. What was that? Then again a crack and a whine. Good God, I was being shot at, the Jap sentry was about 150 yards away - I slid down the ladder - the other two were away through the fence, I picked up one of the precious nuts and ran back through the fence, I hid the nut in the long grass. Serve that sentry right he was a damned bad shot. I was afraid a report would be made and I, or we, would have to own up that we had been outside the fence. If this was the case, we would be in very deep trouble. I went to fetch the coconut that I'd hid in the long grass, the milk was delicious, the nut helped to flavour the rice for two or three days after but, through this episode, we learned that the Japs did not stand on ceremony, they fired first -then asked the questions.

At about this time, we were given a lecture by Major Nicholson. "My Escape and Capture". He made his escape from Singapore, he was OC HQ Coy RE. He pushed off in a small boat. He got to Sumatra (Dutch East Indies) where, with other men, he got a small motor launch and set off toward India, he got within 600 miles of Columbo (Ceylon) when a Japanese oil tanker passed them, it got almost to the skyline, they began to breathe more freely - then it returned to pick them up and brought them back to Singapore. The Jap Navy were quite good to them but the mood changed with the Army - what hard luck.

It was about this time also that a ginger cat happened to walk into the area of our billet. We killed it and prepared it as one would a rabbit, we then curried it - it was delicious. The cat had belonged to a Sergeants wife who lived here before the War. What hunger will make one do!!

We were taken to Singapore. One day we may be working in the docks at Kepple Harbour, at other times we were repairing the power lines or getting the water supply working again. Of course all the water supply for Singapore came from the State of Johore across the causeway. This was one of the main factors that Singapore fell, all that General Yamashita had to do was cut the main supply, we could not go long without water, thinking of all the refugees from Malaya. The bombing and shellfire had caused havoc.

One day at Kepple Harbour, a German U boat (submarine) was tied up alongside the dock. One of the Japanese guards picked on a British prisoner and began to beat him up as was their pastime. We were of the opinion that he was showing off to the German crew, who were watching for some time. Suddenly, without warning, one of the Germans ran down the gangplank, he got hold of the Jap, disarmed him and proceeded to beat him up, he knocked him to the ground, picked him up and knocked him down again. The guard did not get up, the German gave us the thumbs up and wentback aboard the U boat. We were delighted. The U boat was there for a few days and the crew gave us cigarettes and tobacco. We asked if they could smuggle one or two of us aboard but because of diplomatic relations, they could not do this. If it had been at all possible, I am sure they would have helped us. Japan had signed a pact with Germany - they were part of the axis powers. I have often wondered about that U boat - did it survive the War? Or the sailor that beat the Jap?

During this period, we worked on the docks, loading the loot destined for Japan, scrap metal, the guns etc that they had captured from us, not that they could be of any use only as scrap as most of them had been spiked or damaged beyond repair.

At this time, we were billeted in River Valley Road POW Camp - a real dump!! Rats from the Singapore River were a real menace, we were also in the company of bed bugs and lice.

One day we were on our way to the docks when we were horror struck at a sight by the Singapore cricket ground. On the spikes of the railings were five heads of people who had been beheaded by the Japanese the day before, they were Indian-Chinese. One - his turban had been put back on - underneath was a notice "These people had been caught looting".God what sort of people were these??
On another occasion, four Chinese ladies came and threw tins of fruit and bread over the fence for us. The Jap Guard chased them away, later they came back and threw more food. Again the Japs chased them away, one of the girls had a baby on her back, she was slower than the others, the Jap Guard beat her then put the bayonet in and severely wounded her, he kicked her into the storm drain, still with the baby on her back - he left her to die, we were helpless - we could not help her as she had tried to help us. The baby cried into the early hours of next day, those cries will be with us forever. Both girl and baby were left in the drain for days. This lady so brave - she died for us.

It wasn't long after this that we went, or I went, back to Changi - to V Block. Five of my friends made an escape attempt. They were absent for about five days and had hoped to get in contact with the Chinese Guerrillas who were known to be operating in Malaya. They were making their way to the north of the island, when they ran into a Japanese patrol, who were resting in the rubber plantation. They hid the weapons they had, which was lucky for them. They were surrounded, searched and taken into custody. They were taken before a Jap Officer. He told them to kneel, their hands were tied behind their backs, they were told to look to the ground in front of them. He then withdrew his sword from the scabbard - they thought "this is it, in a few short minutes it would be oblivion". This was the cat and mouse game they liked to play. Eventually he asked them "Where were you going"? They all replied that they wanted to go to Singapore to work for the Imperial Japanese to earn money for food and cigarettes. Well, they were very lucky - they returned to Changi to be dealt with by our own administration, they were given seven days cells - with rice and water. How lucky they were.

Back in Changi, I was detailed to the gardening party. We tried to make a garden to help out our meagre rations. We grew onions, sweet potatoes, melons and a bit of green stuff, it did help a little but not to the extent we should have liked.

We had been prisoners not more than about five months when we received Red Cross supplies from South Africa. A Red Cross ship had docked in Singapore, we were all very elated. This ship came to Singapore on 20 August 1942. There were clothes, tinned food, i.e bully beef, tinned peaches, a lot of milk powder but most of all there was great tins of marmite, this was a great help to those suffering from beri beri. As I explained before, a vitamin deficiency disease. All these stores were distributed around the cookhouses. These did not last long, there were so many of us taken into custody.

We had been in the BAG about seven months when the IJA (Imperial Japanese Army) brought out an order that all prisoners would sign a (non escape) document. Our Commanders refused this request, the IJA became very irate. This took place on 3 September. This is an abstract of the Order:-

Special Order Selerang No 3 dated 3 September 1942

(i) On 30 August 1942, together with my Commanders, I was summoned to the Conference House at Changi Gaol.
There I was informed by the representatives of Major General Shimpu-Fokuye, GOC, POW Camps Malaya that all POWs be given forms of promise not to escape and that all were to be given the opportunity to sign the form.

(ii) By the laws and usage of war on land, POWs cannot be required to sign by the holding power or give their parole and in our Army those who become POWs are not permitted to give their parole. This was pointed out to the IJA authorities.

(iii) I informed the rep of M.G Fokuye, that I was not prepared to sign the form and that I did not consider that any Officers or men in the Changi camp would be prepared to sign the form. In accordance with the Order of the IJA authorities, all POW were given the opportunity to sign. The result is known. NOT ONE MAN SIGNED.

(iv) On 31 August 1942, I was informed by the IJA that those personnel who had refused to sign the certificate would be subjected to "measures of severity" and that a refusal to sign would be taken as a direct refusal to obey a regulation which the IJA considered necessary to enforce.

(v) Later on the night of 31 August 1942, I was warned that on the 1 September 1942 all POWs insisting in refusal to sign were to be moved by 1800 hours to Selerang Square. I confirmed on my own behalf and in the name of all POWs our refusal to sign.

(vi) The move to Selerang Barracks was successfully accomplished the same afternoon.

The Order goes on to say that Colonel Holmes pleaded with the IJA authorities to either abolish or at least modify the form, this they refused to do - and made even more threats of punishment. The Jap Government backing the IJA.

The conditions under which we had been placed could be described briefly that in a few days an epidemic could break out causing many many deaths.

After three days we were ordered to sign the form. I signed Sapper Ackroyd's and he signed mine - so we did not give our parole.

The Order finishes:-

I wish to record in this Order that of my deep appreciation of the excellent spirit and good discipline which all ranks have shown through this very trying period. Thankyou all for your loyalty and co-operation.

Signed

K.B Holmes
Commander

Here are a few statistics:-

SELERANG

Period from approximately 1500 hours 2 September 1942 to 1300 hours 5 September 1942.
Dimensions - Selerang Barracks gutter to gutter 250 x 150 yards or = to 37,500 sq yds or approximately 7.74 acres
if upper stores are counted and roof area 21,000 sq yds

Personnel - 15,019 men signed the certificates.

Comparative - there were 1,940 men per acre, which is equivalent to 1,250,000 men per sq mile, each man had 2½ sq yds or 3.9 yds with latrines chow houses etc. All floors and roofs included.
Additional personnel - 6 goats, 1 pig which were wrapped in clothes to protect from the sun.

Weather - first day, very hot as it was most of the time.

Day of departure heavy rain - night cool.

This was not the whole story of Selerang.

Whilst we were holding out and refusing to sign the non escape forms, the Japs had taken senior British and Australian Officers to a nearby beach where they were forced to watch the execution of four soldiers who had been taken from hospital.

The Japs told the Officers that they were to watch and witness the executions of the four as an example to the men holding out on the square at Selerang.

The four were stood in front of shallow graves. They were an English Officer and his batman and an Australian Corporal and a young private. The Corporal appealed for mercy for the private. The Japanese Lieutenant shook his head.

The firing squad was composed of Sikh riflemen. These had been among our allies when war broke out, one of these was an Officer holding the King's Commission.

After these men had been put to death slowly, the Jap Lieutenant said "You have seen men put to death for trying to escape against Japanese orders. The great Japanese own all the lands in the South and anyone escaping will be put to death".
This I am sure was one of the main reasons why the Selerang Incident ended. More of our number would have been executed.

SPIES - ESPIONAGE - THIRD COLUMN

I should have written earlier on these subjects but will try to explain one or two cases that I knew about and have come to know about in later years. Spying and the third column was very rife before and during the fighting down the Malaya Peninsula and on the Island of Singapore.

There were many photograph studios and shops where one could go to have your photo taken to send back to the folks at home, you always had to leave your Regimental or Corps name and address. These places were nine times out of ten run by the Japanese. It didn't take long for them to fathom out where every unit was stationed.

Then there were the houses of ill repute. As mentioned before, where men at times would frequent, these men would take off their tunics, no doubt leaving their pay-books in the pockets, the books would be looked at while the owners were otherwise engaged, all information gleaned would be recorded and sent back to Japan. During the Battle of Singapore, Japanese aircraft dropped leaflets on our lines with such messages. "Gunner Jones Sidney, your wife Mary is at home while you are here fighting for nothing, no doubt she is being entertained by an American soldier - give up the fight". All this information must have been got in the way I have just described. These leaflets were always true.

Quite some time ago, I read a very good book - "Singapore". The Japanese version by Colonel Masanobu Tsuji. I think it was in this book we are told of the preparation for the assault on the Peninsula of Malaya and Singapore. As we know, our interests in Malaya were mainly tin and rubber. Many of the plantations had Japanese staff, even some of the managers took charge of building warehouses etc. They ordered steel structures from England, which were sent out and no checks were made. During the retreat down Malaya, bridges and other structures were demolished by our engineers but within very little time they were repaired, we could not understand how this could be done in such a short time. Well, it appears that the steel structures that had been imported from England were not used in the plantations but were secreted away in the jungle very near to these bridges, made to the exact dimensions to do these repairs. Why was no check ever made in these orders for steel? After the Selerang Incident, we soon settled into the old routine at Changi in our old billet at V Block.

On 20 September, or thereabouts, we buried one of our L/Cpls, he is the third of our Company to pass away, we had lost a Sapper and our CQMS (Company Quarter Master Sergeant). It was all very sad, they were all young fellows, lads we had been very close to.

At about this time, two or three of us were allowed under guard to visit Roberts Hospital. One of our number, a Sapper Broadbent had been involved in a very bad accident, while felling trees to make way for gunfire before the fall of Singapore, a tree fell on him, he was very badly injured and he had a fractured spine, pelvis and hipbone, together with several broken ribs. I have previously mentioned this accident on page *117*. As you can guess, he was bedridden. It was a pitiful sight that greeted us. He was in a plaster cast from his armpits to the waist, his right leg was in full plaster. He was totally immobile, laid on his back. To crown it all, he was in a bad attack of dysentery. Can you imagine how he was situated? It was a pitiful sight to be sure, yet he was quite cheerful and he kept on saying "Don't worry lads, I will get out of this, these B's will not beat me".

Well I think, at this stage, I should complete the story of "Doc Broadbent, to tell you the spirit of this man, by God what spirit. On the day that we visited him, I think we left the hospital feeling very sad that this should have happened to one of the fittest of our number, he had played in all sport, rugby, football etc and could box quite well, he also liked his Tiger beer. As we left the hospital, we could easily have cried. The medics were doing their best in spite of no help from our captors – a sick man in their eyes was a liability. They couldn't work so got no pay or rations.

At a later date, about two months, we went to see "Doc" again, his plaster had been removed from his leg, he had recovered from his attack of dysentery and he looked very frail in his plaster cast, he was still flat on his back. He said that he could feel his feet, he in fact moved his toes. He was still very cheerful, we said after "God bless him, what guts".

After about another month, the plaster was removed from his spine or back. He was allowed to sit in a chair at his bedside. We had a WO II Mechanist Engineer who went to visit the "Doc", he said that he thought he could help him. He saw the Medical Officer and they told him to go ahead as anything was worth a try. He made the "Doc" a pair of special shoes, with leg braces and springs. "Doc" had great difficulty in trying to walk as he dragged his feet behind and could not bring them forward enabling him to take steps.

This invention was the answer. "Doc" took his first steps. Two wires were erected just about shoulder high, he used to cling on to these and the springs flipped his feet forward. It wasn't very long before the Doc was discharged from the hospital to join us at V Block. The wires were erected outside the block, he got stronger as time went by.

Then he took to arm crutches, he could be seen going around the camp, very slow but very determined. Always had a laugh and a joke for anyone.

As Doc was allowed to wander around the camp, he got involved in the black market, he timed his routes to get near the fence and buy tobacco and cigarettes from the natives. One day Doc ran into the Japanese Guards, he was escorted to the guard house, still laughing and called the Japanese all names under the sun, I'm glad to say they did not understand him. He was searched and found to have a quantity of tobacco and tinned food on his person. The Jap Commander sentenced him to seven days - rice and water in solitary confinement. He came out laughing and said "Well, twas a bit of a rest".

Doc never left Changi but was liberated - he came home to his beloved "Smoke" (London). I did hear that he took a job as a night watchman.

GOD BLESS YOU DOC BROADBENT - YOU HAD GUTS.

We had many stories to tell. One such story. One of our number used to go through the wire as we called it, otherwise the perimeter fence. He went at night to a village named Bedok, there he bought flour and other goods which he brought back to the camp and sold at the same price as he paid to our Messing Officer. We asked him why he did not charge more and make a profit for the risks he took, he said that he liked to do it, as he liked the thrill of outwitting the Japanese, it had always got the adrenalin flowing in his veins.

A number of men were caught outside the wire, most were taken to Curran Camp, it was a barbed wire fence all open with no shelter from the sun during the day or the cold at night, all open to the elements. This camp had a number of Indian Guards who were part of our Army, these people defected to the enemy. At times they took great pleasure in beating or torturing the white prisoners. In some cases, when they wanted information such as the whereabouts of a radio, these people would put a prisoner's head in a vice and tighten it until he gave the information or fainted with the pain. These guards were responsible for the deaths of many of our men. This was the chance these people took when going through the wire.

Time was passing very slowly, it was now about the end of November 1942. The rations were terrible.

Each man got approximately 18ozs of rice per day. Vegetables were very poor, issue consisted of pumpkins and sweet potatoes. Now and again, we may have got a few carrots or onions.

We got very little cooking fat, at times a supply of ghee or goat fat. Mostly we fried some of our special rissoles in palm oil or coconut oil.

The meals were as follows:-
Breakfast:-
½pt rice pap, two rissoles and onion gravy.
Dinner:-
1¼ pts rice with coconut sauce or brown sugar.
Supper:-
1½pts dry rice (jungle stew), pumpkin and green soup, jam rice or a rissole.

The rice pap consisted of rice boiled until it resembled porridge (ahhh!!).

The rissole was made of rice and whatever, it was baked on a hotplate, maybe fried in coconut oil.

At times we had a fish issue, this was very handy. One day we had four small sharks and two dog fish. It all helped to make the rice taste a little different.

Most times it was the dregs of the catch.

Some we had to throw away, it had been left in the sun and gone bad, but it always counted towards poundage in rations.

So life went on.

WE BUILD A STILL

It was early December, we started to think about Christmas. One of our number, a Corporal, had a good idea to make whisky. We built a still. This was how we made it:-

Sweet potatoes, partly cooked, pumpkin peelings, partly cooked. Any rice left over - all thrown into an earthenware jar and left to ferment for one week having added sugar after one day. It was quite a brew, all foaming on the top, we then distilled.

It was a success. The first brew we put a small amount in a tin and put a match to it, it was alcohol - it caught alight. We all tasted some, it was like methylated spirit, it burnt the inside of the mouth, when taken down, one could feel it all the way down into the stomach. We came to the conclusion that it had to be watered down.

We made several brews, experimenting. I drank very little of it!! It was too hot for comfort.

Well Christmas again and we had all looked forward to being released by now - it was not to be.

The Japanese had given us all the day off for Christmas Day.

We had been issued with little Red Cross rations that had been held back for this day.

Meals were as follows:-
Breakfast:-
Melba porridge with milk and sugar, two fried rissoles made with bully beef and one slice of bread.
Dinner:-
Rice pudding with milk and sugar, hot cocoa, two meat veg pies made with rice flour, meat and veg stew.
Supper:-
Dixie rice with m-v stew, sweet rice, rice pasty with m-v.
At night:
Hot sweet cocoa, sweet rice cakes and, last of all, a drink of IJA wine.

Just at this time I was employed in the cookhouse as the rice cook.

We held a Christmas Service and we all prayed for our freedom. We prayed for you at home that you would be spared from the bombing by the German Air Force. Before our capture, we had heard of the bombing of London, Coventry and Plymouth.

It was lovely to hear the lads all singing the carols, "Silent Night" - Holy Night". It brought tears to my eyes, I thought of my old village Church, where I had sung this as a choir boy. We all thought of home. "God bless you all" and happy days.

One of our Corporals had returned from Singapore, he had a radio - we may get news. Things looked very black and bleak for us at that moment. Quite a few parties had gone up to Thailand (Siam as it was then) to work on the building of a railway into Burma. Conditions there were said to be very good (I wondered).

So 1942 slipped away. A terrible year it had been for us all.

1943

It was 1 January 1943. Would it be victory year for us?

The Japanese celebrated the New Year, they had given us extra rations of rice and a little meat and wine to drink to their Emperor, we raised our tin cups and said "******** to him".

It was 20 February 1943. Quite a few letters had arrived and I looked for one from home but no luck.

One of my friends, Bill Ackroyd, got one from his wife, she was evacuated from Singapore. It was very bad news, his little son had died due to enemy action, their ship was machine gunned by aircraft and they were all on deck waving to their loved ones. The little chap died on arrival in South Africa. It was his only child - six months old. My dear friend was very upset, he cried most of that night. I tried to console him but to no avail.

23 February 1943. I found myself on draft to Siam with a lot of my best friends, God be with us all. The Japanese told us we would work for pay, there were good hospitals. We should be looked after. I wondered how true this was to be!!

24 February 1943. The draft for Thailand had been published. Major Jack Marsh was our OC, he was in the RASC, quite a character. He had taken part in quite a few of the concert parties and was very good as Hitler. We could not have a better man in charge of us.

Nobby Clarke and myself were on it, Bill Ackroyd had asked to go with us. Would it be better or worse? We were on very low rations here.

We had had medicals and were all graded A1? Had inoculations for TAB, cholera, dysentery, ATT. Or was it water they injected us with?

We were a very mixed bunch, a Battalion of 500 men, RE, RA, Gordon Highlanders, Vol Corps, RAOC, RASC.
Our Second in Charge was a Captain Tuxford SVT, the interpreter was another Captain. We were known as "Y" Battalion.

OFF TO SIAM AND BURMA

26 February 1943. We had been given a medical examination by the Japanese medical people. Most of us were supposed to be A1 (God forbid some were swollen with beri beri, some had had relapses of malaria).

On 8 March 1943 at 0700 hours, we boarded trucks at Changi Village. We had pumpkin and meat pies to take with us. We had loaded our haversacks with all we could take. It was a very hot sticky day. We had a Major in charge of our party, he was a fine Officer and he had done a lot for our welfare in Changi. Major Jack Marsh was a real gentleman.

We had Jap drivers on the trucks, a sentry to each truck with loaded arms. We passed through the camp, past the hospital and we saw a lot of the wounded - some were blind and we waved to them all. We passed Curran Camp, a horrible place, God help the inmates - poor devils. We passed Changi Prison, the civilian internees were digging up the big grounds and turning them into gardens.

They shouted and waved to us as we passed, they too had Indian guards (the traitors). We travelled on along the old Changi Road, along the East Coast Road, we entered Singapore City - how quiet it seemed, very little traffic on the streets, all the cars were carrying Jap civilians. Quite a few of the cars were charcoal burners, the fuel situation wasn't too good. We saw too that very little of the bomb damage had been repaired.

At last we arrived at Singapore Railway Station, we were detailed off in groups of thirty men with kits to each small railway wagon - this was going to be great?? We entrained and had to wait, the trucks were all steel and as we waited, they became like ovens.

At 4.00pm we moved off, we were all sweating profusely. We passed the Krangi oil tanks, the Japs didn't get a lot out of them only scrap metal - we saw what a good job our Corps the RE had done in destroying them.

We crossed the causeway into Malaya. Then in Johore Bharu, we stopped for quite a while. The civilian population looked very dejected, they wanted to speak to us but dare not - our guards could shoot them, or us in fact.

On this journey, we had one Japanese guard to two trucks, they were shouting and bawling most of the time, not very handsome men I must say, all looked like a bunch of cut throats, they were vigilant at all times, don't know why? There wasn't any place to escape to - only jungle. Of course there were Chinese guerrillas operating in most of Malaya, perhaps this was why the guards were so alert, they may have been thinking that the guerrilla forces could rescue us to join them - who knows?

We had several cases of dysentery on the train, it was a pity to see these poor fellows, of course there were no toilets on the train. We had one young soldier in our truck, he had this awful complaint, we took it in turns to help him when he wanted to relieve his bowel - he took up the squat position in the truck doorway - we held his arms - it was quite an operation. Whatever the inhabitants must have thought when we passed through these little kampongs.

I think every truck had one or two of these unfortunates - it was so humiliating to see us degraded to this standard.

The train was now speeding up, just before we got to Kuala Lumpur, the track had been fully repaired and all the bridges were intact. We stopped at Kuala Lumpur for a meal, we got a full mess tin of rice with pork and veg and other meat all fried in together, the best food we had had for quite a while.

We saw the areas where very heavy fighting had taken place, the area was scattered with fighting vehicles from both sides Japanese and British, we also saw that very few of the buildings had been repaired.

At Gemas Station, it seemed people had been told of our train going through, they were waiting to sell us their foods etc but the train did not stop, it went through very slowly, so the awaiting people threw their goods on to the trucks, they cheered us and wished us well, the guards were pointing their weapons at them and shouting but the people did not heed them. We had bananas, bread and cakes, all were shared between us.

We continued on to Siam. The journey had taken us four days and four nights. Can you imagine - thirty men, being holed up in a steel wagon, they were like ovens with temperatures in the high 90s. We then arrived at Nampradok after a night at Bampong.

SO THIS WAS SIAM (NOW THAILAND)

The Japanese gave us about thirty or forty skips of bananas, we each had six bunches of 15 to 20 small "monkey" bananas. We were then given water, we were so thirsty that we drank six to eight pints, we had all lost so much fluids in the long journey from Singapore.

At this point, we met a Sapper from our old Company. He had been in Siam for about six to nine months and had come up the line with an early party from the River Valley Road Camp in Singapore. He told us that many of our old friends had already died from malaria and dysentery. Conditions were very bad, the further one went up the railway and into the jungle, the worse it got. As supplies could not be got to camps because of the floods and bad roads, most supplies went up by barge on the River Kwai.

After a few hours of waiting, we moved off to the railway such as it was, the train came in and we embarked on open trucks. We moved off onto the new laid track - it was like a "swish back" - up and down, squeaking and grinding along at about four or five miles per hour, our destination was Bampong. This was a terrible journey - men were fainting with fatigue and we were all bathed in sweat. Men had dysentery and other kinds of sickness, the smell was terrible, this was a terrible journey. Chinese and Thai people were running along the tracks by the train with buckets of water which we threw over each other, the sun was blazing down on us all. These people were so kind to us, their pity was shown in their eyes, so different to our captors. To add to our misery, the track was so bad that, on three occasions, as we went over the uneven track, the trucks became unhooked from the engine and started to run back the track, we had to all jump out and run back to catch the run-away trucks, put the brakes on then re-hook them to the engine. We were all beaten up by the guards, as if it was our fault (the low brained twits). At this point, I would like to mention that most of the guards in Siam were Koreans, perhaps about a dozen of them with a Japanese soldier in charge of them, at times they were much worse to us than the Japs - that is saying something. So our perilous journey continued, some of the bridge structures were very rickety and squeaked and groaned as we went over them.

At last we reached Bampong - in total darkness, we had reached the railhead. We unloaded our kits, suddenly the train pulled away with some of the Red Cross supplies we had taken with us from Changi, that was the last we were to see of it, it was done on purpose, those supplies were destined for Japanese bellies. We shouted and tried to stop the train, the drivers took no notice, they were on to a good thing.

We then fell in on a parade of sorts and were marched off into the undergrowth about three miles from the station. We slept under the open sky and we made our beds down on the undergrowth. We were told that our food would be served in about one hour. We had gone forty hours with only four bunches of bananas and pails of water. At last the food arrived -never have I seen rice look so welcome, it was accompanied by a lovely stew with pork, beef, kidney and vegetables. I was starving, we all were, I had two mess tins full of the stew and three mess tins of rice. Then to our beds beneath the stars, we were all deadbeat.

It was now about 14 March 1943. We awoke to a lovely bright sky with beautiful sunshine. We had to supply our own cooks. The cookhouse was very Heath Robinson, all in the open air. The food was cooked in giant saucer shaped woks about three feet in diameter and about one foot deep in the centre, they were perched on a base of mud and stones with a fire underneath.

This was how all our food was to be cooked throughout Siam and Burma. In the big camps, as many as fifteen or twenty of these woks would supply the camp with food. We called them "quallies".

At about Midday, the Japanese guards detailed us off for work, we were told to build ourselves shelters as a temporary measure, as we would be moving out in a few days time. We set to work, we dug latrines and laid out a cookhouse. Six of us Sappers built ourselves a shelter, we put bamboo poles in the ground, put cross members and we made a roof of palm and banana leaves and our groundsheets, it had no sides.

Whilst we were at work an old Thai gent asked if we could sell him any of our kit, we had a few shirts and shorts. I sold him two shirts and two pairs of shorts. I got thirty Tickles (the currency is now Bhats).

My friend sold a blanket - thirty Tickles. Now we would have to try and buy some food. We were allowed to walk to the River to bathe. En route we would meet Thai hawkers. We would buy fruit and eggs. This was great and it would be nice if we could stay here!! After a day or two, we got around and found we could buy cigarettes, eggs, even bacon. We would soon get fat if we could stay here I am sure.

About 16 March 1943!! We had one hell of a storm the night before, it was quite a monsoon. We awoke to find water running right through our hut and underneath our blankets, the hut we took so much pride in building had blown all around us. At daybreak, it was still pouring with rain and the wind was howling around us. We tried to re-rig our shanty afresh. We fixed it after a while, then lit a fire inside to dry out our clothes and blankets. Now the Japanese wanted a working party to build an embankment. Amid much cursing and swearing, we went to work on the railway embankment. The sun came out, so we dried out a little.

We returned to our camp, those of us who had them put mosquito nets up and shared them out, perhaps three to a net. This place was infested with the dreaded mosquito, there seemed to be millions of them.

Most of our kits had dried out, the blankets were still damp. We had to start work at full speed the next day.

A party of Australians left camp this day, they were going up into the jungle.

On the works parade, the Japanese asked for two engineers. I stepped forward with another Sapper, they took us to a captured British Ford V8 truck, they told us that, if we got it going, we would get "good presento". We worked on it all day, we found the whole of the petrol system was choked with sand, it had been sabotaged!!! We cleared the whole system from the tank to the carburettor and we assembled it, pushed the start and away it went. The Japanese were delighted, they gave us cigarettes and a tin of bully beef each. They said that they would try and get us to work in the garage as mechanics on a permanent basis. I wished to God they could, we all dreaded going up into the jungle. By what we had heard, it was dreadful - disease was rife. We went to work there the next day, we did one or two jobs on the trucks. We were told they could not keep us there and would not be required the next day. I felt quite upset, it could have been a good job.

WE WERE NOW KNOWN AS "Y" BATTALION

18 March (or thereabouts??). The Japs asked for any cooks. Two of us stepped forward, our only thoughts were food!!! We were taken to the Japanese cookhouse and we had to work under a Jap cook, washing dishes and preparing vegetables etc. The food was good - the cook gave us a full basin of pork each, it was lovely, tasted like honey. While the cook was out, we pinched some of their eggs.

That night I got back to the camp, I had the runs, the pork was too rich for the weakened stomach. I took two hard boiled eggs but it didn't help. The next day the Jap gave us both creason tablets, we both still had the runs.

Some of the lads came back that evening, they had met one of the lads from up in the jungle, Jack Evans. He had gone up from Singapore on an early party. It was bad news they had brought. Four of our very good friends had died at Tarsao Camp 4. They were always very fit men. This was a great shock to us all.

Orders had just come through that we had to march out of here and go north into the jungle to join No 4 Group at Tarsao. Good God!! That was the same camp where the above mentioned had died - I wonder how many of us would come back??

About 22 March, I thought about our birthdays. My dear brother was 17 March - he would be twenty years of age. I wondered where he was. My cousin was 19 March. My own birthday 21 March - I was 25 years of age. Should have been back with you all if it hadn't been for this awful war. Please God help us all.
We left Bampong that morning at 7.00am. We got on to trucks and what a journey we had - by road - a mud and dirt track all the way through the trees. We hit tree stumps that had been left in the middle of the road, we hit trees on the side of the road, it all added to the spice of travel. The trucks could only travel at 7 to 8mph. I had now seen real jungle and we were fifty miles from the nearest civilisation - nothing but thick jungle all around. We hadn't seen a sign of Tarzan. Some wag put a piece of paper on a bush "Dorothy Lamour around the next bend"!

We arrived at Tarsao late at night. I met Sapper Hydon and Sapper Kennard. They told me that things were awful, a lot of our lads were very ill. There were no medical supplies.

The night before we had slept in an old petrol store, it was full of old cow skins and didn't they stink!! The place was full of great rats, we had had little sleep, the rats kept running over the tops of our bodies.

Sapper A and I found a four gallon tin of coconut oil in a shed, we had taken quite a few pints, if we could get any eggs, it would do to fry them in.

About 23 March. 350 of our Battalion had gone on ahead this day. We were 150 left here, we were to go off the next day. We marched the rest of the way, trucks could not get through because the road had been washed away in the rains. Mud in places was about two or three feet deep.

We had a long march ahead of us, so we had better rest up a bit. We knew we were on our way to Kanu I - the Death Camp.

153

KANU I

Well here we were at Kanu I. We started our march up through the jungle at daybreak - we arrived at dusk, only the 150 of us came here, the other 250 were further back the track, they were building a new camp to be called Kanu II. They were very busy cutting down the virgin jungle, where no man had ever trod before. There were giant bamboo thickets, giant teak trees 40 to 50 feet in height. Creepers as big as a man's leg. The thick jungle we were unable to see through the undergrowth - my God - a railway has to pass through here!! Kanu II was to be built, huts and tents were to be erected. First to be built was the Japanese guards quarters, latrines to be dug, water supply to be organised, some task. This was the eutopia they promised us before we left Changi, with all the good food, hospitals and supplies, sports facilities. This was more like the end of the World. We were all very tired but, before we slept, we had to clear a cutting to bed down for the night, before we did so, we had a very poor meal of plain boiled rice and one piece of dry fish. It was revolting, the smell was awful but we ate it - we were all hungry. We made the clearing, it was dark by this time, we were fatigued. We laid our blankets on the ground and were soon fast asleep. I awoke in the early morning to find that I had been bitten all over by mosquitoes. I was covered in small bumps where these insects had sucked my blood. We found that we were all the same, we all thought of the disease malaria and what it entailed.

As to the lads who came here six months before us - they were very sick people, they looked like zombies. They had all lost weight, their eyes were sunk back into their heads. They looked as if they had lost the will to live. We saw men who were so fit who had played in all sports, rugby, football, swam for the regiment, they were just shells of their former selves. Some had already died of dysentery and malaria, whatever was in store for us.

The Japanese were so cruel, both the guards and engineers. We had not been there long and I am sure we had all been beaten up for some small infringement, perhaps not saluting a guard. The Korean guards were the same. If a Jap guard saw a Korean beating us up, they thought he was doing his job very satisfactorily.

The first means of supply (food stores etc) was by very poor roads. These were dirt tracks on which you travelled slowly. A lot of the trucks used were captured GMC (General Motor Company) of USA. We had a few of these in Malaya and Singapore and most of these had a winch on the front. If they became stuck they could winch themselves out of the thick mud. I can tell you they were a great asset, a few supplies got through in the monsoons.

The second means of supply of course was the River Kwai. Food etc was brought up river on barges towed by little tugs. The tugs we called "put puts". As that was the noise the small engines made when towing through the rapids. During the monsoon season of course, this supply was at a very low level. With the river in full flood, it was impossible to navigate it at all. It became a very wicked river then and took all before it.

The British Camp Officers had opened a kind of canteen here, there was not much for sale, a very poor stock. Our pay when at work was 25 cents per day, so for a full seven days, we can earn up to 1$ 75c. If one was sick, the pay was stopped. Our pay was taken by the purchasing officer, he went to the barges on the river and brought back supplies. We got goods to the value of our credit. We of course looked after our sick. We got sugar, eggs, tobacco (we called the tobacco hags bush). It was awful stuff but it kept the pangs of hunger at bay. Some of the stores went into the cookhouse, such as it was.

End of March. We had built our huts after a style, we had eight to our hut and we had a big green mosquito net, all eight of us could get underneath it. The hut was built of a bamboo structure tied together with creepers from the jungle.

We had to go on parade in the jungle clearing that we had made. We had to learn to number off in Japanese

Ichi	nee	san	see	go	roko	suhi	hasi
que	jue						
1	2	3	4	5	6	7	8
9	10						

We also had to drill by Jap commands. We could not understand half they command, it was quite a pantomime. We did quickly learn, if we hadn't, we were beaten up with bamboo poles.
Then like a bolt out of the blue, the Japs told us to pack our gear, such as it was. We had to move into Camp Kanu I.

From here we started work on the building of the railway. The Japs asked for any tradesmen, my friend Ackroyd and myself said that we were blacksmiths. They then asked for any stone-masons. We marched out to work three miles away on a jungle track. We reached the rock face, the stone masons were told to drill the rock by hand. A drill about 1½ metres was driven into the rock with a 10lb sledge hammer. They worked in pairs, one held the drill and turned it as the man with the hammer hit it. We called it hammer and tap. It took quite a while to drill a hole one metre deep, depending on the rock formation. Dynamite was then forced into the hole with a detonator and safety fuse. When about ten holes were complete, we all retired for blasting. The loose rock was then picked up in baskets and carried as fill for an embankment. I might add the blacksmiths did this task, walking round all day carrying rock and spoil in the baskets on our heads. It was all very very fatiguing. All men were kept at their tasks, non stop, the Japs were slave drivers. They only shouted once, after that you were bambooed, otherwise slammed on the head with a bamboo pole.

We who had just arrived from Changi managed quite well but the old hands who came up with the early parties were very weak with disease. All had some illness, they could not stick the pace. They were beaten all the time, some too weak to stand up. We saw some of our friends collapse with exhaustion and we could do nothing to help. A person had to be totally bedridden before he was allowed to stay in the camp. Then he was expected to get out and do a light job. Malaria and dysentery were rife.

We stopped at 2.30pm for dinner, we had a mess tin full of cold rice and a kind of Japanese pickle called mesau, it tasted awful but if filled a hole in a starving belly.

The sanitary conditions in the camp were very primitive. The latrines were deep trenches about 15' deep, 20' long and 6' wide. Bamboos were laid across the top on which one had to squat to do ones natural functions.

This camp No 1 was a terrible place, the men who were here before us had been moved up the river to work further up on new clearings and cuttings. They had moved to Kanu III which was about five miles towards Burma.

The huts here were full of bugs and lice, the roof leaked and when it rained we had to put our blankets over the holes. When we had good weather, it was better to sleep outside under the stars, then we risked attacks by mosquitoes.

After a days work we, at times, had to go to the river to bring up rations that had arrived by barge and "put put".

About mid April. Things here had deteriorated very markly. The food was very poor and we had very little strength. The stamina I once had was leaving me day by day. My once twelve stone frame was done, I was now about eight stone, if that!! We had hardly the strength to walk let alone work but still we went to bore the holes for blasting and carrying the baskets full of rock and rubble.

This was our usual diet daily:-
Breakfast:-
1pt plain rice pap.

Dinner:-
1pt rice boiled with a little sugar.
Supper:-
1¼pts of rice and a mug jungle stew.

Boy, was I starving - you could hear my belly button grating up and down my spine!!

A few days before, we caught a snake, we took the skin off and roasted it on an open fire. It tasted different, we cooked frogs and snails.

If one was lucky enough to catch a snake, you killed it and lay it across the palm of your hand. Let the sun shine on its belly, if you saw the colours of the rainbow in its reflection, it was poison - do not eat.

During this past fortnight, it had been raining non stop. Monsoon weather, we had worked right through non stop. The thunder and lightning had been terrific and frightening. The lightning came with the crack of a big gun. Then the thunder, right behind it. It felt as if it was all around us, very frightening. We were all wet through but had to keep going. The Jap engineers and guards were shouting all the time "Speedo - Speedo"!!! This was hell itself.

A lot of our number were going down with sickness - dysentery, malaria, beri beri and others were going insane, staring ahead not saying a word to anyone. As I have said before, these men were becoming zombies.

End of April. During the last few days, it had been raining like hell - non stop. The mud outside our hut was about 2' to 3' deep. We walked through it in our bare feet (tried to make our boots last out). The Japanese had their huts on the top of the hill, their latrines were half way down the hill. As the rain poured down, it ran through their huts down the hillside and through their latrines and into our huts - the smell was terrible. We never knew what we were walking in when we went out to our latrines at night. Maggots and blue bottles were everywhere. We also stubbed our toes on hidden tree stumps, one had to be in this situation to realise how degrading it all was. To the Japanese our lives were not worth a second thought. With all the mud and flood, the ration trucks could not get to us, the River Kwai was in full flood. The "put puts" and barges only got to us every few days, so our rations were very poor and we were all virtually on the point of starvation.

We had had a bad outbreak of dysentery. It was of a mild form but still very unpleasant. Of course we had no such thing as toilet paper, the low bushes had been stripped bare of leaves to be used as same.

So time went by, the rain was getting even worse, pouring all the time, visibility was down to about ten yards when it poured really hard, the wind was howling as well. When on the way to get our food, we got stuck in the deep mud, we had to rescue each other. To crown all this, we still had to go to work and be expected to drill holes and clear the rocks after the blasting.

I had not had a good wash for about three weeks, one was kept clean by the cold pouring rain, my hair had grown long and I now had a goatlike beard.

Food was at its lowest, just a diet of rice and more rice boiled with perhaps a piece of stinking maggot infested fish. At times we got dried whitebait (small fish).

Our working numbers were on the decrease, a lot of men had been admitted to the hospital, such as it was. These men tried to keep on at work and not go sick. They knew that their pay would be stopped and funds to the hospital would drop but disease took its toll and they had to succumb.

One man died the night before in our hut, it was heartbreaking to see him being carried away, he would be buried as soon as possible in the small cemetery overlooking the River Kwai.

We always had a lot of rumour on the loose, false news laced with good news, one had to pick the bones. It left a lot to the imagination. We heard that the Americans had won a battle here and there, a big arm had come across from India into Burma and the Japs were on the run. The Germans were also on the run. It was good to hear these things - but - was it true? We clung to anything.

We were still cutting through the rock to make the Kanu cutting for the railway track to go through, would the railway ever get that far? Could we be rescued by some good fortune? God only knew!! Dreams! Dreams" Dreams" It was an escape from the world of reality.

We often wondered how the gangs further up the track were doing. We knew that other groups were coming in towards us from the Burma end.

When we started this cutting, we had to put down or drill a hole one metre deep with the hammer and drill, the shots would be put in position, then blasted, we then cleared the rock and rubble to the embankment. The Japs told us if we worked hard and got the tasks done early, they would let us go back to camp early to "yasami" (rest). At the time, I said to some of the gang that we should not be drawn into false hope of an early finish, knowing how they did the same in Singapore and then added to the tasks they had set us until we had to work non stop. We worked hard to finish early, they kept their word for one week, they then added to the tasks. Whereas we at first drilled the ten holes, one metre deep, then cleared the rock blasted into the embankment area. For the gang the task was raised to 15 one metre holes. It wasn't long before we were working all day. As men became sick, men went to the camp hospital, the gang became smaller and the tasks were eventually raised until we were working from dawn to dusk.

Still it rained, we worked, fed and slept in the mud. OH! HOW I HATED THESE JAPANESE.

We returned to camp that evening and it was found that we were one hammer short, the guard had counted!! We were all bambooed, I was hit in the face and nose, my nose was bleeding and my shins were kicked. God!! If only I could retaliate, I could have killed that guard, we were all in a shocking state. The guard, who was Korean, was "Donald Duck", our nickname for him. Well, after all the fuss, the hammer was found, the idiot couldn't count. There was not one word of apology.

These guards were treachery itself. These beatings were going on all the time, one had to be in it to realise what it was like. For instance, as I have mentioned before, we had to salute and bow to this scum. They hid behind trees and awaited some unsuspecting prisoner to pass by, they then attacked with rifle butt and bayonet. Some had been in a very sorry state after these beatings. Our Camp Officers had complained to no avail - and so it went on. The Japanese and Korean guards were sadist.
I was taken off the hammer and tap and put on to rock shifting, thank God!! A whole day on the hammer took all of ones strength and such a great strain on a weak, starving stomach. Quite a few of the lads who were employed on this work had been passing blood, they said it was due to the strain on the stomach.

At all times of course, the topic was FOOD! FOOD! Our rations were at the lowest ebb, the bulk of course was rice. At times there was a good ration but rice alone gave no nourishment, we wanted meat and vegetables to support and to provide the vitamins that the body required. We were up at dawn on these days, we got back to the camp at dusk. It was dark when we queued for our breakfast. I got in the queue as early as I could, at times there was a chance of "legi-mishi" (extra food), so I queued again. I tried this at the evening meal as well. It filled ones stomach - if not for long - it was 2/3 water content. A lot of the POWs just could not take to rice at any cost, they just hated it - but - I felt I must eat as much of the damned stuff as I could. I hoped to get out of here alive - my God - I prayed so.

At this point, I must say that I said my prayers every night and every morning when I awoke - I thought of the good life I had - I thought of you all at home, little did you know what we were all enduring - were we in hell??
We felt very sad, every day now we found that our friends were dying from the terrible diseases.

There were different views amongst us as regards to religion. Some said "Why pray"? "If there was a God, he wouldn't let us suffer like this". I suppose they had a point to some degree but I knew where I looked for comfort. I had seen and heard men who said that they were atheist, non believers of God, they had died - when dying their last words had been "Please dear God, help me".

We were now into May (so they said). We had lost all count of time. We used to get a "yasame day" (rest day) every tenth day. That had gone by the board, it was work every day, all day from dawn to dusk.

Thank goodness - the weather had improved a little, the roads had dried a bit and the River Kwai was not so swollen, so more food had been getting through. In due course, our food had improved.

One night a canteen barge came up river - so - after work we had to go to get the rations or goods. This consisted of gula malacca (dark brown cane sugar), Thai tobacco (we call it hag's bush). There were cigarette papers, also a large amount of duck eggs, all these extras went to help out food ration 100%. We could have a little sugar on the rice or a boiled egg, we could take this to work with us.

As we were coming up from the river with our canteen supplies, we passed "Smokey Joe's". It was a small hut between the river and our camp. It was used as a store for a black market racketeer "Smokey Joe". He had a barge of his own, he bought stores down the river at Bampong or maybe Bangkok. He brought them up and sold at 200% or 300% profit, it was very very dear. He had sold goods to POWs, they paid with watches and rings - he was a robber. Bill Ackroyd, a friend and I looked inside the hut as we passed and saw a big pile of eggs and other goods. We decided that that night we must get some of that gear. Well!! Was it worth the risk? We talked it over - we thought of our empty stomachs - we must get out of the camp, go through the jungle to Smokeys and help ourselves, we had to watch out for the guards. We decided that we would get out at about 1.00am or 2.00am, it would be very dark but the guards might have been taking it easy!!

I went off to sleep, I was always so tired, then my friend Bill shook me awake. "What the hell is going on"? I asked. He said "Come on let's go - that is if you're not scared". I must tell you I had butterflies in the gut, the adrenaline was flowing through my veins but afraid - I don't know, was I?

We took a sandbag each and made for the fence, we saw no guard so we made a hole in the bamboo fence and crawled out into the jungle to whatever we were going to meet. We made our way along the jungle track, very alert and not saying a word to each other. At anytime, we could have bumped into a sentry but we saw none. I did see a pair of small lights and thought "What the hell is that" but it was fire flies, they light up like glow worms, a bit uncanny I must say. We plodded our way on, I was in quite a sweat, the night was so hot and we travelled barefoot, so as not to make too much noise. We slipped down the narrow track to the river and we reached Smokey Joe's hut. All was quiet, Smokey must have been away. We forced the bamboo door and entered, to us Aladdin's Cave, we put the sugar in the sack and we found tobacco and the pile of eggs. We did not say a word as we pilfered the place. We tried to silence our excited breathing, our sacks were full. We shook hands and left to return to the camp. It was uncanny, we did not say a word to each other. We slipped and slid on the uphill trek, with our sandbags full. We knew that we had to get into the camp again. Would we find the hole made to come out? Boy! Was I sweating - was it fear? No! Let's say excitement.

We wondered back on the track, the night was so still bar for the barking of a deer.
We found the hole, Ackroyd went in first and I waited to hear of any shout or challenge from a sentry. I then struggled through the fence and back to the billet.

Our mission had taken us two hours, it was now 3.00am. In 1½ hours dawn would be here, then out we got again. Boy! Did I feel good. Mission accomplished. We had a smoke, we had a few eggs and we had sugar to put on the rice. We did give some of the loot to a few of our friends but one must not say too much. No questions were asked, so no questions were answered. So back to the grind again, but I did feel good, we had pulled it off - we had robbed old "Smokey".

The POW Battalions in the Kanu area were "E", "J", "W" and "Y" each battalion had a strength of 500 men. I hated to think how many were left, we were the strongest left here.

Quite a few of the other units had been moved up the line to Kanu 3 - a new camp. We had taken over the vacated huts. We moved in to find they were infested with lice, bugs and rats. At night, it was impossible to sleep here, so, weather permitting, we slept again under the stars. At all times, we had the malaria carrying mosquitoes to put up with. In the huts, we slept shoulder to shoulder, tossing and turning. One felt an insect crawling, you found it and squatted it between the fingers. The smell told you that it was a bug, it was fat where it had gorged itself on human blood. It was disgusting, the smell of sweating bodies and the smell of dysentery. God - were men ever expected to live in these conditions? There was nothing we could do about it.
The guards and engineers were more brutal than ever. "The rails must go through - speedo, speedo". The Officers here were working under the same conditions, most of them were in "J" battalion.

Japanese billets had all been rebuilt, they were very strong and more substantial than our rickety old dumps.

It was in this camp that I got to know of Colonel Weary Dunlop the Australian surgeon, truly a great man, he did so much for us all.

We were all looking toward the day when we would be liberated and these pigs were the underdogs, would we do what we had in mind?

One little point I would like to mention as a matter of interest, you see my regimental number was 5619438. I had said to the lads that they should watch my number, it gave the date when we should be liberated, the 5th of the 6th 1943 at 8 o'clock. 5 June 1943 - 8.00am and I didn't mind if it was 8.00pm. We must wait and see!!! We had two months to go.

Quite a lot of the sick had been evacuated to Tarso. It was pitiful to see the state of these lads just skin and bone, unable to stand, decimated by these terrible diseases. The killers malaria, dysentery and beri beri. These evacuations were very few and far between. Some were too ill to be moved to the little better conditions, many were dying. It was disgusting how the sick were treated. When the working parties had been depleted through sickness, the Japanese had ordered that they be taken to work on rice sack stretchers. They laid by the roadside and had to crack rocks with hammers, the Japanese were disgusting people.

Mid May, or thereabouts?? We went to the Japanese Medical Centre one night to get quinine, it was about midnight when Bill Ackroyd awoke me from a very deep sleep. "Blackie" he said "we must pinch some quinine from the Jap Hospital". I was startled "Bill, is it worth it, they will cut our bonces off if we are caught". "Well" he said "if you don't get the quinine we shall die of malaria". So off we went and we were successful. We had enough for a week or two. I always got a buzz on these raids, the adrenaline started to pulsate. I always felt good afterwards, it was such a thrill!!

Quite a lot of men were on their way up the line, having finished their sector. This was now ready for the laying of the railway track. A special gang was picked for this important work. They were fit and big fellows and they were supposed to be well fed - they certainly needed it to be lifting the rails at 30lbs per yard, 10yds in length, at least that was what they were when we laid railways during our training days. Then there were the sleepers to be laid in position to take the rails. It was certainly hard work, as far as we were concerned, they could not lay them fast enough to get up the line to bring up the foodstuffs.

When we came up into the jungle at first, fires were lit and kept going at night to keep the wild beasts away from the camps. However, no animals had been seen, the blasting during the day had kept them away.

Bill Ackroyd and I broke into the Japanese store a few nights before and stole a few pounds of sugar and half a bag of dried fish. It added a bit of flavour to the rice. We took these risks and we only knew too well of the consequences if we had been caught. Starvation gave the urge to take these risks.

Quite a lot of our fellows had passed away with these terrible diseases. They seemed to be at work one day, then some person said "Bill passed away last night" a chap you played football with or swam with. It was surely getting worse. We had all got this haunted look, not knowing if we too would be dead the next day. These lads were only 21 to 24 years of age. Death stalked us all, we just took it as it came. Bugs, lice, mosquitoes, the beatings we took every day and the tasks they set us were impossible.

No story we tell will ever be believed. No book will ever tell the stories. No film will ever depict the full facts in this hell upon earth. What we had endured and would have to endure in the future was well beyond belief at the hands of these sadistic people.

At about this time Ackroyd and I were on our way to the work site. We both had the runs, so had to relieve our bowels. We went into the jungle undergrowth, we kicked a skeleton, it must have been there for a month or two. The bones were bare, the eye sockets were full of ants and, by the looks of things, it was probably of indian origin with the clothing around. A cooking pot was nearby, so we took that as it may come in handy to cook rice in. We did use it afterwards for quite a while in fact. Were we getting to be callous?

Another task had started now that most of the cutting had been completed. There were gaps to be crossed by the rails when they arrived in this area.
Now timber had to be taken from the jungle to build structures for the trestle bridges. Before these could be put in position, the tree stumps had to be dug out with picks and shovels and the surrounding bases made level. They said they could not spare explosives to blast them out, as it was required for the rocks that had to be moved. So we dug and dug for hours on end to expose the stump, then ropes were tied to it and we all pulled about twenty or thirty of us. The stumps were of bamboo, this was tough stuff indeed. It's roots tangled in every crevice of the rock for moisture. We were again given tasks but we never got back to camp before dusk. Many times it was very dark. So it went on.

THE KANU KID

He was a Japanese Officer, one of the most hated in the sector. The story went that he was in the Japanese Air Force and he had, in some way, disgraced himself. As punishment he had been sent into the jungle. He became widely known as the "Kanu Kid". When he first came into the jungle, he made a speech in broken english. He said "We want your toil, we want your blood and sweat, many men will die but the railway will go through and be successful -we must win the War". He was true in many things he said but we knew for sure that they would never win the War. Defeat was always on the cards but how long would it take - who knows?

This man always carried or wore his samurai sword. This was the Jap weapon, a two handed sword. Many of these weapons had been handed down through the years from father to son. The kid was very proud of his. He could be seen exercising with it early in the morning outside his quarters. Near the camp was once a small banana plantation, the banana tree is very fibrous at the trunk. The kid one day started to cut with his sword at the trunk of one tree, he found that with one or two swipes, he could cut through and fell a tree. To his delight and to the applause of the guards, he went every morning to exercise his cuts and thrusts, this went on for some little while till all the banana trees had been destroyed - such was his intelligence.

He "the kid" once got us all on parade, he said that too many men were sick and he would detail all men for work that he thought were fit to "go shagoto" (go to work). He detailed men who could hardly stand - leave alone work. As he made his rounds, an Officer our Medical Officer (Captain Lee R.A.M.C) said that the men were very unfit and should in no way be expected to work. The kid then made us all stand to attention and he took Captain Lee to the front of the parade for all to see he made him stand to attention. He then withdrew his dreaded samurai sword from its scabbard - we were all afraid of what was going to happen. He then swung the sword in circles above the Captain's head, getting nearer and nearer, some of us turned our heads away - thinking that we were about to see another cold blooded murder. He kept this up for about eight or ten minutes but Captain Lee, a very brave man stood his ground, he kept a very ice cool head, he didn't move an inch he just stared at the kid. Did he think that Captain Lee would pray for mercy - but he did not - a very brave man. The Jap withdrew, replaced his sword in its scabbard and strode off to his billet, very "down in the mouth", we could have cheered our

Captain. This shows how these little men like to show off. We all at some time or other had a bash or two from the "Kanu Kid".

End of May 1943:-

Things did not improve by any means. In fact, I think it was worse, you may not think that at all possible. Men were dying at the rate of four or five a day, with all the aforesaid diseases.

I had been down with my first attack of malaria, it is a terrible disease. I did not, or could not, sleep the night before the attack, my body ached all over and I had the fever. I felt boiling hot all over but was in a rapid shiver, I could not control it in any way, then I started to have hallucinations. I imagined that I could get a boat on the river, let it take me out to sea where I could be picked up by a friendly submarine. At the time, it was raining very hard and as the drops came down on to the roof, it sounded as if one was putting a small stick onto the spokes of a bicycle wheel, each drop gave a ringing sound, it was the most peculiar feeling. I went to see the Medical Officer and he prescribed quinine, lucky for me there was some available. Two tablets to be taken twice a day. A bout of malaria lasts about ten days.

Quinine was very valuable in the camps. Some foolish men sold it for cigarettes. They would recover from the malaria but they would get so many bouts - then they would go down with severe cerebral malaria, this attacks the spine and brain. They fell into a coma which lasted ten days. If they came through the crisis on the 9th or 10th day, then they were lucky to survive.

If one should get malaria and dysentery together, one was also lucky to pull through as the treatments for these two diseases combat each other.

The very sick were left in the camp, they were the ones that the Japs did not think fit to work. Even these had to do tasks in the camp such as grave digging. After the task, they were returned to the camp, many of them to die within a few hours, to be laid in the graves they had dug. They had been made to dig their own graves. Such was life!!

DOWN THE RIVER

Went on the work parade this particular morning. A Japanese, a stranger to us all, went through the ranks and picked out four of us - Ackroyd, two others and myself. We all wondered what was in store for us. The Jap went on to tell us that we would be working for him - he was the gaffer. He said that he did not want any nonsense or we should all be for it. We were going to Tarsao to fetch stores to build the railway. We were then taken to the food store where we were given food to last us for two days. We had half a sack of rice, 1½lbs of brown sugar, five dried fish and a handful of salt.

It would be a good break to get away from this hell for two days. We looked forward to the prospect, just like going on leave!! We picked up our stores and made our way to the River Kwai. We reached the landing stage to find that we had to wait for our barge and put put. The Jap was a bit annoyed about this and said that he wanted to get away early.

We settled down to await the arrival of our transport, we sat on the landing bay with our feet in the water. The water, which had been so muddy for the last two months was now beginning to clear. Ackroyd looked up river and said "What the devil is this floating down"? It was quite black and round in shape, we waited for it to come close and found, to our dismay, that it was a dead water buffalo. It looked as if it had been in the water for quite a while. It was all blown up and beginning to decompose. It floated by like a great land mine with its legs pointing skywards. To think we had just a while ago swam in the river and drank some of the river water. It floated by and disappeared around the bend in the river to continue its journey.

It was quite peaceful by the river, no shouting in agitation "Hiako Hiako" "Speedo Speedo" of the Japanese pacemakers, we sat and pondered at our lot.

To our amazement, we found that our Japanese keeper had fallen asleep, he was snoring quite loud, so he was in quite a deep sleep. We said to the others in the gang "Give us a shout if he comes around - we are going for a scout around". We made our way to Smokey Joe's once again. No-one was at home, we moved a few bamboos to one side in the wall and entered. Smokey was well stocked for his next rip-off. There was tobacco, eggs, sugar and of all things cigarette papers. We took off our lice ridden singlets, tied the bottom with a piece of string and proceeded to loot. We fetched a three gallon tea bucket and filled it with duck eggs. We had made a haul worth about $40. We returned to the landing bay to find our Japanese keeper still asleep. He was non the wiser about our little excursion. Once again "Thankyou Smokey Joe, your profits will be down this week"!! Of course we shared the loot with the other prisoners in the gang, after all they kept watch while the Jap was akip.

In the distance, we saw the barge and put put coming up the river. We woke our sleeping guard and he began to laugh and say "Taxan nero" (long sleep). We then said that we were glad for him to have had plenty nero.

The barge pulled alongside the landing bay and we put our stores aboard, together with the loot. We pulled away from the side and got into the main stream. The river was flowing at quite a rate, it was still partly in flood. We got down river at quite a rate of knots. It took us 3½ hours to reach Tarsao. We arrived at approximately 1.00pm. Most times we told the time by the position of the sun, most had sold their watches, mine had been broken for quite a while. I still had it in my kit, I guessed I would have to sell it one of these days.

We sold some of our loot to the barge men. They were Thais, most of them treated the Japs with contempt but we didn't trust them.

We made about $25 between us. We had had quite a profitable day.

When we arrived here, we were shown where we had to sleep in a clearing on the river bank. We put our sacks down, these were our blankets. We erected a frame to put our mosquito net over, this was our tent.

We now started our task, we had to load the barge with railway lines or rails. It was quite hard work in our very weak state of health. The rails were thirty pounders i.e 30lb per yard. The length ten yards, so they were each approximately 300lbs. We struggled to load them on, when the barge was about 3/4 loaded, the Jap began to shout and scream at us. The barge was beginning to take in water, so in quick time we had to off load before it sunk completely. God, after all that hard work. The Jap had quite an argument with the crew of the barge, in fact, I thought we were going to see blood spilt.

Another barge was brought alongside the landing stage, so we started to load again. By about 6.00pm, we were loaded and ready to move out. Most of all we wanted to eat and sleep. First of all, we must get the grime of the day off our sweaty bodies. We had a lovely swim in the river, the water was so inviting. We put the floating buffalo out of our minds and dived in. We cooked our rice and some of the dried fish. After the Jap had gone, we boiled some of our eggs. So we had a lovely meal to finish the day, then we all had a nice smoke - compliments Smokey Joe.

Our Japanese keeper told us to stay where we were and to behave ourselves as he had to go to the Jap HQ to get another put put to tow us back up the river as the one that had been allocated was not powerful enough to pull the heavy barge full of rails. He returned before dark to say that we could rest the next day as they had to get a tug from down the river to do the job. We were quite pleased to rest. We bid him goodnight and got to sleep, we were all very tired.

Next morning we awoke, we had breakfast. The Jap went away to the headquarters once again and he told us to behave ourselves in his absence.

We had a look around and found that we were quite near to a British POW Camp. We got in to find quite a few of our old company friends. It was lovely to see them again. The railway had reached here and it had become a base. They got all supplies by rail and were living quite well, they had a good canteen service and there were also a lot of rackets on the go. With the money we had made the day before, we were able to buy a small piece of beef steak for 30c, we also bought liver. We had quite a good feed up. Roll on when the rails got to Kanu, we may then get a better deal in life!!

Our friends told us the food here was quite reasonable - as food went.

Breakfast:-
Sweet peanut pap, a fried cake, egg and sugar.
Dinner:-
1½pts dry rice, pumpkin and sweet potato stew with meat.
Supper:-
Mess tin full of dry rice, thick stew with plenty of meat, two rice cakes or a pie full of meat.

God! What we would give for food like this at Kanu. All the lads that remained here looked quite fit. Of course, they had a very rough time before the railway arrived. They went through same as we were now going through at Kanu. Quite a lot of our men had died here. There was quite a large cemetery which was enlarging all the time, as more sick were brought down from up the line. Before we left our lads at Tarsao, they gave us things to take with us. They filled our slouch hats with peanuts etc. We bought two beef steaks and had a good meal at breakfast, our eggs had lasted well. All we thought about here was food, our bellies were first and foremost.

We left Tarsao at about 10.00am the motorboat towed our barge out into mid stream and we fought against the speeding flow of the river. We were on our way back to "hell" again. We looked on it as being a bit of luck to have been able to come down on this job, it had been quite a change.

Our Japanese minder was not at all well, in fact he was quite ill. We were of the opinion that he had dysentery. He kept running to the end of the barge and hanging his backside over the stern to relieve himself. One should feel sorry for him but I couldn't because he was a Japanese, they had never shown the least bit of sympathy for us in all the suffering we had had to endure.

It was very slow progress against the swift running waters as the tug fought its way up stream. It came almost to a standstill in the rapids but it wasn't too bad in the very deep waters.

At one point early on, when we hit the rapids, the barge was almost at a standstill. The Jap shouted "All men push" he told us to push on the gunnels (the sides of the barge). "All men push" he kept shouting and gave us a demonstration of what he wanted us to do, so we all did as he wanted and pushed like hell on the gunnels - but - a very big but - we were all standing in the barge. He was quite pleased with our efforts and, in fact, he helped us to push himself standing in the barge. We quite enjoyed this episode. After a while of this pantomime, we POWs all jumped over the side and pushed. Gradually we made headway.

We were of the opinion that the Jap was so ill that he just left us to it. The bottom of the barge kept dragging on the rocks and stones of the river bed. Each time we went over the side to add a little power to the tugboat. It was almost like being free with the half dead Jap in charge of us. He was ill but we had seen so many of our own like this and we could find no sympathy. He was laid on the deck groaning all the time.
We arrived back at lower Kanu at about 5.00pm, we were all very tired. The Jap said that we could rest, he kept going into the undergrowth to relieve his bowel.

I stood here in this position for eight hours

*En route to Japan, battened down on the Hakosaka Maru.
Some of the men suffered with dysentery, we buried them at sea*

Bull elephant charged through the hut at Hintock

Kanu camp, 1943
We had to put our blankets on the roof to keep the monsoon rains out

Hintock railway station, Siam/Burma railway

Railway is completed, this is the new base camp at Tarsao, nb. Japanese platform where the office took salute, they do not like to be looked down upon, we tow the line

Early cemetery

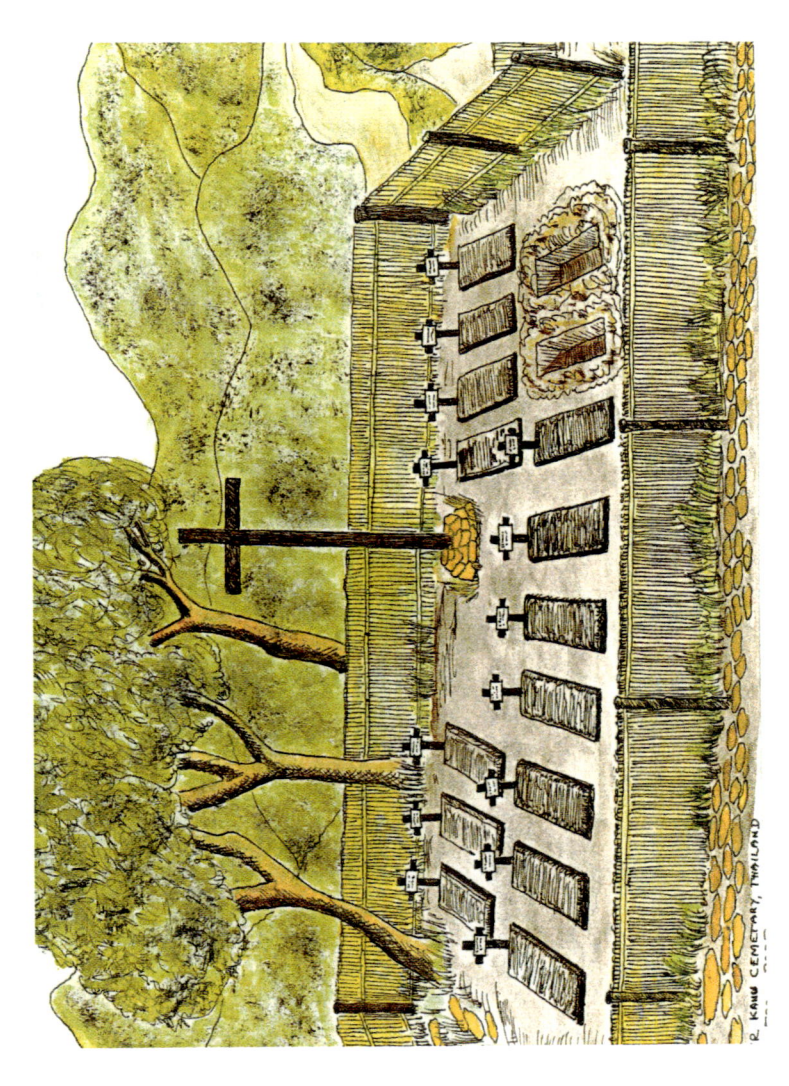

The coal mine at Onahama

Ackers and myself made a further raid on Smokey Joe's. No-one was about, it was like a magnet to us, we again pinched about $25 worth of his stock. The Jap told us he was going to telephone the top camp and ask for transport to take us back up the hill to our camp. We would have to off load the barge in the morning. After a wait of thirty minutes, the lorry arrived to take us back to the hell camp again but we had experienced a little freedom of sorts, having a sick Jap in charge of us. We got aboard and set off up the hill, it was a very rough ride.

As we got up the hill, the lorry pulled into a siding to allow a funeral party to pass on their way to the cemetery. One of our Company was a bearer, we knew that it was one of our friends taking his last trip through the jungle.

On arrival at camp, we were told that it was our 41st Company Orderly Corporal. He had died suddenly during the night, another man that had been worked to death.

We went through the camp entrance to be counted with our escort. We carried our loot from Smokey's in the three gallon tea bucket, we were not searched.

We made a good supper and we had about six eggs each. We sold the rest of our loot and we had in hand $25. We would be back tomorrow Smokey - if all went well. We slept well and very contented.

The next day we returned to the river site to unload the barge and put the rails on to lorries, they then took them up to the main camp ready to be laid when the time came. It just could not come quick enough to save lives before the next monsoons came. Finally the last of the rails had been off loaded and were on their way to the camp. We were told to wait an hour and the lorry would then return to pick us up. Our Jap escort was very sick and went up to the Jap camp on the last load of rails. So, for an hour, we were free. So - we paid another visit to Smokey's joint, again we took loot. We filled the tea bucket with eggs and filled our stinking singlets with brown sugar and we also took some tobacco. When we left, we put the bamboo slats back into place. We arrived at the camp gate and the guard waved us through, much to our relief. We off loaded and went straight to our filthy huts. It was about 6.00pm. We had had a change, a good outing with good hunting. As our lorry was making its way up the hill, we saw Smokey Joe on his way to his store, we had been in luck. Did he believe in the evil spirits of the jungle when he found his depleted stock?

It was now about 8 June:-

During the past few days, we had had a few canteen barges arrived at the river. Ackers and I found ourselves on the fatigue party to fetch the stores up. We stole two dozen eggs between us, these had been destined to the Japanese store. We dropped them about fifty yards from the camp in the jungle to be recovered later that evening. We were very lucky, the guards on the gate took the first three men in our party to one side, they were searched and found to have stolen goods on them. They were severely beaten with bamboo poles until they were almost unconscious. Buckets of water were then thrown over them to bring them back from the brink. When they did recover, they were made to stand to attention outside the guardhouse all night. We had to stand and watch the beating as a warning to us. Dear dear, and we had a dozen eggs out there to be recovered at a later time.

We waited until about three in the morning. Ackroyd shook me awake - "Let's go" he said. Again we moved the bamboo slats in the fence and went through. We could not at first find the eggs, it took us about fifteen minutes and at last he said that he had found them. We took a dozen each and were making our way back to our hole in the fence when we heard a shout - we laid flat in the undergrowth. We heard footsteps, they came nearer, we laid dead still and we dared not breathe. I could feel my heart pounding in my rib cage. Did I sweat. Then there was the guard, he was just two yards from us, he passed by. We waited until we could not hear the footsteps any longer and we crawled all the way back through the fence to our billet. Out of the two dozen eggs, we only had six left, the rest were lost or broken. Was it worth the effort? Well, yes! I suppose we still got that thrill. To think, as a young lad, I was afraid in the dark.

The lads who had been caught the night before with their loot were, in the morning, beaten up again then released to get their breakfast and report for work. Then the guard gave them a packet of cigarettes each, they were very downcast but not broken they were laughing about it.

It had been raining again very hard these last few days. The roads had become mud ridden and in parts unpassable. Therefore our rations had to be cut down again. We were living mostly now on rice and salt, we were slowly starving to death.

The mud was about knee deep all slurry.

Japanese soldiers were passing through here on their way up the road into Burma. At times we saw mounted troops go by on horses. It was shameful the way they treated these poor beasts. Some units had small ponies, like the small dartmoors. They pulled little carts loaded with gear, the mud came up to their little bellies. They slapped and kicked them and they pushed and shoved them at times. The soldiers were pushing both horse and cart through the mud, the Japs were pure beasts and so cruel.

It was impossible for motor transport to get through, our only hope was the GMC and Chevrolet trucks that they had captured - they had winches to get them through.

A few nights before, I set a snare over a hole and caught a lizard, it was soon skinned and put on a spit to be toasted over a fire. It smelled good and it tasted good. The two of us shared it. It was nice with an egg. What were we coming to?

We were all beginning to feel the strain now and our stamina was going. We must have been strong to last this long, one could feel ones soul ebbing away.

THE DEATH TENT

The dysentery isolation tent was next to the latrines. We called it the "death tent". One had very little chance of coming out of there alive. We said the chances were one in ten. We saw men there so low in body weight, skeletons about five stone. It was awful to watch - sights no human eye had ever seen the like of and never wanted to see again. If there were photographs, I am sure they would never be published in any country.

These men, human beings, just laid on the slats of the platforms completely nude, covered in a mass of flies, blood and excrement. The maggots were crawling over them and the walls of the tents. The poor souls vomited and cried for help. Oh god, please help them. Good honest men - what a state we were in, dying like flies, such heroes as these to suffer. As far as the Japs were concerned, they were all heroes and they died for a cause - "The railway must go through".

The working hours had once again been increased. We were supposed to be behind in our sector. We worked from dawn to dusk - bed to work, bed to work, rice, rice and more rice. We were miles into the jungle and miles from food or civilisation. We were cut off from the outside world, all we saw was sickness, death, bugs, lice, rice and Japanese sadists. The rains poured all the time and thunder and lightning. Few of us had any clothing, just a "Jap happy", maybe a hat. I had an old slouch hat, tattered and torn. I had no boots or shoes. We slipped and slid in the mud, it was almost knee deep in places.

The sanitary conditions here were the cause of most of the troubles in health. The Japanese staff, their camp was above ours on the side of a small hillock. Below this they had their ablution area and below that came their latrines. These were deep pits 12ft deep, 5ft wide and the length approximately ten yards. Below that they had a pig sty. Below all this was our camp. The stream that we used for our ablutions came down from this hillock and the water was comparatively clean. So you can see when it poured with rain, the stream overflowed at the top of the hill, the water rushed through the Jap latrines and overflowed down the hill into the pig sty, then through our camp - the cooking area - by the time the stream got to us, it was completely contaminated with all the muck that one can imagine. After a good downpour, maggots were crawling all over the camp. Our cooking must have been contaminated all the time with this filth. What could we do about it?

A lot of the lads here hadn't a stitch to their backs. They had exchanged their clothes for black market goods. Yes, there was a black market here. Thais came out of the jungle to buy shirts or anything that was going. I think at times some of these people were in league with the Jap guards. They chased some away but others were allowed to the fence, no doubt they had given back handers. The only clothes some had was a "jap happy" as we nicknamed it. This was just a strip of cloth with a long tape. The tape was tied around the waist and the cloth was tucked around the tape, only just enough to cover the most private parts. We had all kept our hats of sorts, there were trilby hats, peaked hats, slouch hats and even little woolie hats. Many now had discarded their footwear. We were a disgrace to the civilised eye but the Japanese did not wish it to be any other way.

About Mid June 1943:-

I had had terrible stomach troubles, I had had to go sick. I think I must have had a touch of dysentery and I had been passing blood. I have been given a small dose of epsom salts. The doctor thought it may clear the bug out of the system.

I also had treatment for leg ulcers. They had become quite deep. These ulcers had been caused by cuts on the legs. When chopping the bamboo, they split and the edges were sharp like razors. The cuts bled profusely, we had no bandages and it wasn't long before dirt got in or they became covered with flies. Within a matter of days the ulcers formed. I had been given saline dressings (salt and water). All bandages had to be washed and returned to the medical centre (such as it was). The bandages were very discoloured and I don't know how many times they had been used, washed and returned. The doctor said that I should have a day or two off on light duties - but - the Jap task master had said "Shagoto Hiako" (to work hurry hurry). I had felt awful all day and had had to force down the ration of rice. I was in pain with my tummy and kept running into the jungle, it was awful.

Our doctors were in conference with the Japanese Officers, begging for any medical supplies. This was an every day occurrence, all to no avail. The two faced pigs, they smiled and then made promises but it was all in vain. The railway must go through. They were not worried how many men died - the yellow bastards and I mean it!!

Early one morning I went to the latrines, I saw four bodies laying by the death tent covered with a union jack and a very dirty white ensign. Both flags were very dirty but still full of honour covering these poor souls. After we had been to work, I had cause to visit the latrines again and I happened to mention that the bodies were still by the tent. I wondered why and asked why they had not been buried. I was told that a burial had taken place earlier on and that these were another four who had died within a few hours. When these poor souls were buried, they were buried in the nude or maybe wrapped in banana leaves. The medical orderlies just had no time at all to prepare them for the grave.

About Mid to End June:-

Fever, dysentery and beri beri was fast on the increase here now. Men were going down like flies and they had no resistance against these dreaded diseases. The Japanese had just started to give us one quinine tablet when we returned from work on the railway. If you did not work you got no quinine, what a pity the mosquitoes were not so benevolent in picking out their victims.

Sapper Price died - he was in my section at Changi. Another fine fellow to die in such degradation.

On this day a batch of men were evacuated down the river to Tarsao, so lucky to be leaving this hell hole but so unlucky to be in such bad health. I didn't know how many of them would survive the illnesses that they had, as they were in very poor shape.

My stomach had been very bad during the past few hours, I had been passing a lot of blood so I had been put on light duties.

We had a new Japanese Colonel posted in, he was to take over the command of group four. Later I found out that it was Colonel Ichie. Being on light duties, I had been posted with a gang to build the Colonel a new house. We pulled bamboos out of the jungle to build the structure, it was quite a nice place and we had put a new attap roof on. It looked quite nice. The Colonel supervised the work throughout. We all hoped that he would in fact improve conditions throughout the area. He was an older type of man and seemed quite a good guy as Japs went.

We had to go back to put a few finishing touches to the place. Before we went to work that morning, we filled small tins with bugs and lice and when we visited the house to finish off, we scattered these little presents around. We hoped they would enjoy the Colonel, he was still a Jap anyway.

We had finished the Colonel's house and he had moved in. He had a good look around.

We were detailed to go the Colonel's house again that afternoon to pick up the building materials around the site. When we had finished Colonel Ichie sent for us. We were lined up outside the house. I thought about the bugs and the lice we had scattered around - had we been caught out? No, the Colonel gave us a few Japanese cigarettes each, together with some fruit and sugar. We were delighted and bowed to him and thanked him sincerely. We were rotten sods planting those bugs!!

This particular day my stomach felt better, I had had a few doses of epsom salts. I guess it had cleared out the germ, I hope so.

The Colonel had detailed a large gang to improve the camp conditions. He had put plans forward to rebuild the camp and dig new latrines. The other Japs in the camp were scared stiff of him, let's hope things would improve now.

At this point, I think that I should say that Colonel Ichie was executed at Changi as a war criminal at the end of the War.

What could have gone wrong? Was his hands tied by those higher up in command? No doubt he was hounded to get more men to work by the railway engineers!

26 June?:-

Seeing that my stomach was a little better, I had been returned to heavy duties.

27 June?:-

So tomorrow I would be back on the cutting again and blasting the rock face from dawn to dusk on hell fire pass.

Supposed to have started work this day - ha ha!! I went on to the work parade at dawn. The Japs did not shout out my number, so I hid in the jungle all day and took a rest, an easy 25c earned. Of course you always took a great risk when you did this, some had been caught and accused of trying to escape. The punishment was terrible, beaten and starved, it was a hazardous game to play but we all, at times, took the chance.

July:-

Ackroyd and myself had a bit of luck one day - or was it luck? We were detailed off to work in the Japanese cookhouse. The Jap in charge was a thorough pig, he beat and kicked us terrible, the only thing about it was that we had plenty of food - but what was the use - this Jap knocked it out of us as fast as we ate it. Our duties were to fill the boilers with water, peel all the veg, wash the rice and cut firewood for the cookers. We said "Fancy being on jankers in a bloody prison camp".

There were two Japanese that did the actual cooking. We got plenty of food. It was the first time I had been able to eat my fill for months, we got plenty of pork with the rice, it was good rice and I might add not like the rubbish we had been given in our stores. The Japs were very wasteful. They killed a pig then just kept the meat, from the body and legs. The rest they threw into a pit and it was buried. They disposed of the head, liver, kidneys etc. Our lads in the camp would give anything to have what these Japs wasted. It was not to be. The Japs lived very well.

The two Jap cooks had a small monkey, it was supposed to be tame. They had it tied to a tree on a very short lead. These two took great pleasure in tormenting or torturing this poor creature. They each had a short bamboo pole and lay bets. The money was put on the table, they then proceeded to hit the monkey on the head, taking it in turns, until the poor little beast was unconscious. The one that took the last tap was the winner and picked up the money -it was great fun! These are civilised people. If they were well they had escaped from some madhouse in Japan.

The cookhouse job didn't last long. Ackroyd was in the hospital with a bad bout of malaria. They were unable to get his temperature down. I was in with dysentery and malaria and had been on nine quinine tablets a day - I felt awful. I said my prayers but would we ever get out of here. I was off my food - what a state we were all in. Have no idea of the date!!

I had been through quite a lot and had lost so much weight. I must have been under nine stone, I was 6'2 in height and I looked like a piece of string. I did feel so ill.

IN THE DEATH TENT

One day I felt so ill - God what was happening to us all?

I had been put in the dreaded tent but I didn't care, I just wanted to lie down. I felt so weak and exhausted. Let me rest, the fever was racking my poor under-nourished body. I also had the runs. Others were moaning all around me, some had died and were laying outside. Their poor emaciated bodies, laying there in the rain. They were beyond all this, they were at peace. These were respected British Army soldiers, so proud, so brave - what an end. What a way to leave this world.

I fell asleep to dream the dreams of the damned, I was hallucinating and racked with the malaria fever. I felt I was fading away, where was I? I slept and slept and slept, blessed relief.

When I awoke I found that there were only two of us in the tent, laid on the bamboo slat platform. The others that were here had been discharged or had died, dead and buried. The other fellow opposite me was in a very bad way, I knew him to have been very brave in the battles for Malaya. He was one of those to bear the brunt of the first Japanese invasion force and he had distinguished himself in battle. He was captured and imprisoned at Kuala Lumpur. He joined us many months later after the fall of Singapore with many of his comrades. He was a Corporal in the Argyll and Sutherland Highlanders. He was opposite me in this tent or hut. He had fought to live and was now just skin and bone, a mere shadow of his former military self, laying on these slats covered by a rice sack with flies buzzing around his poor emaciated body, covered in blood from the dysentery, just a skeleton. He fought on for 48 hours, then the Roman Catholic Priest came and gave him the last rites. I said "Padre, he fought to live, he didn't deserve to die like this". The Priest took out a small alter, he opened it and it contained a very small chalice and bread. He set it up and gave the Corporal absolution. I felt I was honoured to have witnessed this religious act. The Corporal passed away peacefully. I said "Padre, I feel so humble to have been a witness to the passing of this brave man". The Padre asked how I was, I said that I felt very ill. He then put his hand on my head and said "Bless you my son" he then left the hut. I felt very elated and the next day I felt better and I left the "death tent". I never went back again. Was it my faith? I felt as if I was back from the dead!

My stay in the death tent at this point in time I am sure, if my will had not been strong, I could have easily slipped away from it to eternity. So many did just that. Ackroyd came to see me in the death tent "Come on you daft bugger, get out of here". He brought me food, he was a good mate.

Date unknown July?:-

Thank goodness I was on the list for evacuation but I still had to go to work on the line.

I was at work this particular day clearing the debris after the shot firing. I filled my basket and put it on my head and carried it to the cutting and tipped its contents on to the embankment. Then I thought "To hell with this, why should I do this all day"? So for a considerable while, I walked around with an empty basket on my head and went through the motions of emptying it, I thought that me being tall the short Japs on the site would know no difference. It got to mid afternoon and I had a good run. A Jap on top of the heading had been watching me. Unfortunately I had not seen him and as I passed underneath with the empty basket on my head he picked up a good size stone, you could call it a small boulder and dropped it into my basket. Well the blow knocked me out and when I came round there were three Jap gentlemen kicking hell out of my poor weary body. I passed out to be brought around by them pouring water over me, then beaten again with bamboo poles. They knocked me down but I got up again to take more punishment. Eventually they let me off the hook and I joined the working party again but I ached all over. The next day I was black and blue all over. To add insult to injury, on the way back to camp one of the guards gave me two or three Japanese cigarettes, he said "You velly bad boy"? So it went on.

Date?? - I just do not know:-

One particular day I found that I was on the list for evacuation in the morning. We got down to lower Kanu to await barges to take us down the river to Tarsao. One of my friends, Bluey Holmes, was now working in the Jap cookhouse with the monkey bashers. He brought me a full mess tin of rice and pork stew, a tin of sugar and tinned meat which he had stolen. I was lucky to have good friends around me, we had been through so much.

The sun was shining and, as the sun rose in the sky, I looked up and saw the big black clouds of flies hovering over the camp like a cloud of black death. Every morning it was the same, they were giant blow flies just waiting to pounce on food, these were the dysentery carriers. When the sun rose up into the sky and became hot these germ carriers landed or pitched on the leafless trees and the branches were black with these terrible insects. They hovered around the latrines breeding maggots, then death and destruction. One would never believe it unless one was here in this terrible environment.

Well I packed my kit for the evacuation and I found that I had quite a wardrobe. Two shirts, one pair of shorts and a blanket, these had been acquired through fiddles in the camp. I had no boots, they were discarded quite a while ago, they just rotted on my feet. I had my old hat and a few personal belongings, some of which I hid on inspections. My old photo album with a few photos of you all at home. I still had my Royal Engineers cap badge (issued as a recruit). The Japs liked to get hold of these as souvenirs.

Our evacuation was off, we counted our chickens too quickly. The Japs had made a further check and put a lot of us back to work again, were we browned off?

I was on my way to work this particular day and it had been raining. Most of us were all in bare feet and slipping all over the muddy path through the bamboo thicket. As I passed under the trees, something fell on to my back, cold and slippery. I felt it crawl over my neck and down my bare back, the chap behind me shouted "Look out Blackie" and swiped it off, it was a green bamboo snake. It slithered away into the jungle. I still cringe to this day when I think about it.

I had another dose of malaria again and was lucky to get quinine. I got over that and had a touch of dysentery again but had a couple of doses of epsom salts. I had every faith in them, 1p an ounce in England but worth a fortune here.

I seemed to be getting the malaria every month, it lasted about nine or ten days. These diseases were with us all the time, I think it was well into our systems now and we would never be better until we got full treatment to cure it all.

Quite a lot of our lads had passed away with cerebral malaria and a lot still did not take their quinine. It was courting trouble and foolish not to take the medicine when it was given, just for a cigarette or two.

We had been taken out on working parties again now. We got into the jungle to fell trees, mostly teak to build the trestles. These were erected in the cutting to take the railway lines.

The Japanese employed elephants at first to drag these large logs out of the jungle to the clearings. The mahouts (elephant drivers) were Siamese and, at times, the elephants found the logs too heavy to drag in the undergrowth. The Japanese started to beat the elephants, so the mahouts and the elephants kept away. So the prisoners were brought in. If you cannot get an elephant, get ten POWs!!

When we had got so many logs in position, we were given hammers and wood chisels to shape the trestles and to fit them together. It was quite a good job once the logs were in position. We could sit down to do the cutting.

The Jap engineers took them to the site to be erected. They seemed pleased with our efforts. We had to do the work to suit them or be beaten up. We knew only too well that this kind of work should not be done by POWs. I was on this work for about three weeks.

I had had quite a bit of sickness again, fortunately it had only been in a mild form of fever. The tummy had been playing up but I had to try to keep going until the evacuation came along. I had been cheating as regards to food. Early in the morning and at dusk I had been going to two feeding points. I did not want my weight to go any lower as I was like a beanpole.

Days later - date unknown:-

My friend Ackroyd was evacuated, he was destined for lower Kanu. A few nights beforehand we made a raid on the Japanese cookhouse and made quite a haul so we shared the spoils. Four tins of salmon, four tins of meat, half a kit bag of dried fish, dried meat, eight small tins of vegetables and two tins of white sugar which was very rarely seen. So I said cheerio to my old friend. We had had quite a few adventures together. I did so hope that I would see him again soon.

DOLLY GREY

One night all was still in the camp and I heard a voice in the dark shouting "Blackie, Blackie". It was coming through loud and clear, then one of the lads said "Blackie, do you hear that? Someone is calling your name". It came nearer and nearer, then I recognised the voice, it was my old mate from Changi days - Dolly Grey. I shouted back "Dolly - Dolly, I'm over here". Then we homed on to each others voices. He was in a camp about three miles up the track and he went on to tell me that he had heard that I was down in Kanu so he decided that he would come down to see me. So he broke out of his camp, evading the guards and he walked alone along the muddy track to Kanu, where he had to break into our camp, again evading the guards. when he got near the centre of the camp he started shouting my name. We were both so glad to see each other, we hugged each other close and we told each other all the latest camp news - who had died and who was still around. We talked well into the morning hours. He then had to go so we shook hands and wished each other well. He had to get out of our camp, walk back to his camp and break in again before daybreak. He had taken a great risk to do this as I have mentioned before. If one was caught outside the compound, he could be accused of trying to escape and the punishment could be death by the sword, as we saw during the early days at Changi. So what price friendship, when a man takes such a risk. Dolly Grey, you will be my best friend for life, I shall never forget this act of courage, some may say foolhardy but not I. A true friend if ever there was one. All the friends I had at Kanu were so full of praise for this act of courage.

Quite a lot of coolie people were marching up through the mud, they were on their way to work up the line to help get this railway working. They consisted of Chinese, Indians, Tamils and quite of lot of Malays. They were supposed to be going into the Burma sector. They all looked very dejected and poor in health. They told us news of the outside world - that was when the guards allowed us to get near them. According to them, Malaya and Singapore was in a state of famine and starvation. The Japanese had been very cruel to all the population. Most of all to the Chinese, many of them had been executed around the coastline and their bodies left for the tides to take away. Many of the coolies who had worked in the tin mines and rubber plantations under their British bosses had been in contact with them here, as a lot of the rubber planters and tin workers had joined the Federated Malay States Volunteer Forces and were here in the camp as prisoners of war. They could speak the languages of these people. They asked for any glimmer of news and hope. The European situation did not look too good as there had been no second front yet. We knew only too well that Hitler and the Axis Forces had to be defeated in Europe before we ever stood a chance of liberation. Burma was not too well, though the Japanese had been halted, they had not got into India as they expected to do so.

There had been bitter fighting in Burma. Such was the news from these poor dejected people as they trudged their way toward Burma. These poor souls had been told that Siam and Burma were lands of milk and honey. How well we knew.

Kanu III camp had been evacuated. The great cutting of 60ft deep in the hardest rock, cut out by hand, hammer and tap for 75%. The Japs then saw that the target time could not possibly be met and they brought up a compressor and air drills. It was much too late for all the poor devils who had died and other ruined for the rest of their lives.

It was a great shock to hear that our RSM (Jack Restall) had died after only four days sickness. Before becoming RSM, he had been our Company Sergeant Major. A good man and a good soldier, what a waste this was. So many of our old friends had passed away, I had lost count.

More very bad news had been passed to us, cholera had broken out down the river from here. God! Please help us! Don't let it break out in this camp, we were all so weak. We had to take all precautions, dip our mess tins in boiling water and to keep them covered when not in use away from the ever hovering blue bottle flies and the common house fly. They were responsible for carrying all these terrible diseases. When we entered the camp, we had to wash our boots in disinfectant - well, those who had boots. I just washed my feet in the solution. A lot of these precautions should have been carried out before, perhaps the dysentery epidemic which had caused so many deaths would not have been so bad.

Our CQMS died one morning (Sammy Southern) he received a letter from his wife just before he passed away. So tragic, another good soldier.

A few letters had been received in this camp, what was happening to our letters. I had received none at all yet. I was sure you at home were writing to me. Since we had been captured, I had written three cards, often wondered if you would ever receive them. They were all pre-printed "I am fit and well, I am working for pay". What a load of rubbish but at least you would know by the date that I was still alive at that time.

My stomach had been very bad during the last week. I was now in the new hospital (a bigger bamboo hut - some hospital). It was a terrible place to be, there were terrible cases here from up the line and Kanu III, diseases of all kinds. The tropical leg ulcers, the smell was so terrible, some had gangrene - poor devils were just rotting away. The death toll was on the increase, we were seeing twelve or thirteen die each day, all we were able to do was say "Sorry, we cannot help you".

The Medical Orderlies were doing their best with what they had. A lot of the orderlies were Anglo Indian, they were brave and kept going as best they could. It was terrible to lay here and listen to the dying men, shouting to the orderlies to help them. A cry of "Mother" or maybe a wife or sweethearts name called in agony. A curse upon the Japanese, they twisted in agony. Then the silent stillness, the orderly cam to cover the still body with a rice sack or torn blanket - and so - another of our comrades had gone beyond it all. This was a picture of what we saw here all day long. The mind was almost at bursting point "Is it worth fighting to endure this torture"? One got off the bamboo slats and walked, smoked if you had tobacco, anything to take the mind away from the hell of insanity. There had been suicides, poor devils just could not take any more. Some were demented with malaria and they dashed into the jungle, they were found wondering by the Japanese who punished them. Punish them! Yes, they had means. One man found wondering was put in a cage, he was in the sitting position and he wore no clothes. A hole under the bottom of the cage allowed him to relieve himself. He could just move his hands to take the rice ball and water that was passed through the bars of the cage. He could only just feed himself and he was in that position for 84 hours - yes! 84 hours.

Others had been put in the oven, a cubical, just big enough to squat in, built of corrugated iron. Placed in the blazing sun, they had three or four of these cubicles in this camp.

Another chap was led around the camp with a chain around his neck, his hands were tied behind his back. He would be taken to the latrines and another POW would be called to take his shorts down, then do all that was needed re his ablutions.

Was it any wonder that so many gave up and could not find any hope to get out of this hell. Surely they would be made to pay the price at some time or other. Let's blast them off the face of the earth!! They had so much to pay for!

Two new medical officers had been drafted into this camp to help Major Driscoe our overworked Doctor. The Japs I feared were getting a bit worried about the death rate among our men. The two officers were Australian.

The Japanese came into the hospital and took men out to work. They said that they were fit enough against the wishes of our medical officers. I hid away so missed it. Some had to go to the cemetery to dig graves, later one or two of them died - to be buried in the graves that they had dug earlier in the day.

The Japanese had now come up with a new idea, they said that they would give extra milk, salt and sugar to any POW who put in a whole days work. This was extra to a days pay. Later that day, the extras promised were given as a bonus for working a full day.

Many of the hospital patients had fallen for the play and had discharged themselves from the care and attention that they so badly needed. I was not interested in their promises.

Another evacuation was supposed to come off the next day. I had to try and get on it to get out of this hell camp.

During the past few days, we had had a meat issue, the cattle were driven up through the jungle and they were slaughtered in the camp. Poor beasts were in poor state before they began the hazardous journey. They were beaten to keep them on the move and they were not fed. They drank from stagnant pools full of disease. It was a pitiful sight to anyone who did or had loved animals. All seemed to suffer in this hell hole, man and beast together at the hands of the Japanese. They were a cruel race. The poor beasts, that they tried to escape into the jungle were beaten back onto the trail. They were nothing but skin and bone. Some, when they were slaughtered and cut open, had to be buried and were unfit for human consumption. Their insides were full of TB - so much for the meat ration.

The railway was reported to have reached Tarsao. Rations should have got better if this was true.
The cholera epidemic was on the increase, rumour had it that it had broken out in a camp about two miles from here. I hoped it would not break out in this camp. It is a terrible disease. A man could be fit one day, be taken and be gone in a matter of a few hours. It was very frightening.

I had been told to stand by to be evacuated the next day. It would depend on the Japanese gentleman who inspected us as we lined up. I had to try to look my worst to get out of this hell hole. I did not know the date, I had lost all count of time or date, nothing seemed to matter much now - only survival.

The evacuation came off, we were lined up one morning. A Jap inspected us all, some he told to get to work - poor devils. I put on my "hung dog look" and he told me to join the evacuation party. I was lucky to get out of Kanu I, it was a terrible place. We had had to march to lower Kanu camp to await a barge to take us down the river to a rest camp.

I forgot to mention the Jap that inspected us that morning was only a two star private. He had the power to say yea or nay, it was a pitiful situation. One officer, British that is, was being evacuated with appendix trouble. This little Jap said "No" and the Medical Officer tried to explain the trouble but was beaten up by this little Jap pig for his trouble, a matter of life or death. Many of the men had gaping tropical ulcers, as big as a mans hand. The bone showing through and the smell was awful, the flesh just rotting away, all it needed was a small scratch from bamboo to set it off. Finally gangrene set in. If possible the limb was then amputated (if one was lucky enough to be in a base camp and the medical staff were able). Many men had lost their limbs in the rest camps down the river. Some very good work had been done with old knives. Some said the meat saw was often sent for from the cookhouse, it was sterilised in boiling water. Such operations had been performed by that great Australian Colonel "Weary" Dunlop, a hero to us all.

Well here at lower Kanu we had actually been excused heavy duties, we had to do a few light fatigue jobs for health's sake and the cookhouse.

The camp had been out of action and not used for eight to ten months. So repairs had to be done, paths had to be cleared and we had to repair the roofs before the rain started again. There were two Japanese in charge, they were both so important strutting around the place. The POW and British Officer was a Captain from the Singapore Volunteer Force, some say he was a stickler against the Japanese and fought for prisoners rights, as far as possible that is!! It was said too that the two Japs had a certain amount of sympathy for us.

At this moment, I had managed to keep hold of some of my own kit, I had one pair of KD shorts and two KD shirts. I had kept hold of these items and hoped when (a big when) we were liberated to look a little presentable. As I had said before, my size 9 ammunition boots had long since gone, rotted on my feet in the terrible mud and rain soaked Thailand. I had walked bare foot for many months and had got used to the burning dust and the hard rocks in the cuttings, my feet were so hard. We often joked with each other and said "You could sole and heel my feet, putting in the army regulation 13 studs!! All most of us had was a strip of cloth approximately 6" wide to cover our nudity. We tried not to worry too much about the terror that surrounded us - death and disease - the mind was so evenly balanced, as we had seen so many suicides that happened at odd times.

We had been detailed to our billets, I found that I had been allocated next to two Officers of the Singapore Defence Force - a Captain Ralt and Captain Wright. Rank meant nothing to the Japanese as far as they were concerned, we were all slaves together. Officers were paid on a regular basis and they received regular weekly payments. These Officers were nice gentlemen, I cooked a bit of food for them when I cooked my own. They looked after me for the trouble I took. They tipped me at the weekend when they were paid.

I sold a shirt one particular day and a singlet, I had about $25 in hand, this would keep me going for a day or two.

We had been here four days and the flies were on the increase. Dysentery had broken out. Cholera had broken out at Kanu 2 and Kanu 3 camps, it was gradually getting nearer.

It had not rained for a day or two and the mud had started to dry up a little.

A small camp had been erected about a quarter of a mile from here - it was a cholera camp. All cases of the disease were to be brought here from the other camps, so we had another death camp, brought here to die. There was very little treatment for this dreadful disease, one must drink plenty of saline, salt water drink, to replace the fluids passed to help stop the cramps this disease caused.

So far most of the cholera deaths were among coolies that were making their way up the northern end of the railway toward Burma. Many of these poor souls were falling by the trackside to die, some crawled into the undergrowth and there were women and children with some groups. Their pitiful bodies were torn to pieces by the ever present vultures. What was left was devoured by the giant ants. They lay unburied, white skeletons bleached by the burning sun. Poor souls claimed by this mad existence. Relatives would never know what happened to them or how they died. Would the Japanese ever be brought to task for all these crimes to humanity.

Two or three barges came up the river, they were moored at the stage. They had brought eggs, cigarettes, tobacco, cigarette papers, white and brown sugar, palm oil and coconut oil. I got a supply in with the money and I got for the shirt etc that I had sold.

The railway had definitely reached Tarsao. So rations were coming up by rail, the barges had a bit of competition and the prices were dropping. The damage had been done, too many lives had been lost at this stage. "Hell firepass" was finished, the cutting through solid rock, one of the biggest projects on the line. God knows how many lives it cost.

Men left in the Kanu camps were being sorted out, the sick were to be sent down to base camps. The fit were to go up the line or river to more working camps, to other hells I suppose.

Kanu camp had finished, it was being fitted out as a coolie camp. Coolies were also moving in to this camp or another part of it. There were a lot of sick amongst them, they were most unfortunate as they had no doctors with them or medical supplies. They had very little fighting spirit left. We saw them just lay down and die, they seemed to be able to will themselves to die in a very short time. They gave up all hope very easily. We had tried to coax some of them to fight, all to no avail.

They had started to bring the cholera cases into the camp just up the road from here. They passed just a few yards from our billet. Six cases were brought in this day, one died on the way. They had to be carried on makeshift stretchers, shoulder high, as the road had almost been washed away in the terrible monsoon weather that we had had in the past few months. The poor fellows were in agony, some having rolled off the stretcher in their agony and some had cried out in pain. We at times could see no end to this hell upon earth.

Quite a few of our lads had passed through this camp on their way to Tarsao from the other Kanu camps. I wished I could go with them!!

During the past few days, I had had a lot of stomach trouble, I had been passing a lot of blood and mucus, the pain was terrible. I was sure I was having another attack of dysentery. I was unable to get any salt, I had to see the doctor the next morning.

I had not written anything during the last day or two as I had been in pain and feeling awful. I saw the doctor and he had no salts, he had put me on ground charcoal, it was supposed to stop the runs. God I felt so weak.

Later that day, we heard that the medical people had had a small supply of epsom salts. I had to get down there first thing to get some if I could. Epsom salts was like gold dust.

I saw the doctor again and he put me on salts. I had had three doses that day and was beginning to feel better, the runs had eased off. Thank God, it was so worrying.

The canteen barge came up the river and I bought a bit of flour and a few eggs. I mixed the two together and hoped to put a lining on to my poor old stomach and get a bit of nourishment.

Still had no idea of the date, it was about August I suppose.

More fellows came in to camp from Kanu 3. They were in a very sorry state, a lot of them were Australians and they had all the diseases - dysentery, malaria and beri beri. One of the Aussies looked as if he weighed 16 to 20 stone. He was blown up with water and he could hardly move around, blood was pouring from his private parts and his testicles were blown up like footballs. He was laying there nude, it was one of the worse cases I had seen of beri beri. It was hell to have to watch this suffering and being unable to help the poor wretches. Then to watch them die at your side after weeks of agony, afraid at times that you might be next. On the other hand, we had put these feelings to one side, the sadness must be overcome - be callous - take no notice - let things take their course. Make up your mind that you were going to survive and to pull through whatever happened.

My stomach was much better, what luck, to get those epsom salts. But all was not well and I had had two or three bouts of malaria and was getting it every ten days. I had been able to get quinine, thank God.

Three Australians had moved into our billet and we had become very friendly. Poms and diggers got on quite well and there was always a bit of leg pulling. One of the Aussies was a Sergeant from the 2/26 Machine Gun Battalion. He had in his possession a large cooking pot. We went on a scrounging expedition and we got potatoes, pumpkin and small portion of meat. All this went into the pot together and we had a lovely supper.

After the supper, we had a very interesting conversation, he told me a lot about Australia, his home town and his work. Then he took out his folder, he showed me photographs of his wife and family - he had two lovely boys. He said how he was looking forward to getting out of this hell hole and back to these wonderful kids and his wife. It was all he wanted to get home to them.

We were detailed to go into the jungle to cut bamboo for the cookhouse fires. This was quite a task, the bamboo was in very big clumps. One must be so careful not to cut ones limbs for fear of the dreaded ulcers. After cutting the wood, we had to take it all back to the cookhouse. We had cut quite a large pile which would last a day or two.

The Australian Sergeant that I had the conversation with was taken ill at breakfast. He was very ill, vomiting a white fluid and passing blood. He was getting terrible cramps. He was then taken to the cholera tent. It looked bad for him to be sure. Five hours later the poor Sergeant died. I could not get over it, the evening before he was showing me the photographs of his wife and two boys. He was so full of getting back home with them again, so full of hope for the future just last evening, now about twenty hours later he was dead - God why?

More barges came up the river and tied up at the landing. An Australian and I went down to see what was on offer, we took chances and came back with quite a haul. Three tins of biscuits, two dozen eggs, a stack of sugar and tobacco. Yes! We did well that day, we didn't spend a cent, just lifted - then left. I wondered at times would I ever break the habit of being a thief. Perhaps I would give up the habit in different circumstances.
Three or four days later, the Aussie friend was evacuated. He had gone down the river to Tarsao, I wondered if I would ever see him again - who knows - he was a good lad.

I hoped to go soon, I had been here almost a month. A lot of good lads had died in the cholera tent. The funeral - a pile of bamboo was placed in position crossing the pieces to the height of 4 or 5ft. The body was placed on the top and at times there may have been two or even three at a time. These fires were going all day long and the smell was terrible. The men employed on this work were (it was rumoured) on extra pay and rations. They could have that job, they were quite welcome.

My name had been called for the next evacuation barge. I hoped it would go soon, I had just about had enough of this camp and the cholera. More were dying every day, it was a terrible disease. From being taken ill they were dead within hours. Those fires were burning all the time. The stench was terrible when the wind was this way and it seemed to hang in the air. God let us get out of here. I had a feeling that, if I didn't get out soon, something was going to get me.

TARSAO

Thank my dear God, I was out of that dreadful place. Lower Kanu, any of the Kanu camps for that matter with all the diseases, mosquitoes and flies breeding in their millions. Not forgetting the lice and bugs, then the flea carrying rats with their typhus.

We left by barge at approximately 9.00am. The River Kwai was calm and we had a pleasant trip down, so very peaceful. I had a feeling that all was well, so relieved to get out of there. It was about 11.00am when we arrived. We were a ragged lot, all skin and bone.

The first thing that happened was that we were all inspected by one of our own Medical Officers. We were split into three sections:-

(i) Hospital (at once)
(ii) Medical Treatment
(iii) Working Camp

I found myself in (ii) group. Working in camp to get medical treatment three times a day. Such as the treatment was but better than at Kanu.

The camp had altered a lot since I was last there. The huts had been improved and certain gangs were building new ones.

Working arrangements were the same as anywhere else. The Japanese do not like sick persons and pay was stopped for the sick. When working, we got 25c per day, we were paid every ten days (I guess it made it easier for the Jap paymaster, just add the O). They were not very bright. When the ten days were completed, we got

$2.50c and we got this in our hands, no credit, no debit. We all gave 25c to the hospital to buy food and drugs for the sick poor devils needed it. We also donated an amount to the canteen fund to help out our poor rations.
The canteens here were quite good, I don't think we had a NAAFI - far from it!!

WORKING PARTIES AT TARSAO

Most of the parties were employed on road making, camp repairs and railway maintenance, there were other <u>odd</u> jobs. The hospital was being rebuilt. This in fact was one of the main tasks as they were expecting an influx of sick from up the line, they said some were even coming in from the Burma end of the line. Quite a lot of extreme sick were due in at any time.

The food here was very reasonable as things were. We got rice cakes etc. The cooks were quite good at trying to make the rice look palatable with a little help of extra titbits, we had to be thankful for small mercies.

This will give you an idea of our meals (this was all we thought about):-

Breakfast:-
Rice Pap, a watery rice gruel with sugar or salt with perhaps a few peanuts. At times we got boiled rice.
Lunch:-
1½pts dry rice, fish or sambol (paste), boiled sweet potatoes, or beans or a pea and meat stew.
Supper:-
1½pts dry rice with a kind of vegetable stew (very watery) a savory rissole, made with whatever was going???
I was employed in camp cleaning in the morning, I got 10c a day. At that moment I was on light duties. A little spending money.

On the way to the River Kwai to wash oneself, we had to pass the Jap Store, a large atap building. It should be a comparatively easy task to get access to some loot by removing a few panels of the atap. I must keep this in mind!! We would no doubt have a go before very long. Must keep the place under observation.

A few of the Aussies were running a racket or two, I had been watching points and would have to get involved in some way or another. I had to try to get a bit of cash by me.

It was, I believe, about October, I know it was 1943 - but even the month I was at a loss, the day or date - well who knows??

Things had been going at a very steady pace as I have said before, the camp was kept very clean and the huts were bigger and more airy but of course were still homes for vermin, rats, lice and bugs living in the cracks of the bamboo slats on which we slept.

We had had quite a few cases of typhus, this was extremely contagious, often a fatal fever. It is transmitted by lice and rat fleas. It is mostly caused by filth and over-crowded living conditions. We had had one or two die from this fever.

The Japanese had rat traps around the camp. I saw one Jap come out of their store. He was carrying a rat trap cage, with three live rats inside. He called his friends around, there were about six or seven of them, he then poured petrol over the cage and set light to it. The rats were running around the cage screaming in agony, it lasted about a minute to a minute and a half until the rats died. The Japanese were all screaming with delight, it was the highlight of their day. Such were these people, brutal, callous and sadistic, it was bred into them!!

Since being in Thailand, we had not only the Japanese guards but also Korean guards. Toward us they were as sadistic as any of the Japanese, at times even worse. They were beaten and kicked around by the Japanese, then they took it out on us.

The Japanese guards had been thinned out considerably, rumour had it that a lot of them had been sent to Burma as front line soldiers.

One very interesting guard we had was nicknamed "Oklahoma Joe". He had lived in the USA for quite a few years and was said to have been a car salesman. He had the bad luck to go home to visit his folks in Japan as the war started and was drafted into the Army - well Joe couldn't care less, he tipped off the British Officers when to expect a search. In fact he was quite friendly with some of the Australian troops. He took watches and rings outside the camp and sold them for some of the POWs and brought the money back to them. It is said that he got radio parts and such. He used to chat with the lads, have a smoke but he had to be very careful not to be caught or shopped by the other guards. Anyway, one day Joe was having a chat and a smoke with the Australians, we had an influx of POW strangers from up country. They didn't know Joe, so they pinched his rifle, it happened to be a .303 Lee Enfield, captured from us on surrender I suppose. Joe of course was in some state but not to worry Joe!! The Aussies pinched a rifle from one of the other guards, so all ended well. They could not have had any check on the numbers. I often wondered what happened to the stolen firearm.

I had another bout of malaria, so I was on quinine for another ten days. My stomach seemed to be keeping free from the bug, I dreaded getting the fever and dysentery at the same time, it was a killer, it had done for so many.

As I have mentioned before, the rackets were rife. So out of my little pay packet I bought myself a four gallon square oil can. I boiled it out and cleaned it well, so I had gone into business with an Aussie who slept opposite me.

There were five big cookhouses here, HQ, L and M, Aussies, Convalescent Depot and the Main Hospital. We had a meat issue to each cookhouse. The poor cattle were brought up the tracks from down south on the hoof. By the time they got here, they were so pathetic and thin. I thought it was so cruel, if only we could do without this cruelty, we had to live and try to get fit.

The slaughter place was in the open air and about seven to fifteen of these very poor beasts were killed in a day. I don't think they looked anything like the good old English beef cattle. At times I thought I had seen bigger greyhounds than these poor, starving "Yak" as we called them.

The method of killing was so cruel - this is how it was done. We roped the beast and lead it into the paddock. A rope was tied around its horns and passed through a staple in the ground. It was then pulled tight and the animal was brought to its knees, with its head pulled down to the ground. It was then hit upon the head a number of times until it was unconscious. Its throat was then cut. It was then slung up by the hind hooves on a kind of scaffold. We skinned them and the head came off with the skin. We cut it off and put it to one side. We then helped to carry the meat to the different cookhouses, after it was cut into portions. At times we were given a piece of meat for our help. When the stomach was taken out, we were given the fat (if any). When the throat was cut, we caught as much blood as possible. On an average, we got about a gallon of blood.

After the work was finished at the slaughter place, we went to the river to wash the meat and clean the heads a bit, wash the fat and the tripe. We got quite a bit of this at times.

We now made our way back to the camp huts where we lit a fire and began the process of cooking our bits and pieces.
First job was to render down the fat - we got quite a bit.

We then boiled the heads in a big oil can or tin. We put vegetables in, which we had stolen from the Japs - **it smelt good**. One of us then took the four gallon can (converted with carrying handles) around the camps and sold hot meat soup 5c a pint, we always got buyers.

The blood we put in a tin and brought to the boil - it then solidified, we took it out and cut it into slices and sold it at 5c a piece, it looked a little like Aero chocolate.
To finish the day, we fried the pieces of meat, which at times was as tough as old army boots. It helped to pass the time just chewing.

The Aussie and myself were making quite a bit of money, with which we bought eggs, sugar and tobacco. It all went to make life a little easier and so to bed as such to feed the hungry lice and bugs.

When we rendered the fat down, we could sell that at 50c a pint, we could make four pints a day - on a good day!!

The tripe we fried or boiled and sold for 5c a piece.

On a good day, we could make about $10 each.

Our doctors wondered why we did not want to go out to work. Why kill oneself to work for the Japs.

Other rackets were hot sweet coffee. Some of the Aussies had 4 or 5 oil tins on a fire brewing up. They had to lay out the money for coffee and sugar, which they got on the black market. We had no such outlay.

About two weeks later - date unknown:-

My Australian friend had been taken very ill and had gone into the hospital. I thought he had had a very bad bout of malaria and dysentery - I did so wish him well, he was a lovely fellow and very genuine.

Anyway, life had to go on. I had paired up with Corporal McDonald of the Gordon Highlanders. We were continuing the business together but not on such a big scale.

Quite a lot of our "Y" Battalion had collected here. They had tried to keep the old battalion together. We were now known as 16 Battalion <u>No 4 Group Thailand</u> or Siam.

I forgot to make this entry before but my old friend Bill Ackroyd went right down south to Chunkai. That was on the day that I arrived here. Bluey Holmes had also gone straight down but did not stay here at all. We had been told that Chunkai was a "death camp" of the River. All the very sick were sent there from as far up as the Pagoda Pass on the Burma border.

At one time they blew the "last post" at Chunkai when a man died. They had to stop it - there were so many, the bugle was driving men insane.

Chunkai finished their sector some time ago, that sector was in <u>No 2 Group</u>. We believe they were very well organised and had got things going. They said that it was a good camp. I would love to get down there to join my old friend Bill Ackroyd. Our Medical Officer here was a Dutch Naval Officer. I thought I would ask him if he could get me on the evacuation list when I had my next bout of Malaria.

Date unknown:-

Touch wood I was keeping fairly well bar for the malaria. I got the attacks quite frequent. At times I went a month no trouble, at other times I only went a fortnight.
  Thank God we could get the quinine, it kept it at bay for a while.

We knew that quinine had an awful taste but it was our only hope against the dreaded fever.

I was afraid a lot of the men here did not take it. They were issued with it but then hoarded it to sell to the natives. Each tablet would fetch 15c to 20c. The money they got they would spend on food to fill their empty stomachs, or buy tobacco. They were so foolish.

The Medical Officers kept telling them that failing to take the medication to combat the fever would, without warning, at some time attack the spine and brain - otherwise cerebral malaria. We knew that hundreds of men had died in this manner when the camps up country had had little or no medical supplies whatsoever.

We had known of men who had robbed our own hospitals of quinine which they had sold to natives at a very big profit. If caught, these people would have been shot, they were putting their own comrades at risk. We knew that it was every man for himself but not to this extreme.

At last I had found out the correct date. It was, I had been told

10 August 1943:-

How time had dragged along. I thought it was nearing the end of September.

We were now having to feed with the Australian Cookhouse. Quite a lot of men had been sent down south. This was the usual daily diet:-

Breakfast:-
Salt peanut pap (a mess tin full).
Dinner:-
1½pts dry rice, pork and bean stew. Sometimes a rice cake (kind of rissole).
Supper:-
1½pts dry rice. Good thick veg and meat stew and always two rice cakes.

One would not give this diet to a pig at home.

This cookhouse also turned out a queer kind of jam. It consisted of pumpkins and grapefruit boiled together, or perhaps pumpkin and limes.

They also experimented to make a custard. It was made with rice flour and eggs or egg powder. It helped to give the rice-rice-rice and more rice a better taste.

Mrs Beeton had nothing on this place!!

The Japanese had made a purge, they had a blitz. They had banned all except the butchers from the butchers shop. We had to start work. They were demolishing the old huts, these were to be replaced with new ones.

There were many different tasks for the works parties. Some went into the jungle to cut bamboo, the tasks were to cut and carry back to the camp fifteen lengths on a trip. Doing two trips before lunch and two after. When the job started, we carried only five lengths per trip -so much for fairness.

Other gangs ripped down the old huts and prepared the sites for the rebuilding. The old buildings were infested with rats, we thought nothing of killing twenty or thirty in a day and quite a few got away. So this was what we had been living in. It was a wonder that we all hadn't had typhus. A lot of the rats we killed were infected with the disease. One could tell by the fact that the males had great swollen testicles. This slowed them down when they try to get away, they were killed and burnt on a big fire.

The Japs had also started gardening parties, trying to cultivate parts of the jungle. The task at first was to clear the undergrowth and the bamboo thickets. Trees had to be felled. It was very hard work. After a week or two, we started to plant Chinese radish, onions and cabbage, would it all grow??
A few months before, the Japs issued some of us with rubber boots, similar to the ones we used to wear at the seaside. The big toe was kept separate from the others. They had got to the stage they were useless. I kept them tied on with string. We tried our

best to protect our feet from the bamboo thorns that caused so many leg ulcers.

A few days before, an English lad was caught with a young Thai girl. She was from one of the barges that brought supplies up the river to the camps. It is believed that one of the Japanese guards was trying to get friendly with her but to no avail. When he caught the young lad, I guess it upset his ego. He took him to the guard hut where he was given a severe beating and released after two or three hours. A day or two later he was caught again with the same girl. He was supposed to have been having a sexual relationship with her in an old hut by the river. This I doubt very much on the rations we were having. It was the same guard that caught him the first time. He was beaten and taken to the guard room again. It was terrible what the guards did to him, they tied a long string to his penis and pulled him around the camp. I cannot tell you what else was done to him. Poor lad was set up as an example, if any of us were caught, the consequences would be even worse. He was released after a day or two. The next day he was found dead on the railway line. The Japs said that he must have been a suicide victim but those who had to go and recover the body said that it was too clean a cut - he must have been beheaded. One will never know.

Two men were found stealing from the Japanese store. They were taken to the Guard House, a rope was tied around their necks, cards were hung on their heads "I am a thief". The guards got the band out such as it was, fell these men in behind. They were marched around the camp, the band played most of the time "Colonel Bogey". We sang the Army version "B******s and the same to you". We were all cat calling and laughing. The Japs thought we should have booed the victims, it was quite uplifting for them.

I AM A THIEF

As I have said before, I had the Japanese store under surveillance with a view to helping myself to an item or two.

I had one very successful expedition. I found the door open, I just walked in and acquired a large portion of dried fish, known at home as toerag. In the camp, we called it banjo fish because of its shape. I took the fish back into the camp and shared it with the others. One could not keep it too long, or the guards may have sniffed it out.

A few days after this episode, I thought I would have another run out to see what I could find. No-one would come with me to keep a lookout for the Nips. (This is where I miss my old mate Bill Ackroyd). I got in through a hole in the wall (the wall was only atap). I had a good look around, all was quiet. My eyes fell upon a partly used tin of pig fat, so very handy for cooking I thought. Yes, I would take charge of it, it was only a quarter full. So I made my way to the hole, I listened, there was no sound. OK lets go, I got through the hole. I looked and my eyes fell on two puttee covered legs and brown boots. Yes! you have guessed, it was a Korean guard. He beat me up and took me to the Guard House, where I was welcomed by flailing fists and kicking feet. I took quite a beating, I was tripped and pushed over and kicked again. One must never stay down. Oh to retaliate just once but one must hold on. A platform was then taken out of the Guard House and I was made to stand on it, my arms above my head holding the tin containing the pig fat. I was there for about six hours in that position. Every time I lowered the can onto my head, I was prodded with a bayonet up the backside. As the working parties went past, they said the placard around my neck read "I AM A THIEF", they all shouted out "you thieving bastard Blackie". The Japs thought this was good. It gave me quite a lift up. Tomorrow I may be shouting at one of them on this box. As darkness fell, I was allowed to go back to my billet, with the guard Corporal telling me that I was a no goodee soldier - no goodee man - pinchy pinchy soldier. This is a mad hole.

THE BURIAL PARTY

The death rate had been very high in this camp of late. The cemetery was growing in size all the time. The gravediggers were kept very busy. It had been said that a few days before 25 were buried in 24 hours. It was a terrible waste of life and good men, surely somebody would have to be punished for the treatment we had all had to endure.

A few days before this, I was on such a burial party. Four of us had to go to the hospital and bring the bodies to the cemetery and bury them. The grave was only four feet deep, the ground was sandy. We carried the poor souls on bamboo stretchers, the bodies were covered in rice sacks. We lower them into the grave, the padre said a few words of blessing etc. The rice sacks had to be recovered to cover others coming later, they also had to be recovered for another reason. A few weeks before, natives came out of the jungle at night, dug up the bodies, stole the sacks or blankets that covered these poor souls, then dashed back into the dark jungle leaving the bodies outside the grave exposed to wild animals etc. No-one else wanted to get down into the grave to recover these sacks - so I did. They were only young lads about 21/22. I shall never forget that task, or the looks on their faces. In death, one looked so at peace, the others I think died fighting to the last. The thing that made me sick, was as we were bringing the bodies from the hospital, we saw one Japanese guard and he saluted in respect. A great shame they could not show a little respect before this happened.

A NEW GAME FOR LITTLE MEN

Anyone caught stealing, or any other misdemeanour, then the victim was made to raise his hands above his head and stand against a tree with the tip of his nose just touching the trunk. If he moved away just a fraction, he got a bash on the back of the head. The results - bleeding noses, bruised heads and black eyes, much to the delight of these sadistic little men. Would we ever get a chance to beat them up??

OUR WONDERFUL DOCTORS

We had nothing but praise for our wonderful allied doctors. They were all worthy of their profession with the medicines and equipment at their disposal. During this last month or two, they had performed operations here in this camp. To see men coming into this Tarsao camp from up country as the railway neared completion. They were in terrible states, you would think they were all going to die very shortly but, within a few weeks, they were up and about.
Colonel "Weary" Dunlop, an Australian Doctor had performed brilliant operations, so many leg amputations. Tropical ulcers were the cause, a cut from bamboo and the poison got in and massive ulcers were formed. Gangrene set in - the only cure was amputation. These operations were carried out in the most primitive conditions. Very little anaesthetic was available. The op table was a bamboo structure under an atap roof surrounded with a big green mosquito net to keep the flies at bay. As we passed, we could see the surgeons performing. When an amputation had to be carried out, the meat saw was brought from the butchers room. These ulcers were terrible things. I had seen mens legs, the flesh just eaten away to the bare bone, the whole of the shin eaten away.

Some who had lost their limbs had had artificial ones made of bamboo. It was amazing how they got around, it was all clever stuff.

Even these fellows were not excused work. The Japs found them odd jobs like rolling their cigarettes or repairing their boots. The spirit of these men was terrific, they were an example to us all.

The huts were almost finished. A lot of parties were being evacuated down south to Bampong and Nampladok, the base camps, it was supposed to be great down there. I wished I could get down with all my old friends.

It was now the end of August 1943.

I had not written anything for some time. Life was much the same everyday. Hut building, cleaning camp, cutting bamboos.
6 October 1943:-

Here we were all looking forward to being evacuated down to camps in the south.

Two Sappers (including me) three Gunners and three Gordon Highlanders had been detailed for a weeks work up north on the line. We had to catch the train in the morning. None of us knew what was in store for us!!

7 October 1943:-

First thing that morning, we went to draw rations. Fish, rice (200lb sack), 30 stinking fish, 3lb sugar, 50lb beans and 2lb salt. Quite a good ration for one week!! Or was it being a longer job?? It had set us thinking. We could never trust a Jap, cunning little sods, they did pull some queer gags.

The Jap who was supposed to take us north failed to turn up, so we had to wait till the morrow morning.
We asked the Japanese if they could supply us with quinine to last us while we were on this mission. They said that they would think it over.

8 October 1943:-

A Jap came this particular morning to collect us. Before we left, we were given 200 tablets of quinine and a few other odds and ends of medical supplies. The Jap said "Japan very goodie ka"! All the stuff was marked "International Red Cross". You would have thought the little man was giving us out of his own stock. I wonder how much had been pilfered from us.

9 October 1943:-

On joining the train, we found that there were a lot of Australians going up north as well. They were put off at a station. Their work was to cut down trees, which had to be cut into logs about 3ft long, stacked by the railway line and loaded it on to the tenders for firing the engines as they came up and down the line. All these engines burned wood. I did not fancy their job at all.

It took us 24 hours to get here along the rickety winding old track. We had been put off at HINTOCK STATION.

We were told that our job would be to fetch water from a spring about two miles from here. We were expected to carry eight gallons between us and to make four trips a day. The Japs bathed in this water. The bath consisted of a 65 gallon drum, stood on end, the other end was cut out. It was then placed upon stones, a fire was lit underneath - hence a Jap bath, this was how they all bathed.

We had no hut to live in, we slept beneath the trees. After a days work, we had to cook our own meals, most of the time we ate boiled rice with a bit of stinking fish. We did not even get a bit of jungle stew.
None of these Japs could understand English and they did not want to try to understand the Japanese that we spoke.
The oil lamps that they burned in their billets would not burn one night and they came in to our area, woke us up and knocked hell out of us.

We tried to keep a fire burning at night to keep snakes and other animals away, as we did not have a lot of protection.

20 October:-

We were getting a hell of a time with these bastards, nothing was ever right and they kept beating us up for the least thing. Quite a lot of our lads were on the way back south from up near the Burma border. The railway had joined up with the others coming in from Burma at the Pagoda Pass, thank God.

27 October:-

The weeks work we had come here to do was lasting out and we had been here three weeks by this time. We had had a bit of good news, these Japs had told us that they would soon be leaving us as they had to go up to Burma to fight the British. They told us they would kill all Engerish Soger. Well I wished them all the best - perhaps a good 25 pounder shell shared between the six of them, a nice chunk each.

Later that afternoon, the Jap Corporal came into our billet and my haversack was on the makeshift bed (we had by the way got a makeshift shelter built with bushes and leaves from the jungle). He picked it up and turned it out, I had hung on to a small photo album that I had brought out from home. He looked through it all the time making Japanese remarks. I had one photo of my late girlfriend, he asked "wifeo wifeo"?. I said "Yes". Then he found the old photo I had of the King and Queen, well he went berserk, called me a fool and he jumped on the photo all the time shouting "King no goody ka". Then he gave me a slapping, he stormed out of the accommodation and threw the picture on the swill pit. So that was that. Later I retrieved the photo and put it back in my haversack.

CORPORAL YAMAMOTO'S CHITTERLINGS

28 October:-

Stores were sent up to this camp from down the line, food stuffs etc.

The Japs were issued with a live pig. They came into our compound and asked if anyone of us was a butcher. Thinking of food that may become available, I said that I was, so I was told that I was to kill the pig tomorrow. I had often thought of the poor beast since the operation.

30 October:-

The poor pig was killed the day before. It was still in a long bamboo strip basket, how long it had gone without food and water, I hate to think. One of its hind legs was hanging outside through a hole in the basket. I put a rope around with a clove hitch and tied the other end to a tree. I then took a large felling axe and I hit the beast on the head, it gave a squeal and went quiet. I took the basket off and cut its throat. We then slung it up to a branch of a tree and I slit it down the middle and disembowelled it, catching the entrails into two big oil cans. The Jap corporal told me that I had to skin the pig, he did not want it scraped. It took a lot of explaining as he could not speak English. My Japanese had been learned by the big stick method but we got there in the end. I then cut the carcass into four quarters. For once, our hosts were quite pleased, they took three quarters and gave us one hind quarter saying "Nippon Presento". I noticed that, at no time during the killing of the pig, did they come anywhere near.

We put our portion in an old disused oil can (four gallon) and soon had a fire going. Feeling very hungry, we kept the pot boiling until it was well cooked. It was time for our supper and a good nosh up it was. We even drunk some of the water we boiled the meat in. Well it was much too rich and we were up all night running to our bog pit, it was a way from the camp and we had the runs all night. Our stomachs were too weak to digest such rich food. We all tried eating charcoal and it worked to a certain extent.

The Corporal we noticed had kept all the stomach parts of the animal. the next evening he told us to take the entrails to the river to be washed, it was getting dusk and we set off to the River Kwai. We had two four gallon petrol tins slung on a pole. The Corporal had decided to have chitterlings for breakfast the next day. Two of us carried the cans, the others, one the candle lantern and the other the knife. I might add that the knife was one of the Corporal's prized possessions and we were told not to leave it behind. If we lost it, we should be for it!!

We had been working about half an hour on the none too pleasant task when we heard a very loud roaring in the distance. Then someone said "That's a bloody tiger - he has got scent of this stomach"!! We became more convinced as it got louder and seemed nearer. We had the runs the night before and, to tell you the truth, I felt a relapse coming on. Then, to make matters worse, the candle in the lantern burned out, we were in total darkness. We at once came to the conclusion that it would be better to get back to the station.

The stomach was strewn all over the river bank, so we scooped it up, slapped it into the tins and made off as quick as we could. I took up the rear position on the pole and pushed the man in front all the way up a very steep, muddy, slippery hill. I just couldn't say where I got the strength from. When we got to the top of the hill, the man who was supposed to be carrying the valued knife told us that he had left it on the riverbank. We were about half way back to the camp or station. We thought for a moment or two and decided that we should have to go back for it, it was better to face the tiger than Yamamoto - the knife was one of his prized possessions. We left the tin on the path and went back to search for the knife. We felt around in the dark and, at last, it was found and we got back to the tins on the path without incident but the animal was still roaring in the vicinity. We picked up the cans and set off once again at a good pace until we saw the camp fires in the distance. We took a breather and examined the contents of the tins, which revealed that, besides the stomach there was grit and ugly black mud from the river bank in them. Corporal Yamamoto would not be at all pleased with this, or us. What were we to do? Harry Goodall, one of the Gordon Highlanders, had prepared a bath for one of the Japanese that day. As I have said before, the baths were a 45 gallon drum with the end knocked out, which was part filled with water. Under this a fire was lit, the result - the luxury of a hot bath. This gave him an idea and we decided that our only chance was to creep into the Jap compound with the stomach and give it a bath and get out again and take it to the Japanese cookhouse (swegeba).

We got into the compound quite safely. The tub had not been emptied. Everything went to plan except for a sentry passing, he was from a detachment on guard at the bridge further down the line. They came around at times to talk to the Japs here. Sweat over, the stomach was returned to its rightful place.

Next morning Yamamoto was up early to cook his delicacy, he was an expert!!!

Harry Goodall happened to be on duty later that morning keeping the fires going in the Japanese cookhouse.

When Harry came back to our compound, he asked me if I knew the meaning of the word "sabon", I told him I thought it was Japanese for soap. Goodall went on to say all the Japs were eating the meal kept saying it.

We were offered the remains of the meal - I think this is the first time, probably the only time I have seen a prisoner refuse food. I have often wondered what would have happened if the Corporal had known the whole story. On the whole, we quite enjoyed it all.

The tiger? We never saw it but a panther was shot about three hundred yards from our camp and elephants tore the Japanese compound to pieces but they are stories for a later date.

As for Yamamoto, we were glad to see him go off to Burma shortly afterwards. I hope some chindit put a bullet through his skull.

It is now November:-

At last some materials had come up by train for us to build a decent hut to protect us from the elements, bamboos attap etc. We could commence building after we had done our daily chores.

The guards we detested had gone up to Burma, they all loaded their gear onto the train and set off. They did not look too happy at the prospects of going into action. As the train pulled away, they glared at us. I shouted "God save the King and bollocks to the Emperor Hirohito. I don't know if they understood.

JAPANESE CIVILIANS TAKE OVER

Just before the guards moved off, five Japanese civilians arrived and, with much bowing and ceremony, they took over the camp. Two were elderly, two middle aged and the other was quite young. The young one came into our half built hut and shook us all by the hand and bowed, he spoke a little english. He went out to join the others. We said "What the hell is going on"? We had already given them names, the older man "Boss", "Glasses", "Gertie", "Bullet Head" and "Satu". He had told us his name "My name Satu, Satu in english is sugar" and he laughed.

They had certainly changed things in this station. All the lamps had been changed and they had given us a brand new lamp for our hut. We had a coconut oil lamp before and it used to stink to high heaven.

They seemed to have plenty of money, tobacco, cigarette, medicines, quinine etc.

We had all had the usual bouts of malaria.

Mid November:-

One of our lads "Paddy" the Sapper had been sent back to Tarsao and got fever and dysentery.

Two days later the two gunners were sent down to Tarsao and they were quite ill. There were only five of us left here now. Harry Goodall, Titch Meldrum a Gordon Highlander, myself and another Sapper.

We told the Japanese about the tiger we had heard (if it was a tiger), so they had decided to light fires around the camp at night, a good idea, one never knew what was about.

"Glasses" and "Bullet Head" came into our billet one day, they spoke pigeon english mixed with their own language which we had learned a little. They told us about how they had fought in China in 1937 etc. I asked if they had been in Nanking, they did not give me a "yes" or a "no". I expect they knew all about it.

The old chap came into the billet, he had been given a captured Lee Enfield .303, he asked us to show him now it worked. It think he only had ten rounds. Harry Goodall said "Don't show him, he may bloody well shoot us". Then the old boy said "Animal come, I give you gun - you shoot", we all laughed.

Quite a lot of troops (Japanese) were going up the line to Burma and they had light tanks and guns and all types of Army equipment. I think the Jap had a manpower shortage, these troops were mere boys of 16 or 17 I guess. They looked at us in awe, I suppose we were the enemy. The train chugged away, I wondered how many of them would come back, maybe in little white boxes!!

Trains coming down the line at times were bringing back sick and weary POWs who had almost been to Burma, some I think had even come in from Burma. Some were in a very sorry state, human skeletons, racked with malaria, ulcers, beri beri and dysentery. Being so far up the line they had had very few supplies of food or medicines. We had seen quite a lot of "F" force on their way back. I saw my old Sergeant, Sergeant Strachino old George. I worked with him on a lot of the demolitions we did in Singapore. Blowing up the 15" guns at Johore Battery. They say 60% of "H" force had died along the line.

Troops had moved into two camps near here, they had AA guns on a big long bridge - there to protect it I suppose. There were about 25 soldiers in each camp, one above us and the others down by the bridge. The bridge of course was built with POW labour. Some of them when they visited this station told us that they had been in Burma. They did not worry us in any way, they did their jobs and we did ours. You did not hear them shouting and bawling at each other, there was quite a marked difference and they seemed to be more disciplined, were cleaner and even wished us "ohio" (good morning).

A lightweight motorised train went down the line this particular day. These trucks were adapted to run on the road or rail. The tyres came off the rims, they then jacked down, locked the steering and ran on the railway lines. They towed three or four wagons behind and they ran on the reinforced brake drums.

The four wagons this train was carrying had attap roofs, white drapes all around and in the centre was a kind of catafalque all draped in white, like a satin material, on which was neatly piled these little white boxes, like nine inch cubes. These contained the ashes of men who had been killed, we thought, in the actions in Burma. At the corner of each wagon sat an armed sentry. They were no doubt homeward bound. We were politely asked to bow in respect, we were then told that these were the remains of Nippon soldiers killed in action. The old man told us this.

20 November 1943:-

We had quite a lot of aircraft flying over here during the last few days and at night. It sounded like music in our ears. I hoped to God we would soon be out of here. I had been saying "another six months we shall be out of here". At night the fires had to be extinguished because of the aircraft overhead. Funny thing I never felt afraid, they were ours I guess.

22 November 1943:-

The old road camp had been re-opened at Hintock. There was a camp there some time before, six or eight months I think. It had to be closed due to heavy rains. During the monsoon the road was washed completely away and nothing could get in or out. Then of course the railway reached here.

The camp was manned by Australian POWs and was quite a big camp.

When the last occupants were in that camp, there were two graveyards, quite a lot of our men and Aussies died there.

The Australians had worked hard and cleared one of these cemeteries of all the undergrowth the jungle had taken the ground back. They could not find the other graves, all the little wooden crosses had gone, termites no doubt.

The Japanese in our camp had been in touch with the Jap administration at the Australian camp and arranged for any of us to go and visit the Aussies. I think this was quite good of them.

On our first trip we went accompanied by the young Jap Satu. He took us to the Japanese Sergeant so that in future he would know who we were. The Aussies told us that he was a good administrator and a good task master. If anyone became sick he was sent back to base camp - down the river at once. The camp was about three miles through the jungle and we went by ourselves. I had the forethought to ask the Japs to give me a letter to carry saying that we were allowed out to visit the other camp. Thinking of Selerang, I did not want any of us getting shot for trying to escape.
25 November 1943:-

Just a month now to Christmas and our second one in captivity. The trees were quite bare in places. With the trees being bare, it was easy to find ones way and to see things. On the way to the Aussie camp this day, we found skeletons in the undergrowth. We saw something round, Harry Goodall kicked it, it was a skull. We looked around and found quite a few skeletons with their belongings by their sides, poor devils, left to die in the unfriendly jungle and the ants had stripped the flesh from their bodies in next to no time. We thought they were people who were recruited to work here a lot and had come up from Malaya and Singapore - coolie people.

At other times, we had seen the very small barking deer or the odd wild boar and, of course, we always saw our old friends the snakes - big and small.

A train loaded with wounded Japanese soldiers came down the line and it had to wait in the siding for another train to come up the line before it could move off. I should think the train had been attacked by aircraft, as some of the wagons were full of bullet holes and shrapnel. Some of the wagons were of the flat type, the wounded were just laying on the wooden floor and their wounds had not been attended to. Some of them were in a very sorry state, I shouldn't have thought some of them would last much longer. Should we worry about them after what we had been through? I suppose, deep down, we were sorry to see them like this! Our Japs gave them water and cigarettes. Well! they started it.

30 November 1943:-

Quite a few of our aircraft were over here, the AA guns down on the bridge put up quite a barrage. The bridge was an all wooden structure about 70' high in sections and 200 yards long all built by soldiers of our army who were POWs. All the timbers were hewn out of the jungle, beautiful teak trees shaped into trestles, stacked one on top of the other. It was so strong it must have been able to take the weight of these great steam trains. They crossed at about two or three miles per hour. If it were put out of action, it would stop all supplies getting through to Burma. One could see why it was so well protected by the AA guns. Just of late the Japs had been tipping loads of earth over the sides of the bridge or viaduct. It would, in time, become an embankment and it would be more stable once the earth had settled around the legs.

10-12 December 1943?:-

The Japanese took us down to the River Kwai on this day. They asked me if I knew anything about explosives. I said that I knew a little. They then produced safety fuse, detonators and primers. They were a little different than our issue but the principle was the same but different in colour. When we got to the river, they requisitioned a small narrow long boat from the Thais by the riverside. Five of us were in that small boat, the Jap handed me the explosives and so I slung together primer, detonator and safety fuse. I crimped the det with my teeth and he then gave me the matches. I lit the fuse, let it go a second or two, then slung it over the side attached to a stone. It sank then exploded. After a while, the stunned fish came to the surface and we POWs jumped over the side to recover them. They were like big catfish with big whiskers on the sides of their heads. We did this about four times and we took a full basket of fish back to the camp, the spoils were shared equally between us. We had had a good day.

One bad point here, we were of the opinion that our rations were very poor and they were being looted further down the track, we knew nothing was safe with British POWs around. It was not only our rations but the Japs as well.

The Japs let us do most of their cooking by this time. Two of them were not very well - I think they had got a touch of the runs, early symptoms of dysentery. Harry Goodall and myself cooked the rice for all of us. We were quite experts as rice cooks. We did enjoy the fish that we caught a few days before. We fried it in coconut oil, after dusting it with rice flour, then we made chips with sweet potatoes. First fish and chips we had had for years!!

14 December 1943:-

Our rations came up from Bampong and, by the time it got here, all we had between us was two pumpkins. Both ours and the Japs had been looted as it came along the railway. All the vegetables had been stolen. Now we had started to loot the trains going up in to Burma. The Japanese here in the camp were feeling the pinch, the same as we were. So we had reached agreement that we must get food from the big trains.

Two o'clock in the morning, a long ration train came up the line. It had to pull into the siding to let one coming down pass by. Satu and the old man took the guards into their cookhouse for coffee. They kept them occupied while three of us looted the baskets of rations meant for Burma Jap Army. We got eggs, cabbages, mangoes, bananas and sweet potatoes. We did very well for the first time. The adrenalin was pulsing through my body. The downward train passed by and the driver, guard and escort bid farewell to our Japs amid much bowing etc. Then they were on their way. The next morning, Satu and the old man were very pleased with our efforts. All went into the cookhouse and we would all cook together now.

The Japs had just told us that it was 15 December 1943.

Just think, it was just ten days to Christmas Day. We were spending another here, I would never have thought it possible. I would have bet anything we should have been free by now. Perhaps another six months. We got little bits of news from the Aussie camp - some good, some bad. I just didn't know what to believe.

We heard beautiful music the night before, it was bright moonlight. I guess it was aircraft following the length of the River Kwai two guns on the bridge opened up with about four rounds. Our aircraft sounded totally different from the Japanese. It was funny how the mind worked when one heard those aeroplanes overhead. If only they could drop a rope ladder and lift us off to freedom to bully beef and biscuits. It was so easy to hallucinate - to dream impossible dreams. I think at times ones reason began to warp a little. It would be so easy to blow ones top.

We were all getting bouts of the old malaria. God only knew how many bouts I had had now - must have been at least eight or ten. Our quinine was getting very low again.

20 December 1943:-

The two younger Japs, Satu and Bullet Head were going down to Bangkok. They had both said that they would bring goods for our Christmas. On the return journey, they would call in to Tarsao camp and get our pay (we hadn't had pay for weeks). I had asked them to get us quinine and epsom salts. We were all so scared of the dreaded spinal malaria. We had only ten tablets between us, that was from a supply that was given to us by an English doctor who was with a party employed on line maintenance. We were lucky to get that.

The Japanese allowed us to go to the River Kwai to swim, it was quite a walk and we had no boots or shoes. The bottoms of my feet were like leather, we often said that when - a big when - we got home we would be able to go to the cobblers and get our feet soled and heeled, it would save having to buy boots. Anyway, the walk to the river was well worth the journey, we all enjoyed a lovely swim.

At times the Japanese came with us. On one visit to the river, Satu asked if I could swim the width of the river, I said that it would be easy, he dived in and swam, I followed and I then realised that I was not at all fit, when I got to the other side, I climbed onto the opposite bank totally exhausted - I was done in. After a rest, Satu dived in and swam back to the home side, I dived in to follow and I did about five or six yards and I got a terrible stomach cramp. I was in agony and I swam back to the bank and rested a while - then had another attempt but again I got the cramps. I waited on the bank to let the pain subside, then I saw six Indians swimming across the river with a big bamboo pole, they came to rescue me. They were from the river camp. I am sure that they saved my life, every time I entered the water, I got the cramps. I could never have swam back, it was foolish of me to try. The next day, I had a terrible bout of malaria, it was I think one of the worst attacks I had ever had, perhaps I had been sickening the day before. I thanked the Indians and Satu gave them cigarettes. I have often thought of them.

22 December 1943:-

The Australians had been very kind and had asked their camp commander and our boss, the old man, if they will allow us over to their camp on Christmas Day, as they were intending to have a slap up feed and a bit of a concert in the evening. Their commander said that it was okay and that we should be very welcome. Our old man would let us know the next day.

The two young Japs had arrived back from Bangkok and Bampong, they said they had brought us back a few things for Christmas. They had given us each a carton of 200 cigarettes each. They had brought back rations and our back pay $15 each, so between us we had quite a bit to spend.

Most of all, they had brought back a good supply of quinine. We were all getting the malaria attacks so this medication was a God send. I think at times these attacks were in some way affecting our mental state. We all said that, during the fever, we had terrible illusions. I guess I was the same but during the cold sweats and the shivering bouts, I heard the others talking gibberish. Oh God, how much longer ??

23 December 1943:-

Our boss man had given us permission to go to the Aussie camp on Christmas Day - but!! only three could go. Two had to stay behind in case of any emergency on the station.

Paddy was back with us again but had gone down with fever, so he was unable to go.

All our names were put into a hat and the old man took them out, I was lucky to be going, the other two Harry Goodall and Joe Goulding.

We were still having a raid or two on the upgoing trains. At anytime in the mornings when it was dark, we were getting quite a bit of food together now!! If the Jap soldiers were getting killed in Burma, they wouldn't need it, would they!!

Another train came down on this particular day, it was full of bullet holes and I should think it must have been attacked quite recently, the damage looked quite fresh.

A lot of our lads were on the way down to Nampradok, they were building a big camp there to look after all the sick who were making their way back. It was terrible to see these men, who were so happy and healthy before this terrible ordeal. Some had got these terrible great leg ulcers with no dressing on. To keep the flies off they had wrapped banana leaves around tied on with any old pieces of string, it was disgusting the way that we had all been treated. Geneva Conventions - Red Cross - non existent!

24 December 1943:-

The boss told us that we could all take the day off the next day - Christmas Day. The three of us would be going to the Aussie camp and we were looking forward to it, pity that the others were unable to go with us.

The Japs had given us two bottles of Thai whisky and a bottle of pineapple wine for the next day, we were okay for a tipple, as Harry Goodall said "A wee dram". They had also given us a chicken, a tin of Japanese biscuits, fruit and quite a lot of other stuff to eat. We just could not understand, these people were so generous to us, so different from the Japanese and Korean guards. To a certain extent, I was of the opinion that they felt sorry for us and the way we had been treated. The military had been real pigs to us, they had tried to humiliate and beat us to breaking point.

CHRISTMAS DAY - 25 December 1943:-

Well we were still in bondage - guests of the rising sun. The year before I thought we should have been out and free by this time.

The night before as I looked through the clearing in this jungle into the sky to see the stars twinkling, I let my mind wonder back, as was so easy to do. I thought of Ilsington Church, I would have been up early as all we choir boys were to attend the 7 o'clock Communion, then have breakfast at the sanctuary with the Rev J.D.H Patch and his wife. We would stay there listening to the wireless until the 11 o'clock Communion. I would get home at about 12.30pm. How we did enjoy our Christmas dinner, lovely carefree days.

I thought of you all at home and, from my heart, I sent you all my love and best wishes. "May our good God keep you safe till I return". This war had brought such sadness, we had so much of it here amongst and around us.
The Japs brought us our breakfast as promised, it was only rice. We found it so hard to comprehend their kindness, of course they were all civilians, just could not understand!!

I wondered what you all had for your Christmas dinner, then I guessed you were rationed with everything.

The three of us went off to the Aussie road camp and they did make us so welcome. We were made such a fuss of. The Aussies seemed such a happy crowd of fellows. They had a good Japanese Camp Commander. He tried to help them as much as possible.

To start their Christmas, he got them four yaks and they were slaughtered the day before, so a good meat issue was a great start.

We had lovely food, quite a blow out in fact with cakes and lots of other stuff they had prepared. Rice in almost everything but it was well camouflaged. A good meat ration and there were tins of milk, goodness knows where it all came from, it was brilliant.

To finish up they got their dance band together, goodness knows where the instruments came from or how they had concealed them till now, it was a good concert. I might add the Jap Commander was in attendance and he quite enjoyed it I think. I know we had a lovely time.

When it was time to leave, they gave us plenty of food to give to the other lads in camp who could not attend.

On our return to our own camp at Hintock railway station, the Japanese had prepared a meal for us. It was fried chicken, so we had another tuck in, it was delicious. We just could not understand the kindness of these Japanese, all the others we had been in contact with had been so sadistic and cruel. Now, to finish the day off, we turned to the wine. We took a drop each, a bit cautious at first but found it wasn't bad at all. The Gordons liked their wee drapee. The wine soon disappeared so why not the Thai whisky - awful stuff - it tasted like methylated spirit. I drew the line but the jocks finished it off. By midnight Harry Goodall gave us a sword dance and the Highland fling, he had two pieces of bamboo on the floor to represent the swords. Harry was quite good and by this time the Japanese had joined us. They quite enjoyed it as well to see this performance. It came to a close all singing "Auld Lang Syne" - us in English and the Japs in Japanese and so happily to bed in the early hours of Boxing Day. We all said it had been the best day we had had as Prisoners of War.

BOXING DAY - 26 December 1943:-

This particular morning we all awoke with terrible headaches and all had a burning sensation in our poor weak stomachs. I guess it was that Thai whisky. We were all wishing we had never touched it!

We had all been on normal duties here at the station.

29 December 1943:-

Satu San, the young Jap came into our billet quite a lot, he was very keen to learn English and, in turn, trying to teach him, he was teaching us the Japanese language. So we had a two way system.

We all said that he was one of the best Japanese we had come across, always very polite and asked if we were alright and did we want anything at all. He would try to get it for us. The other ones, they never bothered us at all.

We still took our trips to the river but I had never been stupid enough to swim to the other side of the Kwai again. When we were down by the river, it felt as if we were free. One could easily escape but where to? We were surrounded by dense jungle on all sides.

So the year 1943 came to a close - I had seen so much - torture and suffering, it had been a terrible year, none could ever be worse than this had been. I did not want another like it. Working on this railway we had seen the worst in brutality and human sadistic behaviour, the human suffering, death had been with us all the way. The sight of the burial of some of our best friends and the smell of the cholera victims being cremated, as the smoke blew across the camp at Lower Kanu.

When we had been able to hold a little church service, men had attended as many as were possible. Just a bamboo cross stood up in some jungle clearing. The padre could be Catholic, Church of England, Methodist, Wesleyan or Church of Scotland, no matter what denomination we attended. Just a crowd of unshaven, unwashed, ragged, wretched human beings, singing their hearts "Abide with me" and "The Lord's my Shepherd". Such a pathetic sight, all praying to God for deliverance from this evil place.

1944

1 January 1944:-

So in came a New Year - what was in store I wondered, God let us be free this year - please! please!

We had another good nosh up this particular day, the base of all meals of course was always rice. Today we had rice, pumpkin stew with a bit of meat. The Japs gave us what was left of their meal. We had quite a lot of chicken and mesau - a kind of Japanese pickle, with a lot of soya sauce, peanuts and a mixture of vegetables. It helped to get the rice down.

The night before the Japanese came into our billet to welcome in the New Year. They brought in some little cakes and sweets and two bottles of pineapple wine and gave us all a packet of ten cigarettes each. Well words fail me at their generosity, not one of us could fathom out why this was so with these people - the others had all been so brutal.

1 February 1944:-

Not a lot had altered here in this place, the routine was the same as ever.

15 February 1944:-

We had one or two air raids during the last week, the guns on Hintock bridge had been sounding off. We did not see a lot of the soldiers down there, I think they had to be on the alert at all times. This railway of course was a prime target for our aircraft. I expect they flew in from India. We all said our aircraft had a much sweeter note than the Japs.

20 February 1944:-

Our rations had been pilfered down the line, I expect the trains were robbed by POWs on the stations farther down. We would have to do something about it, or we would be slipping back and our weight would be dropping again. We all seemed to have put on a bit of weight. I think a lot of it was beri beri, all of us had swollen legs, then when we got up in the morning after laying down all night, our eyes were like slits and our faces were swollen. We had to get fresh vegetables or vitamin B. We would have liked to have got a few jars of marmite.

21 February 1944:-

A Japanese train came up the night before about 1.00am. It stopped in the siding to let another train down. Harry Goodall and I made a recce. No doubt about it, it was going all the way to Burma. The train had about eight steel wagons, the front ones were closed - we could not open the doors so we could not see what they contained. It may have been vegetables, tin foods or even ammunition but when we looked at the rear part of the train, all the wagon doors were open on the nearside and half open on the offside. Low and behold, they were full of baskets of live chicken and ducks. The baskets were of bamboo holding about six or eight chicken, the baskets were in the shape of lobster pots. Well a basket was too heavy to take off the wagon, even if it were not, the chickens would squawk and raise the alarm.

What to do? What to do? That was the immediate question.

23 February 1944:-

We had been in conference re the chicken baskets and how we could get one off the next train.

We had worked out a plan thus:-

We wanted to get a hook and a length of rope, that was the answer.

24 February 1944:-

We had shaped a large hook out of a piece of mild steel and had put an eye in the other end. We had taken a rope from one of the trains just the job - about 12 yards long.

We had put our proposal to the Japs because their rations were being stolen as well. They said yes we could put our plan into operation - but - not to get caught. So all systems go. We had to await another train coming up at night with the baskets aboard, just waiting our opportunity.

27 February 1944:-

Satu told us that a train would arrive this night but he did not know what would be on it.

Midnight: At last the train came, the doors away from the station side were open and there were chicken on board. Our plan went into action and the train was on the loop line, awaiting the down train to pass.

Our Japanese Satu and the old man invited the driver, fireman and guards into their quarter for coffee and smokes.

Now we went. We crawled across the line and under the train to the other side with our home made hook and rope. We got to an open door, put the hook onto a basket containing the chicken and attached the other end of the rope to a tree by the track. We then retreated to our billet. Goodall and I were both shaking with excitement and the adrenalin was pulsing again.

It was almost two hours before the down train came and puffed through the station blowing its hooter as it went. It disappeared around the corner and across to Hintock bridge.

It wasn't long before the train staff came from the bosses hut and much laughter and farewells were exchanged with much bowing and hat raising.

They took up position on the train, green lamps were waved and a blow or blast on the hooter and the train, amid much puffing and wheel slipping, set off toward the Pagoda Pass then into Burma. We waited until it was well on its way before emerging to find out how things had gone. We found everything had been a success, the rope had tightened and pulled a basket containing eight chickens quite clear of the train. We were very pleased, as were the

Japanese. We went into the jungle and built a pen in which to put six of the hens, we killed two. We hid the hook and rope well in the jungle and burnt the basket. None of us could be too careful, one never knew when or where the dreaded Kempei Tai would be in the area. They were of course the equivalent to the German Gestapo. We had had a very successful operation.

3-4 March 1944:-

Satu came in to our old hut this particular day and sat on the bamboo platform which was our sleeping accommodation.

He was asking about England and where in the country did we all live. He was interested in Scotland and he was learning English all the time. Then he asked about religion. Were we all Christians and we said that we were. He then went on to say that he had been brought up in Shintoism, the old Japanese religion. He was telling us the fundamentals and it was quite interesting. Then he told us that he had read a lot about Buddhism and was also a believer in that, it was he said "A good religion". Live by its teaching and you would lead a good life and be kind to everyone, to give and not to take. Then he told us that he had read about Jesus and Christianity - this did surprise us all. He went on about the ten commandments and said they were a good philosophy. He spoke about "Thou shalt not kill" and live by the ten and you will lead a good life. Jesus was a good man.

Later Satu told us that he was a student and was, I think, studying Engineering. He had not finished his studies. He was twenty years of age and would be going back to college when the war was finished. He did not want the war and it had upset his life as he was studying hard at the time when he was pulled away. He said that the old man was a good man and was a teacher. They were surely different than all the others we had encountered.

One day he asked me if I would give him a letter that he could keep to show the Americans or English when they captured him to say that he had been kind to us all. I told him that he had no fear about that, he would be treated well and be looked after by the Red Cross. I did not think that he would put up a fight anyway.

10 March 1944:-

Some Malays had been brought to the station, there were eight of them that had come up from Singapore. They told us that things were very bad down there, no food, nor work and conditions were very poor. They had been told that, to come here, they would get paid and there was plenty of work. Poor devils, I don't know how they would fare. I thought they would be employed in the jungle cutting down wood to fire the railway engines. They had been given supplies to build a hut for accommodation and they had built it on a nice piece of spare ground.

THE JAPANESE PLANTER IN MALAY

It was at about this time that this Japanese person came into the station. I think he was overall in charge of the Malays in the area re wood cutting and he asked me if I could speak Malay. I told him that I could a little. He asked me how long I had been in the Army and how long I had been in Singapore. I told him that I had been there since 1939. He went on to tell me that he had been an under manager on a rubber plantation in Malaya since 1937. Oh! I thought, another bloody spy. God knows how many of them were out there, getting prepared and putting things in order for the invasion. They had been planning for years!

The Aussies had re-opened the old camp by the River Kwai at Hintock.

We heard a lot of men getting off the train at Hintock Station. They were nearly all Australians and from the 2/26 Battalion.

The old camp had been vacated quite a long time before and all the huts were falling down, very little of the attap roofs were left. We could not see the Japanese point for re-opening this place again but stores were sent up and the Aussies were soon shipshape and tidy.

We were of the opinion that they would be employed on railway maintenance, as some of the line sleepers were getting a bit worse for wear and the white ants had eaten a lot away, as well as other termites.

We passed through their camp on the way to the river and we often stopped to have a chat with them. They were a good lot of chaps and we always had a bit of banter about poms and convicts, all in good spirit, a bit of give and take.

Paddy the Sapper had been sent back to the base camp at Nampradok. He was not very well at all and had malaria and dysentery, together with bad beri beri. We had all got swollen legs with this disease. If only we could get some good food with bags of vitamins, especially vitamin B.

9 March 1944:-

An Australian had been posted to us to replace Paddy.

The Aussie was named Wilkinson and he was from Sydney. He belonged to the 2/26 Battalion and I thought he would settle in with us very well. He could not understand why the Japanese were so friendly towards us all. He said that they may have heard news that we knew nothing about.

A train came on this particular day with prisoners of war going back to base camp. I saw two of my friends among them, Dolly Grey and Arthur Fenn. I asked Satu San if I was allowed to speak to them as they were two of my best friends. Satu spoke to the guard who gave permission. They told me that they had been at Niki, a camp almost on the border of Burma. They were both very ill with beri beri, malaria and leg ulcers. Satu came to speak to them and neither of them would answer and told him to f--- off. They said that they would never sink so low to become "A Jap happy". They then went on to say that they hoped that I had not. I told them that Satu had been most kind to us all and was most sorry for the way we had been treated during the construction of the railway. In the meantime, Satu had gone to his hut and brought back cigarettes and tobacco for me to give to them both. I passed it over to them and they both said that they did not want his bloody baccy. I could see that Satu was a little disappointed with their attitude. The train pulled away as they went down south to the base camp. They were both in a terrible state and they had banana leaves tied around their legs to keep the flies off their wounds.

As a matter of interest, I contacted them both after the War and they said that they had both enjoyed the tobacco and fags that Satu had given them.

ANOTHER RAID ON THE TRAIN

A large train came into the station at 1.00am one morning. The front was sealed and we attempted to open the steel doors but found it was impossible. The rear of the train we found contained baskets of chicken. So, once again, we attached the hook to the basket and the other end to the tree stump and again retired to our billet. We did not sleep awaiting the outcome. The Japanese guards and drivers were invited, as was usual, to the Japanese billets for coffee. Then we heard the train coming down from Burma, it would not be long now and it passed straight through the station after the key was passed over from the upgoing train. The crew left the cookhouse and took up their positions on the train. A blow on the hooter, a blast of steam, spinning wheels and they moved away to Burma. We waited until it was out of sight and sound. then ran from our billet to find that we had bagged another basket full of chickens. So we put them in the pen with the other two that were left. The Japanese were quite pleased with our efforts. I think the old man was a bit perturbed and tried to tell us that it was appreciated as they were also hungry because their rations were being stolen from the train as well as ours but what about the dreaded Kempei Tai (secret police). We had better be very careful. I think the old chap was as much afraid of them as we were, so, we had better cool it for a while. So we hid the rope and hook in the jungle quite a way from our billets.

THE OPERATIONS

We went to the river to swim one day and, as we passed through the Aussie river camp, we were told that a man was very ill with a strangulated hernia. He was in great pain and the doctor (Australian) in that camp was also a qualified surgeon but his instruments were in the base camp at Bampong. They had been taken from him before he came up into the jungle. He spoke to the Japanese Officer in charge of their camp and asked if his tools could be brought up to Hintock with a supply of anaesthetic and he would perform the operation. The Officer got in touch by telephone down the line. I would like to point out that Army field telephones had been installed between the camps and stations and they ran along beside the rail tracks. They could have the instruments if they sent someone to collect them. A volunteer was asked for. Several of the Australians volunteered, as did our friend Wilkinson. Wilkinson was chosen to go and he was given a pass by the Japanese Officer. He set off at once and cadged lifts from trucks and on the trains. He did quite well and returned to the camp within 24 hours. Another snag arose, one man was taken ill with appendicitis. The doctor said "Clean them both up - I will do the two as soon as possible". We happened to be passing through the camp, on our way for a swim in the River Kwai, where we also washed our clothes. Just as the surgeon was sewing up the appendix case he started to recover from the anaesthetic before it was finished - he was roaring like a bull. The doctor had carried out the two operations with the anaesthetic that was meant for just one operation. Even then, it was in short supply. Such was life in this jungle. That surgeon deserved a medal, as did our friend Wilkinson who ran most of the way to fetch those instruments. Our doctors were so good. Top of the list of course our beloved Weary Dunlop, a Saint to us all. Within a week, the two patients were up and about. I have often wondered if they got through to the end, they both deserved to.

THE ELEPHANTS GIVE US A CALL - AND A FRIGHT!!

We had heard the elephants in the jungle at odd times before but this one morning dawn was just breaking at about 4.00am. This herd was very close to our camp and suddenly we heard a crashing and screams of human terror. We dashed out of our hut to see the herd, the big bull leading. They were coming straight through the newly built Malay hut and the bull was more or less carrying the hut on its back - it was trumpeting as it went. The Malays who had been sleeping were dashing out from underneath. As the hut went past, I could see one man who was very sick still clinging to the side of the hut and he was terrified and screaming in fear. At this point, the old Jap appeared from their hut, together with the others in a state of undress, he was holding the Lee Enfield .303 rifle. He handed it to me and made meanings for me to shoot the big bull and handed me a clip of five rounds of .303 ammunition, to which I replied "No way". As the herd passed, I counted seven fully grown beasts and two babies.

As I mentioned, the Malays had built their hut on a nice piece of spare and clear ground, it was right in the middle of the elephant path.

The elephants went on their leisurely way, leaving the wreck of the hut on the railway line. None of the Malays were badly injured but greatly shocked by the experience. We helped them recover what was left of their hut and rebuilt it on another site.

A few weeks later, the elephant herd returned during the night but passed towards Burma on the other side of the railway track. We could see them pulling down and chumping at the bamboo thicket. It was said that the herds went well up into the Burma jungle, eating as they went, then they returned down as far as Bampong, the return journey took up to two months to complete.

THE GEISHA LADIES

We were now into April 1944:-

Satu San, the young Jap came into our hut one day very excited. I was quite surprised when he asked me if I would like to "jig jig girl". He went on to tell me that Geisha girls were coming to the camp the day after tomorrow. If I would like to jig jig he would pay the girl. With no hesitation, I at once declined his offer. He then went on to ask the other prisoners, they also declined. We all had a good laugh at the idea and said that we hardly had the energy to tie our boots up, leave alone have sex. Anyway the idea was revolting to think we could follow all the Japs along the railway. We wanted nourishment not punishment. The Japanese were all very excited about the visit of the Geishas. The next day, they all had the oil drum baths and spruced themselves up ready for the event. In the evening, the girls arrived and they were dressed in overalls, they and their baggage were helped off the train. There were four of them and they were all young. I should say about twenty years of ago. One may have been a little older, she was I believe in charge. There was much excitement with bowing and scraping in the greetings. They were taken into the big Japanese hut. After about two hours, they emerged dressed in beautiful kimonos with sashes, their hair all on the top - they looked beautiful. Night fell and they were entertaining through most of the night, we could hear the laughing and it was like Christmas to them!!

The next morning, the Japs did not rise very early, so we cooked up our own meal of rice and beans. We carried on with our chores.

At about 10.00am, the Japs appeared looking bleary eyed but happy. They breakfasted with the girls, strangely they had european type dresses on.

We were in our hut when Satu San entered with and introduced us to all the four girls. They were charming and gave us a packet of sweets each. One I thought had been crying, she was very young and she was shaking her head. I think she felt very sorry for our predicament. I do know that we all felt very sorry for them, what a life for those poor little devils. When they left the hut, they shook hands with us and the little one looked at me so sad and appealing and she started to cry again. That evening they got aboard the train towards Burma. How many nights of lust did they have to put up with at each station en route. They waved to us as they pulled away. We said "Poor little buggers - what a life".

Since the War, I had read a lot about the "Korean comfort girls". I think at times these girls were just that and did they ever get out of Burma alive. Did they ever return to their own kith and kin? Poor little devils!

Near the end of April 1944??:-

I did not quite know the correct date but this day I saw a British Army Officer and two Indian Army Officers being taken down the line under escort, they looked as if they had had a severe beating. All were badly bruised and bleeding. I went toward the wagon but was ordered away. One of the Officers was a Lieut/Colonel. Later I was told that it was Lieut/Col Anderson. He and the two Indian Officers were supposed to have tried to escape from captivity.

JAP TROOP TRAIN

One day we saw a big troop train going up to Burma, it was packed with troops and equipment. I say troops, some or most of these were only boys aged about sixteen and seventeen, just kids. Japan must be feeling the pinch. A lot of the soldiers were wearing straw/rope flip flops, just held on by a string between the toes. What were they going to be like in the Monsoon weather? They looked at us and pointed. We were English or American POWs. They would find that the picture in Burma was very different. No doubt they would be coming back down the line in those little white satin covered boxes.

It was now early in May 1944:-

Not a lot had happened of late, we had made raids on the night trains. A few nights before, we got another basket of chickens - I think about eight. We also got a basket of vegetables, yams, turnips and pumpkins. We had rations for a day or two yet. Every time we made a raid, the old Jap man in charge of the party got worried to death. He was always happy when he had chicken on his binto (mess tin). He came out with "engerish sojer nauty, nauty pinchy pinchy sojer" (Japanese punctuation). We noticed that they always enjoyed that which had been stolen. Our rope and hook method had sure been very handy.

JAPAN ON THE CARDS

Satu came into the hut one day to tell us that we were going back to a base camp in a few days time. The base camp was Non Pladuk. Satu went on to tell us that he thought that we would be going to Nippon (Japan). He said that he wished he could be going as well as he would love to see his dear old Mother.

After a few days, Satu came into our hut and asked us if we could write a letter for him to keep saying that he had been kind to us and had tried to help us, then when the English or American soldiers came, he could show it to them and he would then be dealt with more leniently. We told him not to worry, we knew he would be looked after by the Red Cross. Just to put his mind at rest, we gave him a letter as he had requested - I don't suppose he ever had to use it.

After two or three days, Satu came to me and asked if I would do him a great favour. I said that it depended on what he wanted me to do! He walked away and said that he would have to think it over! The next day he asked me if I would take a letter to Japan and find someone I could trust who would post it on to his Mother, as he would so much like her to know where he was and that he was alright. I gave it a lot of thought and came to the conclusion that, if he was going to England, I would like him to post a letter to my folks. "Yes - I would do that for him". The next day he wrote the letter and he gave it to me saying "God Bless you Brackie (L pronounced as R) but do be very careful". I hid the letter in my very old photo album behind one of the photographs. The

Japanese, when on a search, had often looked into the album, always threw it to one side. It was of no interest to them. Yes, I was sure it would be safe there.

We spent a few days with not much to do, we found that the Malays were doing most of our tasks and we were being relieved of our duties.

After a few days, a message was received, we were to be ready to pack and move out to the base camp at Non Pladuk. We had been told that it was a big camp with brand new huts, very large and airy. Well! God! I would be so glad to get out of this jungle but what would the guards be like down there? It was with mixed feelings that we all packed the bits and pieces that we had left. It was now about mid May 1944. We were to catch the early morning train that would take us down country the next day.

Satu came into the hut looking very worried and upset. He took me to one side and asked me to give him the letter back that I was going to take to Japan. He said that if I was searched and the letter found, we would both be in deep trouble with the Kempi Tai (secret police). We could both end up by being executed. I told him not to worry, it was quite safe in the album but he would have none of it, so I gave it back to him and he tore it up and burned it. It turned out that I was searched a number of times but the album was never of interest to the searchers.

The very next day, we left Hintock Station. We bade Satu and the other Japs farewell. In a funny kind of way, they were sorry to see us go. Who would do thieving from the trains now that the nauty pinchy pinchy soldiers were gone??

At this point, we were sorry to leave Satu, he had been very kind to us and sympathetic to our poor predicament. He was a friend, the only Jap I would ever invite into my home. I, or we, were never to see him or his like again. Under the circumstances, a gentleman, the only one that I ever met, before or after the move out.

We caught the early train and moved out to Non Pladuk. The train chugged down the line passed the camps where we had been. Some were overgrown and the jungle had claimed back what belonged to it. I wondered about the small cemeteries where our dead pals had been buried, would the jungle claim them as well?

The railway was a bit of a switchback in places, we passed one embankment where there had been a derailment and the trucks could be seen at the bottom of the gorge with their undercarriages in the air. We passed Kanu and Tarsao where we had had such a bad time last year (1943). Where we were beaten, starved and seen so many of our friends die of starvation and disease. We passed over the Wampo viaduct, 400 yards of a wooden construction taking these great engines and trains, 70 feet high in places, all built from timbers hewn from the jungle. The River Kwai meandering below. We passed through the cutting at Chunkai, cut through the solid limestone rock, 50ft to 60ft in height and 200 yds to 300 yds long. A great feat of engineering, if it wasn't for the loss of life. We were told to disembark at Chunkai Camp. The camp was now so big, it was full of sick who had been evacuated from the jungle camps up in the north. They said that there were in the region of 8,000 to 9,000 prisoners of war, mostly sick men, it was pitiful to see the poor souls getting around. A lot were amputees, some poor devils had both legs missing, caused of course by tropical ulcers.

We stayed at Chunkai for a day or two. We then had to catch the train again amid beatings and shouting. We were joined by other fit men(?) for Non Pladuk. We had a fresh lot of guards, a mixture of Japanese and Koreans. The railway was finished but their attitude towards us had not altered one bit, they were a lot of sadistic bastards. We were beaten and kicked toward the train and we climbed into the open trucks and set off towards Kanchana Buri. We saw how the area around had been developed in such a short time. The year before, most of this had been jungle, there were now marshalling yards here. A Jap troop train pulled out to go up toward Burma. The soldiers, mere boys, nothing like the ones that overran us in Malaya. We said that it was a pity to take them away from their mothers, they were all packed tightly together, not much better than we were.

We passed Tamarkan, crossed the Kwai Bridge and the Mae Khlong River, another great feat of engineering. The steel bridge replaced the wooden structure that was built in the early days. One thought so many of our friends had died for this. We noted the AA batteries were in place to defend this strategic target against our Air Forces. If this bridge were to be bombed, very little supplies could be sent to the Jap Forces in Burma.

We travelled through Bampong and the line continued toward Bangkok. At last we were herded off the train by the screeching screaming guards. With those, we picked up en route there were about 250 of us on the train. So this was Non Pladuk?

NON PLADUK

We marched into this big camp. It housed British, Australian and Dutch POWs. It was quite a big camp and the huts were much larger than the jungle type that we had been used to at Kanu etc. We had a little more room in which to move around. At first things looked more organised, the cookhouses, washing facilities and the toilets looked cleaner. We were told that we would not be here long as it was only a transit camp. The reception we received at the hands of the guards was not too good. We were pushed around and prodded with their rifle butts. They did not care where they prodded us. These guards consisted of a mixture of Japanese and Korean soldiers, one had to be very careful at all times not to provoke them in any way. As always, the Koreans liked to show their masters how good they were by dishing out punishment at times not called for.

We had a meal of rice and jungle stew, we sorted ourselves out into groups and then bedded down on the bamboo slats for the night.

The main cookhouse here cooked for all the camp, at meal times we had mess orderlies who went to the cookhouse and fetched the meals to the hut, where we stood in line with our mess tins or any recepticals to collect their rations. Some men had lost their mess tins, cups etc and they had to improvise by making containers from bamboo. We saw bamboo mess tins, bamboo cups and bamboo spoons. We had three meals a day here. We did not get a lot but just enough to keep body and soul together.

As we were workers in transit, we were paid with Japanese occupation money, we got about 10c a day. There was a black market here and we could buy the odd egg and bananas. The very small type which we called monkey bananas, it all helped to get the rice down.

One day, out of the blue, we got Red Cross parcels. One between twelve men. Not a lot but a luxury, we drew lots on what we got. The cigarettes were good in the camp, these were a currency, one could buy anything with cigarettes.

Mail was issued, some of it was a year old or even more. I joined the mail queue with high hopes, I had not yet received any mail, once again I was out of luck. Some of the poor chaps had got "Dear John" letters, telling them that their romances were over. Others were told that their wives had left them, I felt so sorry for them, it was a hard life. Engagements were broken and some were told of deaths in the family due to the air raids in the big cities. One of our lads I remember was told that their small village had had an air raid, not a lot of damage but the outside toilet at the bottom of their garden had been destroyed.

NAKHON PATHOM

We were told that there was another big camp at Nakhon Pathom. That was about twenty miles from this camp. It had been built to take a lot of the sick who had and were coming from all the camps to the north of here, some even from the Burma border. We saw some of them passing by here on their way to this so called big convalescent camp. Most were on stretchers made with old rice sacks and they were in a very sorry state. Some I am sure would never last a week at the most.

Here at Non Pladuk, we had had a medical inspection. I had been passed fit for Japan. I was about nine stone in weight and I had been allocated to a party. We were on standby to move by train back to Singapore for embarkation to "The Land of the Rising Sun".

In the meantime, we were employed on the cabbage patch, we were gardeners preparing the ground to grow vegetables for the camp, this included sweet potatoes. We were counted out in fives and had sections of 25 to 30 men to one guard. The guards changed each day and some were not too bad, others were real pigs (I do not wish to insult a pig). They were handy with the bamboo or sticks that they carried. One such ugly guard we nicknamed him "Satan". He was real horrid - a pig from hell and he had very dark skin. We were of the opinion that he was half Japanese and half of some other race, very very dark. We were hard at work one day on the cabbage patch and Satan was in charge of the party next to ours. One of the POW lads lost the head of his digger, the shaft had dried out so the head came off. He knelt down and was trying to replace it, Satan saw him and came charging across shouting and screaming. He snatched the digger from the young lad's hands while he was still in the kneeling position and crashed it down onto his head. He had more or less poleaxed him, outright he had killed him - he stood no chance. He was taken to hospital where nothing could be done for him, he was already dead. About a week or two later, we moved out of Non Pladuk to Singapore. Satan was still in the camp as if nothing had happened. This man should have been hung as a war criminal.

A few days after this episode, I had another very bad attack of malaria. I still got these bouts quite regular about every month, shivers, cold and fever. At times one would get hallucinations, the weirdest dreams and I thought I was going mad. Of course when we were sick, we got no pay. In some ways, food was not too bad here, and improvement on what we got in the jungle camps. A canteen was set up with the aid from outside sources. Sugar, fruit, eggs and tobacco could be bought if one had any cash. I still had my old watch, the spring was broken so I sold it on the black market for about ten tickles (now bhats). I then bought two eggs, bananas and a bit of hags bush (tobacco). There was always a fire burning in the camp on which one could cook. I had made myself a small frying pan from an oval pilchard tin with a wire handle. It was always kept quite handy in case of some windfall which could be stolen or otherwise acquired. All helped the rice go down, so life went on just awaiting things to happen.

I never returned to the cabbage patch again but was employed in the camp cutting bamboo for the cookhouse fires, digging new latrines and other general duties, so time passed slowly.

We had at times heard our aircraft overhead at night and the Jap AA guns had been in action - this was music to our ears.

Mid June 1944:-

Our party was told to be ready to get on the train, so we packed our kits, such as they were. I still had my old photo album that I brought from home. I often looked in it and wondered what you were all doing at home. Did you know the predicament we were in out here? A few days before, one of the Jap guards picked up the album, it had been resting on the bamboo slats as we were tidying up and getting our things together. He was very interested, he saw the photograph of the girl from Bristol and he asked me if it was "Wifo". I just replied "Yes" or "Hai". He said "Velly goodika" he had overlooked the photograph of the King and Queen. Remembering the beating that I had had the last time they had found it, I had a severe attack of butterflies but all was well.

Quite a few of the so called fit men were being sent back up the railway line, some as far as the Burma border to do line maintenance, or to cut wood in the jungle and pile it in heaps to fuel these great steam engines. Our Officers had protested but to no avail, in fact some had been beaten up for their efforts. Things did not alter a bit, we saw some of these parties board the train - a very very pitiful sight. They had that haunted look probably thinking "Would they ever return"?

Whilst at Non Pladuk, I made a few enquiries trying to find my old friend Bill Ackroyd but all to no avail. I was told that he may still be in Tamarkan. I thought that he may have been here. I had seen a few of my old friends from 41st Fortress R.E, we had all been split up and joined other groups. I had been parted from my friends from the Gordon Highlanders who were with me at Hintock. I was now with a completely different group.

We were standing by to go to Japan, the journey by ship across the China Sea. Which was the worse of two evils. These men going back up into the jungle. We thought it was to repair parts of the railway that had been bombed by our own aircraft, another hazard they would have to face. Then we thought of the submarines that may be awaiting us in the China Sea!

WE LEAVE SIAM
(land of smiles)!

We were told to be ready to march off early the next morning, it was I think about 18 June 1944 (cannot be certain). Our few belongings were assembled for the off.

We arose in the early dawn and had our rice pap breakfast. It was a beautiful sunrise as we fell in to be counted in our bundles of five (it was always fives). We then marched off to the cheers of the other camp internees. They wished us luck, all good lads, some we should never see again, all brave men whom one would never see the like of in our history. I have always felt proud to have known them, they were printed forever in my memory.

We arrived at the railway marshalling yard to find our train awaiting us. The same type of steel trucks or wagons that we came to Thailand in from Singapore. We were packed in at 32 or 35 to each truck, it was going to be once again a most uncomfortable journey in the boiling tropical heat. After a lot of shunting and buffeting about, we set off. The door on the inside of the track was kept shut and the one on the outside or station side was only half open, so air circulation was very limited.

Thailand was left behind and we crossed over the border into Malaya, everything looked very dilapidated. Bomb and war damage had not been repaired and all seemed to be in ruin. The population looked very dejected.

It was a terrible journey down the line, we were fatigued. Some had heatstroke and malaria was rife. Quite a few had attacks of dysentery and we were given very little food but, worst of all, in the intense heat of the truck we had very little water. So we were all suffering from dehydration and weakness. Every time the train stopped, men jumped on to the side of the track to relieve their bowels, with the natives looking on, I or we found this a very great humiliation. Men who had been so proud brought down to this level, then to be beaten on to the train with bamboo poles. We stopped at stations to take on food, the usual rice and stew. All the way down through Malaya rundown plantations and suppressed people, everyone looked so miserable.

At last we arrived in Singapore Station, it was early in the morning and we detrained. Trucks picked us up and took us to River Valley Road camp. The camp was run down and dirty, it was merely a transit camp for troops or POWs en route to Japan. I think of the Chinese girl that was bayoneted here when she tried to bring bread to the lads in early captivity.

The next compound was full of Gurkha prisoners, they had remained loyal to the Crown, not like some of the Indian regiments. Their white officers had been taken away and still had some of their own native officers. Their camp was being run in true regimental fashion and with discipline. At night we found stones dropping into our compound and they had messages attached which said "Johnnie keeps happy". "Tommy - we love you". Then there were stones with cigarettes attached or maybe other little treats. This gave us such a lift in morale. We remember they had been stuck there for two years. We thought that no wire made a prison for these brave little men from Nepal. No doubt about it, they went out after dark to visit the black markets and were living as well as could be expected. They were much too crafty for their Jap guards.

Whilst we awaited our boat to Japan, we were sent to work on the docks. We loaded ships with scrap metal, tin ingots, raw rubber, latex and other loot they could take away to Japan. We noticed old car engines, railings that had been cut up into scrap metal, even bags full of empty food tins. Whilst scrounging around, we found a rice store with other objects of interest such as flour and sugar, we must have some of that - we found a container!! The next day, I found an old tin, I thought that I could make a billycan to boil some of that rice. When we returned to camp, I hung it on my waist and entered the camp no bother. I cleaned it out and boiled water in it to make sure it was sterilised. At this point, I had become very friendly with an Australian, who was in the same working party. We found two sandbags, this would do for the rice the next day. We went to work as usual. During a lull in loading the boat, we went to the rice store and half filled the bags. We had quite a haul and left it in a secret place. We would go back to fetch it later at night when all was quiet. It wasn't too far from the camp. At about 2.00am we set off, once again the heart was pounding and the adrenalin was flowing. Sweat pouring, we crossed the river to our hide, all was intact and back we had to go. We crossed the river with the bags on our heads, then into the camp, all was well. We had quite a bit of rice now to cook the next day.

We went to work as usual, all was well, we got back to camp - now to cook our rice. There was a place set aside in the camp where one could start a fire to cook - but we had no fuel. The Aussie and myself went on a recce. Up by the Japanese compound we found an old door, it was green in colour. This would be ideal -

so - we proceeded to cut it up into firewood. We had quite a lot and we gave quite a lot away to other prisoners. We then started our cooking. Me with my brand new billycan, the rice and plenty of firewood, all was going well. Our two cookpots were boiling and the rice was almost done, we were looking forward to a good bellyful. It was at this point that the Japanese guard came along, he looked at the wood, then at us. With a mighty kick he knocked Wilkie's pot from the fire, he then went to kick my pot but the handle caught around his leg and the boiling rice shot out all over his leg, the more he kicked the more he got entangled in the wire handle and he went berserk, he was mad with rage. By this time, the Australian had done a runner, the Jap became free of the billycan, I thought it was about time that I departed so I went with the guard chasing me in hot pursuit with fixed bayonet. By this time, the whole camp was watching, which did not help. He chased me around the camp and was gaining on me. I had the terrible feeling that the bayonet was going to enter my back about the region of my kidneys. He brought the rifle down onto my shoulders and kept prodding me with the bayonet. He brought it down onto my head, I fell and he hit me with the butt of the rifle on the head. I do not remember any more. I awoke in the hut and the Medical Officer was in attendance. I was shaking all over and covered in blood, the Jap had done a good job on me. I was patched up but was in severe shock. The very next day I went down with a severe attack of malaria. I did not go to work again at River Valley Road Camp. I lost my billycan - I lost my rice. The Aussie came in to see me and wished me well and he said "We crossed that bloody river for nothing cobber"! The door was green and was off the Jap Officer's mess for repair.

After the War, whenever I heard Frankie Vaughan singing his famous song "Green Door", I thought of this incident, not that I wanted to be reminded.

Singapore before its fall to the Japanese was a thriving city, with people working and rushing around. The Japanese came in and we saw flags (the fried eggs) flying from windows, the Indian Nationalist Party was rife, all cheering to conquering Army. I saw the INA burning a Union Jack. I was upset to see this. This great city was quiet, a suppressed population. War damage was left untouched and buildings were going to ruin. We saw nothing of Indian National Party. It was not the city that we all loved and fought for. I would be glad to leave it - but for what? We heard rumours of ships being torpedoed in the China Sea. We said that they would not sink ships with prisoners of war aboard!

3 July 1944:-

We had orders to be ready to embark in the morning, so we packed what kit we had left. I said my prayers at bedtime as was usual for me. I asked God to keep us safe on the ocean and the journey that lay ahead. We all knew that this was going to be no picnic. I prayed for you all at home and asked God to look after you all. Would I ever see you all again? I had a sleepless night, my mind was in a whirl. Deep down I thought I was a little afraid of the journey ahead, who knew what was in store?

Before leaving Singapore, we were told that landings had been made in Europe but who knew - we heard such stories all the time.

A JOURNEY INTO HELL

4 July 1944:-

We marched out of River Valley Road Prison Camp at approximately 5.00am and there were about 700 men. We were a mixed bunch of Australian, British and a few Dutch. We passed the gurkha camp, they cheered us and in their way wished us all well. I shall never forget their messages to us during our stay, such courageous and loyal men. To me, everyone a hero, they had stood by our flag, not like Captain Singh of the Sikh Regiments, they joined the INA and became attached to the IJA. Some of them even fought against our Army in Burma.

We arrived at the docks, three ships were tied alongside. We were split into parties for embarkation on to these dirty looking vessels.

Our party was about 400 strong to board the Hakasoka Maru. She was a dirty old and rusty coaster, about 5,000 tons, if that. The first 200 got aboard, up the gangplank to the rear hold. When they had disappeared down to the rear, it was our turn to enter the forward hold. We got on deck then down a narrow set of steps into the hold. We were crammed in and had to live on the cargo of tin and rubber with headroom of about four feet. The smell was none too pleasant, someone said that this ship had just brought Japanese soldiers across from Japan. They were now on their way to Burma.

Before we embarked, we were given a life support in case we were sunk. It consisted of a block of raw latex (rubber) with a rubber handle. The Japs told us that, if the ship was sinking, we jumped over the side and hung on to the rubber float until we were picked up. Some wag said "Yea, they will pick up the rubber and bloody leave us in the water".

We had about eight Japanese Army guards with a Sergeant. He didn't seem too bad, some of our party said that he had been up on the railway and had been as fair as he could be under his superiors.

We were shown the toilet arrangements and if we wanted to go to relieve our bowels, we had to climb over the rails of the ship and get into boxes about the size of a sugar box with one plank knocked out of the bottom. One looked down and could see the sea churning below, such was the toilet. We looked across at the ship berthed next to us, it was a wreck. The deck in the bows had completely gone and the body had been patched up and welded together. A large tarpaulin had been secured to the rails, it was the only shelter for the POWs billeted in the forward position where the hold was! The rear hold seemed to be in tact. Most of the POWs crammed aboard were Australian, poor devils. It appeared that this ship had been bombed, fire had completely gutted the fore part, it was just a shell. The Japs seemed hellbent to get it back to Japan to repair.

About eight men were picked out to assist the cooks who were civilians.

The crew were all Japanese of different ages, some old to very old, some only young lads. The skipper was an old hardened sea dog but looked to be a kindly man. One could never tell how they would turn out.

We were told to get below. The hatches were put on and there was very little light. It was so claustrophobic.

We climbed up onto the cargo to make space to put a bed down. There were tin ingots to the height of four feet, then on the top the rubber bales. There were short ladders to climb to our bed spaces. In the centre of the hold was a space where the food was dished out, that was a space of about four yards square. As the evening drew nigh, the engines were started and ran for a while.

It was a steam ship, burning slack coal. The brass plate on the side of the engine room told us that the ship was built in Glasgow. No doubt discarded by Britain but bought by the Japanese as scrap - they put it into commission.

We felt movement, that first judder told us that we were underway. Our hearts fluttered - what lay ahead?

We were out into the straits and there was a slight swell. The batons were removed to allow our food, rice, stew and a bit of mesau (a kind of sauce or pickle) to be lowered in wooden buckets, one measure of rice per man, about one pint of cooked rice and half a pint of stew. The mesau helped to flavour. About three batons were left off of the hold, so that we got a little fresh air.

We now bedded down for the night and went up on deck to relieve our bladders, we wee over the side. The sea was calm. Some men tried out the sugar box latrines. If it wasn't so pitiful one could laugh to see a mate sat in the box - just his head showing above the rail. Let's hope the ropes hold!!

So we were at sea. We picked our spots to sleep and I had got a place where I could rest my back against the side of the ship. I felt comfortable, covered up with a rice sack with my pack behind my head. I was soon asleep after saying a prayer.

We awoke in the morning to the shouts of the guards, we tidied up as much as we could. The breakfast was lowered in the buckets, dished out as before. One pint of cooked rice and a piece of boiled dried fish, a cup of very watery tea, if it was tea?

We were well out to sea, the old tub was rolling a little. The guards allowed us on deck a few at a time. It was so good to get out of the stinking hold. There were four guards on patrol, two aft and two in the bows. They appeared to be fully armed with bayonets fixed. An artillery piece, a field gun was lashed on a platform on the bows. When we were all below, the Japs did practice on this gun. Looking quickly around, we found that there were about twenty ships in the convoy with a navy escort of two destroyers and two frigates. They kept patrol around all the time rushing here and there. We noticed the Jap guards toilets were tethered on the stern rail, theirs were quite posh with doors, not like our sugar boxes.

With lack of exercise and the diet, we found that our bodies were beginning to swell, the dreaded beri beri was rife. Some were also going down with malaria, a few of the lads were being seasick and we also had cases of dysentery aboard. Buckets were placed in the hold for these poor devils to relieve themselves. The stench down here was nauseating with of course our sweaty stinking bodies. We found some of our men were becoming a little unbalanced in mind and were talking mumbo jumbo!

When we got on deck, it seemed there was always land in sight. We plodded our way through the islands of the Philippines.

We complained about the sanitary conditions, a deputation of our officers approached the Sergeant in charge, the guard and the skipper of this old tub. They gave permission for half of us to go on deck to bath, a deck pump was put into action and it pumped salt water through a large fire hose. With this we hosed each other down, oh dear, this was paradise. We played around like kids at the seaside and we dried off in the sun. Then we went below to let the other half have their bath. It was I suppose the best the Japs could do for us in the circumstances.

The night before we were all below and it was just getting dusk. We had had our evening meal and the batons were pulled over the hold for the night. The alarm sounded. I was in my usual position against the ships steel side. We could hear the destroyers hooting, then we heard the depth charges exploding in the sea, each one gave a ping on the side of our ship. Then we heard louder explosions, which gave a thud to our hull, we all looked to each other in fear. We knew these were torpedoes exploding. Stupidly I said "A bloody tin fish will be through here in a minute"! One of our lads, with a look of fear on his face, said "For Christ's sake shut up you prat". I admitted I was wrong to say that, we were all on a very short fuse.

We had several attacks on the rest of the journey and we were always down below. The field gun was brought into action and we could hear the sharp crack as it fired.

Our officers kept a record of the ships that were missing from the convoy. We lost quite a few en route, some I guess had POWs on board.

We were still allowed on deck about 25% of us each session. The hold was now smelling terrible.

We continued our "cruise", very rarely were we out of land sight and we passed small islands right through where the Americans had fought such battles as Corregidor etc.

We now entered Manila and anchored, it was late evening when we arrived and light could be seen in the city. We did not sleep a lot due to the activity on the shore. It was terribly hot and humid and the batons were taken off the hold, so what little air there was could circulate.

There was much activity and the next day a barge came alongside. Some of us had to go into the bunkers and shovel the coal to the back, it was a very dirty job and lasted two days. The Japanese gave us extra rations to complete the coaling. Fresh water, fruit and vegetables were loaded on.

The guards were allowed ashore two at a time. We wished we could join them and feel free for a while.

The ship that had been bombed and burned out with the POWs aboard had a lot of sickness. We had heard that there had been two cases of cholera. One of the other ships was rife with dysentery and they had had a number of deaths, all had been buried at sea. These two ships were left behind at Manila.

We had to wait outside the harbour whilst the other ships took on stores, coal water etc. We had quite a convoy now as other ships had joined us ready for the "off". There is quite a lot of activity here, ships coming and going. One hospital ship and a liner, left with an escort.

We wondered what date it was, once again we had lost all count of the days or dates. Must have been mid July.

The convoy was now ready and in line, the engines started on full steam and the ships hooter blew and we were away well out into the China Sea.

We seemed to be making good headway when suddenly a typhoon hit us head on. The sea was pounding the bows and breaking over the ship, water had come in to the hold and the wind was whistling. We got the batons down on the hold and we were being tossed about like a cork, this storm had no mercy. Men were being seasick all over the place, some were sitting on the toilet buckets, others were laying on the floor of the hold being sick, this was terrible.

The storm lasted about six to eight hours and we were in a state. We pulled out into bright sunshine.

To break the monotony, our officers had tried to have lectures, talked about what may be of interest.

One young Dutch lad gave us a talk on Holland - my home - and the Dutch bulb fields and flowers growing in general. He was so interesting as he unfolded his story. He had to sit all the time as he had beri beri, he was a typical young Dutch lad and he had beautiful blonde hair.

Two days after that wonderful lecture, the beri beri claimed him and he sank into a coma and died. He was the first to die on that ship and he would never see his beloved Holland again. Most of us who could attended his burial at sea. He was sewn up in rice sacks, pig iron at his feet and he was slid off the stretcher into the deep. Our padre conducted the service. The old captain of the ship attended the service. He was very touched as we all were, I saw him wipe a tear from his eye.

We buried two others after that, both English lads. This was hell.

THE SWIM

We passed through the Luzon Strait. We passed small islands but did not see so much land now. We kept steady progress and we had had a few panic stations. The destroyers did quite a bit of depth charging and we heard the torpedoes exploding. When on deck, we saw ships were missing.

We were a few miles from Formosa which we could see in the distance. Our officers once again had been complaining about conditions. As we had to wait to enter the harbour, we were just drifting. The Japanese guards came out shouting their heads off

"All men can go for swim". A rope ladder was dropped over the side and I decided to have a swim. I climbed onto one of the toilet boxes and dived off into the so calm water of the Pacific Ocean. I enjoyed the thrill of the dive and I entered the water. I went down and down, this was a luxury and I saw the sun shining on the clear water and beaming down. Oh! to be free. I was completely nude, the water was cool - oh! such luxury. Then I thought "sharks" - I panicked and swam to the surface, suppose the Japs set off and left us in the water. I was full of panic as I swam to the rope ladder and heaved myself up, it was such an effort in our weak state. I made it to the deck exhausted and I lay in the burning sun to dry off, I fell asleep - I was so tired. Quite a lot of the lads jumped overboard and had to be helped back, they or we were all so weak.

We pulled into Formosa, dropped anchor in the harbour and stayed for two days. Some of the ships had been damaged. A few were being repaired in the dock, I didn't know if they had been bombed. More stores and water was taken aboard.
We left port and proceeded through the East China Sea. We were still under close escort, the destroyers were in close attendance. We had alarms and hooters blasting, it was a very worrying time for us all.

We still had very sick men on board, some were in a very sorry state. We travelled through another typhoon and it was a very frightening time. We had to contend with seasickness, dysentery, men were using the toilet buckets and the smell was terrible. Men were laying around all over the place, too weak to get on deck - God what we had to endure, let us get out of here! So it went on.

During the voyage, a gang of the lads tampered with the ropes holding the Japanese toilet to the stern rail. The toilet broke free during one of the typhoons that hit us and with a crash fell into the sea - unlucky nobody was in it. So be it.

At last the south island of Kyusho was in sight. We had had a lot of air cover these last two days and the destroyers were still with us but the convoy seemed to be breaking up, going to other parts I guess.

Then thank God, we were docking at Moji Kitakyusho, on the south island of Kyusho.

The date 10 August 1944:-

We had been on that Hakasoka Maru five - yes five - weeks. The only time I was off it was when I dived into the sea off Formosa (now Taiwan).

SO THIS WAS JAPAN (NIPPON)
(Land of the Rising Sun)

A motley crowd, we left the ship. As we got onto the dock, there were Japanese men in white overalls and wearing masks. We had to stand and be disinfected, they squirted the jets all over us, it stung our eyes and they delighted in squirting our faces, it smelt quite strong.

We crossed a small stretch of water on the ferry. We then entrained for Tokyo. We were squeezed into old carriages, the blinds were pulled down and all was in darkness. We pulled into sidings and were left. We were given a meal at one station, fed and watered, like animals in transit.

As we sped through the countryside, I think we were asking ourselves "Where would this all end"? We were all in the very depths of despair.

Then there was quite a stir, the Jap guards told us to open all the shutters on the left hand side of the train. We were told that we could pay our respects to Mount Fujiyama (Fuji-san) -the secret mountain. It was I must say a wonderful sight. We noted that the guards bowed in respect as we passed. What could Fuji do for us - not a lot I guess. From this experience, we worked out that we were about 60 to 80 miles from the capital Tokyo.

We arrived in Tokyo at about lunchtime. We were given the usual buckets of boiled rice, soup and mesau. We did look a bedraggled lot, tired, weary and most of all feeling filthy - our clothes in tatters.

We were paraded and split into parties, our party strength was about 200. As was usual we were counted off in bundles of five, then marched to the underground station. Here we were spat upon and jeered, remarks were shouted at us, it was very degrading. If only we could get at this rabble of all ages I noticed. I suppose we were the lowest grade of life because we were prisoners of war. We found the underground system to be very efficient and very up to date. We crossed Tokyo very quickly and were marched out of the underground station to another waiting train. After very rough handling, we got on board an old train. It had hard seats and very little lighting. The guards told us that we were going to Sendai, this was on the north-east coast of the main island about 300 miles north of Tokyo.

As we pulled out of Tokyo, we all lifted the blinds to have a peep at the surrounding area. We were all very amazed at the closeness of the building, people were living one on top of the other and because of the fear of earthquakes, all the buildings were of wooden structure. Every piece of spare ground was cultivated, in fact we saw some places where crops were in tiers, one on top of the other like giant trays.

We noted that the guards were old men, this made no odds as they were still very surly and quick to beat us if they thought the need be. One told us that he had fought against the Chinese. We had been travelling for some time, all feeling very fed up and getting tired. The train came to a stop amid shouting and screaming, we were told to alight on to the platform. This was not Sendai but Onahama, a small town on the east coast. We marched off with a new set of guards to the prison camp. The date was 13 August 1944. A meal was awaiting us - the usual rice and soup with a little meat in. The camp was occupied by Dutch POWs, a lot of them were Javanese. They were all around us asking where we had come from. They then told us that this was a coal mining camp and they all worked in the coal mine about half a mile away. The Japanese miners had been called up into the forces etc, we were to replace them.

The next day we were given the glass rod treatment. All our kit was taken from us and our aluminium mess tins were piled in a heap. No doubt this would finish up as part of an aeroplane. We were issued with a type of canvas jacket and trousers with ties at the bottom. Last of all we got our miners hats on which to fit the lamps when underground. Then we were given numbers - mine was 307.

At this point, I would like to say that I found that there were only two regular Sappers in the camp. Most of the men here were from the 18th Division, they consisted of the Norfolk Regiment, Northumberland Fusiliers and Suffolk Regiment and I think about four Gordon Highlanders, there were a few 18th Division Sappers.

We were shown to our billets and we had proper sliding doors with shutters on the outside. We slept on the floor with a kind of reed mat. We had about fifteen or twenty to each room, all of wooden structure.

So this was Onahama, Sendai BI. We were administered from the central camp at Sendai.

We had to parade to be counted, we were standing in line with the corridor of the hut awaiting the Jap to count us. Suddenly the whole floor started to shake, I looked through the open window to see a clothes line jumping up and down and the posts swaying. The most peculiar feeling in the stomach, we were experiencing our first earth tremor, a bit frightening at first. In the next year, we were to experience many more, some a lot larger.

We had had quite a pantomime here, the i/c guard came around, the senior man in the hut had to report to him speaking in

Japanese. Our Corporal was beaten for not being able to do this. So we all had to learn to speak in Japanese as soon as possible - we called it "big stick education". It was no better here than in Singapore or Siam.

We got down to sleep in the paper type of blankets. We were issued with one each, all of us were very restless. The reason being the rush floors we slept on were infested with fleas, also a few lice. The miners who slept here before must have been infested. Some of the other huts had a few crab lice. We told our doctor and he went to the Japanese camp commander and asked for DDT, or anything to destroy these pests, we were given flea powder.

14 August 1944:-

We were now paraded in our new numbers and split into three shifts to work in the coal mine. The shifts were 6.00am to 2.00pm - 2.00pm to 10.00pm - 10.00pm to 6.00am as was normal in shift work in the UK.

We now marched off to be shown the coal mine. Another Japanese hell on earth.

We marched out of the camp, the mine was approximately three quarters of a mile. On the way, we came to and were shown a shrine. The Japanese interpreter told us that we must always halt on the way to work at this spot and pay our respects to the spirits of the Japanese miners who were killed in the mine. Their ashes were laid to rest in this shrine and we had to ask them to protect us while we were in the pit. On our return to the camp, we must again pay respects and thank them for their protection during the time we had worked at the mine. We had to always remove our hats, face the shrine and bow. Before we had been there long, the shrine was nicknamed "Bazil" and the comments made when bowing was very funny, such as "Balls to Baz", "Get stuffed Bazil" and a lot of others I cannot print!!

We marched on after "Bazil" to the mine. It was an awesome sight. It was a drift mine into the side of the mountain. There were two shafts - one a fresh air shaft and the other the foul air. The air was drawn into the bowels of the mountain by suction fans and it circulated around all the shafts and was then forced out through the foul shaft. It gave off a putrid stale smell mixed with sulphur and it was like the breath of some monster from the inwards of the earth. After our introduction, we called this "Bazil's breath".

We were next shown the coal tubs, the winding gear, winches and cables. Nothing looked modern, I think we had gone back in time. All equipment was antiquated. Some of our number were from the Northumberland Fusiliers and had worked in the mines at home. They did not put us in good spirits by their remarks, none of us were too happy.

Food in the camp was much the same, rice, beans and stew. At times we got a little fish in stews and the ration of mesau (Jap pickle).

We were given a rest day, then to the mine.

HELL BELOW

17 August 1944:-

We had been in touch with some of the Dutch POWs, they told us that things were not too pleasant in the mine. The work was very hard and the Japs were very cruel and bad tempered, so it was not putting us in a very good frame of mind for coming events.

We paraded at 5.30am, had our breakfast of rice pap and beans and filled up with hot water. We took our bintos (these were enamel mess tins issued for the mine to keep the rats out). They were filled with boiled rice, approximately one pint, on the top was placed a spoonful of mesau (Jap pickle). This was to last us until we came out of the mine. Our next meal would be approximately 5.00pm.

We marched off to the mine, en route we paid our respects to the "Shrine Bazil".

We passed the mine office where we handed in our brass tally, mine was number 307. In return we were given our miner's lamps. At the pithead we were shown how to fit them, the lamp on the helmet and the acid battery fitted to a belt around the waist.

Next we were introduced to the mine boss, his name was "Honda". Through the interpreter he told us that we were expected to work hard and we would be rewarded for our efforts. He then hit each one of us on the head with his hammer, in other words "That is for nothing -so - do not step out of line". We all just stood there, looked at him in amazement and in chorus said "You bastard".
We were then introduced to our "sensies" (foremen). They were a sullen lot and we could see the contempt in their faces. We were now lined up beside the track leading into the foul air shaft, the trucks were lowered by the winch gear and we climbed aboard. The bell rang and we were on our way into the bowels of the earth. I had my back to the shaft as we descended and I watched the daylight at the pithead get smaller and smaller until it was only pinpoint size and then it disappeared. I felt shut in and sick - what lay ahead? At the end of the winch cable we got off at the first landing and from then on we had to walk. We went through dark and dank passages, through blast proof doors and airlocks. Then we came out on to a big tunnel, we walked in, there was plenty of headroom. We came to the face, it was in sandstone and it was the start of a new tunnel to another coal face. This was it, we had to dig into the sandstone face and shovel the debris back to trucks where it was loaded and taken to the surface. We dug and dug, the only light was given by our mine lamps. Some of the lads who had been miners in the north of England (the Northumberland Fusiliers) said that they did not fancy the set up, not enough props were used. They went too far without shoving up the roof. I must say this put us all in good spirits. We stopped approximately thirty minutes for lunch -"binto time" or "mishie mishie" - "yasume".

Our first day ended without mishap!! Was I glad to get out of that hell. We went back to the camp where a communal hot bath was ready for us. We stripped off and all got in together, this was the best part of the day - to get the grime and stink from our bodies. It was then supper time, one pint of boiled rice and a bit of meat stew with veg. I afforded myself half a cigarette then into the flea ridden snooze pit.

This was the routine for the first three months. There were accidents and beatings every day. We noticed the Jap bosses sent us on to the face to dig, they stood back where it was safe and threw stones at us to keep us going. We would dig into the sand perhaps six feet without a prop to keep the head up, it was very dangerous. One of our gang was killed by a fall of sand, it poured in like an egg timer - he had no chance.

Then came the shock, some of us were taken off the sandpit as we began to call it. We had to go onto the coal face. At times the seam was only four feet high, pit props again were used very economically, very few and far between. We were always in dread of the roof coming in on us. In army mining, all safety measures were taken and I had done quite a bit during my field engineering training - so - we were always in fear. The ventilation left a lot to be desired and we were always in coal dust and feared "black damp". We shovelled coal back from the face to the tubs, production always came before safety. If at any time the number of tubs produced began to lag behind, we were beaten and not allowed to stop for our food. We were not allowed to go to the toilet, so we relieved our bowels by jumping into the empty coal tubs. The pit was hell! Some men had dysentery, so it didn't leave a lot to the imagination.

At first we had a "yasumi" day every tenth day. This gave us time to clean up and wash our stinking clothes. All we wore underground was a "G" string or loin cloth, we changed underground. The Japanese miners had the tenth day off aswell. Then this was altered - we, on this day off, were sent to the paddy fields to plant rice and had to work with the old farmers and women. The freezing water was almost knee deep as we slushed around the mud. At least down in the mine we were warm, which was the worse of two evils?

THE SOYA BEAN FIELDS

If we on yasumi day did not work in the rice fields, we went to work in the soya bean fields, collecting the bean pods and, at the same time, stuffing these hard dry beans anywhere we could hide them. We tied the bottoms of our trousers and put them down our legs. We had to soak them well, then boil them, it did help to fill a hole in our empty stomachs.

CLEANING OUT THE BENJOS

The toilets consisted of long deep concrete trenches stretching between eight or ten cubicles. On some yasumi days this was another task that had to be carried out. We were given an open topped barrel with rope handles attached. These barrels were filled to the top from the contents of the latrines and two men threaded a big bamboo pole through the carrying handles. We then carried them to the Japanese gardens where the contents were ladled around their plants. We worked until the latrine trenches were empty. This I found to be the most revolting task of all. On wet days, we slipped on the hillside tracks, the contents slopping over ones person and clothing.

WINTER COMES

It was now about December 1944 and the Siberian winds were beginning to blow across Japan. These were freezing cold and ice was forming on the edge of the stream that flowed through the camp. We noticed too that icicles were forming on the water tank that supplied the cookhouse with water. It was so cold in these winds.

We had overcoats on the shelves in our billets but were not allowed to wear them, they were there for show only. Our clothes consisted of one canvas jacket, one pair of canvas trouser, one singlet, if you were lucky and one Jap happy loin cloth. We marched to work in these clothes, it was freezing. In January and February, we marched through two feet of snow. The boots were of canvas with the split toe, the big toe kept separate from the others. It was a relief to get down underground in the warmth of Bazil's breath. After a shift underground, we came to the surface and got outside the cold, it almost stopped one's breath. It was good to get into that hot communal bath to soak one's aching body.

THE REAPER CALLED AT NIGHT

Due to the very cold at night, most of us got close together and used our two blankets to advantage - to keep warm was the main aim.

I agreed to share with a soldier from the Norfolk Regiment. We had a goodnight smoke, I said my prayers to myself. We wished each other "Goodnight - see you in the morning" and went off to sleep. When dawn came we were woken by the guard. I shouted to my bedmate "Come on - time to get up". I had no answer, so I shook him, no response - he was dead. God knows how long I had been close with my arm around a dead man. By this time he was stiff, we could do nothing for him. The doctor came and he said that he had died from pneumonia in his sleep. My God, what a shock to me and our room mates. We all went off to the mine that morning feeling depressed and sad. We lost quite a few in this way in the months to come, casualties in war, their reward, their name etched on a memorial of war in some town or even little village - the supreme sacrifice.

Sickness had become rife, a lot of colds and coughs and dysentery kept coming to the fore. I am glad to say that I had not had any relapse of malaria since coming here. Some men had, I kept getting the trots and a bad cough, this winter was a killer.

We were in the dining hall one evening when a young soldier collapsed into a heap on the floor, lucky for him our Medical

Officer, Captain Bartlett got to work on him. He gave him first aid and brought him around, he had had an attack of cardiac beri beri. We, I think, all had beri beri to a certain extent. Our legs swelled during the day and, at night, our faces and eyes swelled.

Christmas 1944:-

We had our Christmas 1944. It came and went, our officers told the camp commander that it was usual to celebrate our Christmas. We were given the day off (yasumi). We were given a few apples and oranges. They also issued us with five extra cigarettes. Our padre took a church service for all denominations and we sang the carols and said our prayers. We were just flotsam floating on the tides of life clinging to our God, asking for help and our freedom.

That evening we had our meal with extra rice and cabbage stew. It filled a hole. So much for Christmas Day. On Boxing Day, we were back down in the mine.

TIME GOES ON INTO JANUARY 1945

It was still very cold here, the water tank was still frozen solid with ice and the icicles were about five feet long and about six inches in diameter. It was still bloody freezing.

On New Years Day the Japanese commander allowed us to have a Red Cross parcel. One parcel between six men. We drew lots as to what we would have, the luck of the draw - I had a full tin of bully beef. There were sixty cigarette, so we had ten each. In fact, I think we shared everything out and we had a slice of bully each on the rice. The next day we shared what the others had. In some of the parcels was a tin of mint flavoured tooth powder. After the other things had been used up, we put this powder on the rice, it gave it a different taste.

Date?? February 1944:-

We were on the way to the coal mine. One day, as we passed Bazil the shrine, some Japanese school children were on their way to the school. They stopped and looked at us as if we were from another world. One of them, a rosy faced kid of about eight years of age was stood there with a big apple in his hand. I was filled with intense hunger, I left the ranks and took the apple from him. He was so shocked he didn't move. By the time I had got to the pithead I had eaten the whole of that apple, the core and all. Such was hunger - I will go as far as to say, starvation. I have often thought of that incident and been a little ashamed of myself and my behaviour to that little boy. It was done on the spur of that starving incident. I went down into the mine and all through the shift, I was worried that someone would be waiting for me to return to the surface. I never heard anything about it.

FIRE WATCHERS

A duty had been brought into force. Two men each night would act as fire watchers from the hours between nine to midnight. One to the south of the camp, the other to the north. We just patrolled around and met at times with the Japanese armed sentry. The idea was to report any fires that may be caused by enemy bombers. We knew that heavy bombers had been seen over Japan. I had been paired off with a Sergeant from the Northumberland Fusiliers for this duty. We were on the same shift in the mine. This patrol we put to good advantage, as there were opportunities to steal. The main targets were the Japanese stores, their kitchens and the prize Jap Officers Mess. We got away with petty things like salt, sugar, mesau and the like.

One night I remember only too well. During the journey to the pit, as we passed the Japanese Officers Mess, we could smell the aroma of fried bacon. God our stomachs just rolled over and over, the hunger pangs were intense. I can tell you there was nothing worse to a hungry man than the smell of fried bacon and egg. I would have some of that.

This led to one of the most exciting episodes in Japan. I was on the fire watch, I had just reported to the Japanese sentry that all was well. He went off to the other side of the camp. I next found myself outside the Japanese Officers Mess. I tried the door, it was locked. To my delight, I found one of the windows ajar and I found I could open it wide. I pulled myself up and in, the light outside gave me a little light to work with. I found plenty of rice, salt, sugar and mesau. I wanted some of that bacon! I was in to a good search when I heard footsteps in another part of the building, they were coming towards me - I had to hide. The first place I thought of was under the big preparation table, it was a quick decision. I was under this table when the door opened and the light went on. A Japanese officer walked across the floor and I could see his jackboots and the sword hanging at his side. He went to the sink, took a glass and filled it with water and drank. He leaned on the table, put the glass down and walked across the floor to the door, switched off the light and went out closing the door behind him. I almost drowned in the sweat of fear. I did not get the bacon, or anything else for that matter. I never entered the Officers Mess after that experience.

This winter was taking its toll, about four men had died in our side of the camp. We believed a few of the Javanese dutch had also passed on, cause of death mostly pneumonia, bronchitis and beri beri. These poor souls were taken in a wooden box to the place up by the coal mine to be cremated. I had been up there once with a lad out of the 18th Division R.E. It was a very sad task. The padre went with them to give the last rites.

The water tank was still frozen, it was still very cold and one old Jap told us that the weather would not improve in any way until all the ice had fallen from that tank, it would then improve. The terrible winds from Siberia were killers. They froze one to the marrow. The only respite was down the mine, it was warm but wet with water pouring in through cracks in the roof. After the shift, we had to march back to the camp through two feet of snow. Our old rubber boots were now tied with string to keep the soles on. We had overcoats but were not allowed to wear them, they were left on the shelves in the billets, they were for show only in case a Red Cross representative should visit the camp. They say a Swiss Red Cross rep visited the year before we came here.

The Japanese pit bosses told us that coal production was down and we had to work harder.

They had brought in a new rule now, our shifts did not change on the pit top but down on the first landing. So the extra time in travelling down to the first level gave more working time on the pit face. Crafty swines.

It was not a very good quality coal, it was all loose and slack. It was taken to the coast and used by the fishing trawlers etc. It made a lot of smoke when burning.

Early March 1945:-

I had been in the mine now six months. I'd had a very bad cold and cough and was feeling very weak. I came off the 6.00am to 2.00pm shift and I felt as if I was passing out. The cough was very bad with a very sore throat and I coughed and brought up blood. I at once went to Captain Bartlett our Medical Officer and he at once took me off work in the mine, saying that the dust would aggravate my condition. I was put on light work in the camp and I did this for two weeks. The doctor told the Japanese that I was not fit to return to the mine again. I was to be found work on the surface. They did not agree to this but, after much argument, they relented. I was put to work tipping the coal tubs into the big coal hopper as they came up from the mine. It was still very cold but I was happy to be out of that bloody mine.

We watched the water tank, the icicles would almost disappear. Then the cold winds would come again and they would be back as big as ever. Well, this went on until the very end of March. It was now that we saw some of the beauty of Japan. The ice went from the tank and the beautiful cherry blossom came into bloom. It was wonderful, the harsh Winter over, and Spring was here. Cherry blossom, Japan was beautiful - it was the bloody people living in it!!

I was with a gang of men, we all worked together and life felt a little better but I still had the awful hacking cough. We all had beri beri. Some had relapses of malaria but I kept clear of that.

We worked in three shifts again as we did in the mine. The tubs came out of the mine full of coal, about eight to ten at a time and we tipped them into the hoppers, then rested until the next lot came up. We stayed in a hut with a good fire going, we had plenty of coal. The lorries used to come to the hoppers to load and take the coal to the fishing boats on the coast, there were quite a few drivers and we got to know them.

FISH FOR FAGS

When working in the mine, cigarettes were taboo. We were never allowed to take smokes out of the camp. When working on the surface, we used to take a cigarette in the seams of our jackets to have a crafty smoke in the little hut, we always had a lookout for the sensie, one had to be very careful.

At about this time, we had an issue of Red Cross parcels. One parcel between eight men, there were quite a few cigarettes available, as there were people who were non smokers.

One day one of the lorry drivers came to the hopper and he tapped me on the shoulder and asked me if I had any tobacco. I replied that I did not, at the time I thought perhaps he may have been a plant, to find out if we were taking cigarettes to work. Three days on the trot he asked me the same question. Then he said, through sign language, that he would give me one fish for one cigarette. Well, I though about it and came to the conclusion that I would give it a go. I took two cigarettes to work and I gave him the thumbs up. He went away with his load of coal to the docks and he came back with two big mackerel. So we exchanged, I gave him two cigarettes "Phillip Morris" I put the fish in my jacket which was in the hut. At times when we entered the camp, we were searched by the guards on the gate. So I put the mackerel down my trouser legs, one down each leg.

As soon as I got into the camp, I went into the mess hall and put one of the fish into my mess tin and put it on to the stove. A mackerel will cook in its own fat. It was smelling beautiful and I soon had an audience "Where did I get the fish"? "I'll give you two fags for one". So I sold the other fish for two cigarettes. I saw the Jap the next day and got a further two fish, which I sold for two cigarettes each. I had quite a business going in about a month. I was taking as many as ten fish into the camp, five down each trouser leg. I always sold for two cigarettes to non smokers. Some I gave to my friends, after all, I took the risk of being caught and beaten up. I then asked the truck driver if he could get eggs, hard boiled for carrying. He did get me a few, once again at one cigarette each.

At this point, I would like to say that I was always glad when yasume day came, this enabled me to wash my trousers and to get the fish scales off. They did smell a bit! I took fish into the camp right up to the end. In the end, one of my friends helped to carry some in.

MORE AIR ACTIVITY

We were seeing quite a lot of aircraft at very high altitude. These seemed to be giants and we saw the vapour trails. Later we learned that these were Boeing 17s and Boeing 29, B17s and B29s.

One of our number started to act as if he had gone a little off balance in the mind. He was very convincing and he even convinced the Jap doctor. He was sent to Tokyo under escort to see a psychiatrist and he was kept there in the hospital. At the time, we all said that the Japs would give him a needle or shoot him. He worked his ticket to get out of the mine and he got away with it.

We had forgotten all about him, when suddenly he appeared back in the camp. He had made a remarkable recovery. He told us that in Tokyo he was, as a mental patient, being looked after within reason, it wasn't too bad.

His reason for getting better was the bombing of that city (Tokyo). The high level bombers were dropping great numbers of incendiary bombs, then blasting the fires apart with high explosives. He said that it was not healthy in Tokyo, so he felt much better and he asked to be returned to Sendai.

The news that he brought back gave us a great lift up. We all felt that things were being done. IT WOULDN'T BE LONG NOW!!

After the cherry blossom had died away, we found that chrysanthemums began to bloom, they grew quite wild, most were coloured yellow but there were other colours, they were in abundance everywhere. We could see why the chrysanthemum was the national flower of Japan. We used to say that it was part of nature, these and the cherry blossom helped to brighten our lives. It was something that these bastards could not take from us!! The Japanese picked the heads from the chrysanthemums to make wine. They were also used to flavour different food. We picked the heads and ate them raw, we were careful not to be seen by the Japanese. After a while, we acquired quite a taste for them and found that it filled a hole in the empty stomach.

AIR RAID SHELTERS

About this time, orders came into being that air raid shelters had to be made to protect us from the enemy air attacks. On certain days, we were employed on this task. A tunnel was being driven in the side of a hill. Very little shuttering was being put in to keep the roof up. We thought the props were too far apart. When the tunnel had been driven in about twenty yards, I was outside getting props to be put in position and I heard a scream, the roof had caved in. One man, a Corporal out of the Norfolk Regiment was buried. We all dug frantically with our bare hands but to no avail. Eventually we got him out - the poor chap was dead. The air raid shelter project was shelved after that sad episode. They said that we could shelter in the mine.

Then one day one of the Japanese told us that when the Americans came, we would all be put down the mine and the roof would be blasted down on top of us. All traces of us would be lost forever.

(So we thought, the Americans were expected!!)

They did not want us to take up arms with the Americans to fight them.

After the War, we found this to be true, without doubt the atom bomb saved us from that terrible end that they had in store for us.

EXTRACT FROM THE BOOK "BANZAI YOU BASTARDS"
AUTHOR: JACK EDWARDS

When we returned, we found the old camp was in ruins, the huts were stripped. I decided to poke around in the rubbish left where the Camp Commander and Japanese officers had lived. Someone had made a major mistake and had not burnt the old camp records. We found them, soiled but intact and readable. After working all evening and well into the early hours of the next morning, our interpreters discovered among them the only surviving copy of the written order to massacre all POW's, if the allies had landed. Kinkaseki (Jack's old camp) will go down in history as the only place where this evidence was found. I was deservedly lucky and I am proud to say that I found it.

Below is a copy of the translation:-

Document No: 2701
(Certified as Exhibit "O" in D.c No: 2687)

From the Journal of the Taiwan POW Camp HQ in Taihoku entry 1 August 1945

(entries about money, promotions of Formosans at branch camps, including promotions of Yo Yu Toku to 1st Cl Keibiin - five entries).

The following answer about the extreme measures for POWs was sent to the Chief of Staff of the 11th Unit (Formosa POW Security No: 10).

Under the present situation if there were a mere explosion or fire a shelter for the time being could be had in nearby buildings such as the school, a warehouse, or the like. However, at such time as the situation became urgent and it be extremely important, the POWs will be concentrated and confined in their present location and under heavy guard the preparation for the final disposition will be made.

The time and method of this disposition are as follows:-

1. The Time:-

    Although the basic aim is to act under superior orders, individual disposition may be made in the following circumstances:-

    (a) When an uprising of large numbers cannot be suppressed without the use of firearms.
    (b) When escapes from the camp may turn into a hostile fighting force.

2. The Methods:-

    (a) Whether they are destroyed individually or in groups, or however it is done, with mass bombing, poisoning smoke, poisons, drowning, decapitation, or what, dispose of them as the situation dictates.

(b) In any case, it is the aim not to allow the escape of a single one, to annihilate them all and not leave any traces.

3. To the Commanding General:-

The Commanding General of Military Police reported matters conferred on with the 11th Unit, the Keelung Fortified Area HQ and each prefecture concerning the extreme security in Taiwan POW Camps.

As Jack says in his book "Thank God the Americans dropped the atomic bombs when they did". I am of the opinion that we should have been massacred. The Japanese it seems were well on their way to developing their own bombs. What could have happened then? I ask anyone to realise the mentality of our captors, our oppressors. Just ask any Japanese Prisoner of War, those of us that saw the brutal atrocities carried out by these people, I am sure you will get a true answer.

I am convinced that the Japanese gentleman that told us we would be put down the mine and the roof brought down on top of us and we would be lost forever, was telling the truth.

WE ARE NOW INTO MAY 1945

A party of Canadian POWs arrived in our camp, a lot of them Winnipeg Grenadiers were captured in Hong Kong, as regards to health, they did not look too bad, much healthier than we were. They told us that they had been working in the docks and had not been treated too badly -lucky them!!

They had their own shifts down the mine and they were taught about "Bazil" and had to bow etc.

They had been in the mine about one week when all hell let loose! One of the big Canadians was hit by one of the Japanese with a hammer. Without warning he retaliated, he had been a professional boxer, the Jap did not see him move, he was knocked out cold on a heap of coal with four teeth missing. It was some time before the other Japanese came to pick him up and get him to the aid post.

Then the military guards entered the pit and arrested the Canadian. He was taken to the guard house, there he was put in a small cell and was given rice balls and salt for two or three days. He was then taken before the Japanese Camp Commandant and all the POW officers had to attend the hearing. The Canadian Officer put in a plea of complete ignorance on behalf of the prisoner, in that at no time as POW had any of his men been treated in this manner and no-one had ever beaten them. In fact they had been treated with respect and as soldiers. The Commandant took it - hook, line and sinker. The Canadian had to apologise to the Commandant for his actions, which he did! He got about four days cells, rice, salt and water. If I may say "He was a lucky guy". In Thailand he would have been shot without question.

JUNE 1945

Our humdrum life carried on, never certain what was going to happen next or what was around the next corner. The Japanese were always so unpredictable, we could be pulled out of the ranks and beaten for no apparent reason. One of our guards (the frog) had a nasty habit. When inspecting the men, for no reason whatsoever, we would kick one in the shins. Another guard (one lung) had a nasty habit of practising his judo. For his own delight he would grab the biggest man and throw him down to the ground - a detestable man - he was always telling us he had fought in China. I asked him if he had committed rape in Nankin (he couldn't speak English I might add). He used to look for applause - he was a pathetic wimp.

Another of our guards was nicknamed "Glasses" - reason being that he wore thick lens, like the bottoms of bottles. He was a nasty character, always kicking people in the shins, or hitting one in the face with the heel of the hand.

Another old Jap guard, was quite a gentleman. He used to escort us to work and was very friendly with our Officers. At times he would pass the odd egg or two to them to give to the sick men. He was always kind to us, never a bully like the others. I have often thought that if Satu had let me bring his letter with me, I am sure I could have passed it to this old gent and he would have posted it to Satu's Mother. There were very few like him, we all I think liked him. He was given the odd few rations during the air drops later on.

Our interpreter told our Officers that he had played tennis at Wimbledon in about 1928 for the Japanese team. I hope he was a better tennis player than he was an interpreter. He tried his best but got words mixed up, we used to call him the "Japanese Interrupter".

JULY 1945

The air raid warning was going at least twice a day, we called it the "warbler". It was a beautiful sight to see the aircraft overhead, with their great vapour trails behind. We were now sure that things were happening faster than we knew.

Date late July?:-

I had a great shock one day. We were waiting at the pithead to be detailed for our tasks for the day and my stomach was not too good. I asked the guard to allow me to go to the benjo. To this he agreed saying the usual hurry ak-ko. so I went to the little hut and whilst sitting there, I heard distant gunfire. It seemed very rapid, an AA gun replied with about two shots then all was quiet. I left the little bog hut and I suddenly heard an aircraft. I looked and it was coming right between the hills at low level, it could not have been more than forty feet above me, it flashed by slightly to the right of me and I could see the crew inside. The star on its fuselage told me it was an American and I waved to it but it was gone. I then heard more machine gunfire, it was beating up the docks nearby. I dashed back into the pithead and shouted that I had seen an American aircraft and had seen the star on its side. I do not think they believed me but I knew - it made me feel right good!! The guard came at me saying "Americano!! Americano!!". He then started to wallop me, still I felt good.

After this the raids came more frequent. They came hedge hopping and the Japanese ran for their funkholes, no calls of "Banzai" now.

("Banzai" - their battle cry when they were on the attack).

Some of these planes we were later to find out were of the "Grumman" family - "Hellcats" etc.

We had feelings that it would not be long now. Either way, we should be killed off in the mine or be free. Some even talked of their plans for escaping to the coast and perhaps getting boats to put to sea and being picked up by American ships that should not be far off the coast.

I am sure we all had that terrible fear of being put into the mine, then the roof being brought down upon us. It was a very worrying time. To the end of July, the pattern was much the same, we had been employed tipping the coal on the three shifts, or preparing pit props to go into the mine.

WE HAVE A MEAT ISSUE

It was about this time that I think this story should be told. We were told that a meat issue had come into the camp, in fact, quite a quantity. One or two of us made it our business to have a look see into the cookhouse. We saw the meat being cooked. Quite plainly we could see the horses legs sticking out of the boiler, still with the shoes on the hooves. So much for the excitement of the meat issue. Probably some poor old nag killed in an air raid in the nearby town. In spite of the intense hunger, I did not eat any of the meat supplied in the next two days.

It was now August 1945:-

We saw single planes flying overhead at great heights, leaving their great vapour trails "Reconnaissance" we all said. They were giants, the like of which we had never seen before.

We had heard before that Germany had been beaten and bombed into submission. It had all been rumours but we were now convinced. Our Officers, we are sure, had known for some months.

Thursday 9 August 1945:-

The warbler went at 5.45am. No planes were in the area and we were about eight miles from the coast. At about 5.55am we heard gunfire. We had just finished our breakfast of pap and beans. After a while, we were all marched to the mine and into the fresh air shaft for shelter but we felt no fear, they were our planes. After a time, we took it in turns to ask the guard if we could go to the benjo (toilet). The s***house was just by the side of the mineshaft entrance. We heard gunfire, the planes were gunning the harbour and town at Onahama. It was sweet music in our ears. The air attack kept us all off the working shift. In the mine area we had four or five armed sentries. The Japs were scared as hell, at the least sound they ran like rabbits. We were kept here until 3.30pm and at 5.00pm the "all clear" goes - not a lot of production this day.

Friday 10 August 1945:-

The warbler went early this particular morning - 5.50am. We heard explosions in the distance, the Americans were dive bombing the town and harbour at Onahama again (it won't last long now). Working parties were made to dig deep water pits in the camp in case of fire etc. All the buildings were wood and paper and they wouldn't take long to burn away. Aircraft over all day long - the all clear was sounded at 5.00pm.

Saturday 11 August 1945:-

Went to work at 6.00am and started at 6.45am. Sensi told us to rest and take food (he was getting very kind) everything seemed very quiet. Air raid warning at 11.00am, we saw a B29 overhead and very little work was done on this day. Natterer was very quiet and Walternabi San seemed very upset.

Sunday 12 August 1945 - Yasume Day:-

We paraded at 6.00am for roll call breakfast - rice pap beans and plenty of hot water to drink to fill our empty stomachs, later we had an issue of four peaches each. We went for a medical test and I was almost 63 kilos. Two warbler alarms on this day and we saw two B29s, what a wonderful sight they were!! Supper was 16 to a bucket of stringy stew.

Monday 13 August 1945:-

One year ago today we arrived in this camp. The Canadians had been here for three months. The warbler went at 6.00am today and we went to work as usual at 6.15. The all clear sounded at 6.30am and by 7.00am it had sounded again and we were all marched into the fresh air shaft.

Nine Grummans Hellcats flew over on this day, what a thrill to see them, they were hedge hopping and so low that we could see the stars on the wings.

We celebrated our year here with pumpkin stew and rice again, a little more water in the stew and meals were getting shorter.

Tuesday 14 August 1945:-

Very thin watery stew, half binto of rice.

Worked at 6.00am - straight siren - no air activity on this day and we finished work at 4.00pm. Supper was 17 to a bucket of stew. Got no fags!!

Wednesday 15 August 1945:-

Very early on this morning from about 4.00am until 6.00am, there was the continuous roar of aircraft overhead, wave after wave. Everybody both inside and outside the camp were acting very queer. The Japs had a haunted look about them.

No one seemed to care if we worked or not. We heard that there was a special news broadcast for the Japs at 1.00pm. Rumour was that the War was finished. Our gaffers were very excited about things. "Something we didn't know"?

Supper was 18 to a bucket, ten cigarettes and five peaches!

Thursday 16 August 1945:-

Rations were the same, we were not called to work. So was this the end? I prayed to God above that it was.

Tom Partridge came down the hut passage way banging buckets together and shouting "We have had it boys, it's all over, yesterday 1 o'clock". We looked at him like fools and said "How the hell does he know"? Tom shouted "You sods don't believe me". Well after three and a half years of hell and rumours, who knew what to believe. All the same, I had a terrible shivering feeling in my guts.

After dark, one of the Nips in the camp told one of the lads that the War was finished. We all started to celebrate by lighting up and smoking a whole fag.

Friday 17 August 1945:-

6.00am - work parade but no one seemed to care about us. Natterer kept writing on our backs and saying "All Englishmen OK OK".

Orders came through for all prisoners to finish work and return to camp at 1.00pm. A Jap gaffer came at 12.50pm and ordered us to load a lorry with pit props to go down the mine, we took great pleasure in telling him to stick the props up his ****!! We returned to camp.

That evening at 5.00pm Captain Thornton told us that he and the other officers had been called to the Commandants Office and informed that the War was over. He also told them that we, the Allies, had bombed them with a big gas bomb and that they had no option but to jack it in - "A load of bullshit".

Captain Thornton then took over the camp as C.O and we were sorted out into our own Regiments and Corps and allocated a specific hut. Bill Hay and I were the only ones in this camp from 41st Fortress R.E, so we had joined the 18th Div R.E. I was mucking in with a lad from the 18th called Cyril Welstead. We had both been working quite a long time down the mine and on the surface.

A lorry load of apples arrived in the camp on this day and each man received two apples and ten cigarettes.

The Captain had asked the Japs for all the Red Cross food that they had been hoarding. It ran out at a tin of bully beef and a tin of salmon for every two men, so Cyril and I had a very enjoyable tiffin. During the night, the Japs tried to break into our food store, we now had our own R.Ps patrolling the camp.

I finished my day by getting down on my knees and thanking God for being so good to me, I hoped that he had kept all those at home safe and that Harry Howard had pulled through his ordeal in

Germany. I again thanked God as he was the only one who knew what we had suffered.

Saturday 18 August 1945:-

I had no sleep the night before, I tried to sleep outside to avoid fleas. Cyril and I spent the night talking, it was beginning to sink in that it was all over. We talked like excited kids and when we get back to civilisation, people would think we were crackers.

The Japanese Camp Commander had asked if we could keep the garden going, as soon we would be returning to the land of plenty and they, the Japs, would be left with nothing if we destroyed it. They should have thought about that in December 1941 when they stabbed us in the back at Singapore and Pearl Harbour. But as Captain Thornton said "We are British -we do not kick people when they are down".

Sunday 19 August 1945:-

We cleaned up the drying room to be used as the Coy Office and did a coal fatigue. We were issued with seven apples, which were welcome as rations were low. We were starting very slow and sure as free men. Thank God we didn't have to work, the meals were much the same only more watery.

Monday 20 August 1945:-

Once again same old meal, spiced up with fish to make it taste better but still it wasn't enough. Rumours around the camp were that we would soon be getting out.

Tuesday 21 August 1945:-

We had a sing song in the Canadian section of the camp. Change of menu for supper, we had fried sea cucumber, very nice.

Wednesday 22 August 1945:-

Nothing much happened on this day, no extra food and no fags. I sold a loaf of bread brought up from the village for five fags.

Thursday 23 August 1945:-

Not much happened again on this day, we lay around wondering what our meal would be.

Friday 24 August 1945:-

We had 15 minutes drill on this morning, the Japs looked on in amazement. I think we were showing off a bit with an act of defiance "You tried to kill us off but we have won".

The food was the same as ever but the gen going round was that we may get an air drop of supplies. Some of us thought it unlikely. Later in the day, we were told by radio to put out signs giving the position of our camp.

We tore down blackout curtains from the Jap Officers Mess and removed white sheets from their beds and made the sign:-

P.W

The signs were made and placed on the outside of the camp in a North, South, East and West position. They were quite large. Painted on the roof of some of the buildings was the number of men in the camp - 563.

Saturday 25 August 1945:-

We woke to find the weather had turned dull and dreary, not like it had been over the past few days, it made everyone miserable and we were all waiting for something to happen.

We were issued with British Army greatcoats, tunic and trousers, shirts and mess tins. The Japs had been hoarding this equipment whilst men had been dying from cold and pneumonia. The kit itself was in an awful state and we had to wash it all and hang it on the lines to get the smell out.

Having recovered my English mess tin, a pleasure indeed, I was outside cleaning it with sand and water when suddenly flying in over the horizon were 12 or 14 Grummen aircraft and heading right over our camp.

These were Americans!! They flashed past with such power not like the Japs charcoal burners we were used to seeing. Throwing my poor old mess tin into the air, I could not stop myself from shouting, screaming and waving out to the boys "My God we were free"!!

The aircraft dipped and turned and flew low over the huts waggling their wings in salute, we all jumped on the roofs of the huts waving anything we could find - shirts and blankets and then someone waved a tattered old Union Jack. Where he had got it from nobody knew and if he had been found with it during captivity, it would have been curtains but there it was - our own UNION JACK.

What a sight, it warmed the cockles of our poor weary hearts. Hearts that had nearly been broken, it was the British spirit that had kept us going. The planes circled above the camp for about twenty minutes, we couldn't let it sink in. I am sure that I will never experience such emotion ever again. We had lumps in our throats and were crying, only those of us who had experienced this would know how we felt. These Angels of Liberty swooped over the camp, dipped, saluted and departed.

We returned to our flea ridden billets, lit a stinking Jap fag and talked over the events of the day, we all thought and hoped that they would return before the end of the day. We lay down and rested for an hour but we could not rest, our minds were full of the air display and the wonderful feelings.

After about two hours, everyone began to feel let down and miserable, feeling that they would not return that day and that they would have to wait until the next morning. Then, like a bolt from the blue, we heard them overhead again and we dashed outside shouting and waving our tattered Union Jack and anything else we could find, it was all so thrilling.

Then one of the planes came in very low with its air brakes down, it was followed by two more and they suddenly dropped their bombs - six large kitbags full of food!! Followed by other odd packages. What an uproar, we were all shouting, laughing, cheering and crying at the same time, we had waited three and a half years for this moment.

A few of the Jap civilian guards looked on, they were the swines who had kicked, beaten and bullied us and now they looked like frightened rats unsure of their future.

The planes returned and swooped overhead and we could see the crews waving and taking pictures, they were so low we could see so much, then suddenly they turned and were gone.

Captain Thornton was so pleased to see all his men happy. He knew what we had had to endure during the last winter and he had had a great fight on his hands trying to protect us and those who had been sick. The Nip guards had been real pigs.

We were like kids at Christmas, 600 men who had defied defeat!!

One of the containers had gone right through the roof of the new dining hall, another was out of bounds and landed on a Jap miners house but the boundaries didn't stop us now and an excited mob got it back to the right side of the fence. The remaining containers landed on target on the parade ground. It seemed strange to think that a few weeks before these planes were dishing out death and destruction and now they were being used for the reverse purpose.

The containers were taken to the Officers Quarters. Captain Thornton then asked that three privates from the British Canadian and Dutch groups assisted in the food distribution, this was done to ensure fairness.

When everything was sorted out, we found newspapers, magazines, letters and notes from the crew of the USS Lexington - an aircraft carrier of US Navy. All the stores had been sent by the crew. A copy of one of the notes is as shown below:-

* * * * * * * * * *

COMPLIMENTS OF USS LEXINGTON

Dropped   V194
Pilot   Lt G.M Douglas
Gunner   J.J Jirash AMM I/C
Radio Man   C.W Freeman ARM 2nd Class

GOOD LUCK AND CHIN UP, WE WILL HAVE YOU OUT OF THERE SOON

* * * * * * * * * *

Amongst the supplies dropped were toothpaste and brushes, razors, soap and blades, in fact everything we needed to get cleaned up. The foodstuff dropped comprised of small boxes marked breakfast, dinner and supper. Each box was shared by two men, the boxes contained:-
Breakfast: Chopped ham and eggs
5 Army biscuits

Coffee powder
1 Milky Bar
2 sticks of chewing gum
1 cigar and matches

Dinner: Corned beef loaf
5 biscuits
Lime or lemonade powder
5 caramels
1 box of sugar
1 cigar and matches

Supper: Bacon and cheese
5 biscuits
1 bullion powder
Chewing gum
1 cigarette and matches
1 box of sugar

The Officers went without their tea in order that all the stores were issued. Cyril and I got a supper box, the chewing gum and matches were taken out and put with the other stores, we then drew lots for these items. I drew a toilet roll, razor blades and chewing gum. The best was that we got 17 cigarettes per man.

Though quite a lot of newspapers had been dropped, there were not enough to go round, so the Padre read the news to groups of us. Real news in black and white. We found that the news was quite a different version from what the Japs had been telling us. It appeared that it only took two bombs to finish them off, big bombs I should think but I didn't know what their content was.

We sat talking about the events of the day and we remembered that one of the planes had a package stuck to its undercarriage and tried many manoeuvres to release it before returning to the Carrier.

We sat, not afraid now to smoke more than one cigarette - we seemed to have plenty.

And so to bed, happy and smiling, God thank you for a wonderful day, a day we shall always remember, a very full day.

Sunday 26 August 1945:-

We did not sleep much the night before, whenever you woke you could hear voices and see the glow of cigarettes. Still we can all have a smoke now, though people were still saving the cigarette ends just in case, the last three years had taught us to be frugal.

There had been no sign of any planes on this day, being Sunday they may be at Church or having a rest day.

There was a Church parade that morning, I think most of the men attended. We had continued to clean the camp up and we heard rumours that the Red Cross were coming to arrange for our exit from this hole. I hoped they would come soon as we had some very sick men.

The Japs had brought up a few presents from the mine, a packet of toothpaste powder and a toilet roll, there was also some notepaper and cards.

The food had improved on this day, even the stew was thicker, the extras that were dropped helped.

Monday 27 August 1945:-

Early on this morning, three POWs arrived from another camp ten miles away from us. They had followed the Railway line, the Japanese mistook them for Americans. They told us that the War had finished on 15 August but they had heard no more since then.

They came out of the camp to find out what was going on, I would think that a risky business coming out like that, the Japs could have ganged up on them and bumped them off. One of the POWs was a Sapper from the 18th Div, the other two were Canadians. They told us that there were two Fortress R.E Sappers at their camp, Toodle and Reed.

The aircraft came very near this day but I think they had found the camp next to ours and were giving them a birthday treat.

That afternoon, three lads came in from the camp next to ours and told us that the planes had made a drop on them, in fact they had had a pleasant surprise. They had received 14 bags between just 150 of them, it was a much smaller camp than ours. They said that the Japs had played up hell when one of the bags had dropped through an outside building.

It appeared that the Japs who still had the part of the camp that belonged to the mine were taking rice from the storehouse and were selling or exchanging it on the black market. We all thought this was a sad state of affairs and should be stopped. The NCOs got together and went to see Captain Thornton but I don't think he knew what was going on. Anyway he told the deputation to clear off. They then went to the Japanese Administration and put their case forward. The rice issue was then increased to 705 grams, an increase of 35 grams.

Captain Reed and a Dutch Officer were to go to Sendia, the Japanese Headquarters for this area the next day. We also heard that General McArthur would be entering Tokyo the next day.

During the day, a lorry load of fresh fish arrived at the camp, mostly mackerel "Taxan astor" (plenty tomorrow).

Tuesday 28 August 1945:-

Breakfast: Pap, 14 to a bucket followed by two bowls of thick fish stew, some of the lads just could not eat it all, it was too rich for their stomachs and it gave everybody the runs.

This particular day, General McArthur entered this country. We were all wondering what affect it would have on us, we had great expectations.

There was supposed to be another air display this day, it was a lovely morning. I was writing this early because we had so much time on our hands. Everybody was getting very browned off with the waiting.

We were just cleaning the room when a shout went up "Here they come lads". Sure enough, there they were. They swooped around twice waggling their wings and made a drop, the time was about 8.50am.

Amongst the items in the drop were bread, meat, cigarettes and messages of goodwill from the crew of the Lexington. On the back of one of the message forms was written "See you guys in the States soon". We were asked to put message signs in the middle of the parade ground to indicate clothing, medical supplies and food.

3   Medical Supplies

11   Clothing

1   Food

We selected medical and food.

The bread was issued out and one piece fitted exactly into a mess tin. The bread was beautiful, just like eating angel cake we said. The first bread we had eaten in three and a half years, those long weary years of torture under the Rising Sun. We were all so excited, you just cannot explain that feeling of liberty.

Well dinner was over, what a meal, one and a quarter bowls of rice and beans, three fried fish, a large piece of cucumber and a piece of bread, all rounded off with a fag. I thought I'd lay down for an hour and try and sleep off the excitement. We were like a lot of kids getting this excited over a piece of bread. Before the War, we used to throw it away or feed it to the pigs. How the words at home had come back to me "You'll be glad of that one day my boy". How true, never again.

3.30pm:-

We heard planes in the distance and we all rushed out of our huts. Coming in very low were two four engined planes, "bombers" just cruising around. They were being led in by one of the fighters from the Lexington. They flew low enough for us to read the words POW Supplies printed on their sides. You should have heard the cheer that went up, we all rushed to the roofs shouting and waving anything we could find. They first dropped leaflets over the camp saying "Dropping supplies in one to twenty hours time".

Within two hours, they were back and we watched the bomb bay doors open, it gave one a queer feeling in the stomach remembering back to Singapore when we were being bombed. The feeling soon passed as we saw huge drums of supplies coming down on parachutes. They dropped outside the camp and we dashed out to bring them all in. The Japs were as interested as we were, if they could get hold of some of the stores they would have done.

We were disappointed to find that some of the parachutes did not open and that the containers had dropped dead weight and their contents were spilled all over the countryside. Some had fallen into the flooded paddy fields, we waded in to recover all we could, chocolate, milk, fruit, tomatoes and clothing of all descriptions. In the distance, we saw a Jap with his horse and cart, we confiscated it and loaded the supplies and returned to camp. We had recovered about 80% of what had been dropped and it was all in good condition. Some of the items were about a quarter of a mile from the drop position.

During the recovery, a Canadian caught a Jap pinching supplies from a dropped container (he had been a supervisor in the mine) so Canada let him have it in the mouth. He knocked a number of his teeth out - good on you mate, we didn't forget the coal face and the beatings we had taken.

We learned that the planes that dropped the supplies were B17s, we had never seen these machines before.

During supper we were issued with:-

20 Raleigh cigarettes, 1 box of matches, 1 big bar and 1 small bar of chocolate. We were advised not to overeat, as our stomachs were in such a weak state.

The supper was a bowl of rice and beans followed by a thick pork and meat stew, this was finished off by a small piece of chocolate and then the pleasure of using your own matches to light a cigarette.

Then to bed (the flea pit). We talked about the events of the day and thought of the next day and breakfast, eating was always our main topic of conversation as it had been for the last three and a half years.

We would never forget this day - 28 August 1945 - the day the Americans entered the mainland of Japan. I wish we had had a wireless set and listened to the Forces Network, it would have been nice to hear the military bands.

Wednesday 29 August 1945:-

We awoke to find another beautiful day. Most of us had little sleep the night before, one could not explain the excitement - we were back in the good life.

Breakfast was bowls of pap with fruit and real sugar, cake made with broken bread and a stew using all the damaged tins from the drop the day before. Another thick stew for lunch and, to round off our supper, we had a mess tin full of cocoa made with milk and sugar, biscuits and cheese and chocolate - what luxury. This was the real food we had been pining for.

Thursday 30 August 1945:-

What a lovely sleep last night, it must have been the cocoa and a contented stomach. We had been woken by the sound of aeroplanes, we dashed out dressed in shirt and shorts as they flew over. They came in low and dropped leaflets "Stand by, we are dropping crates". They then circled, came in low and dropped six or seven large crates inside the camp and two others outside the perimeter - they were soon recovered. All the crates contained ration packs, breakfast, dinner and tea and each pack contained 300 cigarettes. Having recovered the containers, we had breakfast including a large tin of peaches eaten eight men to a tin. No sooner had breakfast finished than the planes were back and dropping two more crates of tea rations.

How grateful we were to the Americans, they were sure looking after us. With each drop, we got messages of goodwill from the planes crews, it was all so thrilling.

Our Officers had returned from the conference I'd told you about two or three days before. We heard that the Red Cross would be sending us to Manilla. Later that day Captain Thornton informed us that we were now in complete control of the camp and that the Japanese had no say in any of the administration. We were to stand by to move out at anytime between 2 and 15 September 1945. A train would be brought up to the marshalling yards at the mine and await orders. There would be plenty of room, a seat for each man, we didn't know where it would be taking us but they said it would be a twelve hour journey. From wherever it was, we would then be flown out to Manilla.

The Red Cross would not accept the rolls list from the Japanese, so many men were missing or unaccounted for. We were told that when we got on the boat or plane, we would have to give our names and home addresses, next of kin etc. The American Red Cross would then radio the information to the British. I did hope that you at home would know that I was OK at this point.

This day was very sad, a young Dutch soldier died, if only he could have been got out quickly enough, something perhaps could have been done for him. It was heartbreaking to think that he had got this far and then had to die.

We heard that there were 45,000 POWs in Japan. 35,000 of whom were Dutch and 10,000 American, Canadian and English (I should say British). We were a very small percentage. By all accounts, this was the biggest camp in the area (Sendai) and it had been the worse treated with regards to work and food.

The two Officers who went to the conference told us that they had had a very good time. They had been waited on hand and foot, very different treatment from that the Japs had offered in the past, in fact the complete reverse. They had been guarded all the time in case of trouble from the Nips and they had had four seats on the train and their water bottles had been filled with sterilized water.

When asked by the waiter if he wanted rice or potatoes with his meat, the Canadian Officer had said "I'll have both - I'm damned hungry:.

The Japs had handed over 100 bags of rice to Captain Thornton. It was now in our cookhouse. They, the Japs, had been ordered to remove all their gear and stores from the camp, One Lung and The Frog (two of our ex-guards) came in with a two wheeled cart to pick up the stores. They had loaded up and were going out of the gate when one of our own MPs noticed what looked like a Red Cross box. They were stopped and made to go to the OCs Office. The cart was unloaded. On it was Red Cross clothing and food that should have been issued over a year ago. The store was then searched and found to contain medical and food supplies that these bastards had been using for themselves. The Japs were escorted to the front gate with nothing but what they stood up in, they were jeered all the way. In fact, I think they felt lucky to get away unscathed, they were told not to come back.

The Japs had to account for more than ten shiploads of Red Cross supplies that had entered this country but this was just a minimal detail to what they had to account for, the pigs.

We were not allowed out of the camp. We thought this was for our own protection, as no one knew the mood of the Jap population. On the other hand, we had a few debts to pay back to our old gaffers. I knew two or three I would like to meet - The Frog, One Lung and Glasses to name but three.
Friday 31 August 1945:-

Awoke this day to find it very cloudy and dull, I did not think we would see any planes on this day. At breakfast I exchanged half a bowl of stew for more rice, one of the lads was too sick to eat the rice, maybe the stew would do him more good. We had to start preparing our roll for home.

It had started to rain and I decided to do a bit of sewing on my tattered garments. It was still pouring with rain when we heard an aircraft. We looked out to see a B17 flying overhead, surely it wouldn't make a drop in this weather. We got back inside and continued our chores. Suddenly the plane was back again and, with bomb doors open, it approached and let everything drop on beautiful coloured parachutes. We didn't wait for orders, we dashed out in the pouring rain to recover a harvest of clothes, food and other supplies. We worked until it was all collected. We were all wet through and we put on dry gear and had a smoke. We were exhausted, we were so weak that I found my heart pumping. I think part of the trouble was the excitement of it all. After two hours, the rain had eased and another B17 made an approach and made two drops, then in came another plane and did the same. Five drops so far on this day. It was very hard work getting the drops in and under cover and the rain had started to pour by the time we had finished the task. It would have been lovely if the weather had been fine but we had a good time anyway. Hardly any of the containers were damaged, the parachutes had done their job well. A message on the containers told us that the planes were coming from Sipan - 16 hours flying time from here.

A container crashed through he roof of a house, a little girl aged 5 was injured with a broken arm. We took her to our doctor and he put a splint on her arm. We gave her chocolate and sweets. She was such a dear little girl and we gave her mother some of our food and cigarettes.

Sixty four chutes came down on this day, they were going to be cut up and issued to us. Those crates that were broken went directly to the cookhouse, that would mean a good supper that night.

We always seemed to be talking about food, that is how it must seem to you. Never heard anyone talk about having a good woman, like we did when we were well fed.

We had an issue of 20 Philip Morris, one box of matches, a packet of "Jelly Jojo" and one packet of "mounds" - what luxury.

Saturday 1 September 1945:-

It had rained all day and we called it a browned off day.

Saturday 2 September 1945:-

A great day in the history of Asia, the signing and settling up of the whole affair. The great Nippon Army was no more, they who attacked us with such treachery in 1940 were finished.

TRULY A GREAT DAY!!

I should have mentioned that the day before we were issued with clothing dropped on the previous day.
1 pair boots, 2 singlets, 2 underpants, 1 boilersuit, 1 hat, 2 pairs socks, 4 handkerchiefs, 2 towels, 1 windbreak jacket, 1 jacket, 2 packets cigarettes, 1 toothbrush, 1 tin toothpowder.
We were awoken on this morning to the sound of the giant engines of the B17s and 29 bombers. It was a beautiful morning and overhead were these four bombers. The first plane made its drop and, to loud cheers, parachutes of all colours opened and the supplies floated down to the rice fields of Japan. We dashed out of the camp like hounds after a fox. We had collected all the crates and boxes, including the parachutes before breakfast. The broken crates were piled on to barrows and brought into the camp.

Four cartons of cigarettes, tobacco (Bond Street), bars of soap, razor blades, toothpaste, chocolate bars and chewing gum, two tins of sea rations and a bottle of Multvits. God, how we had longed for these things in the past three and a half years. If only it had come a little earlier, how many would have been saved?

We were hoping that we could keep some of the parachutes that we had cut up during the day.

That night we had a picture show, it was not a success as the Jap projector kept breaking down.

We had three top rate meals that day, though we still clung to having rice, we had soups, stews, fruit and to go with the fruit, we had CREAM! I am sorry to keep on about food and what we had eaten but we knew what starvation was about and we had been looking forward to this so much. God knows every day was Christmas Day.

Sunday 3 September 1945:-

We had had a few more issues on this day, including five great big cigars - Winston would have been proud of them. What a sight to see, us smoking cigars - God what luxury. Some lit up and went green round the gills, they were a bit strong when you drew on them.

Not much happened this day. We were waiting for news of our move away from here at anytime.

General McArthur gave a speech and the Japanese, before they left the camp, had to leave the wireless set behind to enable us to be in touch with the outside world. This was all part of the orders laid down during the Japanese capitulation. The Officers had the radio in the Camp Office.

Monday 4 September 1945:-

A very good day it was this day. Plenty of kit issued along with a good supply of tinned food. We were told to stand by to move out of the camp, what a long time we had waited and how patient we had been.

All the kit issued to us by the Japanese was no longer required. It was a mixture of British, Dutch and other nationalities. We now had the latest American combat gear. We got rid of the blankets by selling them to the Japanese. In our hut we sold five blankets to one Jap (one we did not like, due to past experience) at 40 Yen each and made 200 Yen. Then we tipped off the main gate and, when the Jap went out, they took them off him. The next day we sold them to another guy, quite a profitable business.

We were all mucking in together in this billet and we had acquired quite a pile of Japanese money. We had no idea what it would be worth in the outside world. Some of us were thinking of going further afield outside the camp, hoping to get some chicken eggs and things of that sort, just think - a nice chicken.

We had some bad news this day, a B29 plane supplying food to the camps had crashed into a hillside. Our Officers found the wreckage that evening. Of the 13 on board, one of the dead was a girl. What a tragedy that, in bringing in supplies, they had to die. It was different when it was a bombing mission, it meant that 26 people had died in the past two days flying on mercy missions.

Tuesday 5 September 1945:-

We awoke to find a convoy of lorries parked outside the camp. The Officers found that today was supposed to be our moving day. We packed in haste, selling all our old and unwanted kit to the Japanese. We got 20 eggs and 60 Yen. Enough to buy potatoes with money to spare. We made fried egg and chips as a standby meal.

We were still waiting in the camp, the Grumman Hell Cats returned and dropped four large kitbags of medical supplies and more food.

Quite a number of prisoners from the local camps had been evacuated and were now stranded at the Onahama docks, that being the Port for Tokyo. We did not take any notice of the Japs and now we had no blankets, we had to sleep on flea infested mats, though we had dusted them with the American supplied flea powder.

Thursday 7 September 1945:-

We were still here awaiting further orders. In a broadcast this day, the Americans had asked us to stay put and they would get us out as soon as possible. The trouble was that there were a lot who could not wait and were trying to get to Tokyo. They hoped to get picked up and taken to transit camps.

We heard that Singapore had been re-occupied by the troops of the Commonwealth Army, what a great day for the old "Fortress". 7,000 prisoners had already been evacuated, 700 British were flown out the day before and General McArthur had ordered the whole Japanese Army to disarm.

On this day, we went out of the camp and bartered kit for food. We got 3 chickens, 30 eggs and potatoes and we also got onions, leeks, carrots and tomatoes. No sooner had we got back the hut was dining on roast chicken and mixed veg - beautiful!!

Friday 8 September 1945:-

At roll call on this morning, Captain Thornton, who along with the other officers had returned from HQ at 2.00am that morning, said that those at Onahama docks were being picked up today and that we were likely to move out the next day.

Though the weather was overcast and misty, we still continued to receive air drops of supplies and these, combined with our scrounging missions, mean that we ate well every day. We were gradually being weaned off our rice diet.

Saturday 9 September 1945:-

A very busy start on this day, coal trucks arrived at the mine sidings and by 6.30am we had been loaded onto open trucks and were off. The miners were out in force to see us go and some even shook hands. The moment that stays in the memory though is of the little girl with the broken arm crying as we departed. Her arm had been broken in the food drop.

We were all glad to be away from that stinking camp and the horrible coal mine.

The train was segregated into three parts - Canadian, Dutch and British. We didn't have far to travel to the mainline station where we were loaded onto a passenger train. My mind went back to when we arrived and how the Japs jeered and spat at us, now it was quite different. They bowed and were very polite and they couldn't do enough for us.

The train left at 7.30am and soon gathered speed. There were flags and bunting everywhere, it just seemed one blaze of colour. As we proceeded through the beautiful countryside, the wheels seemed to say "Going home, going home". Towards the outskirts of Tokyo, we passed Mount Fugi Yarma, a sight to remember. Tokyo looked different from thirteen months before, the American bombers had made a great job of it. The fire bombs and H.E had raised most of it to the ground, people were living in a barren waste and we felt no pity for them, they didn't deserve it. We only stopped for half an hour in Tokyo before setting off for Yokohama. It seemed strange that while Tokyo was flattened, the railway appeared untouched.

Our arrival in Yokohama was greeted by brass and military bands playing "Roll out the barrel" and other songs. As I jumped off the train clutching my kitbag, an American nurse grabbed my hand and then kissed me on the cheek saying "Welcome back to freedom". It was then that I realised that I was free. I started to cry for joy and couldn't thank her enough for her kindness. She wished me good luck and moved on. It seemed to me at that time that she was the most beautiful girl I had ever seen.

The Americans directed us to the station exits and we noted that the whole place was guarded by heavily armed MPs and soldiers. They all seemed to be smoking fat cigars and a great number of them were coloured.

Once outside the station, we were loaded into giant TCVs and whipped away through the streets to a Godown or reception centre. All our clothes were taken from us and we were subjected to a spray of what smelt like DDT. Then to the luxury of a hot shower. Whilst we were still naked, a nurse arrived to take our pulse rate and temperature. Then we were in to see the M.O for a thorough medical examination. Depending on the results we received, a "fit for travel" card, the card was in different colours indicating degrees of fitness, some lads were detained in hospital for further checks.

We were then issued with yet another new uniform and processed to the interrogation centre. There we were asked to make statements regarding war crimes and name those guilty of committing them. I named Satan, Donald Duck, The Frog, Tanaka and many others who I encountered during my captivity.

Then what you had all been waiting for, the telegram to send home stating that I was safe and well.

We recovered our personnel kit, photographs, my cement bag diary, my drawing done in Siam and my photograph of the King and Queen which had been kept at some risk for so long. In fact it got me three beatings, it was like a red rag to a bull to them. In Japan I had to recover it from an incinerator and in Singapore they taunted me by saying "English soldier sing God save the King, in Singapore God no bloody come Hi".

The Americans were very interested in my diary and drawings but I would not part with them. Anyway they would all have to be sterilised.

The last stop on our journey was at the food hall and there we had a slap up American dinner. Dinner completed, we were taken to a jetty in batches of 30 and embarked on a liberty boat to the USS Bracken, a troop transport ship. This was the ship that would take us to Manila in the Philippine Islands. The American sailors just could not do enough for us, they all wanted to know what it was like being prisoners and were we ill treated in captivity. We were in good hands, all the medical supplies we wanted, not forgetting the good doctors.

What a difference from the last boat trip we had with the Japanese, when they brought us to Japan from Singapore, all battened down and laying on the cargo of rubber and tin listening to the depth charges exploding and the crunch of torpedoes as they hit ships in our convoy. This was our journey through the South China Sea and the Pacific Ocean.

We now had papers and books to read, plenty of candy and cigarettes. The meals were beautiful, no rice. Bacon and egg for breakfast smothered in maple syrup, cornflakes smothered in sugar. Everyone tried to help us, it was paradise.

Sunday 10 September 1945:-

I went to the sick bay with a small ulcer on my leg. I only wanted it dressed but they took my temperature and, because it was up a little, they confined me to bed. I tried to tell them that it was just the excitement of it all and that I was fine but the doctor said that they were taking no chances with us. "You have got this far" he said "and we are going to make sure we get you home again". So I stayed put and spent most of the day answering questions about the past years. I felt very old compared with some of these young men.

Monday 11 September 1945:-

At 8.00am we set sail for Manila. We were now sailing through the Pacific Ocean and we heard that it was planned for us to fly out but, because of a typhoon warning, we were travelling by boat.

This ship had fitted bunk beds with reading lights, it was nothing like sleeping in hammocks as we did on the Lancashire on the way out from the UK. This ship was so up to date, the galley was all shiny chrome and food was served in a cafeteria system and, what's more, you could always go back for more food.

Monday 18 September 1945:-

On this day we arrived at Manila and the city was in shambles. When we passed through on the Jap ship, there were a few sunken ships in the harbour. Now it was full of them, ships of all different sizes with their masts sticking out of the water. It must make navigation difficult. On shore most of the buildings were wrecked. The B17 and 29s had certainly left their mark.

The next day we were to leave the Bracken after what had been a pleasant voyage. The first few days we travelled flat out to avoid the typhoon. The weather was pretty rough and some of the young sailors were seasick. In the last few days, we had sailed in fine weather and enjoyed all the entertainment provided.

Tuesday 19 September 1945:-

We were landed ashore on this morning and loaded into large American trucks ready to be driven to transit camps. As we disembarked, military bands played "Roll out the barrel" and "Colonel Bogey" and all the other old favourites.

The driver of our truck was coloured and weighed about 16 stones. He was smoking a big fat cigar and he drove like a nut case. We all hung on as he cut corners and reached speeds of over 60 mph. The British Official travelling in the front was terrified, as we all were. He said "Take it easy old chap, you'll wreck the truck". To which the driver replied "Uncle Sam's got plenty of trucks boss". The Official then said "But what about your own life". "Well boss, Uncle Sam's got plenty of niggers too" he replied. He then continued to drive like a madman, horn blaring and it did not do our dysentery any good at all.

We entered the transit camp and were checked in. It was a large tented area with the tents set well off the ground. We were eight to a tent and we had to sign for our beds. The camp was being run by the Australian Army, supplied by the Americans. The main buildings were of wood and comprised the cookhouse and stores etc.

Our first stop was the Admin building where we were vetted, supplied our names and addresses, next of kin etc. We made out another telegram form which would be sent as soon as possible. I wondered how you were getting on at home, we had heard of the bombing of Plymouth but never knew how things had gone. I wondered whether there was anyone at home to receive this telegram.

The Carrier HMS Illustrious was offshore waiting to take some of the lads home. I found that there were quite a few of the 41st Fortress R.Es here. They had come from all parts of Japan and some from Manchuria. I met up with John Collins and Sgt Ben Brisco, they were in the lines next to us. We talked of the latest news and of old mates, quite a lot were not as fortunate as us.

We were issued with perforated ration cards marked B, D, T. The B indicated breakfast and entitled you to two packets of cigarettes. D was for dinner and included two bottles of beer and the T (for tea) issue included two fat cigars.

The Australian Red Cross ran the canteen and they supplied coffee, tea, cakes and other light snacks completely free of charge.

We found that the Americans had employed a lot of Japanese POWs as labour in the camp and they treated them quite well. The Australians treated them a lot harder, even after a few days our lads gave them some of their issues. I gave them nothing, not after the way they had treated us.

As usual the food was first class and we got used to the good life. The feeling of freedom to light up when you wanted to was wonderful, though the bottles of beer gave me a blown up feeling.

Although we were able to leave the camp, very few did. The camp entertainment was superb with cinemas and canteen readily available. The hazards of going out were pointed out to us and included bars selling wood alcohol. They told of some servicemen going blind or dying of alcohol poisoning.

HMS Illustrious was waiting to take POWs home via America. Other POWs were going via Canada, the Illustrious would be leaving in a few days. To the Americans, our aircraft carriers appeared very small.

We were now meeting up with a lot of old friends, friends whom we had known since the days of our recruitment at Chatham. Others from R.E camps at Haslar, Gosport and Blackdown before the War had started. They were coming in from everywhere, even Jap occupied China. All had tales to tell about Japanese brutality and they told of friends lost in mine tragedies or explosions. Some had survived being torpedoed by the American and allied submarines during their transportation to Japan. We heard many stories of friendship and bravery and many sad tales too.

Several of our lads had been told that they would be leaving in two days time on the Illustrious. The meal tickets they had would have several days of rations yet to be claimed, so they suggested that we might find a use for them. We had no need of any extra food but the beer and cigarettes would come in handy. We planned to have a farewell booze-up with the extra beer and we would certainly smoke as many cigarettes and cigars as possible. We knew it sounded greedy but we felt that all these luxuries may suddenly disappear.

HMS Illustrious left the next day, our mates were ferried out on this day ready for their trip home. They passed us their ration cards as planned and now all we had to do was to wait until the next day.

At breakfast on this day, we worked our meal ticket scheme, using our own cards we got our meal and our cigarette ration later. We rejoined the queue and said that, though we were not hungry, we would have our cigarettes. We did this twice and so finished up with 60 cigarettes. At lunchtime we did the same and ended up with six bottles of beer and in the evening six cigars. We managed to do this over the next four days and the four of us in our tent had acquired quite a little haul of beer and cigarettes. We were told that we would be travelling on HMS Implacable the Carrier that relieved the Illustrious. We, Ben Brisco, John Collins and myself decided to have our booze up. Boy were we ill after that nights binge. Our stomachs were not yet ready for eight beers in a sitting. Our throats were not much better with all the smoking. To make matters worse, I had to get up at least three times during the night with stomach cramps. The toilets were about 100 yards from our tent and it was separated from us by a large storm drain (the tale of that night will have to appear under a different cover).

WE BOARD HMS IMPLACABLE
MANILA TO VANCOUVER 25 SEPTEMBER - 11 OCTOBER 1945

We leave the transit camp at breakneck speed driven by these crazy coloured american drivers, smoking their fat cigars (remembering the journey here - "Uncle Sam got bags of niggers sir") we head to the docks for another leg of our journey towards home.

We see ships sunken in the harbour, both by the Japanese and the Americans, just rusting hulks.

It was not long before we got aboard lighters, they convoyed us to the aircraft carrier the mighty "Implacable", it lightened our hearts as we saw the "white ensign" blowing in the slight breeze as we drew closer.

We were told that this was the biggest carrier in our fleet 31,000 tons. Her master was Captain C.C Hughes-Hallett CBE. She saw action in the sinking of the German battleship Tirpitz along the coast of Norway 1944, Truk in the Pacific. She ended active service with Admiral Halsey's third US fleet last August off the Japanese coast. She had destroyed 122 aircraft including some Kami Kasi pilots. She had sunk 220,500 tons of enemy shipping. So she had seen plenty of action.

A hospital had been fitted to the lower flight deck, all aircraft had been removed. The hospital was never put to its full use. So it was turned into a vast dormitory holding 500 men, the upper flight deck was crammed with beds for 1,750 men. So there were 2,227 ex POWs on board, plus a band of RN nurses plus crew, a total of 3,718 in all.

We soon settled down, everyone was so kind to us, our every need was tended to by the crew and the nurses.

The food was excellent, again we were told not to overeat, just enough to keep one going. We had been starved for so long, it could cause untold trouble if we over did it.

We were given cigarettes, round tins of 50 Players, tins of Ticklers tobacco (roll your own) and there were sweets and chocolate galore.

We had concert parties laid on by the crew, band concerts by the ship's own Royal Marine Band.

We went on to the flight deck for exercise, or to laze in the Pacific sun. We sat on the stern of the ship and watched as the giant screws thrashed through the blue tranquil sea, throwing up phosphorous waves at night, we watched the dolphins play in our bow waves. All so restful to our tortured minds and bodies.

Our ship travelled in a north easterly direction. It was announced over the tannoy system that there would be a firework display on the flight deck that night, after dark and it would be worthwhile attending. So we all trooped on deck as darkness fell to find a table had been erected in the middle of the deck. After a while, a Petty Officer approached the table with a large roman candle, he shouted "stand back" and lit the blue touch paper, a few stars shot out with a bit of smoke. He then said "That's it lads", we started to boo a bit and said "rubbish" he, the P.O, then said "Don't blame me, we couldn't find anymore". We were so disappointed, he then said "hold on a minute". Then all of a sudden all hell was loosed off as every gun on the ship fired out over the sea - 4 AA guns, heavy guns, machine guns firing tracer bullets, pom-poms, firing skyward, flaming onions. It frightened the daylights out of us all. It was without doubt the best firework display I had ever seen, or have seen since.

I was wondering around the ship one day and I saw the D.U.W.K. This was one of the amphibian vehicles, used on land or on water. It was the first I had ever seen, in fact I was fascinated and wanted to find out more. There were two Royal Marine operators aboard it and I got very friendly with them. A Marine K. Yendall from Exeter and Marine W.H Symons. I spent a lot of time with these two gentlemen. They were giving the engine of the "duck" a decoke and I helped them grind the valves in amongst other things, just to keep my hand in.

We crossed the International Date line, we knew then that we were well on our way.
Then we were told that we would be calling at Honolulu - Hawaii and Pearl Harbour where the Japanese committed that terrible act by attacking the Harbour when War had not been declared. "The Day of Infamy".

The two Royal Marines, Yendall and Symons told me that the beer in Honolulu was terrible and full of gas, they would give me a drop of the hard stuff to go ashore with, do not drink the beer!!

We awoke early to hear the anchors being dropped, so we guessed we were laying off. Early breakfast and shower, Yendall and Symons gave me a bottle of grog to put into my water bottle to take ashore. We were loaded on to tenders which took us ashore and the ship was anchored approximately one mile from the shore. I went with three other POWs. At the landing bay, we found American servicemen to show us around the place. We were told to be back on the ship by 2100 hours to get settled in as we should be leaving port at about 2300 hours. The two guides took us around all the sights, beer houses, dance halls etc. As I had been warned, the beer was terrible, so to spice it up I put a lot of Nelson's blood in each of our drinks. I had my photograph taken with two topless Hawaiian girls - one for the lads back home. Two of our POW friends went missing, so there were just four in our group, two Brits and two Americans. I didn't drink a lot of beer, we were afraid for our weak stomachs. The rum we topped up the "Yanks" drinks. As the day wore on, they were getting very tired and speech became slurred. By evening we had lost them. We had to find our way back and it was getting very late. We wondered around for what seemed hours - we eventually reached the dock area. We could see Implacable out to sea all lit up - it was a lovely sight. There were no liberty boats around, there were a few American sailors. I had no idea of the time. Then "four white mice" appeared and I asked them the time, they said that it was 9.30pm or 2130 hours. God, we had missed the last liberty boat. I asked the American Military Police what we could do. I said that our ship was sailing at 2330 hours. They hunted around, phoned from their office at about 2200 and they got us a lift back, we arrived at the landing, went up the stairs to the deck - the Master of Arms was there - "Where the hell have you been?" etc etc "you were just in time, we are about to cast off" - "you will be on orders in the morning". I heard no more about the incident. The two of us were very lucky. My friend was Cyril Welstead R.E. He left the train in Canada and he said that he could see no future in the UK. He was a good motor mechanic, so I guess he stayed in Canada.

We set sail on time and the rest of the voyage went well - next stop would be Vancouver, Canada.

THROUGH CANADA

After a very pleasant journey from Manila on board one of the biggest Aircraft Carriers "HMS Implacable" we awoke at dawn to find that we had stopped to pick up a pilot and newspapers. We were just off William Head and the sea was covered with a very thick fluff like mist. Our giant carrier nosed her way through the calm waters, her guns bristled with the usual pride of the Royal Navy. Just a few months before, these guns spelt death to the Japanese forces in the South Pacific.

Many reporters came aboard, taking photos as they were shown around the ship. They also asked us about our experiences during our captivity. Then the great rush began to get the parade ready on the flight deck to enter Vancouver Docks. Shortly before 10 o'clock, the fog lifted and the sun broke through the clouds and we glided passed Point Atkinson, the flight deck was now lined with our sailors in their glittering white caps, the Royal Marine Guard of Honour marched while their band played "O Canada" and other stirring marches. We then passed under "Lions Gate Bridge" and the bridge was crowded with cheering people as they threw streamers of all colour on to our deck. Ships sirens blew to welcome us, then Implacable answered with a great blast of her own horns, like a mighty animal answering her cubs, this was only part of the welcome already our hearts were lost to Canada. Such things had been shut away from us for almost four years, tears came, lumps in our throats, what joy this was, all we had was brutality at the hands of our Japanese captors.

The tugs took our ship in tow, buildings became plainer as did the streets as we neared the dock. The marine buildings and streets were a sea of faces to welcome us and our giant carrier - this vast floating aerodrome. "A more precious cargo" as one reporter explained in a Vancouver newspaper. 2,127 freed Japanese prisoners.

We docked at the C.P.R Pier "A" at 1145 while thousands of Vancouver citizens watched and cheered. The R.C.N.V.R Band played a string of stirring music.

When at last we were docked and the ship tied up, we exchanged some of the useless Jap money - Yen-cen for Canadian souvenirs, we threw this useless money to girls on the dockside. I remember "Blondie", she got a wad of mine, she threw me cigarettes. Only wish I could have spent a few hours with her, I thought she was beautiful!! I must be getting stronger.

We had not been docked long and our lads began to leave the ship and were boarding a train (Canadian Pacific Railway). I found that I was in the last group to leave. We spent time watching points.

Now our group had been called to leave, we said our farewells to the ships company - they had been so good to us on the journey across the Pacific Ocean, "Give our love to Blighty" they called.

Down the gangplank and I set foot in Canada at 3.30pm. We were mobbed by the Canadian Red Cross nursers who gave us writing paper, cigarettes and chocolates, they even had tables we could sit at to write cables home, which they would despatch for us. We were then put on to the train and we had every comfort. Two giant C.P.R steam engines to pull and push us, the whole 2,227 ex POWs on this long journey across Canada - "VANCOUVER, WE THANK YOU ONE AND ALL".

So we pulled away from Vancouver and we had a good supper, plenty of fruit, candy etc provided by the Red Cross of Canada. We were shown how to make up our bunk beds by our ever obliging attendants. We retired for the night after such a lovely exciting day. The giant steam engines seemed to be singing "Going Home - nearer and nearer to home". I dropped into oblivion in the early hours - it had been such a good day.

At daylight, I awoke to the sound of excited voices of my friends admiring the beautiful scenery of the Rocky Mountains, it took one's breath away - no artists paintbrush or pencil could ever give these snow capped sunkist mountains their full credit. I have travelled the World, seen sunsets, sunrises and beauty, but this was fantastic, it was breathtaking - as we glided by the beautiful pictures were changing all the time, as we passed over bridges, through valleys and dales the evergreen firs, the air so fresh and clean.

We took breakfast, such wonderful food and all our diets were prepared, we were not to overfeed and we kept to what the doctors had advised. We sat back and took in these wonderful views - they were a tonic in themselves. We passed through small towns en route with lovely names such as Lauretta, Albert Canyon etc.

Just as lunch had finished, we had a 15 minute stop at Field and we were allowed off the train to stretch our limbs, again the generosity of the people of Canada was poured upon us - fresh fruit, cigarettes, chocolate. I bought photographs of the Rockies to show the folks at home who were waiting for our return. Girls loved to chat us up - life was so good. The children with their rosy cheeks, they looked so healthy and happy. The doctors still insisted that we took our anti malaria medication - most of us had the "yellow" look caused by this medication being in the pigment of our skin.

We all admired these giant CPR engines in the way they pulled this long train up the steep inclines at speed. We thought of the hard working firemen stoking the fire boxes to keep up such a good head of steam. The track ran by the roadside, everywhere we looked people were cheering us on our way.

We now crossed the Great Divide 5,332 ft, the boundary between British Columbia and Alberta. We were told that the Great Divide was a small stream that split into two parts, one half goes out to the Pacific Ocean and the other into the Atlantic Ocean. We cut through the rocky mountains via "kicking horse pass". A wonderful fete of engineering, where the railtrack corkscrews up through the mountain to gain height. It goes in a complete circle and travels over itself, like unto a giant thread cut through this mountain pass. This scenery was fantastic. Later this particular afternoon we left the Rockies in the distance, we then came upon the plains of Alberta, we now saw the cattle grazing on the great ranches, yes and cowboys. Our train passed the great lakes, all adding to the beauty of this country.

Now we were crossing the great plains, where cornfields stretched as far as the eye could see.
Later that afternoon, we looked ahead of the train onto a big city. the setting sun was reflected back to us from the windows of the tall buildings, making a perfect picture, we were told that we were entering Calgary. As we pulled into the station, a big military band was playing its welcoming music, so uplifting. Once again we were showered with gifts, cakes, coffee and cigarettes. Banners were flying "Welcome Home" and we were given cards.

We stopped at Regina and were treated like royalty. It was wonderful after what we had been through "Welcome Veterans of the Far East". Gifts were showered upon us from all quarters.

As we travelled eastwards, we found that the land structure began to change and we found that fields were the same as at home in England. Brandon then on to Winnipeg. We had quite a stop here and could get off the train for a while. I met a gentleman who gave me his card, he was an executive on the CP Railway. I told him that I was a regular soldier in the Royal Engineers. He asked if I had any experience in railways. I told him that I had laid tracks and knew about packing etc. He then went on to say that if I found that I could not settle when I returned to the UK, I could contact him in Canada at the address shown, he would ensure me employment on the CPR (Canadian Pacific Railway). I was very touched by this offer but, as you will see later, that I never again contacted this gentleman.
Our next call was in Winnipeg, we had the usual welcome and gifts again were showered upon us. The Lord Mayor gave us a

speech of welcome. As one of our lads said "It was like Christmas every day". It was here while we were in a siding that a train travelled west, it was loaded with Canadian forces that were returning home from the War in Europe. They said that they had disembarked from the French liner Il de France. Stories were exchanged re our experiences. Some of these men had landed on "D" Day and went right through to Berlin. I would like to have stayed in Winnipeg a lot longer. There were pictures in all the national Canadian newspapers of our ship HMS Implacable as she entered Vancouver Harbour. We set off eastwards again.

Later than night, we entered Kanora with its beautiful starlit lake, the Indian translation for this place is "Laughing Lake". We met two girls who came from Scotland, they had married Canadian servicemen and arrived here the previous July. We set off again and were soon asleep as the train clacked its way eastwards.

It was 14 October 1945 and we journeyed on eastward. We arrived at a small town of Nipigon, to the right we saw Lake Superior. Ocean going steamers were sailing here going about their business. What beautiful pictures we had seen, was it I wonder because we had been locked away for so long? We found it was getting cooler and, at times, we had had flurries of snow. We had snow in Japan.

We travelled on through White River, Chapleau, the pictures ever changing. This particular evening, we arrived at Sudbury, we left the train to stretch our legs to the usual reception. There seemed to be so many girls, all asking for souvenirs. Unfortunately we left our kits on the train and when we returned, we found that a lot of these girls had made a raid on the train. I found that I had lost my bush hat as issued to Australian forces, quite a few had been stolen. One of the lads wasn't feeling too well and he was asleep in his bunk, his hat, shirt and trousers were missing - so that was Sudbury.

15 October 1945, we arrived at Smith Falls. We were here for only one hour and a Canadian soldier offered to show us the main street and we had very limited time. We were showered with the usual generosity and we found a small Woolworths and we bought boxes of chocolates to take back to the folks at home. We wished we could have stayed longer. Before parting, our guide told me that his mother came from Devonshire, my home county and she had married a soldier just after the First World War. We took our farewells and left Smith Falls.

We now carried on to Ottawa and passed through at night, so we did not see much.

We then stopped at Montreal, it somehow did not seem too friendly. We went outside the station and we asked questions in english - but were answered in french, not so good here!!

We stopped at Sherbrook Field, it was like at home, with hedges and there were orchards, roll on Halifax now!!

As we passed Ottawa then on to Montreal, we travelled along the banks of the St Lawrence River, it was breathtaking.
At every stop, people spoke to us in french. So we chugged on past rivers and lakes and at last we entered New Brunswick - then into Nova Scotia and Halifax. It had taken us four days and five nights to complete the journey.

We de-trained in the dock at Halifax and British officers and NSO started to scream "Get fell in". I thought for a moment that we were back in Japan. This treatment was in contrast to that which the Americans and Canadians had given us. Some little upstarts!!

IL DE FRANCE
("The Flower of France")

We were marched along the dock - left, right, left - swing those arms - get 'em up. These little upstarts - been nowhere, seen nothing - give us a break will you? Not a very good start for the last leg home.

There she was the once proud great liner that we used to watch sailing up the Solent. Now a drab grey hulk, it looked a little depressing. We were numbered off into sections and then each section taken in turn - we went aboard. The accommodation was not like one would have expected. Still the old tub had been trooping all through the War and been all over the world - she was in a sorry state. With a blast on the ship's siren, we slipped away and were soon in the Atlantic Ocean. The food was very poor, as was the service by the all French crew. Some told us that it was the ship's last voyage before going into her home port Cherbourg. So I expect they were glad to be going home, getting "paid off" this being their only interest. This voyage was not at all like it had been on the USS Bracken or HMS Implacable, perhaps we expected too much. I thought at times we were being treated like cattle in transit.

As we got out into deep water, we found that the ship had a list to the port side, this was quite obvious when on the top deck. "Keep going old tub". So we were well under way.

It was good to get up onto the top deck - cold - but the fresh air was so good, it was good to get away from the smell below. I met John Collins on board again - as I had seen him in Manila. We used to meet on deck every day. While on deck one day, he pointed to a gentleman who was leaning on the rail and he said "Isn't that Jimmy over there"? I looked - yes it was Major James Boyle our O.C 41st Coy R.E. We went up to him and saluted. He looked at us and said "Thank God, I have met someone from my company - how are you? I'm so glad that you have survived". He went on to tell us that he had been imprisoned in Formosa (now Taiwan). After this, we met him many times on the top deck and he once said how he was looking forward to getting home to his wife.

So we ploughed our way across the Atlantic, it was now getting much colder and we were glad of our overcoats, scarves and gloves.

At last - what we had been waiting for - the coast of England came into view. The patchwork quilt of green fields. "Green fields that will be ever England". We passed the Needles. My heart was heavy when I thought of those left behind in those "foreign fields that would be forever England". So many of them scattered all over Asia. My friends - the finest a man could ever wish for. Tugs came and took us in tow to tie up at Southampton. We could not get off quick enough, down the gangplank - no bands of welcome. No-one to meet us!! How different to Canada's welcome. A letter of welcome was thrust into my hand - it was from the King and Queen.

We awaited our kit bags - being offloaded and mine was packed full of clothing, cigarettes and chocolates to take home. I went straight through customs to the transit camp. It was 31 October 1945. It was so good to feel blighty under one's feet. We had been overseas six years and nine months. In this camp, we were documented and we had further medical examinations. We sent telegrams to our homes, we just couldn't get away soon enough.

Just outside the camp, John Collins and I found a public house and we went into a bar and ordered a beer each. It tasted awful, so we tried a drop of rum to flavour it up. Suddenly a large number of American soldiers entered and we got into conversation with them and found that they had just come from Berlin. A few of them said that they had gone in on "D" Day and had fought all the way through. They were going back to the USA the next day. I bet they got a far better welcome there than we had had here. They did say that they were glad to have fought in Europe and not been in our situation as POW Far East. We had another drink with them and bade them farewell and good luck.

HOME AGAIN

On 2 November 1945 we were paraded, given leave passes and railway warrants for our journeys home. I said "farewell" to John Collins, he was going on a later train for Yorkshire, we promised to keep in touch. I caught the train for North Road Station, Plymouth with my two kit bags full of goodies. The journey was quite straight forward and I arrived in Plymouth on time - it was about 1400 hours and my cousin's wife was there to meet me. I struggled onto the platform with my kit bags. It was great to be home. A railway porter came to my assistance and he said "Welkom 'ome me der". I knew I was in Devon. He asked me if I had been in the Burma fighting and I said that I had been a Japanese POW. He said "Dear God, you be lucky to be yer, you 'ave 'ad a rough time" and he shook my hand. I then noticed that he had a row of medal ribbons on his GWR waistcoat from WWI, the first one was the Military Medal, I felt very humble. We left the station by taxi and was soon in Plympton where I had never been before. I did not go back to my old village at Liverton. I was told that my Auntie with whom I had lived had died a week before I was taken a prisoner. I felt sad and remembered her words before I left to go away, that she would never see me again in her lifetime. My Uncle had married again and remained in the old parish. Everyone was so kind to me in Plympton. On my first night home I met the girl who was to become my wife five years later.

I was introduced to all the neighbours. One old lady, a Mrs Scoble, was over 80 years of age and when she was introduced to me she took a step back and looked very hard at me. I was very thin and full of quinine, mepacrine and we were well dosed with this medication to counteract the malaria that we still had in our bloodstream from the jungles of Siam and Burma. A side effect was that the pigment of the skin turned yellow. Mrs Scoble went down into the village and met another neighbour and it was mentioned that I had returned from Japan. Mrs Scoble said "Yes, tiz sad, poor boy, he's bin with they Japanese that long, he's got to look like 'em - he's all yeller" - dear old lady!

There was a "Welcome Home" laid on at the Plympton Senior School, I was invited and it was attended by - Royal Marines, Royal Navy, RAF and the Army who had been away in the War. I felt a bit out of place as I was the only Japanese POW there. There were quite a few German POW, some who had been taken in Dunkirk. We had a lovely evening and at the end of which we were all presented with £25 of Premium Bonds, all given by the residents of Plympton.

I had been home about three weeks when I received a Post Office Savings Bank book - it contained my back pay for the 3½ years in captivity - the amount £285, all on flat rate.

Having been home in the UK about a fortnight, I thought it time to go and see old friends and my Uncle in the small village of Liverton, Devon.

One of the first places on my list was Ilsington Church where I sang as a young boy in the choir. I sat in one of the pews and offered a prayer of thanks to God for my deliverance from the awful days. I went then to visit family graves, my mother's and grandfather's. I often wondered if they had been near me in the days of crisis, at times I had felt that there was some guidance very near.

Next on my list was my Uncle, he was so glad to see me and he said that he was glad to see that I still wore the Royal Engineers titles on my shoulders. I don't know why he should have thought they would be any different! As I have mentioned before, he was always proud to say that he had been a Sapper in World War I. He went on to tell me that my release had been announced over the BBC Radio. The Church (St Michaels) bell ringers went into the Church and rang the bells in Thanksgiving. It brought tears to my eyes when I was told this. One of those old bell ringers had lost his son (who had also been a choirboy with me and a great friend) in the War. He was one of a bomber crew lost over Germany with no known grave. How brave of this old bell ringer. I was very touched.

My next call was on my old friends. Mr and Mrs Howard who had been so good to me during my school days, I was always made welcome in their house. The kindness they had shown me I will never forget. My great friend Harry, their son, had been a Prisoner of War in Germany for almost five years, he had been captured in Crete. I was so glad to hear that he had survived his ordeal. We had so many tales to tell each other. He had made two or three attempts to escape. In his last episode, he had been on the run in Poland for several weeks before being handed over to the Germans, he suffered terrible frostbite to his toes and feet.

Then I visited my old Church School in the small hamlet Blackpool. My old Headmaster, I was told, had gone to another school in North Devon. I would very much like to have seen him again, he had done so much to set us on to the right road in life in our young lives, in spite of the occasional cane on the hand for small misdemeanours, across the bottom for more serious misbehaviour. The old oak trees were still standing as proud as ever in the playground, to my amazement the birdbox that I had made in the carpentry class was also in position in the largest oak as I had put it there so long ago. I hope it has brought pleasure to the birds as well as the pupils over the years, it must have been there fourteen years at least.

After a while, I thought I had better get irons in the fire as regards to my future employment. As I have said earlier on in this account, I had ambitions to join the Police Force after having completed Army Colour Service. I went to the Greenbank Police Station to make enquiries re Plymouth City Force, to my utter disappointment I was told that I was too old - the age limit was 25 - I was 27 years and 9 months. That was the end of the Police for me. I did not want to return to the potteries, so the only conclusion was to get back into the Army. So I applied to go back into the Royal Engineers. After a medical examination, I returned in February 1946 and we had had three months leave on full pay, I must add as a Sapper.

On returning, I was posted to the 2nd/5th Welsh Regiment at Trowbridge in Wiltshire. I found that there were quite a number there who had been in Singapore with me, some in other companies. We were brought up to date with all the modern weapons that we had never seen i.e Bren and Sten guns, the anti-tank guns P.I.A.T and other weapons. Field craft had also altered from that which we had been taught. It was a good course.

At this time, I became very worried about my mental outlook and I was getting terrible nightmares. I found others were the same. Many times I had dreamed that I was back in the camps and could hear the screams of torture, then wake up in a cold sweat - so relieved to see the electric light bulb hanging from the ceiling. Another thing I found when being questioned orally, I panicked and started to sweat - why? I felt as if I was being interrogated by the Jap Guards. Then giving the wrong answers - it was a set back on some of the courses that I had been on. It worried me at times very greatly and I am certain that, at times, it would have had bearings on promotions. So be it!

At this time, I found that I started to drink more than was good for me but it steadied my nerves a bit. Men who had been in Burma - we had Chindits and men from the 14th Army.

DRINK WAS OUR VALIUM

We finished the course at Trowbridge and we had become proficient in all small arms. I was now posted to Barton Stacey - a training battalion. Here we learned all the new drills and a refresher course on Field Engineering. We moved down to Pangbourne near Reading. A bridging instruction, this is where we came upon the dry and wet Bailey Bridge. We had to cross the River Thames in flood. All very exciting stuff, we had never seen Bailey Bridge before and we found it hard work and very cold in March - not quite the place to be when one has just returned from the tropics.

We finished the wet and dry Bailey and I had quite enjoyed it and learned a lot, we had good instructors. We now went back to Barton Stacey to finish the rest of the refresher course. Drill and other Field Engineering skills, mine warfare - demolitions and such like, time soon passed by April and we were ready to "pass off". This was a great day and all went well. Then we got our different postings. After leave, I was detailed a posting to T.B.R.E (Training Battalion Royal Engineers), Fulwood Barracks, Preston, Lancs. Local acting unpaid Lance Corporal it was a Cadre Class. Plenty of spit and polish and more study. I was fitting in quite well and getting good marks when I was taken ill, coughing blood. I was rushed into the hospital at Whittingham, Nr Preston. I was there about two months and I was given all the very best of treatment and tests that one could wish for. The doctors and nurses were top rate. One of the nurses I might add I got on very well with and, in fact, I took her out on several occasions when my troubles were cleared up. I was given every type of test one could think of.

(i)   It was found that I still had malaria in my bloodstream;

(ii) dysentry (amoebic);
(iii) a disc was misplaced in my neck (cervical spondylosis);
(iv) helminthiasis (worm infestation);
(v) duodenal ulcer;
(vi) acute bronchitis, suspected at first as TB;
(vii) beri beri - malnutrition.

At once I was put on courses of drugs to combat all these diseases, they had to be treated one at a time and eventually, with time, I had a clean bill of health to return to duties. God knows how I should have fared had I not been in the forces and got the best of medical attention. I must add that, in later life, I have had set backs in the stomach and neck.

My next posting was to Chester on a rehabilitation course. Assault course, 5 mile route march - 10 mile route march with full marching order etc etc.

Then a posting to Engineer Stores Depot, Long Marston, Stratford upon Avon. Whilst here I met some of the best friends one could ever wish to meet. A lot of ex POW both Far East and Germany. Ex 14 Army Burma, ex Chindits, ex 8th Army Mid East. All had been through the mill as it were in one way or another. It took me just over a year to reach the rank of Full Sergeant. I took Cadre courses under the watchful eye of R.S.M J.H Pavey. I taught drill, weapon training, mine warfare and demolitions (my favourite subject). I had many happy years at Long Marston. I then had a posting to West Africa, Lagos and had all my inoculations. I went to Barton Stacey ready to fly but was taken ill with influenza and went into hospital, again the malaria bug was in attendance. So to hospital for further treatment, so I missed the draft to West Africa. I was disappointed at this as it was a very good posting. I was then returned to Long Marston. Shortly after this, I was posted to the Territorial Army as a permanent Staff Instructor. I went to 251 Field Park Squadron, Norwich. It was a very enlightening posting and I enjoyed it, those of the Squadron were very keen to learn.

We had several demolition exercises. One that gave me satisfaction was the completed demolitions of Havering Hall - at one time a very impressive building. I should think Georgian and it had been used by the RAF during the War as an Officers Mess and Hospital. An airfield surrounded it and one old gentleman told me that he had seen spitfires take off from there at twelve abreast. He went on to say that it was a very sad day to see the hall demolished, as his father had worked there as man and boy and he had spent a lot of his childhood there.

It was here that Field Marshall Lord Ironside came to Nelson Barracks and presented me with my Long Service and Good Conduct Medal. I was very highly honoured. In the Mess after the presentation, we had a long chat and he was very interested to know about my experiences as a Japanese POW. He said that one day I should write a book - the World should be told of what happened.

I completed my service at Ripon, Yorkshire having reached the rank of Staff Sergeant in September 1959. I left many good friends in the Army, some I am still in very close touch with.

I hope to have told my story to the full and you will all understand the pain and suffering that was experienced, please give a thought to those left behind in those foreign fields that will be forever England - and those below the seas. I dedicate that story to them and especially to the 87 of my Company the 41st Fortress, Royal Engineers.

AN UNUSUAL PET - JOE THE DUCK, Sapper R.E

In February 1939, I was posted to the 41st Fortress Company, R.E in Changi, Singapore. Six months later War was declared against Germany. We were employed to strengthen the defences around the coast of the island. This meant the digging of trenches and gun positions, as well as anti aircraft gun positions on the airfields.

It was late in September when we were employed in the Katong area of Singapore digging weapon pits. To our amazement, four little ducklings waddled across the parapet of one of the pits. We fed them with worms that we dug from the pits. They gobbled them down with delight, they seemed to be starving. They stayed with us most of the day and we had become attached to the little fellows. At this point, we decided to take them back to our barracks at Changi. We found some straw and put them in a cardboard box. They were then loaded on to our truck for the journey to Changi.

We were cleaning our tools and getting ready to depart when an old Chinaman came on the site. He was looking in the lalang (undergrowth). He then approached us and made a quacking sound. It was obvious that it was the ducklings that he was looking for. We took the box from our truck and let him see that we had his ducks and he was quite pleased to find them. At this point, the Corporal in charge of our section offered the old Chinaman fifty cents for the four. The old man turned this down and said that he wanted two dollars and quite a bit of bartering went on. In the end, the old chap accepted one dollar. The Corporal had clinched a deal. When we reached our accommodation, the Corporal had doubts as to how he could manage to look after the four ducklings. After much thought, he decided to sell off three of his charges. One of our Sergeants bought one, the other two were purchased by two Sappers. One of the Sappers let his little duck wander from the barrack room. it was savaged by a semi wild dog and was killed instantly.

After a few weeks the Sergeant had his little pet on the bed with him and he rolled over in his sleep, the poor thing was suffocated. The other one owned by the other Sapper I did not quite know the fate of but I think he was posted to an out station and he took the duck with him. When he returned, he was without the duckling and I never knew the fate of it.

The surviving duck developed quite well and very quickly. It got the best of food from the Mess Hall, together with a good diet of worms as we continued digging the gunpits etc all over the island.

In the meantime, the last remaining was named "JOE".

He became quite intelligent and would answer to his name. We took him swimming, both in the sea and the pool at Selerang Bks. We used to take him to the top diving board and we would all dive off into the water then shout "come on Joe" and he would hesitate for a while and then fly down into the water, ducking and diving, quacking all the time. He really did enjoy his swims.

In the canteen he always had his drink of "tiger beer". He would never leave a drop and at times he got quite tipsy, which was funny to watch. Joe, trying to keep his long neck straight, would curl up and go to sleep under the Corporal's chair.
Time went by and Joe grew into quite a big duck. He slept in a box full of straw in the Corporal's locker and was never any trouble. He was always up early and would be seen accompanying the Corporal quacking his way to the showers at the end of the barrack room.

Then came a bombshell, the Corporal was cleaning out Joe's box and he shouted "bloody hell, Joe has laid a bloody egg"! We were all shocked - what now? It's a "she". The Corporal made the decision that she would be renamed Josephine but she was still called Joe.

Saturday mornings were, by tradition, the Colonel's barrack room inspection. We stood by our beds, the bedspace and lockertops tested for dust etc. The Colonel would ask questions regarding our well being and were we happy in the Company?

On one such Saturday morning, the Colonel approached the Corporal's bedspace. After a few questions, he asked the Corporal to open his locker. This the Corporal did, turning a pale shade of green, at the same time thinking "this is it, I am in deep trouble"! On opening the locker, the cardboard box was in full view, Joe poked her head up and began to "quack quack", as if she was glad to see the Colonel - who asked "what the devil is that?", to which the Corporal replied "it is the Company Mascot Sir", expecting an explosion. "Good God" said the Colonel, he then laughed, turned and walked away. The Sergeant Major and RSM were dumbfounded. From that moment on, we knew that Joe had been accepted as our Company Mascot.

There were many adventures after that involving Joe. In fact she became well known wherever we went.

On one occasion, our section was employed at Sembawang Airfield. The Airfield was manned by the Royal Australian Air Force. We were employed there to install anti aircraft gun positions. The aircraft on this field were Hudson Bombers. We became very friendly with both the ground staff, as well as the air crews. We were "Cobbers" and "Pommies". We had been on the Airfield about a week when the Sergeants invited us into their Mess. We accepted and were made very welcome. Seeing that most of us were Sappers, this was unthinkable in the British Army. We were all settled in and beer was served. We exchanged jokes and spoke about England, our homes and Australia. Suddenly one of the Aussie Sergeants, who had placed his beer under his chair, shouted "who the hell has been drinking my beer?" He looked at one of the other Sergeants and more or less accused him of the offence. Just in time to save a punch-up, Joe came out from under the Sergeants chair, the culprit had exposed herself. "Well I'll be damned" said the Aussie. "I have never seen the likes of that", he then went on to offer our Corporal twenty dollars for our duck.

"No way" said the Corporal. Joe became quite popular at Sembawang Airfield.

To cut my story short, I will jump in time to the end of 1941. The Japanese were massing in Indo China. At this time, we were employed on building beach defences all around the East Coast and to the South. We were camped at a place called Bedok. We were there for several weeks, going to and fro every day. Joe of course was still with us and in fact a major part of our Company. We had been working hard one day, when we were packing our tools on the truck. Joe was missing, she could not be found anywhere. We spent an hour looking around, our mascot could not be found. Reluctantly we had to leave. We all thought "she would end up in a Chinese curry" - I can tell you, we were very upset. We returned to our camp, had our meal, showered and retired to our canteen for a beer or two. We sat talking until late, it must have been about 11.00pm, when suddenly we heard quacking coming up the rough old track. We just could not believe it, it was Joe. She had found her way back to the camp mostly in the dark. The distance she had travelled was well over half a mile.

As we all know, the Japanese invaded Malaya and within a short time Singapore was under seige. We were being bombed from high level, shelled from the sea and from the mainland of Malaya, we were hemmed in. We were then moved to the City Centre. Our HQ was now established in Amber Mansions, Orchard Road. Our Company was split into two. One half went to a pineapple factory and they took up positions as Infantry. We at Amber Mansions were laying mines and booby traps. At night we did street patrols, mostly looking for snipers, there were plenty of these. We made a little pen for Joe on the lawn at the Mansions and we kept her well fed on worms etc.

On 13 February 1942, we were coming back off a patrol when we happened to pick up three stray turkeys. As rations were getting short, we confiscated the said birds. We put them into a very large laundry basket and they would be in the pot at a later date. We then had a terrific air raid and barrage from the Japanese. Joe had somehow got out of the pen, so we picked her up in the laundry basket with the turkeys. At this point, the Japs intensified their barrage. Mortar bombs were landing and exploding all around us and all we could do was to take cover as best we could. The bombardment lasted about 45 minutes. When all was quiet, we took stock and saw that the laundry basket was tipped on its side. We opened it and out flew the turkeys but Joe did not move, one piece of shrapnel had cut through the basket and decapitated our dear old pet. We wrapped her in a ground sheet and buried her in the lawn at Amber Mansions, Orchard Road, Singapore, with the Epitaph "Joe - killed in action 13 February 1942". Two days later Singapore fell to the Japanese Forces. It was 15 February 1942.

At no time have I mentioned any names of persons in this little story, as many of them died in captivity on the Siam/Burma Railway or were torpedoed en route to Japan.

Anyone who served with the 41st Fortress Company, Royal Engineers, Changi will all remember dear old Joe.

In 1995, I returned to Singapore and, while travelling on a coach along Orchard Road, I asked the courier what had happened to Amber Mansions. She told me that they had long since gone in the new development. She then asked why I had enquired about these old buildings. My partner then told her that I wanted to put some flowers on a duck's grave.

I do so hope that you find my little story of interest.

LIST OF MEN LEFT BEHIND

	Camp Died	Rank Reason	Name Location	Regmt	Age
471	KB80 30/01/44 -	L/Cpl	Armstrong K.J KB 2 A 11	RE(41F)	25

507	Lab10 19/07/45 -	Spr	Arthur A Lab F B 10	RE(41F)	39
942	SK20 09/04/45 PoW	Spr	Bantin G.R SK 25 D 8	RE(41F)	30
1299	CK100 03/11/43 B/B-Mal	L/Cpl	Beardsworth E CK 6 J 2	RE(41F)	27
1507	TZ460 22/09/43 -	L/Cpl	Bennett S TZ B3 U 1	RE(41F)	28
1895	CK100 22/10/43 -	L/Cpl	Boakes S.R CK 6 P 1	RE(41F)	23
2435	SM100 12/09/44 DaS	Spr	Brookbanks E.W SM 40	RE(41F)	28
2464	TZ460 26/11/43 -	Spr	Brooks J.S.R TZB3-Y16	RE(41F)	25
3054	SM100 12/09/44 DaS	Cpl	Butler E.A.D SM 39	RE(41F)	34
3194	SM20 21/02/42 DaS	Spr	Cameron L.J SM 40	RE(41F)	24
3196	SK10 03/12/41 KIA	Spr	Cameron R SK 35 G 9	RE(41F)	23
3486	TZ461 22/08/43 -	Spr	Cate A.A TZB4-G12	RE(41F)	25
4463	TZ461 14/07/43 -	Spr	Cooper W.H TZB4-L14	RE(41F)	24
4552	#43 01/06/43 -	L/Sgt	Cottingham L.E SM 39	RE(41F)	26
4742	KB240 30/06/43 G 85	Spr	Credland L.C KB 8 L 47	RE(41F)	26
4928	KB82 03/11/43 -	Spr	Cundy J.D KB 2 B 23	RE(41F)	24
5121	Lab10 26/08/45 -	Cpl	Davey H.H Lab QC 13	RE(41F)	36
5432	SM100 12/09/44 DaS	L/Sgt	Dengate J SM 39	RE(41F)	27
6044	KB200 09/04/43 G 50	Spr	Dyson H KB 4 F 26	RE(41F)	34

6381	SM120 Spr 21/09/44 DaS	Englefield D.G SM 40	RE(41F)	28
6620	TZ460 Spr 13/09/43 -	Fawkes F.S TZ B5-A-6	RE(41F)	27
6733	KB80 Spr 20/03/43 -	Finch A.A KB 2 F 48	RE(41F)	28
6894	KB201 Sgt 10/08/43 G 113	Flower C.F KB 4 B 1	RE(41F)	30
6934	Lab10 L/Cpl 15/08/45 -	Forbes E.R Lab P D 15	RE(41F)	28
7327	SK20 Spr 14/10/42 PoW	Furness A SK 13 E 7	RE(41F)	29
7425	KB230 L/Cpl 12/05/43 G 23	Gardner F.H KB 8 J 17	RE(41F)	29
		412		
7792	SM100 Spr 12/09/44 DaS	Glover N.M SM 40	RE(41F)	28
7831	Lab10 Spr 21/07/45 -	Golden H Lab R A 2	RE(41F)	26
7893	KB220 Spr 19/07/43 -	Goodger R KB 8 H 72	RE(41F)	32
8008	KB60 L/Sgt 01/06/44 G A1	Goulstone F.A KB 2 L 34	RE(41F)	37
8053	SM100 Spr 12/09/44 DaS	Graham R.N.I SM 40	RE(41F)	25
8474	SK20 L/Cpl 14/09/42 PoW	Gunnell J.J.H SK 10 C 8	RE(41F)	31
8845	SM100 Cpl 12/09/44 DaS	Harding R.G.S SM 39	RE(41F)	31
9395	TZ690 Spr 12/10/43 -	Hek R.A TZ B6-P-5	RE(41F)	-
10384	TZ461 Spr 11/08/43 -	Humphreys G.W TZB3-D11	RE(41F)	24
10796	CK100 Cpl 27/08/43 Debility	Jarrold L.H CK 5 J 2	RE(41F)	28

11005	TZ461 30/05/43	Spr G B 1-7	Johnson L.A.E TZ B3-N2	RE(41F)	41
11047	KB470 06/06/43	Spr Cholera	Johnston N.R KB 9 M 4	RE(41F)	-
11166	KB201 13/10/43	Spr G 239	Jones J.H KB 4 B 73	RE(41F)	32
11222	CK43 02/11/43	Spr -	Jones V.H CK 6 K 7	RE(41F)	-
11252	CK100 25/09/43	L/Sgt B/B-Pleur	Jordan T.S	RE(41F) CK 1 M 9	37
11275	KB230 06/03/43	Spr G 47	Joy B KB 8 J 24	RE(41F)	25
11426	SM100 12/09/44	Spr DaS	Kempton J.A SM 40	RE(41F)	29
11439	SM120 21/09/44	Spr DaS	Kennard F.J SM 40	RE(41F)	32
12291	KB240 25/06/43	L/Cpl G 72	Lilley J KB 8 L 36	RE(41F)	24
12356	TZ461 24/08/43	Spr G A51	Lister A.N TZB3-G14	RE(41F)	23
12599	KB769 04/08/45	Spr -	Lucas A.C KB 6 F 35	RE(41F)	33
12601	SM100 12/09/44	Spr DaS	Lucas A.J SM 40	RE(41F)	27
13016	SK20 28/04/42	CQMS PoW	Marshall A SK 7 C 13	RE(41F)	38
13817	TZ580 22/05/44	Spr -	Menton S TZB6-J-8	RE(41F)	25
13882	KB90 16/08/43	Cpl -	Middleton F.D KB 2 H 65	RE(41F)	27
14293	SM20 16/02/42	L/Cpl DaS	Morley A.J.W SM 39	RE(41F)	27
14341	SK10 07/02/42	Cpl KIA	Morris L.C.B SK 13 A 4	RE(41F)	39
14394	KB360 14/08/43	Spr -	Morton E KB 2 N 38	RE(41F)	26

14510	SM120 Spr 21/09/44 DaS	Mullins R.R SM 41	RE(41F)	26
14582	SM100 Spr 12/09/44 DaS	Murray R.P SM 41	RE(41F)	25
15004	SM10 L/Cpl 14/02/42 KIA	Nunn A.J SM 39	RE(41F)	25

413

15782	KB230 L/Cpl 02/08/43 G 10	Penfold J KB 8 M 10	RE(41F)	23
16079	KB250 Spr 09/06/43 -	Plant J.W KB 8 D 42	RE(41F)	28
16229	SM100 Spr 12/09/44 DaS	Poulton J.W SM 41	RE(41F)	33
16317	SM100 Spr 12/09/44 DaS	Price G.R SM 41	RE(41F)	25
16326	KB230 Spr 19/05/43 G 66	Price L.D KB 8 J 42	RE(41F)	23
16563	SM100 L/Cpl 12/09/44 DaS	Randall R.E SM 39	RE(41F)	26
16814	KB230 WO1 01/06/43 G 41	Restall L.J KB 8 J 73	RE(41F)	37
17079	KB230 Cpl 02/02/43 G 50	Roberts E.H.O KB 8 J 27	RE(41F)	32
17236	CK100 Spr 09/09/43 A.Dys-B/B	Robinson S	RE(41F) CK 5 C 1	26
17905	SM100 Spr 12/09/44 DaS	Scott C SM 41	RE(41F)	26
18217	KB201 Spr 22/11/43 G 404	Shepherd C KB 4 D 9	RE(41F)	28
18950	CK100 Spr 09/11/43 B/B	Soars W.H CK 6 G 5	RE(41F)	28
18973	KB240 Sgt 15/06/43 G	Sothern J.F.S 90KB8L51	RE(41F)	39
19023	KB240 Spr 08/06/43 G 13	Spatchett D.V KB 8 K 62	RE(41F)	24

19626	TZ461 Spr 18/06/43 -	Sunderland H.A TZB4-K12	RE(41F)	23
19763	SM100 Spr 12/09/44 DaS	Tallon J SM 42	RE(41F)	25
19848	SM20 WO2 26/02/42 DaS	Taylor F.E SM 38	RE(41F)	51
20422	HK106 Spr 12/01/45 Dys-B/B	Tracey A.A	RE(41F) KSWB6H7	30
20741	TZ460 Spr 26/08/43 -	Vaughan N.J TZ B3V13	RE(41F)	26
20818	HK112 Spr 16/08/43 -	Wadsworth W SWB6B10	RE(41F)	24
20937	HK112 Capt 08/09/42 -	Walker S.W KSWB7C8	RE(41F)	-
21217	KB220 L/Cpl 06/07/43 -	Wathen S.G KB 8 H 54	RE(41F)	-
22244	TZ461 Spr 30/08/43 G B 1-4	Winter A.L TZ B4-E-3	RE(41F)	24
22316	CK100 L/Cpl 19/08/43 B/B	Wood H.G CK 5 N 5	RE(41F)	25

JAPANESE HELL SHIP "HAKASOKA MARU"
sailed from Singapore 4 July 1994
arrived Moji, Japan 10 August 1944
journey six weeks battened down for most of the journey

Information which has come to hand since writing this script.

This ship was built on the Clydeside, Scotland in 1894

NAMED:"The Glasgow Belle"
TONNAGE:4,000 to 5,000
Sold to Japanese Government in 1934
Then named "HAKASOKA MARU"

So when we were put aboard this stinking hulk she was already fifty years old.

There were 750 of us packed into the two holds, one forward and one to the stern, we laid on the cargo of tin and rubber.

The "HAKASOKA MARU" sank in a great storm in the China Sea off the coast of Formosa (Taiwan) when she was returning to Singapore. How lucky we were as we had passed through a very heavy storm in the same area on our journey to Japan.

When we arrived in Japan, we were to face the hardest Winter of 1944, the worst they had known for eighty years. Snows two to three feet deep and terrible winds blowing in from Siberia.

How lucky we were, those of us who survived this terrible journey followed by such a Winter.

415

During these ill-fated convoys, 15,000 POWs were transported. Only 3,000 survived (as listed below):-

LISBON MARU: Hong Kong to Japan. Sunk by submarine 2 October 1942, six miles from Tung Fusham Island off China coast. Total prisoners on board 1,816. Missing or dead 839. Survivors 977, plus two survivors died Shanghai.

NICHIMEI MARU: Singapore to Moulmein, sunk by submarine 15 January 1943. Total prisoners 1,000. Missing or dead 53. Survivors 947. Lat 32.43N, Lon 97.27E.

SUEZ MARU: Amboina, Java, torpedoed near island of Kangean 29 September 1943. Total prisoners on board 548. No survivors. Lat 660.20S, Lon 116.30.

TAMABUKO MARU: Singapore to Japan. Torpedoed off Goto Nagasaki, Japan 24 June 1944. Total prisoners on board 772. Dead or missing 560. Survivors 212.

HARAGIKU MARU: Belawan/Pakabame, sunk by torpedo south of Balawan 26 June 1944. Total prisoners on board 720. Dead or missing 177. Survivors 543. Lat 30.15N, Lon 99.47E.

SHINYU MARU: Manila, sunk by submarine 17 September 1944 of Mindanao. Total prisoners on board 750. No survivors.

JUNYA MARU: Java/Sumatra, Japan, sunk by submarine 18 September 1944 off Moaka Moakao. Lat 20.53S, Lon 101.11E. Total prisoners on board 2,200. Dead or missing 1,477. Survivors 723.

RAKUYO MARU: Singapore to Japan, torpedoed off East Hainan Island 12 September 1944. Lat 13.0N, Lon 114.0E. Total prisoners on board 1,214. Dead or missing 1,179. Survivors 135.

416

KACHIDOKI MARU: Singapore to Japan, torpedoed by aircraft 12 September 1942 off East Hainan Island. Lat 18.0N, Lon 114.0E. Total prisoners on board 950. Dead or missing 435. Survivors 515.

TYOFUKU MARU: Singapore Japan, sunk by aircraft 21 September 1942 at the point Battan N.W Philippines. Total prisoners on board 1,287. Dead or missing 907. Survivors 380.

ARISAN MARU: Manila/Japan, torpedoed in Bashi Straits 24 October 1944. Total prisoners on board 1,782. Dead or missing 1,778. Survivors 4 died later.

MONTEVIEDO MARU: Torpedoed by submarine 1 July 1942 off Bagador lighthouse east of Luzon. Total prisoners on board 1,053. No survivors.

ORYOKU MARU, ENOURA MARU, BRAZIL MARU: Torpedoed by aircraft in the Bay of Takaa 9 January 1945. Total prisoners on board ships total 1,620. Dead or missing 1,002. Survivors 618. 58 died later from illness and exposure.

This information was given to me by John Wyatt, who was on this ship at the same time. To him I am very grateful.

WHEN I LEFT JAPAN IN 1945

After the treatment we had received at the hands of our captors for three and a half years, how do you think I felt? My whole being was full of hate for both Japan and its people. This hate has stayed with me for over fifty years, then things began to change.

MY ATTITUDE CHANGES

On the 13th November 1997, I went to Thailand on a pilgrimage with the Royal British Legion, to visit War Graves of the friends we had left behind, I went with an old friend of mine who had been one of my very best friends from Singapore until we parted company in 1944. He had come over from South Africa to be with me on this pilgrimage.
On this trip was also a Japanese lady, Mrs Keiko Holmes. I had heard about this lady though POW grapevines, how she had gone and asked to go into a big POW conference being held in London, she was not received very lightly but her insistence paid off and she was allowed in. She told the packed hall that she wanted Reconciliation, this lady was admired for her will but was taken with a pinch of salt.

While we were at the war cemetery at Kanchanaburi she spoke to me, she did so again at the Chunkai Cemetery. She said that it was such a waste of young lives, she went on to say that she was so sorry that it had happened and wished to apologise for the way we had been made to suffer. She spoke to me again at Nam Tok station and at Hell Fire Pass, she said that it must have been a terrible place, as she spoke she looked terribly sad.
Here, I thought, was a Japanese lady full of compassion and love asking forgiveness. This had a great impression on me. Could I forgive, even if I cannot forget?
After meeting Mrs Holmes I found that my hate mellowed a little, but I was not convinced with Japan as a whole. During the trip to Thailand, I told Mrs Holmes that I had been in

i

Japan during the last year of my captivity, she then asked me if I would like to go back one day. I had very mixed feelings about this, I knew it to be a beautiful country but would I like the people? She then went on to say that she would put me on the list for a "pilgrimage of reconciliation" with an organisation called AGAPE.

I GO BACK TO JAPAN, 1999

At the end of August, my partner and I were invited to join a group to Japan with AGAPE. I knew the scenery in Japan was beautiful, but I was a bit apprehensive at first.
We flew out of Heathrow, London on the 6th October 1999. We found the cabin vrew most helpful and friendly, it was a very pleasant flight with ANA, All Nippon Airways. We flew at business rate which made the journey so much more enjoyable and very comfortable.
We arrived in Tokyo to a great reception, people with welcome banners, they waved Union Jacks together with the Japanese flags, so different to the welcome we received in 1944. So far so good.
We stayed at the New Otani Hotel, the latest and most up to date in Tokyo. The staff were most helpful, nothing was too much trouble.
In the Monday we were to meet our host for the day, Mrs Kozue Komatsuzaki, a lovely lady, she took Katie and I on the underground system, all so up to date. She then took us to the Tokyo Tower, 45 stories high, such wonderful views of the city from this vantage point. In the afternoon we went on a shopping expedition in the lovely shops, Katie loved this!
We then boarded a bus to go to the ladies house which was across the city. I was wearing my blazer with the Corps of Royal Engineers badge on the pocket, an old gentleman came and sat next to me, he pointed to my badge and asked what it was. Mrs Komatsuzaki went on to tell him that I had been a POW in Singapore, Thailand and Japan, he then told me that he had been a fighting soldier in Burma for three

years until the end of the war, as he left the bus he held out his hand in friendship, he wished me "Sayonara".

We reached our host's house where we met her daughter, she had visited London. Later her husband joined us, he had just flown in from America. We had a lovely meal with them. To finish off the evening we had one or two beers together. We were both very sorry to leave this wonderful family, they were so kind and made us feel at ease. Before we left, we exchanged little presents.

We were having the most wonderful and enjoyable trip. We met many churchmen, and visited some of the Christian Churches in the different towns and cities that we went to. At this stage I should like to point out that "Christians" were persecuted and frowned upon during the war years. We went to the British Embassy, the Japanese Foreign Office, a Mr Watanabe gave us a talk.

Keiko was with us at all times and at hand to help us - surely she is an angel.

We visited Mount Fuji. A very impressive sight. I last saw it from the train in 1944 en route for Tokyo thence to the coal mine at Onahama, I thought it beautiful then. Never did I ever think that I would see it again.

We met the people who look after the graves of the Seventeen IRUKA Boys who died in the nearby Prison Camp. They had worked in the Copper Mine. We held a memorial services, after we left knowing that these "boys" will never be forgotten as long as these good folks in the nearby little town are in existence.

We then met our second Host Family, they were Takao Kawamura, his wife Matsuyo, their two little daughters Mari and Risa aged seven and ten, they also had a son. Takao was a long distance coach driver, unfortunately he could not speak English so Matsuyo did all the talking! They made us most welcome in their new house, she told us that we were the first to use the guest room, a great honour indeed. We exchanged presents, the little girls were so excited and laughing as all children do the world over. This house was so full of love and kindness, I began to think to myself, are these the same people that treated us badly during the War?

No, they can't be! We slept in the guest room a very restful and happy sleep.

The next morning, Sunday, we had a beauiful breakfast, Matsuyo had prepared a wonderful spread, she must have worked so hard for our sakes.

Then the two little girls asked their mother if they could take us to the river to feed the fish, I was not too keen but Katie said that we should go, I picked up my Video Camera and we set off for the river. As we walked along the lane all seemed so quiet and peaceful, then I felt a little hand in mine, I looked down and saw the happy face of this little seven year old girl smiling up at me, I felt the warmth in my heart, I felt so at peace. Then I thought, God I cannot go on with this hate in my heart, these were not the people who gave us so much torture and cruelty. At that moment, the hate seemed to leave me completely. I looked back down the lane and the other little girl was holding Katie's hand. I shall never forget those two little girls, they brought peace to my heart and the power to forgive. To forget, I know not.

The little girls fed the fish, they were full of laughter and excitement as the fish jumped to the food, like children of any nation. I took some very good pictures on the video camera, these I shall treasure. God Bless these little girls that gave me the will to forgive. They too were so trusting, no way were they the enemy I knew.

Another lady we met was Mrs Shuko Enomoto, she was most kind to Katie and myself. As I think everyone knows I have always been known as Blackie from schooldays, and has continued through my life. Shuko I think found this very amusing, she thought it was a cat's name. On our second meeting she brought me a little present, it was a small ornament, it was a little black cat, she said it would bring me good luck. I thought it so kind of her, it is now in place of honour in our house. When I look at it, I shall always think of the lady with so much charm and goodwill, also lifting the burden of the feelings I have carried with me for so long.

God bless you Shiko, I shall always remember you with affectionate memories, and yes, I am very glad that I have been back to Japan.